Bewitch

HYBRID THEORY BOOK 1

Brit Andrews

Brit Andrews

Bewitch

Edited by: Kaila Stoval
Cover design by: Brit Andrews
Cover art by: Hannah Danielle
Character Art by : @annkristen_art

ISBN - eBook: 979-8-9941087-1-0
ISBN - Paperback: 979-8-9941087-0-3
ISBN - Hardcover : 979-8-9941087-2-7

Brit Andrews

To the 8-year-old girl who lost her book but found a calling it took us awhile, but we are finally here

To the mother who would proudly photocopy the words of an 8-year-old, thank you for always believing.

Author's Note

Hi! Just a few notes and things to think about before reading. This is a book about vampires so there will be blood and biting. There is also an age gap relationship, explicit sex scenes, graphic violence, death, decapitation, elitism, bigotry, prejudice, acts of terrorism, mental health struggles, talk of medical testing (off page), mentions of assaults (off page), mention of past sterilization, mentions of miscarriage, mentions of past sacrifice and implied torture (off page), structural damage of an inhabited building. The FMC was adopted as a baby. Also humans are not painted in the best light.

If you find any of the above triggering or harmful to your mental health, prioritize yourself and give it a miss. I tried to cover all potential triggers but it's very possible I missed some.

Brit Andrews

be·witch

/bəˈwiCH/

verb

1. enchant and delight (someone).
2. cast a spell over (someone).

hy·brid

/ˈhībrəd/

noun

1. an offspring of two animals or plants of different subspecies, breeds, varieties, species, or genera
2. person whose background is a blend of two diverse cultures or traditions
3. something heterogeneous in origin or composition: composite

Brit Andrews

Prologue

Danger could hide in the most innocent of places. Such a pitiful looking creature and yet somehow, she was dangerous. The blood was cleaned from her skin, and the wounds were taken care of. Still, she looked so pale, small and fragile. How could something so easily breakable cause this much trouble? She was sitting surrounded by her family, but she didn't look comforted, just haunted. Her tears had dried and there seemed to be a hollowness about her. Putting her out of her misery was an option, even if my wife disagreed with it. What was I supposed to do with her?

"None of this is in her medical records?" I asked the doctor who had been going over the test results.

"No, this isn't something that would have been tested as a child. There were extensive tests done on her, but witches tend to come into power at age thirteen. By that point she would have already had the designation and unless this manifested, she wouldn't have known she had a specialty. I spoke with her father, nothing like this has ever happened before," the doctor informed me. "As she is nearly the age of full maturity it's likely that this is something new."

"Was this some sort of fear response? Maybe a defense mechanism?"

"That is actually likely, many things can manifest when in a stressful or dire situation. Defensive magic often manifests that way."

"And in your opinion is she dangerous?" I asked, holding the doctor's gaze which made her nervous.

"I can tell you that she is a hybrid with high level magical abilities and 98% M-levels. Which is unusual in a hybrid but likely most of it contributes to the vampire half. Based on her history she is not an aggressive person and she was well cared for by her parents. And this is a new manifestation of abilities. What *I* cannot tell you is if she is dangerous or not. She is young and untrained and is clearly lacking predatory instincts. All I have are the facts, the rest is for you to decide," she said.

That was in fact the problem, *I* had to decide what to do with her. Sending her home with her family was out of the question. In fact, none of them would be returning to their home until I figured out what to do. Maybe the girl wasn't dangerous *now,* but she could be and that was the problem. Letting her loose in the world would be very negligent and would definitely come back to bite me. Killing her, though, would end this whole matter and I could get back to focusing on more important things.

Bewitch

"We do not harm children," my wife unhelpfully pointed out.

"She is not a child," I replied.

"Not a child but an innocent, she's a little lost soul who should have been raised by her own kind."

"What kind is that? She's a hybrid, she doesn't have a kind."

"Semantics, she has the same physiology that we do, the other half is just details," she said dismissively. "You have all the reports on her and the medical information, punishing her for something beyond her control is wrong."

"What is it you propose we do then? There is no undoing what has been done, and we can't claim ignorance. Whether she means to be or not she is a threat to our kind."

"I have an idea," she said, and I shook my head. I knew that look, nothing good would come from this.

This pitiful creature was going to bring chaos into my life; I knew it for certain. If I couldn't kill her the options were very limited, and I had a bad feeling I knew what my wife would think was an appropriate action. Sure, it might solve one problem, but it would create others. Unfortunately, I knew that the weaker of us were supposed to be protected, that's how things used to be done. Now? Some things were different, and others were the same, everything could change if you lived long enough.

Was there any value in keeping this girl alive? That, I had a feeling, I would be asking myself for a long time to come.

3

Nothing good would come from this and, on the other hand, nothing good would come from killing her. It was just so much more convenient to do so. Too bad my wife usually got her way...

Freddie

As my back hit the wall, I realized I was looking into the face of a monster, not my husband. His lips came down on mine momentarily distracting me from his appearance. I should have been scared, he was, after all, the stuff of nightmares, his eyes having gone completely black. As I understood it, only the oldest and strongest bloodlines still possessed this trait. It was like the human mask fell away to show you that vampires were indeed predators. Lure you in with the good looks and then the monster would come out. There was a reason vampires were the perfect predators and why they stayed near the top of the food chain.

This hallway he pulled me into was dimly lit and deserted. No doubt the whole staff had been summoned to the ballroom to assist with the damage. The fighting was still going on when he came to find me. Despite all the blood, violence, and screaming I hadn't ever actually been in any danger. Not with our security always at the ready. One of the guards was quick to get me away from any potential backlash from the brawl. I could barely hear the commotion from where we were now, but I knew it wouldn't easily be solved. What was supposed to be the start of a unifying event turned into violence and chaos. If not for the magic dampening in the room, it all would have been so much worse.

"Cannon," I managed to say as his kiss moved to my neck. This hardly seemed appropriate given the situation.

"I *need* you," he said holding my gaze so I knew exactly what he meant.

"Here? *Now?*" I asked in shock, that was not what I expected.

"Yes," was all he said before his lips were on mine again.

A potential war was breaking out elsewhere in this building and my husband wanted to have sex. How did one even respond to that? Technically I didn't need to because he wasn't asking me. His touch always had a strange effect on me, and we both knew I couldn't say no to him. We were in an open hallway where anybody could see us, and his hand was between my legs. His touch moved along the lace trim of my panties before he slipped inside. Using his talented fingers, he awoke a need in me that felt so inappropriate. Public sex was not my kink, and I hadn't been aware it was his, but there was likely a lot I didn't know about my husband.

"We could go to your office," I suggested. Anywhere other than this far too public space where literally anyone could walk by would be nice.

"I love the scent of you, always so sweet," he said burying his face against my neck.

A gasp escaped me and heat pooled in my core as he stroked me to climax. It was quite embarrassing how easy I was when it came to him. Before I could think straight, he was moving the center of my panties aside and picking me up so my legs were around his waist. The silky fabric of my dress was bunched up over my hips leaving me exposed. The air in the hallway was cold making me shiver a little, but my husband, of course, was burning hot.

"Cannon, somebody could see us," I said even though I knew there was no turning back.

"I don't give a fuck, my hotel and my wife," he growled gripping my hair and holding my gaze. His black eyes stayed on mine as he pushed into me.

Pinned between the wall and Cannon I couldn't do much more than hold on as he thrust up into me hard and relentless. It was so easy to forget why this was so wrong. Both his hands fell to my hips with a bruising grip as he thrust harder. His fangs skimmed down the side of my neck making me whimper. For once he didn't bite me, there was likely already too much blood in the air and predators around. Cannon's lips found mine again as he rubbed my clit and increased his pace. He swallowed my moan with our kiss as I came. And with a few more deep strokes he followed.

"Fuck, I needed that," he said leaning his forehead against mine while I caught my breath. Naturally he wasn't winded at all, the perks of being a full-blooded vampire. "We need to get you to the car."

At that he set me on my feet and repositioned my panties, *such gentlemanly behavior.* As he looked at me his eyes glowed, he still looked like the predator he was. Even though his face looked more like it usually did he still couldn't pass as human. Something in his black eyes warned you to be wary. He pulled down my dress before he kissed me again like he might devour me. Being married to this man was so strange, I always knew I was out of my depth with him.

"I need to clean up first," I told him but he shook his head as he put himself back together.

"No time for that," he said taking my hand and leading me back down the hall.

"You came inside me," I pointed out. Not that it was different from any other time we had sex, he always did.

"It's fine," he replied because of course he did, such a man thing to say.

"I'm getting in a car with your mother," I said as he pulled me outside.

"Freddie, it's fine, you are my wife, nobody is going to care. I need you to go home where you are safe," he said.

There was no arguing with him, I knew that so I shouldn't have bothered. Oh, how my life had changed since he came into it. He gave me a quick kiss before ushering me into the waiting car. With a few words to his mother, he sent us off. Was I very aware of certain parts of myself the whole drive? Yes, and was I too embarrassed to make eye contact with anyone? Also yes, who knew this was what married life would be like.

"Fredericka, dear, do stop your fidgeting," Belinda said.

"Yes Mother," I whispered unwilling to look at my mother-in-law.

"Men have needs it's nothing new," Belinda added. "Fights bring out the bloodlust in them, they are simple creatures after all. You are his wife, better it be you than someone else."

"Might be better for it to be somebody else actually," Lucy said sounding bored. When I looked at my sister-in-law, she was looking at her phone like she had not a care in the world. "Trust me, they can get a little wild so it's best they use someone else for those urges. You haven't been married long, but you will learn in time."

"When blood is in the air males can't control themselves, you aren't used to that we understand. Males aren't as in control as we are, it's just a fact."

"A wife is to be cared for, protected and cherished, others handle the less pleasant things. Just the way of the world, it doesn't mean he is planning to replace you. As long as you are a good wife and take care of him, you will be fine," Lucy added.

They were full of this type of wisdom and freely shared it with me so I could be a good wife. I knew going into this that things would be different, but I never fully thought it through. To be fair it wasn't like I chose this life, it was just the best of my options. My marriage was arranged, I grew up rather humbly, and I never expected to end up in a family like this.

Six months ago, I married a man I had only known for three weeks, I was still adjusting. His parents decided we would marry and so we did with barely the illusion of choice. Because really there was only one choice I could make at the time. They essentially gave me to their son, and I was his problem and his property. The vampires were not going to allow me to keep walking around free once they found out what I did. They married me off to their prince and I spent the last six months trying to be his perfect wife.

Now I had to wonder if maybe while I was at home being a good little wife, Cannon was out with other women. Belinda and Lucy made it seem so normal and like something I just had to live with. But was it? What could I really do if it was?

Freddie

No amount of time in the shower could wash away my embarrassment. Or was humiliation a better word for it? No amount of time would take away from that night being the most humiliating moment of my life. Considering it happened after escaping a massive brawl was saying something. I wasn't used to violence. That wasn't my life experience until now. Once it all started people just sort of jumped in spreading it like a virus. In an instant the whole room was chaos, and the guards were having us take cover. Dinner had obviously been canceled despite all the work that must have gone into the preparations. And my husband hadn't been the least bit bothered, no he actually seemed like he enjoyed it. But that could have been my imagination.

Once again, I woke up in bed alone, I hadn't seen my husband since that night. He sent a text letting me know he was busy. Of course, it made sense he stayed there to attempt salvaging the situation. The summit was supposed to be about peace and cooperation between the various local nonhuman factions. How things would go after the brawl at the first event, I didn't know. My involvement with the summit was very minimal as I was still rather new to The Family. Cannon was heavily involved since his parents were hosting the whole thing. Basically, I just had to attend events and look pretty while not drawing any attention to myself.

Part of me wondered if my husband was working or if he was somewhere else. I wasn't typically one for paranoia, but this was something his family thought completely normal. I suppose he never promised me monogamy when we got married and I was foolish enough not to ask. In my mind marriage meant monogamy but not everybody felt that way. Admittedly, despite being a vampire I didn't know as much about vampire culture as I should.

My parents weren't vampires; I was adopted so my lack of knowledge made sense. These days some people had multiple spouses or legally registered mistresses and paramours, so I should have considered that at least. In times long past vampires might have a blood harem for whatever services they needed. Now, that wasn't necessary you could buy blood in the grocery store. Drinking from a live source was typically something one practiced with a partner. It was rather intimate and could be very sexually stimulating. For most people it was a choice, I was not afforded that luxury. Cannon was the only one to ever drink my blood. Obviously, I was not the only one to drink his, he did live a long life before we were together. I never considered if he still drank from others just as I hadn't considered if he had sex with other people.

Right now, however, it was all I could think about, and it was very inconvenient. Just like it was incredibly inconvenient to develop feelings for one's husband. This arrangement was not about love, that was a silly luxury. Cannon needed a wife, and the vampires wanted me, so they gave me to him. Being married was the best option since there were far worse things they could have done to me. It wasn't my fault what happened, but I should have been more careful. Should have done something... *anything* differently. My marriage protected me from a worse fate, a life for a life.

Instead of death I got to live in the proverbial lap of luxury on the arm of one of the most influential vampires in this part of the world. The family was practically royalty and was treated as such. So, what did I really have to complain about? Cannon was good to me and his family accepted me. I wasn't a prisoner; I could come and go as I pleased (though with armed guards trailing me) and I could buy anything I wanted. We lived in a massive home that was fully staffed, I had everything a person could want. Except you know those fanciful people who wanted freedom or a career they worked hard for and loved. Even knowing it was a luxury I couldn't afford, I still wanted it. No matter how hard I tried to remind myself that it wasn't part of the deal, the feeling lingered.

The door to our bedroom opened and Cannon walked in. His hair was wet so he was freshly showered, though he hadn't used our bathroom. His bare muscular chest was always a distraction, even today. There was no denying that my husband with his golden olive skin, grey eyes and perfect dark chocolate hair was very attractive. Broad shoulders and muscular arms rounded out a very nice package. Then again, most vampires tended to be rather attractive. Though his lighter skin was a bit of an anomaly in his rather brown skinned family. Harringtons came in various shades of brown; his parents and sister were not fair skinned like him.

He looked at me still lying in bed and said nothing. I should have been up by now, I usually was. My hair was still covered by the silk scarf I wore to bed every night. Saying nothing, he came to bed. Lying beside me, he pulled me into his arms where I went willingly, and he gave me a tight squeeze. Even though I felt conflicted my body always responded to him, so it happened without much thought. Our bodies just fit perfectly together and always moved towards each other like magnets.

"Are you ok?" He asked. His far too perceptive gaze watching me.

"Yeah," I replied then before I could stop myself I asked: "Where did you take a shower?"

"Oh I used one of the other bathrooms, didn't want to wake you," he replied. "One of us should be allowed to rest, I'll be heading out soon."

"Is the summit still continuing?" I asked, forcing my thoughts away from where they had been heading. My husband was a busy man, and this summit was very important.

"That's the plan, at least for now," he said with a sigh. "I would rather spend the day in bed with you."

"You would get bored," I pointed out.

"I could never be bored with you," he said with no hesitation. "Since I can't stay here with my beautiful wife, I'll try to make this nightmare work. But I need you to stay in for the next few days, maybe longer. Can't have anyone getting ideas about taking my wife to get what they want."

"Would someone really do that?" I asked rather alarmed at the suggestion.

"It's happened before, obviously not to me since you are my only wife but it's not unheard of. At least if you are here, I know you are safe and I don't have to worry about you. I just want to be careful, especially with you," he told me.

"Ok," I said as if I had a choice.

Of course I had no choice, my choices stopped existing that horrible night seven months ago. Cannon didn't order me around which I appreciated but we both knew that I could't fight him if I wanted to. Whatever he says goes that was what I agreed to. Besides he was right that I was particularly of interest. That was why we were married after all because some people thought I was dangerous. Did it matter that all I wanted

Brit Andrews

to do was live my life like any normal person? Nope, so I was now constantly surrounded by vampires after a lifetime of living outside their society. I was given the label of wife, but I was never going to enjoy complete freedom again. A gilded cage is still a cage after all.

16

Cannon

The lackluster job she was doing while riding me was annoying. Any other time her curvy body and beautiful brown skin bare was enough to keep my attention. However, something was very clearly off. Typically, she was more of an enthusiastic lover, not this time. It had been a few days since the last time we had sex; I somehow thought she might at least miss this. But no, it was very obvious that her mind was elsewhere. No matter what else was going on sex was where we connected most. Likely that wasn't saying much about our relationship.

As far as I knew we didn't have any problems but obviously that wasn't true. Was it wrong not to want to deal with whatever her issue was? Probably, since I didn't need any more problems, I had no choice. Keeping peace in my marriage was important, right now was just not the best time. I flipped us over so that I was on top of her and gave her a couple hard thrusts to get her attention. Interesting, she seemed to like that at least that's what her body was telling me.

"What's wrong?" I asked, looking down at her in annoyance.

"Nothing," she predictably said.

"Don't lie to me," I growled at her. That was not something I would permit, I didn't lie to her she didn't get to lie to me.

"Sorry, I guess I just wasn't really in the mood," she admitted. "You can finish if you want."

"Yeah now I'm not in the mood," I said, pulling out and moving off her. "I'm not ever going to force you to have sex, if you don't want to just say no. Is that what you think of me? That I wouldn't listen if you said no?" If that was the case, we truly had problems.

"No! It's not that at all, I don't think you would ever purposely hurt me," she said. Her eyes pleaded with me making it hard to stay mad at her. Though the "purposely" did give me pause, but I would let that go for now.

"Just tell me what's wrong, don't say nothing," I told her, pulling her over to me. She rested her head on my chest for a moment like any other time. But it was very obvious that there was something she didn't want to say. "Talk to me Freddie, I'm not mad at you."

Going home to my wife was supposed to improve my day, not make it worse. I hadn't spent much time with her since getting things back on track after the brawl was a priority. And it was best to keep her in the house away from prying eyes. There was also the fact that I knew at least ten people that would take her to use against me. That was the problem with caring about others, they became a liability. It was my job to take care of her and keep her safe, that's what I promised when we got married. My fingers found their way into her dark hair and she relaxed more against me.

This was always going to be a massive undertaking. The truth was we were not exactly a united people. Many failed attempts to unite nonhumans post-Surge had happened. There were just too many different types of nonhumans to make this happen peacefully. We weren't even trying globally; this was a regional thing. It was a nightmare, but it was also important. Should humans decide that coexistence no longer serves them, we needed to be ready. They are always plotting and planning, we had to be better and a step ahead. So even now my mind was halfway on to whatever task I needed to complete next. Which was likely why her question threw me off so much.

"Do you have a mistress?" She asked, surprising me, I didn't see that one coming.

"Why would you ask me that?" I asked instead of answering her question.

A lot of men had mistresses; it was a common thing these days and less of a secretive type of thing. There was this idea that men had these overwhelming sexual urges and needed to satisfy themselves with more than one partner. Some people believed that females were made for monogamy, but males were not. Mostly it sounded like men trying to justify doing what they wanted but to each their own. Women also had lovers outside of their marriages, some couples even indulged together. Different people did different things, whatever worked for them worked. I could guess who might have put this idea into my wife's head, it was just not something I wanted to deal with.

"I guess that's my answer," Freddie said. "I'm going to go take a shower." She started to move away but I didn't let her.

"Would it bother you if I had a mistress?" I asked though I knew the answer from the look of betrayal in her violet eyes that she couldn't hide.

"Does it matter? You are free to do whatever you want, my opinion is of little consequence," she replied. "Can I go now?"

"When did things get like this? I know I've been busy a lot, but when did we stop being able to talk about things? Why are you afraid to speak with me?" I asked her, confused by this change. It seemed sudden but it likely wasn't and I just hadn't noticed.

In the beginning things were fine, we talked and seemed to understand each other. Was it when we came back home that things changed? I thought she was settling into life here, but apparently, that wasn't the case. Freddie spent a lot of time with my mother and sister but otherwise she was a bit isolated since coming here. Did someone say something to her? Treat her badly? I honestly had no idea and that was a problem. Neglecting my wife hadn't been my intention but it was obvious that I had done so.

"What is there to say?" She asked, her voice sounding so hollow.

"For the record I do not have a mistress and I have not touched another woman since we became engaged. When I say I'm working I really am, I'm not off with other women. We never really talked about monogamy; I guess that was a mistake. With everything that happened I figured being a faithful husband was the least I could do for you. But I need you to talk to me and tell me where this is coming from," I told her.

Seriously, the last thing I needed was marriage problems when I already had so much other shit to do. Seven months ago, my life was a lot simpler, sometimes I missed that. But I did not regret marrying Freddie despite the circumstances of it all. She needed me and I needed her; we served each other's needs. My parents wanted me married and they needed an easy way to bring her into The Family.

Did I know she didn't actually want to marry me? Of course I did, I wasn't stupid, her hand was forced. So, I tried to make things as easy as possible for her. She chose me over death or imprisonment; it was just a fact. Freddie didn't do anything wrong; she was just unfortunate enough to develop abilities that vampires did not appreciate.

"Just something your mother said," she shook her head. "It made me realize that you might have someone else.

Someone you actually want to spend time with as opposed to me who you are forced to be with. I'm just a body here for you to fuck when you want to."

"Freddie, you are my wife, I wasn't forced to marry you, I could have said no. My parents wouldn't have been happy, but the choice was always there. If you recall I convinced you to choose me. All I have is you, there isn't anyone else, just you. I neither have nor want a mistress. Don't take marriage advice from my mother or sister, they have certain views I don't share. I'm fine with having a monogamous relationship. I suppose if you don't feel that way we can discuss it. They pretty much were always going to find me a wife. Which I was fine with because I wasn't interested in trying or in being tied down. Then there was you, I thought we kind of served each other's purpose. But feel free to tell me that isn't the case," I told her.

"What happened after the fight it just… felt kind of weird. In the car they told me at least you wanted me when you could have used someone else. Because men have *urges* that aren't appropriate for a wife. They got in my head, and I started wondering if you have someone else. You never come home anymore, I barely see you and I do know you are busy. I don't know, I guess I'm just losing my mind a little," she admitted. "We never talked about monogamy or any of that because obviously we were just thrown together. And I'm worried about what happens when you get bored with me."

Honestly, I had no idea what being a husband would be like, I never really thought about it. Before her it had been a long time since I was even in a relationship that could be considered serious. I suppose I could see why she might feel some kind of way about what happened between us that night. To be fair I wasn't really thinking clearly at the time, it was chaotic. Keeping from letting my baser instincts rule me had been difficult. We were supposed to be all civilized and shit now. Not that it mattered to those idiots that started the fight at dinner.

Vampires were always supposed to be civil and act dignified. We were supposed to be better than everyone else. So to keep myself calm I may have distracted myself with my wife. Now I had to wonder if there was ever a time she might have wanted to say no to me and didn't. Did she feel like she couldn't because of how we came to be married?

"I'm sorry. That wasn't my intention, I just wasn't thinking. Freddie, I never want you to feel like you can't tell me no if I do something you don't like. And I don't want you sitting here worried about what I'm doing. When I say I would rather be with you, I mean it. I do prefer your company," I told her. Then I braced myself before continuing. "Were there other times when I did something you didn't want me to?"

"No! I wasn't unwilling, I've never felt like you forced me to have sex," she said.

"Are you afraid of me?" I asked watching her.

"Should I be?" She asked, classic deflection.

"Be honest, I need to know."

"I don't think you would hurt me but am I afraid that you might change your mind about this marriage? Yes, I'm stuck here, if I'm not with you they will kill me."

"I'm not so petty that I would get mad at you and have the guards drag you away in chains. Couples fight right? That's normal you shouldn't feel like disagreeing with me will end in your death. I really am sorry you felt like I used you the other night," I told her.

"It was really embarrassing," she admitted. "Just because your mother won't care doesn't mean it's any less embarrassing."

"Sometimes I forget that you didn't grow up around vampires, we don't make a big deal about sex. Humans make it taboo, and we aren't humans, but I guess your parents have absorbed their ways like so many others."

While my wife was a vampire or at least half of one, her adoptive parents were a witch and a water mage. Though we didn't live too far apart she lived in a more mixed area, with both humans and nonhumans. Typically, upper-class nonhumans preferred to live away from human influence. So I've always been surrounded by people who didn't feel the need to hide everything behind closed doors and label things as taboo. Nonhumans tended to be less restrictive and repressed; we didn't shame everyone for every damn thing. Humans tended to have the oddest beliefs and practices.

Freddie and I were still learning each other, we had only been married for six months. The first month we spent on a honeymoon. My mother thought it was important for us to spend time alone to connect. So, it had really only been five months that we were here at home living together and trying to figure things out. There were many complexities to sharing your life with another person. Especially when you barely knew that person. Our marriage was an arrangement of convenience, navigating our life together was never going to be easy.

My mother and sister did take Freddie under their proverbial wings, but clearly, I needed to have a word with them about that. Having a monogamous marriage in my family wasn't quite the norm. It certainly wasn't just my father and brother-in-law that had their urges met outside of their marriages. Something that my mother clearly didn't think to mention to Freddie. Not that I wanted to go putting that idea in her head, I was not sharing her. Honestly, I didn't have time for a mistress, this summit had been taking up my life well before it actually happened. And it would continue to take up my time for the foreseeable future. One woman in my life was enough to deal with; I didn't need any others.

"Are vampire marriages that different from other people?" She asked and I shrugged.

"Probably but I don't know I've only ever been married to you, and most of the people I know are vampires," I replied.

"Ok so I'm willing to admit I'm a little insecure, you were the most eligible vampire bachelor after all," she said. I couldn't help but laugh at that, she wasn't wrong. Before her I did everything I could to evade marriage, so it was ridiculous that I practically begged her to marry me.

"Don't be, it wasn't an enviable position to be in. A lot of people are willing to do all sorts of shit to get into this Family. At least I know I can trust you," I said with a sigh. "I'm going to shower, want to join me?"

"You have to go back?" She asked, looking a bit disappointed about it.

"Unfortunately, once this is over I'll take you somewhere, anywhere that's not here," I told her. "Pick a place and we might not come back for a while."

"Your father would not allow that," she pointed out.

"True but I'm going to do it anyway and kidnap my wife."

"Maybe, but I will come shower with you, and then I'll go spend some time with Lucy and the kids."

"Those little monsters? You must really be bored," I said, getting up and holding out my hand for her.

"I miss teaching," she said with a shrug. I couldn't help wrapping my arms around her, she lost so much in this marriage.

"Maybe after the summit and your planned kidnapping, we could figure out a way for you to teach again," I suggested.

"I would like that," she said almost in a whisper like she was too afraid to want it. Damn, I really needed to do better by my wife.

Marriage changed my life as expected but not as much as hers. It seemed normal that it would take some time for things to settle. My sacrifices though were minuscule compared to hers. Freddie's life changed completely; she had to give up the job she loved and worked hard for. She had to move out of her parents' house to basically live with strangers. And couldn't leave without bodyguards. I needed to work at being a better husband, we were stuck together but it didn't have to be a bad thing.

Cannon

This summit was going to be the death of me. The brawl was
only a week ago and here we were at a party. Each faction was
hosting an event as a way to "bring about cultural
understanding." Really, I think it's because they are long lived
and bored and it's an excuse for excess. I would prefer not to
be there, but I was required to attend and so was my wife.
Nobody got out of it, our family needed to be seen, and we
needed to socialize. If these people couldn't behave for an
opening dinner party, I didn't have much hope for this party.
It was a miracle nobody was killed that night, though not for
lack of trying.

My job was to network and gauge the opinions of the
people who had come for the summit. And to mediate
wherever necessary. The event was technically organized by

a council of elder vampires who had long memories and knew the importance of cooperation. My father, as head of the council, essentially made all the rules for governing vampires in our region. Which was why he was able to work things to get control of Freddie's incident. Hunt Harrington was king in all but name and everybody feared and respected him.

So far it seemed like everyone was on their best behavior, the witches likely cast a spell to keep things from getting out of hand. Some people saw witches and mages as lesser beings because they were the closest to human. Magic in their blood gave them abilities and made them nonhuman. Witches, warlocks, wizards, and whatever else they liked to be called were magic users. Magic users as the name suggested could use magic. Mages commanded elements, like their elemental kin. A smart person knew not to underestimate them, their closeness to human was actually a strength not a weakness. They could blend and hide in plain sight, not everybody could. More of them survived the wars than most other types of nonhumans. Even us vampires couldn't all blend like they did, we were too much of predators for that.

"Cannon," Freddie called when she came over to me. I wrapped an arm around her waist and pulled her to my side. My first indication that something was wrong was the trembling of her body. The second was how she kept looking over her shoulder like someone was following her.

"What's wrong?" I asked her, looking around and not really seeing anyone paying her attention.

"I want to go home," she said, clearly agitated. Guiding her out of the loud room we got a measure of privacy in a hallway.

"We have to stay for a while, it's important we show them how committed we are," I said. Did I want to be there? Not really, but it was a necessary evil.

"I get that but I-I really need to go," she said, becoming increasingly agitated. Her hand was fisting my shirt, and I didn't think she realized she was doing it. The erratic beat of her heart was rather troubling, especially considering her current behavior.

"Tell me what happened," I said, trying to project calm.

"There was a man and he grabbed me and I just really want to leave," she said. Again, she was looking around and despite me holding her she was no less on edge.

"Did somebody hurt you?"

"No, just please Cannon, can you take me home?"

"Just stay with me, I won't let anybody bother you," I assured her. Immediately from her expression I knew it was the wrong thing to say.

"Just once I need you and you can't...never mind, I'll find my own way home," she said, pulling away from me.

"Fredericka, do not make a scene, that's the last thing we need. Obviously, you are upset but you have to remember that in public we are a reflection of The Family. Give it an hour or two and I'll take you home myself," I told her.

"No I can't," she said, shaking her head backing away.

Before I could stop her, she turned and walked away right into the lobby. There were people around, so I couldn't exactly force her to come back. Why was I forcing her to stay? Quickly I sent a message to Lee, who intercepted her at the door. She turned to look back at me with a hurt look in her eyes as he escorted her out. We didn't really fight but I imagined when I got home tonight we would.

"Hey, did Freddie find you?" Gunnar asked when he came to join me in the hall. His expression looked troubled as well, which was very unusual for him. What was going on today?

"She was just here, why?" I asked, trying not to be suspicious of my cousin's interest in my wife.

"Some guy was bothering her, had her cornered by the bathroom. I stepped in and told her to come find you. That guy was an asshole, asked who she belonged to so he might get to borrow her later. I warned him to stay away from her but he seemed kind of off. Is she ok?" He asked, looking around like she might suddenly appear, all I could do was stare at him. Now I had to ask why she didn't tell me anything about what happened? There was only one reason I could think of, and it was also why my cousin was being so vague.

"She asked me to take her home but she wouldn't say what happened," I admitted.

"Your wife tells you some guy is bothering her and you don't think maybe you should take her home? The guy was a vampire, do you recall how it is she came to be your wife in the first place?" Gunnar asked, staring at me like I had lost my mind.

"Fuck," was all I could say.

Too many days of no sleep plus so much annoyance at this summit did not have me thinking clearly. It wasn't really an excuse, and neither was the pressure I felt to hold everything together. She came to me for help and I did nothing. And it was very likely the reason she didn't explain what happened was because the vampire was from one of the other Families. This was a mess especially considering her past, killing one vampire had cost her so much already. She wouldn't have risked doing so here with everything going on. That would draw unwanted attention we really didn't need right now and likely start a war. Nobody outside of our immediate families knew what she could do and it had to stay that way.

"You don't deserve her," Gunnar commented, shaking his head.

"I know," I replied before turning to head for the door. Unfortunately, my father chose then to appear in the lobby.

"Going somewhere?" He asked, watching me in that intense way of his.

"I need to go home, Freddie was upset about something and left," I said, explaining nothing. Giving him more details would not help anything at all.

"What you need to do is get better control of that girl," he said. "You are not leaving here and you shouldn't have let her. She is your responsibility, if she can't learn to be an obedient wife then she can't be part of this Family."

What went unsaid was that if Freddie wasn't part of The Family, she would be dead. Or worse because vampires were really good at making things worse than death. There was no arguing with him, I couldn't leave. Which just meant my marriage was in shambles, but my wife was still stuck with me. What seemed like the best solution to her problem was no longer looking so good.

None of this should have ever happened to her, she was only defending herself when it all happened. It wasn't her fault, yet she was punished for it. Her whole life upended and her family threatened, it was a mess. One that our marriage was supposed to fix because my father believed in keeping her close. Likely it was to use her for something; I wasn't dumb enough to believe he did anything out of the goodness of his cold dead heart.

"Someone made unwanted advances at her, I need to go check on her," I said as calmly as I could.

"Did she kill someone?" He asked, looking more annoyed than bothered by the suggestion.

"No, of course not," I said.

"Good then there is nothing to worry about, you will see her after the party ends. Her absence will be noted but can be explained away. Your absence cannot be and will not be. I assume one of the guards took her?"

"Yes," I replied, feeling what I could only assume was helplessness. What a new and strange feeling that I never wanted to feel again.

"Then there's nothing to worry about, she will be safe and later you can explain to her why her behavior is unacceptable. We need to show a united front now more than ever," he told me. "Do not let your attachment to this girl get in the way of everything we have worked to achieve. If she's too distracting, then she can be removed."

"Why did you suggest we marry if you are so willing to throw her away?" I asked genuinely curious why any of this happened.

"She was pretty enough and seemed rather docile and you needed a wife so it made sense. I'm also curious if she will pass on her ability to her children. You think I am heartless, but I let her live and she has a nice life as your wife. Nicer than she could have ever hoped for. If she's going to be trouble though, I might have to rethink this whole thing," he told me. Though he shrugged like it was casual his eyes said it all. He would kill her if I didn't fall in line, message received.

"Never expected you to be the one to use her against me," was all I said. What I thought was that others would try but I should have known better, my father was never one to miss an opportunity.

"I never expected you to get so attached to her," he countered. "It would be a bad investment to kill her now, besides your mother is fond of her. But none of that matters if she gets in the way of you doing your job. We cannot afford to let this endeavor fail."

"Understood," I said, choosing not to get further into this.

My wife was assaulted when I should have been protecting her, but nothing else beyond this summit mattered. If I didn't know better, I would think that the humans were already planning to attack. The urgency in my father was starting to make me wonder. I already failed my wife; I couldn't fail this too.

Chapter 5:

Freddie

Sometimes I wonder what life was like before. Before when magic was dying in this world along with the planet. Two hundred and fifty years ago an explosion in the ley lines caused an event known as The Surge. The hows and whys of it were still a mystery but the resulting shock wave that spread throughout the universe changed everything. Magic was no longer dying and the polite fiction that nonhumans didn't exist was ripped away. Everything was chaos and, in that chaos, there was a line drawn in the sand: humans versus nonhumans.

Nonhumans of course being all those supernatural beings that only existed in fantasy. They were real and they were always here even if the humans forgot or didn't know. But really where did they think those stories came from? What set us apart from them was magic in our blood even though back then there wasn't a way to measure that. Now every nonhuman knew their M-levels which measured the percentage of magic in the blood. As humans tend to do, they declared war all over the world when the truth came out. For over 100 years the wars went on before they finally came to an agreement to coexist.

Since I was 27, I only knew the world after, where magic was alive and wild. I grew up in the world of coexistence which had its own problems. What must it have been like to have to hide what you were? It was weird to think about especially for someone like me, I was a hybrid. Most of the time when you had two different types of nonhumans producing a child together the child was one thing but not the other it was rare to be both. A hybrid blended both sides, so I was both witch and vampire. I could work magic like a witch and came with fangs, the need for blood and digestive system of a vampire.

Even though it wasn't exactly obvious what I was, I never really hid either half of me. However, I was raised as a witch not a vampire. My life was so much easier before when I lived as a witch. The fact that I had violet eyes marked me as nonhuman even though it was rare in both vampires and witches. Until I came to live with vampires, I didn't have my fangs showing all the time. It wasn't that I was hiding that part of me, I just didn't realize vampires felt a certain way about it. Vampires in a family like the Harringtons did not hide what they are, they wanted everybody to know. So, it was something I had to get used to.

Why was I thinking about any of this? Because crying over a man was so stupid and cliché. Thinking about literally anything else was better than thinking about my life. Maybe it wasn't so much crying over a man as it was frustration at the current state of my life. Mostly I was just angry, and I probably had been for a while without acknowledging it. I knew Cannon didn't love me but I thought he at least cared. Obviously, I was wrong to think that because The Family always came first.

The irony of that wasn't lost on me as I had put The Family first. For vampires The Family is everything and I had only been part of it for the last six months. My marriage essentially was my ticket into the Harrington Family. The Family for vampires was the equivalent of a coven, clan, pack, or pride. In my time here I learned the difference between The Family and family, they weren't really that different. Being part of The Family you didn't need to be related, it could be made up of various people. Mostly with the Harringtons it was relatives because there were a lot of them. But it also included the employees living and working on the grounds of the compound. In the typical sense family meant your actual blood related family or those married in that carried the surname. It was confusing learning the vampire way, but I had no choice in if I wanted to or not.

Cannon didn't come home again, which wasn't much of a surprise. Of course he didn't actually care, I was merely his property after all. I was so tired of everything that happened the past seven months. Was I sorry about what happened to that man? No, he was a predator in more ways than one and he deserved to die. What I regretted was everything that came after. A week of being held captive and then I was offered a way out. Followed by three weeks of time spent with Cannon while our wedding was being planned. There was never much of a question if I would say no or not.

Maybe I was being dramatic or maybe I was just fed up. I didn't want to be here anymore, and I didn't care about the consequences. What was the worst they could do? Kill me of course, but then at least I would be free. Last night I was essentially right back where I started so what was the point anymore? No more dwelling on any of this mess instead I got up and got dressed in a pretty sunflower print dress. Pulled my hair up in a ponytail and took off my wedding rings. Part of me hated to do it after all these months of never taking them off. I always felt they were an unnecessary extravagance; the cost had to be as much as a four-generation house.

Dwarven Martian red gold was on its own expensive as it was imported from Mars. But the black Draconian diamonds? They were one of the most precious gemstones in the universe and damn near impossible to source since dragons owned their distribution. Getting treasures from a dragon was notoriously difficult. How I came to have a princess cut engagement ring and wedding band both haloed with the diamonds, I didn't know. Nothing but the best for

Harringtons, one look told you how well connected their family was. Wealth in this post-Surge world wasn't always about material things; it was about magic and connections.

With how well connected and powerful the Harringtons were, there was nowhere I could go that they wouldn't find me. So why complicate my life further by being difficult? It wouldn't be hard to figure out where I would go. Where was the most obvious place? Back home, I missed my family. My phone, I left with the rings, and I didn't bother packing a bag. Aside from the fact it would be suspicious, I didn't want anything from them. Technically most of the things I had were purchased by the Harringtons because I had to maintain a certain appearance. Nothing was ever really mine, not even myself. Getting out of our apartment was the easy part; it was leaving the house that would prove challenging. This was proven immediately when I opened the door to find Lee standing there.

Lee had been my guard since I fell into the world of the Harringtons. After what happened on the worst night of my life I was assigned guards. Four of them lived in my house for the three weeks that I was allowed to remain there. Last night when Lee brought me home, he didn't say anything, and I didn't think he would. He was an employee of The Family, not my friend, even if he was with me every time I left the house. The fact that he was currently outside my door wasn't exactly unusual, but it wasn't typical either. Whyever, would I need a guard with me within the safety of the compound? So, his presence didn't immediately suggest that he was here to keep me from leaving but it was possible.

"Good morning Mrs. Harrington," he greeted like always. "Do you need anything?"

"Pretty sure it's not your job to cater to me," I pointed out.

"My job is whatever you need it to be," he replied easily. He was rather charming and very attractive, too bad I couldn't have been married to him instead.

As a married woman I most certainly did not notice his muscular arms or the way his T-shirt stretched across his muscular frame. I definitely didn't remember that he had abs to die for. Lee was part of the group of guards that went on our honeymoon with us. So, I had seen him shirtless... all that golden brown skin... No, I wasn't lusting after my guard, but I couldn't help noticing his attractive qualities. Unfortunately, I was so foolish that the only man I had any real interest in was in fact the one I was trying to escape.

"Can you do me a favor? I need to go out; can you have one of the cars ready?" I asked casually, this wasn't an unusual request. Though he was technically a bodyguard, he did tasks like that all of the time.

It would be more suspicious if I tried to leave and took a car out myself. Technically I had a car that was mine, but anybody could use whatever cars were in the garage. Harringtons did not drive themselves anywhere. At least they weren't supposed to, but Cannon did it all the time even with his driver in the car. His driver and guard were his friends so

Brit Andrews

they could get away with things. My situation was obviously different; I had to follow all of the rules all of the time. However, since Lee was my guard not my driver he would likely go find him. I liked Oswaldo just fine; he had also been part of my guard since the beginning. But I wasn't sure if he would follow along with what I wanted if Cannon said something different. For all I knew asking Lee to do this was just going to keep me from leaving. But it was the only way I could get off the property. I couldn't just walk out, that would be very suspicious, and I wasn't allowed to go anywhere alone. Living in this family was like constantly tightrope walking, it was exhausting.

"Of course," Lee said as he usually did.

"Thank you," I replied hoping he didn't decide to tell on me first.

"Give me five minutes," he said before disappearing down a hidden staircase.

Typically, I was mostly allowed to come and go as I pleased but with the ongoing summit Cannon had wanted me to stay home. Since my minder wasn't around, I just had to dodge staff and family to gain my temporary freedom. When he found out I left, Cannon would come after me, I knew that. It's why I was leaving my phone behind. So I set off through the house that wasn't really a house at all. On the outside it looked like a rather large mansion. With a few other smaller houses scattered on the grounds. Inside it was way bigger than it should be and was more like a series of interconnected condos. What was most impressive was that a lot of this had been built pre-Surge before magical architecture was a thing.

There were common areas and a massive kitchen and dining room, even a ballroom for parties. With the summit preparations there hadn't really been much entertaining going on since I moved in. Thankfully our apartment was closer to the front of the house, so I didn't have far to go but I did have to pass through the main house. Side doors were for servants, so I had to use the front door, old vampires tended to be snobbier than some rich humans.

Bloodlines were everything for vampires, the older the more elitist they were. The Harringtons were a very old family and had been around as long as there had been people living in this part of the world. Cannon never seemed to be particularly elitist but by vampire standards he was young at 105 years old. He was significantly older than me, which wasn't exactly a problem with how vampires did things, but I was under the age of 30 and vampires weren't fully considered adults until then. A lot of nonhumans didn't really consider you fully mature until you were 30. Humans sometimes had these crazy opinions about your life being over after 30 but for us that was when it was just beginning.

Almost nothing was known about where I came from or anything to do with my bloodline. At best they might say my blood was of dubious quality. There were worst things they said about vampires like me, being a half blood set me apart. Being a hybrid pushed me further away from all things vampire. No matter what, I could never be good enough for them. Being adopted as a baby by non-vampires made me even less desirable. Vampires were never a part of my life until I got the attention of the Harringtons. If I could, I would have gone all my life never caring and staying clear of vampires, sadly I wasn't so lucky. It wasn't my fault what happened, but I had to live with the consequences. At least for another few hours maybe a day if Cannon didn't immediately come for me. He was of course so busy with the summit he might not even notice I was gone.

"Hey Freddie," someone called and I froze, the front door was in sight.

My freedom was right there but I turned to see Gunnar coming from another hall. Like Cannon he was the rare Harrington with fairer skin, he actually looked a lot like his cousin. His eyes were darker and his hair black, but they had a similar muscular build and walked around with all the confidence of a man sure of his appeal. Gunnar, though, was the fun-loving type always smiling and making people laugh. He never really seemed serious about anything, unlike my husband. Both of them were of course very charming as seemed common in their family.

"Hi," I said maintaining my perfectly pleasant facade

"Are you ok after last night?" He asked almost causing me to crack but I was good at masks after living here for half a year.

"Yeah, thank you for your help," I replied. If not for Gunnar I don't know what would have happened to me last night. Or worse, I knew exactly what would have happened and it would have been very bad.

"Any time, if you ever need anything all you have to do is ask," he said. I knew he was sincere but he was a Harrington so I couldn't really trust him.

"Thanks," I said hoping he would just let it be. Why was he more worried about me than my own husband?

"You didn't tell Cannon who it was, did you?" He asked, making my blood run cold, I did not want to talk about it.

"Neither did you," I countered though it was just a guess.

"I could tell him. I considered it because we don't really keep secrets from each other. But I know why you didn't tell him so I'm leaving it up to you. It's your choice, just know that he's going to ask," he warned.

"The Family comes first, right?"

"In most things yeah but you are his wife, he knows something happened."

"It doesn't matter and I really don't want to talk about it," I said hoping he would let it drop. This serious version of him that was before me right now was unnerving, I hadn't even known he could be serious. Last night though I would go as far as to say he might have looked murderous, but I could have imagined it.

"Fine, I'll leave you alone but he's not going to let it go," he warned, then looked towards the door where Lee was parked waiting for me. "Are you going somewhere?"

"Yes, I just have to run out for a bit, so I'll see you later," I said quickly.

My steps didn't increase as I moved to the door though it was a near thing. He didn't say anything else, but I could feel him watching me even once I was outside. Lee opened the door for me and I got in silently. My driver was noticeably absent from the car. When Lee asked where we were going, I told him to go to my parents' house. In the time Lee had been my guard I don't think he ever drove me anywhere yet here he was. Part of me was certain it was a trap, but we made it through the gate and out onto the road. The trip was completely uneventful.

"How long will you be, Mrs. Harrington?" Lee asked when we arrived.

"You could just call me Freddie," I said and not for the first time.

"I value my life so I won't do that ma'am, your husband wouldn't like it," he replied.

"Of course," I said with a sigh. "I'm going to be awhile so you don't need to stay."

"He would like that even less," he pointed out.

"What if I'm not planning to go back?" I asked him though I knew I shouldn't, but I was so tired. He could very well lock me in the car and take me back and I couldn't do much about it. Using magic on him would be wrong since he was just doing his job.

"Then I would say that I especially couldn't leave you," he said, surprising me. "My job is to keep you safe. I'm not going to drag you back to your husband, that isn't in my job description. As long as you are here, I will keep watch. Should you need anything I'm here."

"Are you sure you are willing to risk Cannon's wrath?" I asked, just because my life was a mess didn't mean I would mess up someone else's.

"As I said, my job is to protect you," was his reply before he got out and came to open my door.

"Is that why Oswaldo isn't here?"

"Yes, I got the feeling that you didn't want another person here so I didn't call for him."

"Thank you," I said and he nodded following me to the door.

Before I even reached the door it opened, and my sister came running out. The magical connection my family shared with the house always alerted us when one of us arrived home. Ollie hugged me like she hadn't seen me in years. We talked all the time but with all the summit stuff going on I hadn't been able to come home in a while. Next my mom came out, and she hugged me too, I missed them and I missed our life from before. Though I was the wife of a wealthy, important man, I would give it all up to go back to how things use to be. But that could never happen, there was no going back.

"We weren't expecting you, but I'm so glad to see you," my mom said. "I thought you were busy with the summit?"

47

"I was a little homesick," I admitted. It wasn't a lie because I was very often but that just wasn't exactly why I had come now.

"How long can you stay?" Mom asked and I just shrugged, likely it would be a few hours or less.

"Uh I'm not sure, Cannon will let me know when I have to go," I said. Following her I went into the house where she called for my father.

"Is everything ok?" Ollie asked me in a whisper, and I shook my head. My little sister was 17, a whole decade younger than me, but she was also my best friend.

"Later," I told her before going to greet our father.

It was nice to be home, even though I wouldn't be here long. No matter what happened next, at least I got to see my family one last time.

Cannon

I wasn't sure if my marriage was going to last through this summit. Hell, I might not make it, it felt like I hadn't slept in a week or a year or something like that. All I wanted was coffee before dealing with my next crisis. Unfortunately, I found my mother when I went in search of that from the kitchen. She was going over the menu for a dinner party we were hosting for some reason or another. Thankfully the kitchen staff was so efficient that before I could ask, I was handed a mug of coffee made just the way I like it: black with a dash of blood. Technically, since it was vampire coffee, the beans were soaked in blood as part of the process in making it. But a little extra blood never hurt anything, besides I likely wouldn't be seeing my bed any time soon, so I'd need it.

"You don't look so good," my mother unhelpfully commented.

"This summit is a never ending nightmare that makes sleep impossible," I replied leaning against the counter where she sat.

"Your father is determined to make it work this time," she said, though even she looked doubtful. Too much infighting, distrust, and long memories made this task damn near impossible.

"Yeah, after the party last night I barely closed my eyes before he was calling me to deal with another problem. At this point the humans might as well start picking us off; it wouldn't even be hard."

"Don't say that," she admonished. "Where is Fredericka today? I haven't seen her; she should be taking better care of you."

"Last time I saw her she was in bed but that was before I left," I said with a heavy sigh. "Oh by the way, thanks so much for telling my wife that I'm cheating on her."

"That is not what I said, besides it's not cheating to have a mistress. Even so, you were the one to take all your blood lust out on her. She was very embarrassed, couldn't stop fidgeting the whole ride home. Next time use someone else, though maybe you should be trying harder in that department. I had hoped a young bride might be able to reproduce more quickly but apparently not. Though it's possible her affliction is interfering, which would be unfortunate. If that's the case, I don't know what we will do with her," she said shaking her head.

Sometimes talking to my parents was exhausting, they had their views on things and were pretty immovable about it. Yes, my marriage solved a problem for them, but it was also an experiment of sorts. Nonhumans, in general, reproduced much less than humans due to the magic in our blood. With fae it was especially difficult because they were very magical. For Vampires it could be difficult depending on your bloodline, the stronger the blood the better your chance. But not always, that occasionally worked against you.

Freddie was a very young vampire but being born a vampire didn't mean the long life of a vampire. It was complicated and there were no record of her bloodline and no match for her in the bloodline registry. So, there was no way to guess how things would go for us. She was young so theoretically that could help but she also wasn't *just* a vampire, which might be a big problem. Nothing could possibly ever be easy for us, could it?

"Do you think of anything else aside from how we are all under performing?"

"No, not really, there is just so much to criticize when it comes to my children," she said with a dramatic sigh.

"I notice you didn't mention to my wife that she could potentially take lovers."

"While you know I believe in a woman's right to her own pleasure she can't entertain others until after she's done her duty to The Family." She said dismissively, translation:

Freddie couldn't have a lover because we couldn't risk her getting pregnant. It was my parents' who forced us both to get our birth control implants removed, it wasn't a choice we made ourselves. "Your marriage is still new, once you've had a child then she's free to do as she pleases."

"Do me a favor and don't encourage my wife to take lovers. I'm not sharing her with anyone else."

"Since you met her you've gotten to be so possessive," she commented, shaking her head. "For someone who refused to get married, it's rather interesting."

"Do you recall forcing me to marry her?"

"Oh please, you were not forced to marry her. We simply presented options, and you were all too eager to be her white knight. And don't get me started on that stunt you attempted to pull at your wedding. Trying to steal the bride away because one drop of blood from a blood virgin had you going crazy."

Unfortunately, she wasn't wrong, I had become possessive. At first, I thought it was just that I felt protective of her but then our wedding happened. My first taste of her blood... if I could have stolen her away, we wouldn't have been seen again for a few days. Alas that wasn't really meant to be because my mother had to be the voice of reason and say things even my possessive brain couldn't deny. I still had regrets about how our wedding night went but that was a whole other thing. Being possessive was new for me, and it started before I tasted her blood. From the moment she agreed to be mine I was screwed. Without her doing anything, I was bewitched the moment I looked into those violet eyes.

The way she looked at me last night… she trusted me to protect her and I fucked up. No, I couldn't have foreseen what happened, but I knew she needed protection. This all happening right after our discussion helped nothing. My wife likely believed she couldn't trust me to keep her safe or probably in general. I was trying to be more present for her, but it was hard when I had so much shit to do. How did other people manage to juggle responsibility and marriage? I would ask my mother but for one, she likes giving advice too much and two, there was nothing ever normal about my parents' relationship.

"You said you haven't seen my wife today?" I asked, steering her away from any invasive questions.

"No, but I would like to know what is going on with her? Your father wasn't happy she left the party early."

"She wasn't feeling well," I lied and of course my mother stared at me. I should have known better than to lie to Belinda Harrington. "Honestly I don't know, something happened and she wanted to leave, Gunnar said some guy was bothering her. Before I could figure out what was really going on she left, she's mad at me."

"Who would dare to accost a Harrington?" My mother asked rather indignant, for all her ways she was protective of this family.

"Gunnar wouldn't say, he was very concerned though especially considering what happened before," I admitted.

Seven months ago, Freddie Miller was living her simple life going to work, living at home with her family and then everything changed. There was a reason vampires often got bad reputations, some were monsters. An incident occurred with her that resulted in a dead vampire. Which was why my father had been contacted as the head of the vampire council. An investigation into the whole thing brought certain things to light.

That information eventually ended in her becoming my wife because what she could do was not natural for a vampire and shouldn't be possible. The only way to keep her safe from everyone else and to protect the world from her was to absorb her into our family. Nobody messed with our family and lived to tell the tale, Freddie was part of our family with every protection that came with the name.

Last night I should have taken her more seriously when she first told me I knew something was wrong. I failed her, it was my job to protect her and I didn't. Was I dragging my feet a little on facing her? Yes, I deserved her ire. Not that she would get overly mad at me because no matter what I said she still had it in her mind that if she did the wrong thing we would cast her out. However, that wasn't the case, I would never let anyone hurt her because no matter what happened between us, she was family. And she seriously underestimated how my mother felt about that. Once you belonged to Belinda Harrington there was no going back.

"Why are you here? Go to your wife and deal with this or I will," my mother predictably said. In another life it wouldn't surprise me if she was a bear shifter.

"I'm heading up now," I said just as Gunnar came into the kitchen.

"Did you know your wife isn't here?" He asked and I just stared at him.

"What? No, she should be upstairs," I said. Hadn't I asked her very politely not to leave the house? Sure, she was pissed at me, but she wouldn't do anything to put herself in harm's way, would she?

"I watched her walk out the door and get in a car," he informed me.

"Why didn't you stop her?" I asked while pulling out my phone to call her.

"Uh cause she's your child bride not mine and I didn't know she wasn't allowed out of the house," he said with a shrug. "Guess you haven't started groveling yet after last night?"

"Don't call her that, and I just got back, I've been gone. Another fire to put out though at least not literally like the last one," I replied. Her phone rang but she wasn't answering so I tried texting but of course that got me nowhere. Tracking her phone told me that the phone was here in the house, which meant she left it.

"Go find that girl and bring her home," my mother ordered as if I hadn't already planned to.

"I will," I assured her. "Gun, was she alone when she left?"

"No, one of your guards was driving I think," he answered.

The only one of our guards that would dare take my wife anywhere without my permission was Lee. Which was now its own problem because he didn't say anything to me. I could guess where Freddie would go, and I should have anticipated it. When I texted Lee, his response was slow to come. Yup, that was a problem on its own. Though he had been working for us long before she moved in, he clearly had some loyalty to her. The last thing I needed was for one of the guards to become overly familiar with my wife. His response confirmed what I knew and that I was never going to get any rest.

"She's visiting her parents," I told my mother and cousin.

"This isn't the best time for that," my mother pointed out as if I didn't know.

"Yes I am aware, that's why she didn't tell me, she's still pissed at me," I said with a sigh. "I'll go get her, I doubt Lee will make her come back. I need to fire him now; he's become too attached if he's taking her out without telling me."

"No, don't do anything so foolish, a loyal guard is a good one to have," my mother suggested. "As long as you make things clear there's no harm in it he would likely protect her with his life. You can't buy that kind of loyalty and you are already in enough trouble, she would just resent you."

"Having a wife seems like a lot of work," Gunnar commented a little too amused.

"Your time is coming," my mother told him. Naturally to that he shook his head and made a disgusted face. "Cannon, go bring her home and fix whatever you have broken. Your father cannot find out that she's out roaming around with a single guard as protection, not now. It's not safe, especially for her."

"I know, I'm going," I said.

After handing my empty mug off to one of the kitchen staff I headed up to our apartment. It was as pristine as it typically was, the bed was made, and everything was in its usual place. Nothing was really out of the ordinary, no clothes that I could tell had been taken from the walk-in closet we shared. Even the scarf she wore on her head at night was still beside the bed like usual. I could even catch faint traces of her apple and vanilla scent. As expected, Freddie wasn't there and her phone was on the dresser.

What I didn't expect to find beside her phone were her wedding rings. It seemed that my wife didn't just go to visit her family, she left me. This day just kept getting better and better. Too bad for her I wouldn't be letting go of what was mine.

Freddie

My plan got me this far, everything else was up to fate. I loved spending time catching up with my family. I talked to them daily, but it wasn't the same as physically being together. This was the house I grew up in, where all my memories began. Where I was just the daughter of Vivian and Bernie Miller and sister of Ollie. Five months living with Cannon and the Harringtons I never really felt at home. This would always be home for me, I didn't need luxury and a staff, I just needed my family.

After lunch I went up to my bedroom with my sister. Nothing about it had changed since I moved out, it seemed to be waiting for my return. If I could just come back here and pick up my life where it left off I would. Everything happened so fast after that night. I was suddenly engaged and moving in with a man I barely knew and his family who were my jailers. Belinda and Lucy never treated me badly; they actually seemed to want to help me adjust and fit into their way of doing things. We went places and they introduced me to people, so it wasn't like I was locked away in a tower like a princess in a fairytale. But they were the vampire elite and I wasn't.

The worst part about leaving was that I couldn't see Ollie, we had been inseparable since the day she joined our family. Like me, she was adopted, though unlike me, she was not a vampire. She was a witch like our mother, what I wouldn't give for the simplicity of being just one thing. If things had been different, I wouldn't have moved out of this house or left her. When they finally had a child, my parents invested in a two-generation home. There was enough space for us to have our own families all living under one roof. When the world changed, being closer to your family and support system became very important. I did have a couple friends who moved out on their own, some liked it and some didn't. This was my home and my family; this was where I wanted to be.

"So what's really going on?" Ollie asked when we settled on my bed.

"I can't do it anymore, can't stay with him," I admitted with a sigh.

"You never told me you were unhappy," she said, taking my hand.

"Not unhappy exactly, I just always feel like if I do or say the wrong thing then I'll be punished for it. Cannon doesn't hurt me or anything but I'm just constantly aware that my life is tied to him and his family. Last night I saw for myself it's never going to be enough, I can keep being the perfect wife, but they could still turn on me at any time. If they decide it's safer for everyone if I'm no longer living nobody would do anything I don't even know if Cannon would care. So I would rather take control of the situation myself even though I know the consequences," I told her.

"You think they are going to kill you?" She asked because my sister was smart, I just shrugged and she threw her arms around me. "That's why you are here? To say goodbye? I don't accept that!"

"Once Cannon realizes I'm gone I don't know what's going to happen but I do know he will come to retrieve me. Either they kill me or confine me to the house or toss me in a cell somewhere. There's never been a happy ending for me not since they decided that I'm dangerous," I explained. If I wasn't so worn down by my life I would be alarmed at how I was just calmly accepting my possible death.

"We can leave," Ollie said, sounding so young.

"Where could I go to hide from the Harringtons? Besides Lee is outside, I don't think he would turn on me, but I can't be sure, they pay him not me. He brought me here when he shouldn't have."

With the kind of power the Harringtons had they could literally do anything they wanted. Proven by how they took over my life and nobody could have stopped them, even though my parents tried. But they had no power, not when the Harringtons were ordering around law enforcement. Laws didn't apply to them; I saw that firsthand. I wish I could go back, maybe there was something I could have done differently. Something that didn't put me in the sights of the Harringtons. After that night I was essentially their property. Last night I was right back where I started, the worst part is that they are right, I'm not safe. I've never been safe; I just didn't know it.

"I'm not going to lose you!" Ollie told me, of course she was upset, but I was just numb. "I'll kill Cannon, I won't let him take you away."

"Oleander, you can't kill Cannon, he's a full blood vampire over a hundred years old."

"You could do it," she pointed out but I shook my head.

"I don't ever want to do that again. I'm just tired of everything."

"What happened? What did he do?"

Explaining to her what happened did not make me feel any better. At this point, though, at least I didn't feel worse. With everything that Cannon said to me I thought he would at least care. No, I didn't tell him what happened because I knew nothing good would come of it. Taking myself out of the situation made the most sense at the time. The summit is important, and The Family comes before everything. Right now all I had left to lose was myself, but did I even still belong to me?

"How long before he comes?" She asked, sounding resigned and sad.

"Don't know. He didn't come home last night but that's not unusual these days, he's always working. The summit takes up all of his time."

"None of this is fair, somebody hurts you and you get trapped in this marriage! And you can't breathe without bodyguards following you around. I want you to come back home and forget those people but of course they made that impossible," Ollie said, her eyes glassy with unshed tears.

My situation wasn't just frustrating for me; it affected my family too. Being powerless to stop any of what happened did take a toll on my parents. There was nothing to be done, if I didn't marry Cannon I wouldn't have seen them again. Cannon was good at getting people to like him, and he promised them that he would take care of me and I would be safe. While he did one of those things, that no longer mattered. Six months ago, my family had to let me go and send me off with strangers.

For families like the Harringtons arranged marriages were common practice and even expected. Those with power kept it by carefully building it. This was always going to be his reality but not so much for me. Depending on who you asked, we either fell in love in a whirlwind romance or his parents decided we would marry after he saved my life. Both things were ridiculous, especially since under normal circumstances they would never let someone like me into this family. But my circumstances were anything but normal.

Funny thing is, I didn't even meet Cannon until days after what happened. Our very first conversation was deciding if I was going to marry him or not.

When humans married, they loved to draw things out by months and years, nonhumans didn't waste time like that. Speedy courtships were rather common, but three weeks from meeting to the altar was something to talk about. For some nonhumans they met their fated mate and that was it, instant connection. As far as I knew vampires didn't tend to have fated mates, but it wasn't impossible. Making Cannon the hero and me the damsel was just distracting enough that some people wouldn't question it. Maybe it even implied that the hand of fate was at work. But these were the Harringtons, and it was their only son who was heir to the empire. No matter what story you heard, our marriage made no sense because something as silly as love could never sway a Harrington.

My family and friends were also skeptical considering my status and the fact that I never had any meaningful contact with vampires. Yet, I was marrying the vampire prince like some twisted fairytale. The extravagant wedding Belinda planned did help to sell the illusion. Though the marks had long since gone I looked down at my wrist at the place he bit me for the first time. Of course, a vampire wedding required blood. And well our marriage came with a side of lies and secrets.

"Life is famously unfair," I told her. "I'm sorry to burden you with all of this, but I knew you weren't going to let it go.

And I guess someone should know what's going on if I don't come back. They might not kill me, but they will likely lock me up."

Was I truly so numb to everything that I felt nothing at all when talking about this? Right now it seemed like it, and I knew that was probably freaking Ollie out the most. Calmly facing my doom seemed to be the only way I could handle this. I didn't know what was going to happen, my husband already didn't care about me. All the time we spent together I had thought we were getting closer, but I was wrong. Last night he looked at me like I was a nuisance, and it hurt. What was funny was that I was still trying to do right by The Family in not telling him who that guy was. Because I did know, Belinda made sure I knew who all the prominent vampire families were at the summit.

Laying on my bed with my sister was so familiar, we had done this so many times. We talked about everything; there was never any secrets between us. At least before there wasn't, recently I kept a lot to myself. As time went on more and more, I was feeling off and unsettled, and I didn't know how to articulate that. I also hated to burden my little sister with my problems. She was still in high school, and she had her whole uncomplicated life ahead of her. My best friends would listen if I called, but I barely got to see them anymore. They thought I was crazy to be marrying a man I didn't know and even once attempted to stage an intervention. Cannon sweet talked them into liking him though, he was very good at that.

"Why is it that life seems to be particularly unfair for you?" Ollie asked and I shrugged because I didn't know. Apparently, I was just that unlucky. After 27 years of a regular life fate decided to rip mine apart like I did something I should be punished for.

"The universe has decided that I don't deserve a peaceful life," I said. It was something I had thought about and it felt true. One stupid night changed the whole course of my life forever and there was no going back.

"I tried to find someone who could time travel," she admitted and I stared at her. "What? I had to try; you are my sister. Unfortunately, anyone who has that particular gift is exceedingly rare and would likely refuse to use it. If they did, I doubt even the Harringtons could afford it."

"Messing with time can have serious consequences so that makes sense. It's for the best that you didn't find anyone. Altering things could just make them worse. If someone else had tried to help me they might have ended up dead. It was a bad situation and even if it hadn't happened how it did, I have a feeling that I would have been found eventually. Better for it to come out this way than for somebody who didn't deserve it to be hurt.

"Trust me I wish I could go back and do something different, but I know logically that's not possible. There was nothing I could have done differently; it wasn't really down to me what happened. Sometimes I feel like there should have been something and then I wouldn't be in this situation. But it's also possible I could be in a worse one," I sighed.

"Are you in love with Cannon?" She asked and I sat up looking away from her. "That was telling."

"My feelings about Cannon are complicated, it's hard to know where things stand with him. Sometimes he's so loving and attentive but other times I feel like I'm just there to service his needs. We have talked about some stuff, but the best thing I can do is leave any emotion out of this thing between us. It's hard when we live together and we have sex but it's necessary. I wasn't promised love, and I don't even know that I want it," I admitted. "Last night I just felt so alone and maybe I overreacted. But you have to understand that with them, The Family has to come first. That's what was drilled into my head The Family first, no individual is more important than the whole. And nothing is more important than this summit. They will probably think it was my fault anyway."

Last night when that man came at me, I froze and could barely breathe. All I could think was: is this really happening again? What is it about me that makes vampires feel like they can do whatever they want to me? No matter what I did it didn't seem to matter. Even being part of the Harrington family didn't keep me safe, so what was the point? Everything felt pretty pointless and yes, I was hurt by Cannon not caring. He, more than anybody else, promised me I would be ok then I wasn't and he didn't bother to care. So now I would pay the price for trusting these people, funny how it was always me that was paying for things. My life was so damn exhausting.

"Do you really think he's going to lock you up?" Ollie asked and I shrugged, I didn't know what he might do or what his father might do.

"We are about to find out," I said with a heavy sigh. "Don't do anything Ollie or say anything to him, it's not worth it."

Cannon was here; I knew it. I could feel it in my bones before the doorbell rang. I could hear his voice as he spoke with my mother who had answered the door. I looked at Ollie who looked panicked. Saying nothing more I hugged my sister tight, then got up and went to the door. With a deep breath I went down the stairs where I found him chatting with my mother like nothing was wrong. When he finally looked at me, I knew he was pissed. But he smiled like this was any other day and that sort of terrified me. I was never afraid of Cannon before but now I was starting to question that.

"You forgot your phone," Cannon said by way of greeting. He pulled it out of his pocket and held it out to me. His intense gaze stayed on me as he waited for me to take it.

"Thanks," I said, taking it from him.

"We were hoping to have Freddie here longer," Mom said with a disappointed look.

"Sorry about that, it's my fault entirely. The schedule with this summit is always changing," he said.

"Can you two at least stay for dinner?" She asked, looking between us with a hopefulness that broke my heart.

"Of course," he answered before turning his gaze back to me.

No matter how this ended there was no way I would be allowed to freely roam ever again. If I ever truly was to begin with. I had seen Cannon angry before I just never had his anger directed at me. I did everything I could to be a good and agreeable wife, we didn't fight about anything.

That was going to change though because even if this ended in the worst way I didn't regret leaving. For the first time in the last seven months, I attempted to take control of my life. A short-lived freedom was still a win.

Chapter 8:

Freddie

Time was the most precious thing in the universe, once lost you could never get it back. Like the perfect son-in-law, Cannon took the time to chat with my parents. He even asked Ollie about school; she surprisingly managed not to glare at him. This was all on purpose; he was being his perfectly charming self, making me wait. My parents didn't see the simmering rage hiding behind every pleasant comment. They didn't notice the ring of black around his grey irises, I did. Maybe my time was well and truly up, and still, I couldn't feel anything about that. It bothered me more than having to deal with an angry vampire.

After agreeing to stay for dinner he excused us to talk in private. With little choice I brought him up to my room and no sooner than the door was closed did he have me pinned against the wall. This was probably the second time he had ever been in my room and oh how things had changed since then. As he glared at me his eyes went full black, I was actually impressed he held it off so long. With strong emotions, a vampire's eyes could change black and sometimes red. Black didn't always mean anger, it could also mean lust. As for red, nobody wanted to be near a red-eyed vampire.

"Have you lost your fucking mind?" He demanded all traces of the person he pretended to be for my family gone in an instant.

"I'm done," I told him simply.

"So the answer is yes, you have."

"What? Do you want an apology? I'm not sorry I left, I'm only sorry you noticed so soon," I said with a shrug.

"Fredericka, did it occur to you when you decided on this ill advised course of action that you put yourself in danger? That by coming here you put your family in danger?" He asked and I just stared at him, I didn't expect that.

"Why would my family be in danger? I know that if I'm not with you then my life is quite literally over and I accept that. It's preferable than to continue this charade of being your wife. When I say I'm done I really mean it," I told him.

"For one thing you don't get to be done, I don't accept that. I am sorry for what happened, and I would have told you that last night, but my father wouldn't let me leave the party. I wasn't trying to be dismissive of you, and I wish you would have actually told me everything. But aside from the fact that you would rather die than stay married to me, the summit is still going on. There was a reason I didn't want you going out, you more than anyone aren't safe out here. If anyone had any idea what you could do, they would have you in chains and use your family to get you to do whatever they wanted. Your sister is very young and very vulnerable, you don't want to know what someone might do to her," he told me.

"I wasn't thinking about that," I admitted.

"Yeah that's fucking obvious," he said.

Mostly I had been thinking that I couldn't trust my husband, and I just wanted to be away from him and his suffocating family. Everything in my life is either planned or observed in some way. I have to ask permission like a child to leave the damn house and always under supervision. Why Lee had helped me leave I couldn't guess but he also likely told Cannon where I was too. Which I didn't blame him for, it was his job. Did I consider that this stupid summit might make my life even more difficult? No, I didn't. I wasn't thinking about that at all.

"Does it matter now? You are here, I'm recaptured, nothing happened," I pointed out.

To be clear I didn't want to die I did not have a death wish, and I wasn't suicidal. But I was tired of fighting the inevitable, my life hadn't been mine since that night. I was an unwanted obligation to my husband and essentially existed now to give him children. That was my only purpose as far as the Harringtons were concerned. It was not the career of my dreams, all of that died that night all those months ago. Crazy how one moment could change your life so completely and so permanently.

All I wanted that night was to get home, funny how it ended up being the reason I lost my home. There was no reason I shouldn't have been safe there just like at that damn party. Before living with vampires, I never fully understood that there were different types of predators. Vampires by their very nature and need to feed on the blood of others to survive makes them predators. But there was also the type of predator that went after the weak and vulnerable.

That night a stranger decided that he could take what he wanted without consequence, and I proved him wrong. What I did wasn't intentional, but it was life altering. Part of me knew I should feel guilty about it but truth be told I hadn't been feeling much since then. Agreeing to marry Cannon hadn't even really been to save my own life. No, I did it so my family wouldn't have to suffer my loss.

Living had just become more trouble than it was worth. Men did what they wanted with you, and you just had to take it, wasn't that what Belinda and Lucy had been saying? Be a good wife, do what your husband wants and turn a blind eye to everything else. This wasn't the life I wanted or asked for so what else could I do but give it all up? Consequences? Nobody else cared about those so why should I?

"You aren't my prisoner, is that really what you think? I'm not doing this to be an asshole; I'm trying to protect you. That's all I've ever tried to do," he said, sounding less angry.

For some reason I wanted him to be angry because I was angry. Apparently, I was also irrational too and maybe I had lost my mind completely. At some point don't we all snap? Bend enough and you break, and I was coming apart. With those insane thoughts in mind, I grabbed him and pushed him against the wall reversing our positions. This naturally surprised my husband as I would never do such a thing under normal circumstances. I was sweet and quiet and did as I was told.

"Maybe you should be protecting yourself from me," I told him. I held his gaze as I placed my hand over his heart.

"Maybe," he replied, surprising me by grabbing the backs of my thighs to pick me up, my legs automatically wrapped around his waist. "You are so sexy right now."

"I just threatened to kill you," I reminded him. His response to that was scraping his fangs against my neck which made my traitorous body shiver.

"Sometimes I forget how young you are and how little time you've spent around vampires," he said like that explained something.

"Are you saying vampires like to threaten to kill each other?" I asked only half as surprised as I should be, vampires were weird.

"Yeah," he admitted with a laugh. "I like you like this, I've never wanted a subservient wife."

"Um but I could really kill you, you know that," I said, still stuck on that.

"Yes I'm very aware that I've been sharing my bed and my life with a woman who could very well kill me in my sleep. Or when I'm awake and piss her off enough. Could have saved me a drive if you had just expressed your anger like this," he said like it was nothing.

"Why doesn't it bother you? I mean aside from the fact that vampires are weird."

"Do you waste time thinking about the fact that I could kill you?"

"No, I never thought you might kill me. Even leaving I assumed your father would do it or pay someone to do it," I said with a shrug.

"Nobody is going to hurt my wife," he vowed. "Last night I was tired and stressed and it's no excuse for not listening to what you were trying to tell me. Protecting you is my number 1 priority, even when you hate me. You were upset and I did not react in the way I should have, and I am truly sorry for that. Nobody touches you without your consent, even me."

"It reminded me of before," I whispered. He walked over to my bed and sat down with me still wrapped around him.

"Who was it?" He asked, and by his expression I knew I couldn't escape this.

"Doesn't matter," I replied.

"Fine, don't tell me but you will tell Belinda."

"You told her? Why would you do that?"

"Because everybody noticed that you were gone and my mother cares about you. She's the one I'm most scared of, she will not tolerate something like this. Neither will I, so talk to me Freddie," he said.

This was not the way I expected any of this to go but nothing about my marriage was. With a sigh I wrapped my arms around him and buried my face against his neck. Cannon smelled of cedar, bay leaf, blood, and a tiny bit of magic, so familiar so grounding. His scent was more calming than I expected, and I really appreciated him wrapping his arms around me. Why did I feel safe with him? Wasn't that why the first thing I wanted to do last night was go to him? Except he didn't act like this, of course not, we were in public after all. I just wanted to leave to avoid any problems, but he was never going to let it go. Harringtons were vengeful, I knew that and that was why I didn't tell him everything. The summit was important, and I wasn't selfish enough to ruin it.

"I was coming back from the bathroom and this guy came out of nowhere. He grabbed me and asked whose pet I was and said he would make a better master. If Gunnar hadn't come he would have bitten me," I admitted and he pulled me back to look me in the eyes. Yup there was that Harrington rage I had seen in action quite a few times in my time with them.

"Who," he demanded he didn't ask.

With little choice I leaned in and whispered the name in his ear and his whole body tensed. Before he could get up and storm off in a rage I kissed him. I knew my husband and how to work him, maybe sometimes my fear kept me from admitting that. If this was just an arranged marriage of convenience, then my heart would be safe from him. And maybe I did use what happened last night as an excuse to escape my life. Nothing good was going to come from telling him the truth, but now he knew.

Of course, Cannon kissed me back, he couldn't help it, we always had sexual chemistry. And he was already turned on when I threatened to kill him. That was something to think on later, now I needed to distract him. It wouldn't last but it would keep him from running off and doing something crazy. Did I rock against him just a little to keep him very distracted? Yes, really sex wasn't a problem for us pretty much from the start.

There were a lot of things we needed to work on if we were going to be together. Not that I really had a choice in that. But that was also something I needed to let go. Cannon wasn't going to hurt me or throw me away or hand me back to his father, I did know that. I even believed it, but I was still worried about it. I never felt secure in my place with his family because the slightest thing could have them turning on me.

"Keep that up and I'm going to fuck you," he warned since I was still moving against him.

"Do you promise?" I asked with my lips against his ear. Then I sank my fangs into his neck and he growled.

"Fuck," was all he said while he ripped my panties, rearranged his clothes and pushed inside of me.

Cannon was the only person I had ever drank from, it was intoxicating. With his blood on my tongue and his dick inside me I could almost forget all of my problems. Almost because he was one of those problems. Trusting him with my body and my life were one thing, but I couldn't trust him with my heart. That was way too much. His fingers tangled in my hair holding me to him as I drank. I only stopped when he made me come from his relentless thrusting up into me. One of his hands stayed on my hip and he used the one in my hair to guide my lips back to his. He flipped me on my back without pausing his strokes or our kiss. He used one hand to pin my arms above my head before pulling back from our kiss. Without pause he slipped my rings back on my finger and looked down at me.

"Don't fucking take those off again, you are *mine*, I will not *ever* let you go," he growled. Why was it sexy when he got all growly? His eyes were all vampire black as he looked at me; while holding his gaze I gave him a little internal squeeze. A groan from him was rather rewarding so was the harder thrust. Still with his eyes on mine he released my wrists and brought one to his mouth. The sting of him sinking his fangs into my wrist had me bucking under him. Blood drinking was possibly better than sex, I came while he drank from me. Though to be fair we only drank from each other during sex. He came before he let go of my wrist licking his fang marks.

It was only after we had been laying in my bed tangled up in each other for a bit when I realized what we had done. I just had sex with my husband in my childhood bedroom while my parents were downstairs. How much noise had we made? If I thought being freshly fucked and having to ride home in a car with his mother was embarrassing...this was worse. He laughed as if he could hear my wildly spinning thoughts.

"It's not funny," I said and he didn't even have the decency to stop laughing.

"How many unsuspecting boys did you lure to this bed?" He asked and I stared at him.

"None! My parents would never permit such a thing," I shook my head.

"You never did anything a little sneaky?" He asked, watching me with a skeptical look.

"Not really, I was always very much a good girl. The only guy that has ever slept in this bed was you."

"Ah so there you go, you lured me to your bed."

"Lured you? Do we need to talk about what you did while I was asleep?" I asked, watching him as he shook his head.

A couple of days before our wedding he came over and we fell asleep in my bed. Nothing happened; our first kiss wasn't even until we were married. He leaned in nipping my neck in an obvious effort to distract me. That nip turned into a nuzzle and then a kiss. Next thing I knew I was beneath him again and his lips were on mine. This was not the time or the place but when he kissed me it sometimes felt like the world seemed a little more colorful and brighter. Was I using sex with my husband to feel something? When we were together, I felt connected and grounded. I didn't notice it before but now that I did, I wasn't sure what to do about it.

"If we don't leave this room soon, we are going to miss dinner," he said, pulling back. "Please Freddie, don't take off your rings, there is a tracking spell on them."

"It's not enough that I'm watched everywhere I go and you can track my phone, but my rings too?" I asked, staring at him though I shouldn't have been surprised, it was such a Harrington thing to do. Privacy was a precious commodity in this family, I hated it.

"Everybody in the house has guards, it's not just you. Nobody is spying on you or anything, it's just what's required. There was an incident that happened before I was born that nearly broke our family. After that, no Harrington family member can go out unguarded. It's all about safety, it's not about if I trust you or not. If it makes you feel better there's also a spell so that only you can take them off," he informed me.

"Why didn't you ever mention that?" I asked, looking at the rings like they were foreign objects.

"Because I didn't want you to get upset about it, we were trying to figure things out in the beginning, I didn't want it to be an issue. No matter how mad I make you and let's assume given my current track record I'll be doing that a lot, don't take the rings off. For one thing we aren't getting a divorce, ever, and I do need to keep you safe. You are my wife and you will always be my wife just as I'll always be your husband. Only humans divorce and you signed away that particular right should you have been so inclined."

Our marriage came with a contract which was pretty typical these days. Especially with an arranged marriage, it detailed what was expected of us for our marriage. Like that I would have the full protection of the Harrington Family. And I wasn't to reveal my ability to anyone outside of The Family who wasn't already aware. There was something about living in their family home and children because they are a necessity. Continuing the bloodline was our duty as Harringtons. I do recall there were things that were required of Cannon I just couldn't think of what they were.

My parents and a lawyer looked over it before I was ever allowed to sign it. Basically, it was just a legal document stating that I had to give up my life to be pampered in the lap of Harrington luxury so that nobody killed me or used me as a weapon. Breaking the contract by say, leaving Cannon, should have resulted in a "reevaluation" of my situation. If Hunt knew I left, he could very well decide to terminate the contract and remove me from his family.

"I won't take off the rings," I said because I wasn't that foolish. I didn't actually want to die or become an enemy of the Harringtons.

"Thank you," he said, laying on his side and pulling me against him. "Can we agree that next time you are mad you don't leave, just scream at me and threaten my life?"

"Why so we could end up having sex?" I asked and he shrugged, which meant yes. "Sometimes everything just gets to me and I panic. I think I'm afraid you will abandon me and at the same time that you won't. None of it makes any sense, I don't know what I'm doing."

"Everything changed in your life pretty quickly after…after what happened. Maybe we should revisit the idea of therapy," he suggested.

Things moved rather fast after I killed a man and was taken into the custody of the Harringtons. They detained and interrogated me and my family. There was also looking into my medical and adoption records and running different tests on me. It was stressful and traumatizing, I was never locked in a cell or anything, but cages came in luxury too. Then came the proposal that I marry Cannon. Three weeks passed between that decision and our wedding. There was never really time for me to fall apart. So maybe that was why I was coming apart at the seams now. Cannon had suggested therapy and so had my parents, but I declined. I was fine. Except obviously I was never fine, I didn't get over it. And last night… was definitely triggering.

"Ok," was all I managed to say. He hugged me tighter, obviously noting my distress.

"Everything is going to be ok, if you want to sit out of the summit for a few days then you can. I don't care what my father says about it, I need to take better care of you," he said.

"It's fine I'll go, it is important, and I can get through it."

"Are you sure? Because you don't have to, Belinda will make sure of that."

"Your father already hates me, I can't go screwing with his image of the perfect family. Or distracting you from what needs to be done."

"He doesn't hate you, if he did you wouldn't be part of this family. You are just an anomaly he can't quite figure out, so he doesn't know what to do with you."

"Will I even be allowed to go to therapy? Who knows what I might say or how much weakness I might reveal."

"Going to therapy doesn't make you weak, and I don't care what anybody else thinks this is about you. Something very traumatic happened to you and it changed your life, it makes sense that you are struggling," Cannon said, being the perfect husband again.

"Will you go with me?" I asked because I was a pitiful soul who needed him to hold my hand.

"Of course," he said with no hesitation. "We should probably get downstairs, your parents probably think I corrupted you."

"They love you," I said dismissively. "But yes we should go have dinner and go home."

"Stay the night, I'll come get you in the morning," he suggested.

"You shouldn't be driving," I replied, giving him a look. It was far more likely that he would be driving his car not his driver.

"I got like an hour or two last night, and before you ask, I slept in one of the other rooms. Didn't want to wake you," he said.

"You could just stay here with me," I suggested, earning me a raised eyebrow. "We could spend time with my family and you would have the peace of mind knowing exactly where I am and who I'm with. Besides, you need to sleep, and you deserve some time off."

"I'll stay," he finally said.

"You should send Lee home, there's no need for him to sit outside all night."

"Oh no he's staying there and he should be happy he's just out there for the night. I should fire him for taking you from the house without telling anybody."

"Would you prefer it if he used force to make me come back?" I asked and he growled, proving my point. "I promise I won't leave without telling you while the summit is still going on, just don't fire Lee."

"Should I be worried that you are so fond of him?" Cannon asked, watching me and I couldn't help but to laugh.

"I'm not having an affair with my bodyguard that's so cliché," I replied.

"Happens more often than you would think," he said. "Just in the future if you start developing feelings for someone else, talk to me. We can deal with it if it becomes necessary."

"You think I'm going to cheat on you?" I asked, shocked by the very thought of it.

"No but things happen," he shrugged like it didn't matter but the black ring on his irises said something else. "I would just prefer to know. I don't want secrets between us."

"Would you tell me if you met someone?" I asked, this conversation reminded me of the one we had before.

"If there was something to tell then yes, but I already told you I will be a faithful husband. And it's not that I think you wouldn't be faithful, I just know that life in this family hasn't been easy for you. None of this was of your choice so seeking comfort from someone outside of this family makes sense," he told me.

If I wasn't a coward, I would tell him that wasn't possible because I was very likely in love with him. Cannon was a good man, and he did care about me, I believed that. But he didn't love me, and that was perfectly fine. Love was a complication we didn't need, especially right now. Now we had to survive the rest of this summit and a night here at home with my family.

Love was a silly indulgence, that wasn't what our marriage was about. We respected each other and cared about each other and we learned to live together in relative peace. Sure, everyday wasn't sunshine and rainbows, and I may have found that me threatening to kill him turns him on. But life wasn't supposed to be perfect, it wasn't a fairytale. Yes, I got my prince and he was charming, but that didn't mean there would be a happily ever after.

"We are in this together," I assured him. "I don't need anybody else, just you."

"As long as I live and breathe you have me," he promised.

Why did I suddenly have a bad feeling hearing his words? Was something bad going to happen to him? Would it be my fault because I told him? The last thing we needed was for me to spiral out again; I had to trust that he could handle things.

Chapter 9:

Cannon

In human mythology, once your children turn a certain age, they are considered adults and no longer your problem, that wasn't the case for nonhumans. Us people who are long lived get the joy of having our parents around to nitpick and dissect our lives and choices constantly. Leaving home was often not something we did, you stayed with your family, that was the way of things. Most nonhumans lived in multi-generational households. My family thought far ahead and built a house that had its own apartments so that we could never be free of each other. Magical architecture made fitting more people into a space easier. Someone would notice that we didn't come home, so I decided to just call my mother and update her on the situation. My family was so different from my in-laws, and I don't know how Freddie could stand it.

"Did you find her?" My mother said by way of greeting when she answered the phone. I stepped outside to make this call and deal with another problem.

"Yes, she is at her parents' house as expected, we had a talk and we've straightened things out," I informed her.

"Good, when will you be home? I want to see her," she said.

"We will be home tomorrow, can you cover for me?" I asked knowing it might not happen, my father needed me constantly.

"Why? Is she refusing to return?" Mother asked, her voice devoid of emotion. For all that she liked Freddie she valued The Family way more than a single life.

"No nothing like that, she misses her family and I told her I'll spend the night here with her. She thinks I need to get some sleep," I replied.

"Of course you do, your lack of sleep is starting to show, dear, no woman wants to deal with that. I suppose since you are together and you are bringing her back home, one night won't be a problem. But she needs to know she can't miss any more events."

"She knows and is just as committed as we all are to making this work."

"Did she tell you what happened?" She asked because of course she did, my mother never let anything go.

"Yes," was all I would say on that matter.

Freddie was an unusual vampire and upon first glance or scent you couldn't always tell what she was. So, I could understand how someone might not know what she was. However, attempting to drink from an unwilling person was a violation akin to rape. To do this at a party during a very important summit was in very poor taste. I knew who did it, and I would make him pay for the transgression, nobody got to touch what was mine. Freddie was my wife; I promised to protect her and I would. Someone who would do such a thing, especially in such a public setting, was someone who thought they could get away with it. And it was likely they did far worse in private. It was probably for the best that I hadn't known what happened last night, because I would have killed him.

"Gunnar said that he didn't manage to bite her, is this true?" My mother asked her tone was now one I knew well, she was in mama bear mode. Hell hath no fury like a vampire mother.

"She said he didn't, but there is something else we need to deal with. I think Freddie would benefit from therapy; she's been struggling with things in a way I failed to notice. After what happened to her before this new incident has her feeling out of sorts," I said. Best to give her attention a different focus to keep her from doing anything rash.

"Oh! Of course, poor girl, she's been suffering in silence this whole time. Don't worry, I will set her up with someone we can trust. Though this trauma might explain why she hasn't gotten pregnant yet," she said thoughtfully.

"What does any of this have to do with her getting pregnant?"

"Her body is still reacting to the trauma she suffered, it's not conducive to creating life. Once her mind is right her body will comply, then you will finally have a child."

"You recall that you have other grandchildren right? Three of them in fact, you aren't hurting for grandchildren," I pointed out. It was best never to argue whatever wisdom or insane beliefs she had.

"Yes, yes I know I have them but they are older I want a baby to spoil," she replied. Lucy's youngest was 4 years old so older was rather subjective.

"We will get on that as soon as possible," I said.

"It's been six months you could be trying harder," she said. Never one to miss an opportunity to tell me what I was doing wrong, that was my mother. "Home tomorrow no more detours, we have important work to do." Without waiting for a reply, she hung up.

The idea of children was one I was actively avoiding; I didn't mind if this took awhile. We were still trying to settle into life together; we didn't need to add a child to it. Freddie would be a great mother; I knew that for certain I saw her with her students before we were married. She loved kids but had to give up teaching because allowing her to continue was a security risk for her and for the children. It didn't seem fair that the only way she could stay safe was by staying away from her old life.

"Cannon," Ollie called when she came out of the house. My sister-in-law obviously knew more of what had been going on than her parents. She wasn't good at hiding her emotions, she didn't want me here or anywhere near her sister.

"I don't know what Freddie told you but everything with her will be fine," I said. Of course this was what she wanted to talk about, what else was there?

"Do you love her?" She asked, surprising me enough that I wasn't sure I could answer.

"No," I admitted because it was the truth. "That doesn't mean I don't care about her and want our marriage to work. You are young so you don't know that love is a luxury a lot of people don't get to enjoy. Freddie is my wife; I will always take care of her and protect her. Love is a fairytale; it isn't ever quite what you think it is."

"My parents love each other," she pointed out.

"Yes, that seems rather obvious and it's a rare thing that should be cherished. Obviously, I didn't marry your sister out of love, I had only met her once before we were engaged. We are still learning and adjusting to being together, it takes time. Which I do not have a lot of these days," I told her.

Love was a fanciful idea, but it was not my goal at all. A partnership with mutual trust and respect? That made more sense than whatever love was. I cared for Freddie more than I did any other woman I had a relationship with. Moving her into my apartment hadn't been as bad as I thought it would. I looked forward to going home to find her or going out with her on my arm. As long as we were honest and communicated, we would be fine. Hopefully she could soon feel more secure in our relationship and about her place in our family. That was what was important, love was not.

"Freddie deserves to be happy," she told me and I nodded.

"Yes, I agree she does and hopefully we can work on that once we get back home."

"Why did you let that vampire hurt her?" Ollie asked, looking so very young as she glared at me.

"I didn't know and she didn't tell me but that's no excuse. From now on I'll be taking more precautions with her safety. Ollie I'm not going to let something like this happen again," I assured her.

"Why can't she just come home? She didn't do anything," she said, sounding a little desperate. Likely it was something she had been struggling with for the last seven months.

"Because what she can do is dangerous and other vampires would not like knowing she can do that. And people who hate vampires could use her as a weapon against vampires. Either way, once she revealed that ability, even accidentally it put a target on her. My father did everything he could to keep this quiet, but he isn't infallible, though he would never admit to that. Someone could find out and likely they wouldn't be offering her what we did. She's safe with me; nobody is going to use her or force her to kill for them. Being my wife gives her far more freedom than she would have otherwise, and she doesn't have to be worried that she will be found out," I told her. "Right now things are just difficult because of the summit, once it's over things will be less tense."

"Is it really so bad to have her ability? Couldn't we just get it bound? Then nobody could ever make her use it," Ollie said. She had obviously been giving that a lot of thought. I underestimated just how much she wanted her sister back.

"No, it would draw too much attention in getting the power needed for that. We would need a very strong witch or a coven and even then, it might not work. But even if we could find any of that there's still the matter of revealing the truth. Do you know any witches other than your mother that you would trust that much?" I asked and as expected she shook her head. "I don't either so the best we can do is protect her.

"Do I believe this will stay a secret forever? No, but I'm in a position to keep harm from coming to Freddie because of this. My Family will protect her; she is a Harrington now and that means something. Namely that anyone meaning to do her harm might hesitate. This thing that happened last night is a separate thing from what she can do. She could have killed him, and it would have been deserved. For that reason, I would also hesitate to bind her ability because she could need it. Vampires like to play at being better than everyone else, but the truth is that we aren't. Some of us have zero impulse control and that's how things like last night happen."

"I just want my sister back," Ollie sighed looking defeated. "I do get what you are saying but I want her to come home and for things to go back to the way they were."

"We can't go back but you do still have your sister she's just not living with you. If I thought it would help, I would say you should come live with us, but I doubt your parents would be ok with that. Maybe after the summit is over you could come stay for a while," I suggested. Likely something I should discuss both with my wife and her parents, but the offer couldn't hurt. We had the space, our apartment had 3 bedrooms, which of course is for future children.

"I still have school," she pointed out.

"We have drivers," I said with a shrug. Besides, we both knew she didn't need to physically be at school in order to attend her classes.

"Maybe," she finally said, looking at least a little better. "Do not let anyone hurt my sister, you promised all of us that you would protect her. Do your job, no excuses."

"I will," I vowed, a tiny bit impressed that she would stand up to me like she did. Most people wouldn't dare but Ollie was fierce, much like her sister. At least when Freddie stopped worrying about everything, she did being a reflection on the Family. I mean she did threaten to kill me.

"You better," she said, then turned and went back inside the house without another word. Maybe our families weren't quite as different as I thought.

Family was complicated and so was marriage, I knew that firsthand. Freddie had put our Family first and herself second last night at that damned party. She might deny it but she was becoming a Harrington, which was likely my mother's fault. It was actually mildly disturbing, and I wasn't sure I liked it. What she deserved was to be put first and to not have to worry about our family. Someone attacked her, again, and she could have killed to defend herself, but she didn't. No, instead she just left the situation and mostly kept it to herself in order to protect The Family.

What was worse was that she probably believed that nobody would care about how she felt. And I proved that misconception right which is how we ended up here. Nobody ever said marriage was easy, but they also never said how complicated it could be. Then again how many people actually had to navigate through a forced arrangement like this one? Things had to change, and I needed to show Freddie that she could trust me to be there for her. I wasn't yet sure how I would handle this situation because it was complicated, which was exactly why she didn't want to tell me. Now that I knew I would seek retribution not for my Family but for my wife. Somehow without me noticing my priorities had started to shift when she came into my life.

With a lot on my mind I walked over to where Lee was standing outside the car waiting for me. He knew I had some things to say to him when I came outside. Though dealing with my mother and sister-in-law gave him a moment's reprieve.

What was I supposed to do with him? Both my wife and mother didn't want me to fire him, and I could see the appeal of a loyal guard. However, if he was developing feelings for my wife then it was an issue. Sure, I could trust her not to do anything stupid, but he might be foolish enough to try. It wouldn't be the first or last time a bodyguard seduced or was seduced by the person they should have been guarding. That was the last thing I needed, my life was already complicated enough.

"I should fire you," I told Lee.

"And I should apologize for doing something I knew you wouldn't like," he replied. "Fire me if you want, I deserve that but she doesn't deserve your anger."

"You presume to know what my wife does and doesn't deserve? You admit that you knew better and yet you broke protocol and took her from the safety of our home, why?" I asked genuinely curious as to what his excuse was for his actions.

"Because I don't know what happened last night, just that she cried the whole way home and after I left her at your apartment," he said, daring to hold my gaze. "Nobody was there for her when she needed it so why would I say no to bringing her to see her family? Even knowing that she didn't necessarily plan to go back home I still figured she should get some time away."

Did everybody on the planet know that my wife was unhappy? I suppose Lee would notice more than most, he spent a lot of time with her. Hearing that she was so upset and alone last night made me feel worse than I already did about that whole thing. I should have tried harder to slip away. Firing Lee would not solve my own problems and maybe my mother was right. Though Hell would freeze over before I admitted that to her. He tried to help when Freddie was feeling most alone. How could I punish him for that? Some might because it highlighted my own inadequacy, but I wasn't so insecure that I couldn't admit I was wrong.

"From now on don't let her out of your sight. Especially around vampires outside of The Family," I told him and he nodded. "Also if you value your life don't ever do this again I won't be so understanding should it occur. My wife needs to be where she is safe and protected."

"Of course Mr. Harrington," he nodded.

"Keep watch, we aren't leaving until tomorrow," I informed him.

"Yes sir," he replied and I turned and headed back towards the house.

It wasn't just Freddie who had to leave the house under guard, I wasn't exempt from it either. My guard was parked in my car having already received his instructions. In my annoyance earlier I left the house without my driver. Two guards would have to be enough for the night. I wouldn't be able to fully relax until we were back home, where I knew she was safe. Who knew a woman could change your life so completely? Obviously not me but I didn't hate it, she was mine and I would protect her.

Belinda

Some things never changed, no matter how much time passed. The universe does have patterns, and history does repeat itself, something you see firsthand when you live as long as we do. I wasn't even 100 years old when everything in the world changed. One moment we were discussing having children and the next we were fighting for our lives. Five years after leaving my home and Family in what was then called South America for my new Family and the world just ended. That was what happened, it was an end and it was also a beginning, but the beginning had a very rough start.

At the time I didn't know if I would ever see my family again, it was difficult. My loyalty was to my family, but I was part of a different Family then. Sure, I could have left and abandoned my husband, who would blame anyone for a thing like that? The problem of course was that I didn't back down from challenges, so I stayed and I helped him defend our Family.

While my family was old the Harringtons were much older, some might even say they are natives of this land. Not that the surname suggests such a thing, but they have been here for a very long time. Humans had this idea that all vampires were of a European creation, they knew far less than they thought they did. All vampires were not the same and there were creatures roaming this planet once that didn't even have names.

One thing all vampires shared though was that we are an adaptable people. No matter the type it's just built into our DNA to be able to blend and move about undetected. History shows it wasn't as easy for our paler kin from across the ocean. If humans were smarter creatures though they wouldn't have forgotten our existence. They let all nonhumans become fantastical beings because they thought if they could ignore us enough, we would simply vanish.

I suppose it was much easier to control knowledge in the very old days but that was before my time. When I was born it was the mid-1900s, so I watched as the world became far more connected. Technology was a fascinating thing, more so once magic was involved. Though that too made it harder to hide the truth. We once had to live in fear because throughout history humans showed us what type of monsters they truly were. Survival meant existing in their world but also existing in our own. That was one thing I didn't miss about before, we were better why should we have had to hide? Of course, the answer to that was because humans outnumbered us and they had no problem killing and destroying. Hell, they did it to other humans, we knew from experience how they were.

Now the world that rose from the ashes of war looked pretty much exactly the same as it had back then. When peace was agreed upon and reconstruction began people felt nostalgic for what was before. So, the world was remade to look like it previously did, though not exactly. There was no more hiding, no veil between our worlds and magic had reshaped the planet in interesting ways. Borders and nations changed, some places returned to names that existed before colonization. People took back what was stolen from them once upon a time. The after wasn't easy; it took a long time for things to truly settle. Maps could be redrawn, and agreements were made and we all seemed to have moved on. Except that wasn't true of everybody.

In my 3 centuries of living I have never met anyone like my daughter-in-law. That girl seemed destined to find herself in trouble, through no fault of her own of course. Still, I had to wonder if someone placed a curse on her. Someone so young should have always been protected. I didn't blame her parents; they did the best they could, all things considered. She just wasn't raised right, maybe if we found her earlier things could have been different. There was no use dealing in whatifs, she was ours now and we would protect her. At least that was what we promised, yet not even a year had passed between what happened before and now.

"Have you seen your son?" Hunt asked when he came into my office.

"What do you need him for?" I asked instead of answering the question. Of course, I knew exactly where our son was.

"He's better at dealing with the shifters, at this point I'll end up slaughtering the lot of them," he growled, shaking his head. "Everybody is demanding something from everybody else and all these concessions need to be made so that we can agree to work together. Never mind that the point of this is to protect all of us from those greedy humans who are always out to get what's ours. Peace and coexistence are fine for a while, but it won't last. I mean think about it, they kill each other regularly."

"You could send Gunnar," I suggested. I didn't even point out that at the end of this he would be leading whatever nonhuman council that was established. Giving him more power and influence than ever before.

"Where is Cannon?" He asked, glaring at me having finally noted I wasn't answering his questions.

My marriage was not a silly match made out of emotional sentiment. It was arranged because Hunt needed a strong wife with an impeccable bloodline and that was me. Finding a husband for our Lucinda was easy, his family did business with ours. When it came to Cannon it was a challenge, he made excuse after excuse to get out of finding a suitable bride. Just when I was almost ready to let him choose one for himself Fredericka came into our lives as if sent by the hand of fate. Marriage, like all things, took work, that was what he was learning now. While she was not exactly someone we would have chosen had things been different, she was still the right choice.

At this point I had invested too much into making her part of this Family to replace her. It was always an option of course but I was fond of the girl and so was Cannon. He was likely a little too fond of her considering his scent was constantly all over her. One should never be overly fond of their spouse; it could lead to complications. Though I feared it was too late for them, the poor girl should have been raised amongst her own kind. Vampire parents would have raised her very differently, but the poor thing never could have been placed with vampires. Most vampires would not take a half breed child, especially not a hybrid. We might have had we known about her but it was all rather moot now.

"Our son needed a night off," I said simply.

"That's too damn bad, this is more important than anything else," he predictably said. "I went by his apartment he wasn't there, neither was that girl, so I'm guessing this is her fault. Worst decision I ever made was allowing her to marry him; she is a distraction we don't need."

"She was attacked at the party last night, a vampire attempted to violate her," I said. That gave him pause, no matter how he felt about our daughter-in-law he wouldn't allow anyone to harm someone in this family.

"I suppose that explains some things, why hasn't this been handled?"

"Because she wouldn't tell him who did it, she was protecting The Family and your precious summit. All of this is putting a strain on their marriage."

"Guess she's smarter than I've given her credit for," he said thoughtfully. "Who was it?"

"Gunnar refused to tell me and Cannon only just got her to admit to it, he also won't tell me. Which means that this vampire is someone of a high station," I said.

"That won't save them, we can't let this go unanswered."

"Of course I know this, I'm not sure our daughter-in-law does. You should be nicer to her; she put The Family before herself even after what happened to bring her to us in the first place."

For my husband, who was used to controlling everything and everyone around him, someone like Fredericka confused him. She was chaos, even though she didn't mean to be. In his perfectly ordered world something like her could not exist but she did. Vampires loved to believe that we were near invincible but that wasn't true and this one girl proved that just by existing. Whoever her parents had been played with fire in their pairing. If they had known what she would be I wonder if they wouldn't have brought her into the world? I also wondered about the exact circumstances because was this intentional?

So many questions about this one girl, a girl who was now one of us. Giving her to Cannon was the right call, our son needed a wife, and the girl needed protection. And maybe I was the one to push for that particular idea. Seeing that girl bruised, bloody and terrified hurt my heart. Nobody deserved to be treated that way and it made me very angry that it had happened to her again. Had bringing her into this family only brought her to the attention of more dangerous predators?

"She is married to our son, lives in our house and spends our money, how am I not nice to her? Maybe I'm just immune to whatever makes people like you and Cannon want to rescue her," he replied.

"You rescued her first," I pointed out. "Anyway I already put in a request to pull the video footage from that hallway, we will be able to see exactly what happened and who it was. But we should allow our son the chance to handle it his way first, this is his wife after all. It's only right that he should be allowed to seek retribution."

"Fine, but if he doesn't handle it to my satisfaction then I will step in. These people need to know they cannot get away with targeting our family. It's bad enough we have been forced to play peacemakers constantly for all this whining going on. Murder is not off the table to get this done," he said with a heavy sigh.

"We cannot accomplish this task through fear and intimidation, you know that. Would it be easier to make the halls of the hotel run red with their blood? Yes, it would likely even be satisfying though also wasteful but that's not the approach we need. You more than anyone have to appear calm and willing to care about their petty nonsense. All of this will be worth it when we have their signed agreement," I told him.

Because we were generous, we were giving this summit no more than six weeks before drastic action needed to be taken. Six weeks where the delegations from the most powerful factions in our region would be taking up space in our hotel. Hotels were our family business; Harrington Hotels catered mostly to vampires but also other nonhumans. Currently the hotel was filled with a variety of different types of people. More than the hotel could typically fit so we had to bring in 3 magical architects to maintain the extra space that was created. Magical architecture was a fascinating magic that destroyed the laws of physics and science in general. It also required additional staff, so needless to say the financial cost was staggering. If this did not end in an agreement, there was a far less pleasant contingency waiting to be enacted.

Of all the various groups attending there were five other vampire Families: Gordon, Smith, Lang, North and Wentworth. All of whom resented the power we had, and half were determined to be tedious about everything. If we couldn't get our own people together then how could we get the rest of them? Vampires were of course not a monolith; we were not all the same. Thinking of that made me wonder if maybe the vampire who dared step out of line was *turned*. They were not known for being good with control.

"They are all drawing this out to freeload off of us," Hunt grumbled.

"Cut off the liquor and let's see how fast things get done," I suggested which actually made him laugh.

A notification came up on my phone, and I clicked on my email. The security had sent me the requested footage, so I played it. Hunt watched with me as we saw exactly what happened. All traces of the brief humor he showed evaporated like it never existed. I only realized how hard I was gripping the phone when the glass broke. No one wanted to be the enemy of the Harringtons, it wasn't good for one's life expectancy. It appeared that someone truly didn't value their life.

Freddie

Why couldn't this be my life? Home with my family and my husband? I wondered if Cannon could be happy here? Obviously, it didn't matter, his family had their ways and living away from the compound was not an option. But I wondered if he could or would ever desire living a more normal life. What would our life be like if that was a possibility? Likely if Cannon was free to choose his own life, we wouldn't be together. But what would he be like as a regular person? Well, he was a vampire, and I never associated with my own kind. There weren't many around when I was in school and the ones that were looked at me and saw a witch. Fangs or no fangs, even with blood in my lunch box.

I grew up mostly around witches, things weren't exactly segregated here but a lot of people kept to their own kind. It wasn't until middle school that I had friends that were not magic users. So obviously I never dated a vampire, but I was married to one. Which in itself wasn't odd but the fact that someone from such a distinguished bloodline would marry someone with no bloodline was. When it came to vampires, bloodlines mattered above all else. Skin color, ethnicity, nationality and all those things that bothered and divided humans were unimportant, everything was about blood. Harringtons especially refused any racial identifiers and had them stripped from my records.

My blood should have automatically disqualified me from being part of the Harrington Family. Not even because I was a half-blood it was because I had no bloodline. At least not one registered or anybody could find a link to. It was exceedingly rare not to have a single trace of bloodline in the registry. The registry was vast, covering Earth, Mars and some other worlds. Only my unusual ability made me worthy of their notice. I often wondered what my life would be like if all of this hadn't happened. Where would I be now?

I wouldn't be married and likely wouldn't be seriously dating anyone. The drawback of being a hybrid was finding a long-term partner that didn't care about what you were. Some other magic users thought my blood tainted because I was part vampire. They didn't want to end up with vampire children. Other types of nonhumans weren't as against one part or the other but being a hybrid meant who knew what my children would be. So, another mark against me, basically I could only really date mages and even they had problems with hybrids.

Humans weren't really an option, I wasn't against them or anything. The one time I went on a date with a human he was a little too interested in my hybrid status, it was giving fetishization. Some humans were like that and wanted to be close to nonhumans for weird reasons. I had pretty much given up on dating and then the universe decided that I should marry Cannon.

"Freddie, is something going on with you? Don't deny it, you have been acting rather oddly today," my mother said. We were alone in the kitchen after dinner, Cannon went outside to make calls, and my dad was called in to work at the hospital. I had no idea what Ollie was doing, I was surprised she wasn't there too.

This was a familiar scene of us in the kitchen chatting. I was leaning against the counter having just finished doing the dishes and she was at the table. Until I was 5 years old, I didn't know that I was different from my parents or adopted at all. Both my parents had lighter brown skin than mine but only by a shade, I looked like I could belong to them. But because of my dual nature they couldn't really pretend that I was biologically theirs. They told me the classic story of a birth mother who couldn't take care of me, so she wanted me to have a better life thus adoption. It was a lie, a kind lie but a lie nonetheless.

Nobody knew anything about my birth mother so who knew what her intentions were and why this was the best option. Honestly, I never gave that much thought, did it truly matter why she gave me up? Didn't feel like it should when I had the best parents in the world. Who did their best to explain to me why I was different from other witches. And later after an incident, had to explain it to my whole elementary school.

"Um Cannon thinks I should start therapy," I admitted. Did I want to tell her everything? No, because I didn't want my parents to worry more than they already did. I knew they felt some guilt over what happened and how things went with the Harringtons.

"Have you been having problems?" She asked, immediately worrying which I wanted to avoid.

"He thinks I'm still struggling with what happened and how my life changed. I don't think he's wrong about that, it has been hard, and I am constantly waiting for things to just go wrong."

"If you are having problems why didn't you tell me?"

"Because I didn't really fully realize how much things have been bothering me. Sometimes I just feel like I'm one wrong move from them locking me away or deciding I'm not worth the effort. Cannon told me it's not something I have to worry about but how can I not? I married him so that I could have some form of a life so how can I not worry that one day they will decide to take it back? In Cannon's mind, if I could work through what happened to me then maybe I could accept that my position in his family isn't temporary," I told her.

"Hmm, and how are things going between the two of you?" She asked an eyebrow raised, giving me a look since everybody knew what we did upstairs.

"It's complicated, we kind of had a fight that's really why he followed me here. I guess we are fine now, he agreed to go to therapy with me. The summit is just really stressful for everybody, and he's worried somebody would kidnap me to use against him. So I'm technically not supposed to leave the house," I admitted.

"If it's dangerous for you to be here then why did you come?" She asked, staring at me like I had lost my mind.

"Because I couldn't stand being in that house with those people, especially Cannon," I said with a sigh. "Last night a vampire was harassing me, tried to bite me. I was trying to be a good Harrington and just get away from the situation without making a scene. Gunnar stepped in and I told Cannon I wanted to leave and he refused. If I had told him exactly what happened and who it was there would have been problems, so I just wanted to go."

"Are you ok? Why would someone do that to you?" My mother asked, reacting exactly how I knew she would. I had been trying to avoid all of this, but it seemed impossible. Keeping secrets from my parents did not come natural to me, I told them almost everything.

"He didn't bite me so I'm fine, had he done so I don't know what the Harringtons would have done."

Would they care about what actually happened? I honestly had no idea, I knew how Cannon would react though. Did they consider me family enough to care about such a thing? Cannon did suggest that his mother cared, but I wasn't sure if it was because of me or because of The Family. Had he actually bitten me though it would have been catastrophic. Not only for me because I would be violated but The Family would be shamed and embarrassed and it would be seen as an attack on them. They would have to retaliate against this person and their Family, or they would look weak. Vampire politics were not for the feint of heart, and I tried to avoid it as much as possible. Was it ironic that I was trying to protect them when they didn't protect me? Yes, tragically so but that was my life.

"Why would a strange vampire try to bite you?" My mother asked the million-dollar question: why would some random stranger old enough to know better do such a thing?

"I don't know, it's not something they are supposed to do, especially in that setting. Obviously, I haven't spent a lot of time around vampires but from everything I've learned it's not normal behavior," I said.

"It's your scent," Cannon said when he stepped into the kitchen. I wasn't surprised to see him, I knew he was coming. "Vampires are predators and you are not so it's confusing. If I didn't know you were a vampire at first scent I couldn't guess it. That said it's never ok to do what he did or tried to do to you. Maybe there was a time when vampires would hunt people to drink from, but those times are long past."

"So it's my fault vampires want to attack me?" I asked him because that's what it felt like as this was the second time.

"Absolutely not, if they can't control themselves they shouldn't be in public. Doesn't matter if you smell like a vampire or not, it's still wrong and it's not your fault," he said. He wrapped his arms around me from behind and kissed the side of my neck. It still surprised me just how affectionate he always was and how much I liked it.

"Will this person be punished for his actions?" Mom asked watching Cannon like she no longer wanted him around.

For the most part my parents loved Cannon, he was very likable. After we were engaged, he spent a lot of time getting to know me and my family. His attempt at putting their minds at ease was obvious and appreciated. We were all in a situation there was no escape from so we had to make the best of it. There was one time the three of us were in the kitchen much like this when Cannon was worrying over my blood count. The care he expressed for me won over my friends and I think helped my mother to trust him. It showed he would take care of me even though I was an adult and could take care of myself of course. He hadn't been wrong, my blood count had been low, which was dangerous. In my defense my life was a bit crazy at the time what with getting attacked, engaged, ending my career, leaving my home and family and getting married.

"Oh I will personally make sure of that," he promised.

"You told us that you would keep her safe," she pointed out.

"I failed, I will not fail again," he assured her.

He meant what he said and I knew it, that was what worried me. Fighting amongst the vampire Families was bad anytime but now? During the summit? What was supposed to be a peaceful event to bring everybody together against a common enemy was filled with violence. Adding a feud between the host vampires and another Family would be a disaster. When vampires went to war things got bloody and nasty very quickly. Belinda made sure that I knew this among other things. Since I didn't grow up with vampires, she personally saw to it that I was properly educated on their society, history, the rules and how things were. All so that I wouldn't embarrass The Family with my ignorance or do anything that would cause problems. And yet here we were and if something else happened I had no doubt that I would be blamed for it.

Hunt tolerated me, he didn't like me, I was just there so that I wasn't in the way. Though I never understood why he would have me marry his son when he could have pawned me off on another family member. Being Cannon's wife meant I couldn't just meekly fade into the background. I was required to be out and seen with The Family, and I had more access to them because of my marriage. Vampires didn't make sense to me and likely never would. If they ever started making sense then I needed to be worried about my sanity.

"I want to understand this, do all vampires drink blood from each other? At your wedding ceremony the two of you drank each other's blood," she said. It didn't surprise me as she was a professor so of course she was trying to analyze the situation.

"Um it's not necessary for a vampire to drink blood from live sources anymore as you know. Some never do, the desire is there but we don't need to do it. Blood exchanges between a couple in a wedding are standard. It's common that couples drink from each other; it's a level of intimacy that only another vampire would understand. And blood from another vampire is more fortifying than anything you can buy in the store," he explained. "Hunting people for blood is frowned upon because it's so unnecessary. Technically speaking it is now illegal to do so without the expressed consent of the other party. But like with most things people will break the rules and do what they want."

Of course, I knew what she was wondering now and it was embarrassing. How did one tell their mother that they enjoyed drinking their husband's blood when they had sex? Before we were married, I was told what to expect so I knew the exchange was going to happen. Doing it in front of a crowd my first time felt weird. It was from the wrist, so it wasn't anything explicit. Somehow that act seemed to awaken in me some instinct that had been dormant before. After that first time it just became normal when we had sex, not every time but often enough. We didn't need to drink from each other to live, it was mostly for pleasure. My face was flushed, and I could not look my mother in the eye.

"Is this something the two of you engage in?" She asked because of course she did, she obviously couldn't resist.

"Yes," Cannon admitted his attention on me instead of her. "Should I not have said that? I don't always know what's considered as oversharing."

"It's fine," I said, finally looking at my mother who was watching him. Cannon still had his arms around me like he was afraid to let me go. "Yes, we drink from each other."

"Fredericka you are a married woman now you don't need to get so embarrassed about things," she said shaking her head. My mother would openly speak about such things though not as bluntly as Belinda did. Was there something about being a mother that made you want to embarrass your children?

"Mom, we aren't just talking about sex it's... I don't know it just feels different. I never use to do vampire things before, so we never talked about it," I said, my face still aflame.

"You said before that there were vampires at your high school? How did they react to you?" Cannon asked me, rather abruptly changing the conversation.

"Some didn't believe I was a vampire and others believed it and wanted nothing to do with a half blood witch," I answered.

"No other vampires ever came in contact with you?" He asked me but looked to my mom too.

"There aren't many vampires on this side of town so it's possible that none did. Once I tried to get her into a vampire children program, but we were denied as neither parent is a vampire. There aren't many resources for raising a half vampire child when you are not a vampire. We wanted to be able to raise her embracing both halves, but it wasn't exactly possible," Mom said.

"How did you know how to care for a vampire baby?"

"Most of what we knew for how to care for a vampire child came from doctors. Until we had her, I didn't know that there was such a thing as blood powdered baby formula. The doctors though always seemed surprised that she didn't crave blood more actually. We followed strict dietary instructions to keep her healthy, but she never indicated that she craved it."

"If you never drink from another person then you might never crave it," he explained. "I'm just curious, I can't imagine never having contact with others of my kind. If it helps those vampires probably sensed that you were different and didn't understand why. And well teenage vampires are assholes."

"Cannon," I said, shaking my head at him but my mom laughed.

"Now I wonder if our children will inherit your differences? Half vampires are rare, mostly because vampires are elitist and think every other type of person is beneath them. Mixing and diluting the blood is abhorrent to some."

"Any child we had would be mostly vampire though so probably not weird like me," I pointed out. Though I did have to wonder would my nonexistent bloodline hold my future children back? Even if they were vampires everyone would still know that their mother's blood was anything but pure.

"Is that something the two of you are considering?" Mom asked in a rather obvious way, she tried for casual, but it wasn't that.

"If my mother had her way then we would have already done so," Cannon said shaking his head. "When I just spoke to her she indicated that she believes that therapy will help with this particular issue."

"Do I even want to know exactly what she said?" I asked him, assuming that I didn't because it was Belinda.

"Something about trauma and needing to heal mentally so your body is ready to create life," he said. Yup, I really didn't want to know. "But she is supportive of therapy."

"To answer your question, Mom, we aren't exactly trying but we aren't allowed to prevent it from happening. If you recall that was in the contract so it's up to fate at this point," I said. It could take months for the effects of the birth control implants we both previously had to wear off. Which was why we had them removed immediately after signing the marriage contract.

Was it wrong that Hunt made us sign away our bodily autonomy? Yes, but I knew going in that children were required. What was the point of marriage if not procreation? Marriage was just a legally binding agreement that we would have a child and both be responsible for said child. Apparently, it was the same for everybody in their family because it's our duty to carry on the line. Lucy had three children, and she made sure that everybody knew that she would not be having more. I wasn't sure what it would be like to be a mother, especially a vampire one. Unlike my parents though I would have all the vampiric support I could possibly want or need.

Sometimes I had to wonder if my parents ever regretted adopting me. How could anyone really prepare for what it meant to have a vampire hybrid child? It wasn't easy for them with me, but it was with Ollie. Never once did I ever feel unloved, they always made sure we knew we were loved. But I was a child that nobody wanted, that was how I ended up with my parents. They were desperate enough for a child that they took someone like me. If they knew they could have a full-blooded witch as their daughter, would they have waited the decade for Ollie instead? Sometimes my thoughts took a turn for the depressing out of nowhere. Maybe I really did need therapy.

"While you are going to therapy the two of you should consider some couples counseling. It's something else that could help both of you navigate your relationship," Mom suggested.

"I'm not opposed to that," Cannon said with a shrug looking to me.

"Sure, why not?" I replied because I wasn't opposed to any of it though it did surprise me how accepting Cannon was. His family didn't really give the vibe of being interested in therapy or anything that could make them question themselves.

Maybe coming here had done us both some good, Cannon seemed more relaxed than I had seen him in weeks. Part of me still didn't want to go back because once we did there would be no peace for us. Being a Harrington was exhausting and required constant effort, at least for me it did. Once we were back, I knew Cannon wouldn't just let this thing that happened go. Part of me wanted him to because I knew it would lead to trouble. But the other part of me didn't want this man to get away with what he had done.

I was never much of a confrontational person; it just wasn't my nature. It was another way I was less vampire than others because they didn't let things slide. For better or worse it was out of my hands now.

Hunt

When I wanted something, it was typically as good as done.
I wanted to become the head of my Family, so I did. Not an
easy task considering the Harringtons were once a matriarchy.
Proving to my grandmother and mother that I should be in
charge was no easy thing. But I did it because once I set my
mind to something I always accomplished it. Two weeks into
this summit and I was recalling exactly why this had never
worked before. Granted I hadn't been in charge of things the
last time it was attempted so I was in the position to learn from
the mistakes of others. I had to keep reminding myself that
murder was a last resort not the first. We were getting nowhere
because everyone was incredibly selfish and very shortsighted.

Humans were a threat, they shouldn't be since we are more powerful than them, but they are. Complacency was dangerous, I knew that from first-hand experience. That was why it was important for us to unite because it wasn't a matter of *if* they attacked us but *when*. They were already plotting, and the signs were obvious for anyone who bothered to really look into it. Unfortunately, humans and the useless heads of the nonhuman factions were not my only problem. No, there was also this girl I was cursed with.

The smart thing would have just been to kill her. I was never one for sentimentality; it was against my nature. So I can't even guess why I did what I did. Maybe it was seeing this girl in shock covered in her own blood looking so very young and innocent. There was something about her and yes, I did want to figure out what that was. Killing her would have solved a problem but I needed to know if it could happen again. If there was one of her kind, then there could be another. She came from somewhere and I needed to know where to assess the threat properly. And make no mistake she was a threat; the most innocent looking things usually were.

"You claim to want this cooperation to work while you keep a weapon at hand," Kono Lang was saying.

Kono was one of the heads of the Lang Family with his cousin Marius. Families almost always had two heads, for us of course it was myself and my wife. Some were couples, but not all were as the Langs were cousins, the Wentworths were led by sisters, and the Smiths were led by brothers. The responsibility of heading a vampire Family was never to be taken lightly. Your Family's wellbeing, safety, security and prosperity were down to you. As well as any triumphs or failures, everything always fell to those in charge.

"A weapon? What weapon do you believe I have?" I asked, giving no sign that I knew what he was speaking of but I did, of course I did. There was literally only one new thing in my life he could be talking about.

"That creature your son is married to," Kono said, nodding towards Cannon and Fredericka across the room.

Looking at them they did make an attractive couple. The whole night Cannon had been keeping her close with a possessive hand on her hip. I knew why, of course, he was being protective. Though my son hadn't been interested in marriage he couldn't resist the damsel in distress. Something about her brought out protective instincts in him that he hadn't shown before. It wasn't hard to convince him to marry her, she was a pretty little thing after all.

A sweet little schoolteacher teaching magic to young children. She never did anything of note in her life, never a scandal or relationship that didn't end amicably. Essentially, she was any parents 'dream wife for their son. She wasn't demanding, wouldn't cause trouble or draw attention and would be an obedient wife, it was perfect. Likely too perfect which I did acknowledge at the time but was willing to take the risk.

"My son is married to a vampire," I said simply.

"Whatever she is a vampire is not it, I have it on good authority that she has some special abilities. Very rare, very dangerous," he said.

"If that were true, why would I have such a being in my house with my family? Sleeping with my only son? Around my wife, daughter and grandchildren? Why would I do such a thing? Have you known me to take ill-advised risks?" I asked, keeping my gaze on him as he started to have doubts.

"The truth is that yes my son was married rather abruptly and she is an unusual girl. She's young and we don't talk about it much, but she was adopted so her bloodline is of dubious quality. A vampire witch hybrid, there aren't too many of those out there. Cannon met her and fell for her, she does have an innocence about her. We allowed it because she is vampire enough and our blood is strong their children will be fine. Poor girl didn't grow up around vampires; it has been an adjustment."

"That girl does not smell like a vampire," he pointed out and I nodded.

"Yes that is very true, somehow the witch half suppresses her predatory side. So unfortunate, but we don't discriminate, the poor girl has a disability, but it doesn't make her less. I wasn't aware that you were so closed minded," I said, shaking my head. "Bigotry is such a human trait, I'm rather surprised you would indulge in it."

"No! Of course not, there's no reason to hold that against her," he said. Nobody ever liked to be called a bigot, especially when they were one.

In my time on this planet, I had seen a variety of hate and discrimination. Mostly it was humans, but nonhumans were sadly not immune to these very human failings. My family was native to this land; our roots stretched back to the first people. We generally looked no different from other native people, which of course was an issue when the invaders came. To protect our family, it became unfortunately necessary to blend in with the colonizers who were a plague upon the world. Magic made it possible to adopt a different appearance to look more like the pale humans. Eventually the name Harrington was adopted so that we could further seem like them. Blending was what vampires did for survival; we adapted it's how we were made.

I lived through being looked down upon and underestimated because of my brown skin. They made assumptions on a race or ethnicity, but we claimed none. Skin color was a weapon created to divide people, if only that too stayed with the humans. For the most part with nonhumans it was less about skin color, more about what you were and what power you wielded. The technology to measure the percentage of magic in your blood sadly became something used to divide.

Everyone knew their own M-levels, it was illegal to ask for that information in a job setting. People still found ways to get around that and discriminate based on it. Hate was so universal and tedious, I wouldn't allow it in my presence. I might not be overly fond of this girl and found her lack of a predatory nature curious, but I never once thought it made her

Brit Andrews

less. Even the fact that she was a vampire tainted by witch blood didn't make me think less of her. She was what she was, as we all are and nobody has the right to judge.

"Why would you think she's some sort of weapon? The girl isn't even 30 years old; she's practically a child. If someone is disparaging my family, then I need to know about it. Rumors like that could prove dangerous if one is fool enough to believe them," I said, still watching him.

Was the girl a weapon? No, but she could be with the proper training. Unfortunately, she was too much of an innocent to even consider trying to practice her ability. I had considered pressing the issue but ultimately decided against it. Nobody should know what she was and Cannon would keep her out of harm's way. Except someone did know or suspected and some ill-mannered vampire also attacked her. Was that a coincidence or part of a greater plot? At the moment that was unclear and irrelevant, any threat to a member of my Family would be answered.

It really might have just been kinder to kill her, then we wouldn't have to worry about who knew what. Wasn't it bad enough that as Cannon's wife she made a nice kidnapping target? That alone was enough of an issue, but she could be used. Someone could force her into becoming the weapon that even I wasn't cruel enough to make her into. Some would say allowing her into my home was a risk, but I saw her with her family and knew once she was accepted, she was more likely to feel protective of my family. Loyalty at a low cost, if she was going to use that ability of hers it would be against others not us. I always consider all of the angles before committing to a course of action.

"The Smiths," Kono finally admitted. He likely weighed his options and decided that he feared me more than them. The fact that it was in question was utterly ridiculous, only a fool would fear or trust them.

"I do not take slights against my family lightly," I informed him though he knew. Everybody knew I wouldn't tolerate such things and yet they were whispering.

The Smiths were a vampire Family of little interest to me and were only invited by default as they were in the area. They wanted more power and more territory, a tale as old as time and quite human of them. No one faction or Family officially claimed any certain territory. However, lines were drawn and we all knew it. Very much like greedy humans they wanted more of everything and until now it was a mild annoyance. Now they upgraded to a problem if they were whispering about Fredericka.

"Darling," Belinda greeted when she came to stand beside me.

"I'll leave you two to talk," Kono said, making a hasty retreat. Smart people knew to fear my wife too; really smart ones feared her more.

"He accused me of marrying a weapon to our son," I informed her.

"Should we be parading her around for all to see? I know hiding her would be more suspicious, but we could limit her appearances," Belinda suggested.

"We should do the opposite, make her presence truly felt. This is a family endeavor, she needs to be more involved," I decided. "You meet with the witches tomorrow, right?"

"You want me to take her? Knowing what the witches did?"

"That's the very reason she should be there, it will unsettle at least half the witches. Better the witches than any predators, her scent confuses them too much."

Was it a risk? Yes, but whoever got things done without a little risk?

Cannon

***Sometimes vampires were the most tedious creatures, I knew
it well.*** Socializing with my own people was often exhausting.
Unlike my wife, I spent all of my life surrounded by vampires.
My family, the staff in our house and staff at our businesses
were all vampires. I attended an all vampire academy for
school when I was younger. In my university days was when
I actually spent time with other types of people and that was
when I learned how annoying vampires are.

The world was full of people with different abilities and
different societies and cultures; I truly found vampires to be
the worst. Not that it mattered as I was a vampire and I would
always be surrounded by vampires. The fact that I could relate
to and converse with other types of people was mostly a fluke.

Diplomacy was somehow something I was good at, but my patience was starting to wear thin.

"You look like the bored prince you are," someone said and I turned to see a familiar face.

"Lisha, I didn't know you were here," I replied. She didn't come with the rest of her Family so I could guess why they decided to bring her in now.

"I was out of the country, I've been doing some traveling only just got back. My uncles thought I should come join them here," she explained. "So I heard that you are married now?"

"Yes, for the last six months or so," I confirmed.

Did I know full and well that she knew I was married and for how long? Yes, did I also know her uncles brought her here to parade in front of me? Also yes, I wasn't stupid and I knew exactly what they wanted. Too bad Lisha Gordon was exactly the type of woman I didn't want. She was beautiful and deadly and could not be trusted. Her Family had been trying to set us up for years now and I avoided it every time. Really Freddie did me a huge favor in marrying me; it meant I was unavailable for those who only wanted to use my family. Marrying Lisha would have been a wise business decision uniting two Families but I didn't trust her not to knife me in the back the moment she got what she wanted.

Even knowing I was married now she was still going to try to seduce me, I could read her calculating intent all too well. Technically speaking I could have a second wife, it was fairly common these days though not really in my family. Though in order to marry a second wife I would need the consent of my first wife, which she would never give. And Lisha would just try to kill her to get her out of the way. Little did she know that my Freddie could kill her easily. If I wanted Lisha, I could have had her at any time in the many years that I had known her. As I valued my life and freedom, I never even had sex with her, she was just one big trap.

"Where is this wife of yours?" Lisha asked though I imagine she knew everything there was to know about Freddie. Well, everything publicly available anyway, nobody would ever find any sort of documentation on what she really was.

"Over there with my sister," I said pointing to where they were.

It was a rare moment when my wife wasn't by my side but she was with Lucy, so I didn't have to worry too much. My sister seemed to be innocuous, but no Harrington was ever that. They were chatting with other women, so my presence wasn't exactly desired. Lee though stayed close to her like a shadow; he was good at moving around mostly unnoticed. After I spoke with him, he absolutely never left her unless we were home and even then, he was usually at our door. When the man slept, I had no idea, but he was committed to keeping my wife safe.

"How did you come to be married to a witch?" Lisha asked, proving that she did know something about Freddie.

"She's a vampire," I corrected, because really vampire was all that mattered. "My wife is a vampire witch hybrid, more vampire than witch I assure you."

"Not a full blood and an orphan at that, how did your mother let this happen? As far as I can tell she was adopted by a water mage doctor and a witch professor, how does that connect to you? There is no valuable alliance there at all," she pointed out. It seemed she was done pretending not to know anything, which was fine by me as it was rather tedious.

"Why do you care so much? It's my marriage, I'm happily married and I have no issue with her background. My parents chose her for me so there was no issue for them either, maybe you shouldn't be so closed minded," I replied. Was she going to let this go? Nope not at all, it was after all the whole reason she was here.

Across the room my sister made eye contact with me and looked rather amused. Then she leaned over whispering something to my wife who looked over too. I couldn't imagine what she must have been saying to her. Of course, Lisha noted this and was watching and plotting. Especially when Freddie got up from where she was and started walking in my direction. Lee as ever was a shadow moving beside her. It surprised me not at all when Lisha turned to watch me and placed her hand with clawlike nails on my chest. She even leaned a little closer to me like we were having some kind of moment. My eyes stayed on my wife who just raised an eyebrow at me and actually looked amused. What had Lucy said to her?

"I don't understand your parents 'decision to marry you to some weakling with no bloodline but I would make the better choice. Let me deal with her and I'll give you a night to remember," Lisha said keeping her voice low.

"Lay one hand on my wife and it will be the last thing you ever do," I told her, holding her gaze. That surprised her of course so did me stepping away from her. As soon as she was close, I wrapped an arm around Freddie pulling her against me.

"Are you going to introduce us?" Lisha said before anyone else could say anything.

"Lisha this is my wife Freddie, wife this is Lisha, an old friend," I said. It was an exaggeration as we were never friends, I doubt the woman had any friends.

"Nice to meet you," Freddie said ever the mannered person.

"You don't smell like a vampire," Lisha said, cocking her head to the side. She studied Freddie in confusion, obviously that wasn't in the information she had on her. "Obviously you smell like Cannon but you don't smell like a vampire."

"What do vampires smell like?" Freddie asked her, she of course wouldn't actually know the difference.

"Like a predator, we are after all the ultimate apex predators. We look like humans and can blend in with them, but we are more deadly than most other nonhumans. Vampires command the top of the food chain, every living being has blood and we can use them all for sustenance," Lisha answered.

"I wasn't aware predator had a scent, though forgive my lack of knowledge. Until recently I never lived among vampires, and I don't typically sniff people," Freddie said with a shrug.

"It's common to get a scent of people around you," Lisha said in a wannabe superior tone. "I can't imagine not living amongst my own people, I've always been very connected to my family. Our bloodline is long and strong, though not quite as long as the Harringtons. What must it be like for you to be an outsider in such a prestigious family?"

"Outsider? Not at all we have all happily welcomed our Freddie into the fold," Lucy said when she came to join us. "Lisha, hasn't anyone bothered to tell you that desperation is so last season?"

"Lucy, how great to see you, how is your husband?" Lisha asked glaring at my sister.

"He is fine thanks for asking, I would inquire about you but you don't have a husband. Such a shame your family can't find anybody willing to take you and you are getting old, aren't you? Maybe you should be more invested in getting your own life together than worrying about the marriages of others. Soon enough people are going to start wondering what's wrong with you," Lucy said. There was so much venom that could be injected into politeness, and my sister was the master at it.

"I'll soon have the man I desire, don't you worry about that," Lisha replied. "Anyway I'm bored, I have other people I need to see. Do tell Markus I said hi." With that parting shot she walked away.

"Did Markus actually have sex with her?" I asked and Lucy just laughed.

"If he did he wouldn't be breathing right now," Lucy replied. "You better watch yourself, she's coming for blood."

"I know," I said with a sigh.

"Is she an ex?" Freddie asked though it didn't seem to bother her. Would I react the same to a man she had potentially had a relationship with? No, I could admit to myself that I was too possessive for that.

"She wishes," Lucy laughed.

"No, she's let her interest be known and her family would love nothing more than for us to get together. However, as I value my life, I would never get in bed with her in any way. Besides I'm a married man now, I have a wife I need to please," I told her. "But she will likely try to kill you in an effort to replace you."

"Vampires are so weird," she shook her head.

"You don't even know the half of it," Lucy said. "She underestimates how loyal Cannon is though and he would never touch her if she tried to hurt you. And well I would hope he is never that desperate."

"Never," I said, then noticed my wife stiffening as I felt eyes on us.

"Cannon," she whispered, looking to me and I just nodded. Well, I couldn't say I didn't exactly expect this.

"Lee," I called and in an instant he was there. "My wife and sister need to get some air, can you escort them?"

"Of course," he said, having noticed exactly what was happening. Our guards had been briefed on the situation already for this reason.

"Cannon, don't," Freddie whispered, keeping her eyes on mine.

"Go with Lee," I replied, kissing the tip of her nose before releasing her.

"Come, I need to call the nanny anyway," Lucy said, picking up on the tension. My sister was also aware of what happened, so she acted accordingly.

The three of them left and I walked over to the bar to get another drink. Dragon Fire Whiskey was the strongest alcohol in existence, and it wasn't strong enough for me to deal with this nonsense. At the bar was where he decided to join me. It could not be a coincidence that people with pale skin, blonde hair and blue eyes were often untrustworthy. Not all of course but enough that there seemed to be something in the lack of melanin that should be studied.

Ferris Smith was the brother of the head of the Smith Family. In theory, he headed their family with his brother; in reality, it was in name only. Their family was an oddity as they descended from turned vampires not born ones. There was a distinct difference that all vampires knew.

It was impressive that they could build a whole Family from such beginnings. Still, they were often looked down upon as their bloodline could never be considered pure. Even if most of them were born now they couldn't shake off the stigma of their past. My family rarely ever turned anyone, that set us apart from most other families. We were born vampires who only married other born vampires. And we employed pretty much only born vampires though that was more coincidence than intentional. Born vampires were often accused of discrimination and a lot of times it was true. But there were reasons to be wary of the turned, they could be dangerous.

"I was hoping to have a word with you Cannon," Ferris said. His eyes shifted in the direction that Lee had taken the women. The bastard was practically salivating at the thought of my wife, and I did not appreciate it.

"What about?" I asked curious as to why he would dare come near me after what he did.

"Shall we sit? I have a proposal for you," he said, indicating a corner where there were two empty chairs. I nodded and followed him with my drink in hand perfectly outwardly calm. "Let's not beat around the bush here, you have something I want and I'm willing to pay for it."

"And what is it you believe I have that's of value?"

"That little toy you keep bringing around, sell her to me I'll pay whatever price you want. Or just let me borrow her for a while," he said.

There was a very good reason that most vampires did not turn people, they often ended up not quite right. Ferris was looking at me asking to buy my wife like it was nothing and he believed he was being reasonable. Even if he wasn't smart enough to know she was my wife, he was still asking to purchase another person. If that didn't speak to the insanity in that family, I don't know what else would. I had done my research on him after finding out he was the one to attack Freddie. Nothing good was in his history, his brother spent a lot of money covering for his crimes. A slight red tinge of vampire specific madness showed in his blue eyes. The vampire that attacked Freddie before had red eyes; it was an indicator of a loss of control. Red eyed vampires might hunt and kill anyone for their blood, and they might do other unpleasant things as well. He was a monster pretending to be a man and a danger to everyone around him.

"By toy you mean the woman I was just with?" I asked, watching him as he nodded eagerly. "That woman is my wife so I'll have to decline your rather disgusting proposal." No part of me wanted to know what he would do with her if he got his hands on her.

"What? No, that can't be your wife, she isn't a vampire."

"She is a vampire, half really but it's not that important. What I do find interesting though is the fact that you attacked her the other night," I said.

"No! No, I did no such thing obviously she is lying women are always lying! She tried to entice me," he said predictably. Of course it wasn't his fault it had to be the woman. Men who blamed women for their shortcomings were pathetic.

"My father has put a lot into this summit and making this whole thing work, that is the only reason you are currently still breathing. Had your fangs touched my wife we wouldn't be having this conversation at all. If you look in her direction again, I will take out your eyes. If you go near her, I will rip your heart out. Since I'm being extremely generous because of the summit I will allow you to leave here with your life. You get one chance to leave my hotel, I don't care what excuse you make to your family, but you will leave," I told him.

What I wanted to do was just kill him; it would save us all a lot of trouble. But The Family was supposed to come first, and this summit was important. Really though the reason I was giving him this chance to leave was because of my wife. She wouldn't like to think someone died because of her. It wouldn't be her fault, but she had a soft heart, she would be upset. The last thing I wanted was to upset her, especially before her first therapy session.

"You have no right to tell me what to do," he hissed, his eyes showing more red.

"That's where you are wrong, I have every right," I said then nodded to Desmond. He was my guard, and he had been waiting for my cue. Two other guards came in to escort Mr. Smith out, which he didn't like. "Take his fangs."

"Yes sir," Desmond said, signaling to the guards to remove him.

They took him away; his eyes filled with rage as he glared at me. He knew he couldn't get away though he tried, good thing there was a convenient hidden hallway for them to drag him through. No reason to cause a scene, that would be unfortunate. Taking a vampire's fangs was both cruel and humiliating, they would grow back but it would take awhile. Maybe he would make better choices next time and not assault women. If only things could be that simple, what was most likely was that he would need to be put down at some point. But that was his brother's problem not mine.

"Did I hear you say fangs?" Gunnar asked when he joined me, taking the empty chair.

"Seemed justified as he tried to bite my wife," I replied with a shrug.

"The Smiths won't like this," he pointed out.

"Should I care? He's alive, isn't he? There is madness in that family, they should all be put down," I replied.

"True," he agreed. "Things ok with you and Freddie?"

"Getting there, I should go find her Lisha was sniffing around again."

"Never one to take a hint," he said, shaking his head.

Between this nonsense with the Smiths and Lisha still trying to get into my bed, I needed a break from vampires. Spending that night away at Freddie's parents 'house was a nice reprieve from this stressful ass summit. The longer this went on the less hope I had for anything to be resolved without more bloodshed. Vampires loved to act like we were better than all others, but it seemed it would be vampires that caused the most problems here. Sometimes it was your own people.

Chapter 14:

Freddie

The trouble with being a hybrid was that you never really fit on either side. My magical abilities made me too witch for vampires and blood drinking made me too vampire for witches. I grew up in my mother's coven like any other young witch fully expecting to join when I was of age. They knew me all of my life, they always knew what I was, it was never hidden. So, imagine my surprise when they denied me membership because I was not a *real* witch.

Never mind that I passed every magical proficiency test and I was at the top of all my magic classes, I wasn't good enough. All of my life I drank blood I had to in order to survive, obviously my parents purchased it from the store like anyone else. Apparently, it was the blood drinking that made them "nervous". As a child I was safe but as an adult I was suddenly a monster they didn't want to associate with. Needless to say, my mother withdrew from the coven, she would not stand for them looking down on me just for existing.

Now when I was in a room full of witches I suddenly felt like a vampire, funny how that worked. These were the people I should feel most comfortable around because it was how I was raised but I didn't. Half a year surrounded by vampires and I felt a bit disconnected from my witch half. Since I wasn't teaching anymore the only witches I spent time with now were my mom and sister. I knew not all witches would behave the way my former coven did, but I couldn't help being weary of a room full of them.

I was told that I was to accompany Belinda to this meeting because as a witch I could relate to other witches. Meanwhile the Harringtons generally only referred to me as a vampire and seemed to completely ignore my witch half. Hunt knew everything there was to know about me, he had me so thoroughly investigated he probably knew things I did not. Yet he wanted me to sit in on this meeting with witches when the coven that shunned me was present? Ahh, he did it on purpose, of course he did.

Throughout the whole summit people gave me looks for various reasons. Because I was an oddity, because they didn't know what I was and of course because I was with Cannon. So many vampires were disgusted that someone like me would be married to him. People flirted with him right in front of me like I wasn't there. Cannon didn't pay them any attention and half of the time I don't even think he noticed. Witches turned up their noses seeing us together, I wasn't good enough to be one of them, but it was also not ok for me to be associated with vampires.

"Harringtons always hold their heads high, dear," Belinda told me before moving to the front of the room. I followed silently and did not look away when some of the witches gave me dirty looks.

There were representatives from 3 different covens, covens could be small or large. Covens were not strictly for witches, other more mixed groups had covens too. These ones were witch only covens. Some families were their own coven, that was how things had to be for us after they dismissed me. I could live with them not wanting me in the coven, it didn't matter that much to me.

What actually annoyed me about them was that they tried to keep me from being hired at the school I used to work at. Even though they watched me grow up they expressed concerns about a vampire being allowed to teach children. Thankfully the school administrators were better judges of character and hired me anyway. Besides, such discrimination would open them up to a lawsuit. I was teaching magic, my vampire half had nothing to do with anything.

"Belinda, it's good to see you," an elder of one of the covens greeted.

"You as well," Belinda said with a smile. "My new daughter came along with me today, our whole family is very committed to coming to an agreement. For anyone who hasn't met her this is Fredericka, my son's wife."

All eyes were on me, and I hated that instantly, I did not want attention on me. We sat at a large round table that fit most of the witches in the room. Others sat in a ring of chairs around the outside of the table. Of the 60 witches in attendance, I noted only two males. Male magic users tended to differentiate themselves from their female counterparts for some reason. Often times they were warlocks or wizards or some other name they deemed not feminine. It was rare that males were actually designated as witches. There was a warlock guild that was a companion of sorts to the coven I grew up in, but they weren't in attendance here.

"That girl is no witch," Susan Reynolds from the Lohan Coven said pointing at me. "I get why you are here Belinda but not her, she shouldn't be here."

"Oh? Why is that? Fredericka has a witch designation, she passed all of her certifications in magic and even use to teach magic to young witches," Belinda pointed out. All things Susan knew quite well and so did her whole coven. My accomplishments were another mark against me in their eyes.

"Her blood is tainted," Susan said and two others in her coven nodded.

"Tainted? By *vampire*? I wasn't aware being part vampire was a crime now. We did not think it was a problem that our Fredericka was part witch," Belinda replied. "I am actually shocked that your coven would participate in such discriminatory practices. Though I suppose that it's good to be aware of it now since we are all trying to work together."

"We see no issue with your daughter," one of the other coven leaders said.

"Girl," a witch elder said looking at me like she could see into my soul.

"Ma'am?" I asked holding her gaze, Harringtons didn't cower. Under the scrutiny of a powerful elder witch, it was not an easy task, but I would do it.

"You are a vampire raised as a witch?" She asked and I nodded. "True hybrids are rare, you should have been valued in a coven. Vampires are good at knowing worth, you stay right there. If anyone disagrees, they can leave."

Silence fell heavy in the room, attention going to Susan and her cronies. Belinda took control of the room and the conversation immediately getting down to business. Every faction in attendance wanted something in order to agree to working together and creating a council. Nobody wanted to compromise, they all just wanted things and that was the problem. And why this thing seemed like it would never end.

The witch covens had grievances with each other, with the shifters, with the mages and some other people too. Everybody seemed to want their own territory to do whatever they wanted. Except if that happened it would just lead to everybody being segregated. And we all knew from human history how well such things turned out.

The moment I stepped into the bathroom I knew something was off. To prove that fact the door closed and locked behind me. Magic crawled along the walls and over the door so I was sealed inside, and nobody could hear what was going on from the outside. Honestly, I didn't think Susan was that powerful or this hateful. She had been close friends with my mother once upon a time. A friend who would smile in your face and stab you in the back. Of all the witches in the coven she had known me best and apparently had been harboring hate for me all of my life. I had been friends with her daughter until high school; we sort of drifted apart like people do.

After the coven shunned me, I learned that her mother didn't think I was the right sort of friend to have. Bigotry and hate would always stand the test of time. Empires rose and fell and everything in the world could change but hate would always linger around. Racism took on a new flavor in the new world; it was less about skin color and where you were from and more about *what* you are. Humans weren't the only ones full of hate; this summit was proof of that. Instead of coming together people were airing their grievances with each other.

"If you are going to try to kill me can we get this over with?" I asked the seemingly empty bathroom; someone was there hiding from me. Maybe I had been spending way too much time with the Harringtons if this was my reaction.

"I'm not going to kill you Girl," a familiar voice said.

Ethel Rosewood was the witch elder from the Highland Coven that spoke up for me. I learned who she was during that truly tedious meeting. How Cannon could stand doing this every damn day and sometimes multiple times I did not know. At the very least when he got home, he deserved a blow job. Not something I should be thinking about in the presence of an elder though.

"You've trapped me in here with you so forgive me for being weary. Nothing good seems to ever happen to me when I'm alone," I said.

"This was the best way to speak with you without prying ears. Tell me now and be quick, why are you with these vampires? Why did they give you over to their son? Don't insult my intelligence by saying it was some fanciful love nonsense," she said surprising me.

"I'm not allowed to tell you that," I replied and she just gave me a look. The long-suffering look of someone dealing with a troublesome child. "I married Cannon because he was the best of my limited options. As for the rest Hunt would kill me or keep me imprisoned for the rest of my life if I tell you."

"I've had my ear to the ether about you, saw you that first day could hardly believe my eyes. Why would someone like you be with a vampire? Makes no sense, why would Harrington let you live amongst his family?" She asked and I just stared at her, maybe she wasn't so approving of me after all.

"Look I'm powerless in this family I have no sway in this summit," I told her. Worst time for me to remember that Cannon said someone might kidnap me to use against him. "This is not about this summit, this is about *you*," she clarified. "Tell me Girl or I cannot help you, what did you do to bring the vampires to your life?"

"I killed a vampire who was assaulting me," I admitted because what did I have to lose? Everything, but she seemed to know something I needed to know. "Hunt found out that I killed him by unusual means and that's why I'm a Harrington now."

"Smart of him to keep you close," she nodded thoughtfully. "They tell you that you are a necromancer? You aren't they couldn't possibly know what you are if they did, he wouldn't have brought you into his house. Though he does like to gamble with the lives of others so maybe. I'm an old woman very old so I've seen things others have not, I've seen your kind before."

"If I'm not a necromancer then what am I? He had every possible test done," I said.

"Death witch," was all she said while watching me. "Never were many to begin with and I had wondered if any still lived. And here you are a death witch hybrid. Not so different from a necromancer, but they do far more than raise the dead. Someone like you could control the dead and the living, and possibly vampires and some types of demon. Harrington likely suspects this and wants you where he can control you. The boy you are married to, is he trying to get you pregnant?"

"Um kind of I mean it was in the marriage contract that I would have my implant removed," I admitted.

My head was spinning with this new information, I never heard of a death witch. Death magic maybe but a witch whose specialty was death? Until the disaster that landed me here, I didn't have a specialty designation. Which was to be expected as I was a hybrid, so it made sense that I was just a general witch. Magic was an element so much like mages who worked with specific elements a witch worked magic. It worked a little differently since magic could do far more than the other elements could. After Hunt had tests run on me, they decided I should have a necromancer designation as my specialty.

There was no existing documentation that said this, Hunt had the records destroyed. Just being a witch in general made vampires weary of me but to be labeled a necromancer? Some of them might be willing to face Hunt's wrath just to kill me. Vampires were not dead like in the old myths, but we had an odd relationship with life and death. In theory a powerful necromancer *could* control vampires. A vampire who was also a necromancer? That was not a combination that should exist, thus the dilemma I was in.

"For you to be a vampire with that type of specialty whoever your parents were must have been having some secret affair. A death witch and a vampire do not go together, though if someone wanted to intentionally breed such a creature…" she said thoughtfully.

"Um ok I have literal seconds before my bodyguard breaks down this door. But are you suggesting that I'm some sort of experiment?" I asked her incredulously. That seemed crazy but then again, did it?

"Give me your phone," she said and I just complied. "We need to talk more but not here not with so many ears about. You'll have to slip away from those vampires always watching you. I need to think, first tell me how old you are."

"Twenty seven," I answered.

"It makes sense, who knows what abilities you might manifest once you are fully mature."

"This is so confusing and I cannot get away from the vampires. Not again anyway, Cannon would never ever let me go anywhere alone. Especially now, he thinks I'll be kidnapped," I admitted.

"The boy is smart then, he has made it clear to all that you are his that puts a target on you. You see it, everybody wants something and someone like you looks easy to use. Even so you must come alone, you can't trust those vampires you live with. If it serves them, they would sacrifice you and I bet you know it. You aren't stupid, you have to know Hunt is ruthless."

"I do," I agreed. "Maybe I can get my guard to bring me to you, that's the best I can do."

"Will he report back to your keepers?"

"I don't think so, my husband thinks he's far too loyal to me."

"If you tell your husband his father will know everything," she said watching me as she gave my phone back. She had done something magical to it though I had no idea what.

"I know," I said with a sigh. "Cannon is near, I have to go."

"You sense him?" She asked and I nodded starting to feel a little panicked.

All the things she said aside I was locked in a bathroom with a strange witch. If I would have permitted it Lee would have followed me into the bathroom. He didn't say anything, but it was obviously on his mind until I glared at him. When I didn't come out, he would have to tell Cannon and Belinda that something was wrong. This encounter was strange but not exactly dangerous though I didn't really know this woman who happened to be very powerful. How the hell was I supposed to explain any of this?

"Come Girl, give me your arm," Ethel said and I just did. Respect for elders was ingrained in us all and why would she hurt me now?

The magic she had been using to silence the room fell away abruptly bringing sound back. There was definitely arguing going on outside the door. She magically unlocked the door, and it swung open, startling everyone outside into silence. Since she started walking, I had no choice but to go along with her. I caught on that she was playing the role of frail old woman though she was anything but. Just because Ethel looked like an old woman with wrinkles in her dark brown skin and her braided hair was completely white, didn't mean anything. In a world where you could glamor yourself to look any way you wanted nobody really could know what you looked like. While this elder witch could likely look anyway she wanted, I gathered that this look served a purpose. Some people were foolish enough to think being old made you weaker, mostly humans believed that nonsense. When it came to nonhumans the older you were the more powerful and Ethel was *powerful*. The power I could feel from her told me far more than her appearance could. She wanted to be underestimated and thought of as old or past her prime, wasn't that why she had be "helping" her? Needing help suggested that she was a fragile old woman, meanwhile I could never hope to be as powerful as she was. As expected, Belinda and Lee were both in the hall. Unfortunately, so was Susan and two of her followers and one of the male witches.

"That girl cannot be trusted! Attacking an elder witch? I bet she drank her blood too," Susan said loudly breaking the silence.

"Who was attacked?" Ethel asked looking at Susan.

"Obviously you why else would she lock you in a bathroom?"

"Susan I don't know what your problem is with me I mean you've known me my whole life and yet you decided I'm some kind of monster out of the blue. Even if I was, I'm not as magically gifted as you seem to be implying, I am," I said. The woman was exhausting; the best part of moving was not having to see these insane witches around town. They loved to be dramatic in public.

"If you can't say anything useful Susan say nothing at all," Ethel said. When Susan opened her mouth again no sound came out.

"What exactly is going on here?" Belinda asked in her polite way but in her eyes, you could see the predator.

"Forgive me, I'm old and I remember a time when vampires fed on the blood of witches. I couldn't live with myself if I didn't make sure this child was ok. No offense meant to you and yours, but she is quite young," Ethel said to her. At the door she released my arm and took the male witch's arm. "Pity she's taken she might have been a good match for my grandson."

"My dear Fredericka has assured you that no harm has come to her in our care?"

"Yes, now if you will excuse me I think I'll rest now," she said and at that her grandson led her away.

"Are you alright?" Belinda asked me scanning me head to toe for any indication that I was hurt.

"I'm fine she just asked me questions," I said. That wasn't a lie, I just had no intention of saying what those questions were. While she was always kind to me, I wasn't quite sure who I trusted at the moment.

"Be careful," Belinda said holding my gaze and I nodded.

Finally leaving the bathroom I walked by Susan and her supporters who were looking panicked because she still couldn't speak. I wondered how long Ethel would leave that spell on her? Did it matter? Not really, though I did note that Lee had disappeared. He moved about like a shadow often appearing and disappearing. What I wasn't surprised to see was Cannon leaning against the wall at the end of the hall. It was surprising that he hadn't come bursting in but I suppose he assumed his mother would handle things.

"Go home, I think you've had enough excitement for the day. You have your appointment tomorrow," Belinda reminded me.

"I'll see you later," I said walking over to Cannon who was watching me.

"Causing trouble?" He asked as he pulled me against him.

"Not exactly," I said with a shrug. "Don't you need to work? I'm fine nothing happened."

"I was coming for you anyway, I'm done for today so I'll take you home," he said.

With his arm around my waist, he led me back to the lobby and out the door. That explained where Lee went as a car was waiting for us. Cannon kept his arm around me during the drive even as he was doing something on his phone. I wasn't sure I could trust the old witch, it would be foolish to blindly trust anyone. But could I trust Cannon? Ever since the incident that led to me leaving he had been *very* attentive. When we had to go out, he was almost always beside me or he was watching me from somewhere in the room. He hadn't spent a single night away from me even though he was still on call at all hours. So, he often had to leave or came in very late.

Aside from that one-time Cannon never did anything to make me question him. But at the end of the day, I still knew why I was his wife. The only people I knew for sure I could trust was my family, but they weren't here. Ollie told me that Cannon said he didn't love me but that wasn't exactly surprising. Though it didn't mean I couldn't trust him. If everything I said and did was going to get reported back to his father, could I ever trust him? Was it even a good idea to see this witch alone anyway? My life never seemed to get less complicated, only more. And tomorrow was not going to be a good day.

Cannon

The world could burn down around us and I wouldn't notice. Not when I was with her. I pulled her back against me while her hips moved in a slow grind. This woman was going to be the death of me. My hand moved from her breast up to wrap around her exposed throat. Her eyes were on me but she did not pause her movement, and I didn't apply any pressure. Most of the time I tried to be more careful with her, lately it seemed like that had been a mistake. She was a vampire even if not a full blood, so I needed to treat her like it. Instead of like she was fragile and I would break her.

When her nails scraped along my legs I couldn't help but to thrust up into her. That fucking sound she made when I did it made me want to do it again. But she was supposed to be in control here, at least that had been the plan. It was torture trying to restrain myself and keep from bouncing her on my dick. We would both enjoy it; I would never leave a woman unsatisfied.

"Play with your pussy for me," I whispered in her ear. I never watched her play with herself, and I wasn't certain she did so when I wasn't around. It was a good day for new things, she hesitated of course.

"Isn't that your job?" She asked, well she wasn't wrong there.

I used my free hand to take hers and brought it to my mouth. She watched while still moving her hips but was otherwise frozen as I licked her fingers before moving her hand down to do what I wanted. My hand moved with hers as she played with her clit. She panted head thrown back on my shoulder. I could feel her getting ready to come so I turned her head so I could sink my fangs into her neck.

Her whole body shook with her orgasm and she moaned. I kept her fingers moving on her clit as I decided to take over thrusting while drinking from her. She came again rather quickly, whimpering against me as I licked the fang marks on her neck. Knowing that I had been the only one to ever have her like this felt good in a possessive primal way. Likely something akin to what other males might feel knowing they were the first to fuck their woman. She was mine only I knew the taste of her blood.

"Do you want my wrist?" I asked her as I lazily thrust into her and she lay limp against me.

"No," she said, then surprised me by getting up on her visibly shaky legs. She turned and straddled me, my dick quickly back inside her tight wet pussy. "I want your throat."

If that wasn't the sexiest thing she ever said to me. I couldn't help bringing her in for a kiss as my hips seemed to move of their own accord. One of my hands tangled in her hair as the other stayed at her hip. Her arms wrapped around my neck, her nails dragging up and down my spine. Apparently, I had been underestimating my little vampire vixen, I no longer would.

"You are so perfect," I told her and I meant it. "It's like you were made just for me. Tell me you're mine."

"I'm yours," she said, holding my gaze with no hesitation. Then she shifted going for my throat.

Unlike her I had on occasion drank the blood of other vampires but none of that could compare to what it was like with her. I thrusted up into her hard as she drank my blood. Her pussy felt so good squeezing me as I fucked her. I came I couldn't hold back with her drinking from me, and she let out a little gasp when she did again too. Pulling her fangs out she licked the marks she left on me. I pulled her in for another kiss, our blood mixing on our tongues. If she was the death of me, I would die with a smile on my face.

We sat in silence for a moment with her head resting on my shoulder and my hands rubbing her back. With her sex was always intense but so was the intimacy after. I just wanted to hold on to her and never let her go. Nothing mattered besides the two of us together. We were on the couch in our living room and there were clothes all over the floor. Any of my annoying ass family with their boundary issues could walk right in. I didn't care; nothing could matter except her.

"I guess we should get up, you might get a call," she said, sitting up after a while.

"Everyone at that fucking summit can burn for all I care, I'm not going anywhere," I told her and she stared at me. "Do you want to have a baby?"

That question really tripped her up, but it was a valid one. There was absolutely nothing preventing us from conceiving the fact that we hadn't yet was just down to luck. Any form of birth control was forbidden for us since the day we got engaged. It was going to happen sooner or later so it was something we should discuss. Maybe this wasn't the time but when was? I didn't really care about having kids before but now I was thinking about a lot of things.

There were some primal urges written into the DNA of males that had us flipping a switch one day imagining our females having our kids. She would be an amazing mother, I knew that. And it was another way to make her mine, there went the primal thoughts again. When I looked at her all I could think was mine, mine, mine, especially when we were around other people.

"That would make your mother happy," she finally said.

"Would it make you happy?"

"I don't know, I guess, it's like a really big step."

"True, not sure I would be any good at it but you will."

159

"Oh spare me Cannon, you keep me locked in this house under constant guard. I feel like you would be much worse with our children," she said, shaking her head.

"Possibly," I admitted because she was likely right.

There was this drive in me to protect her since the day I met her. She had seemed smaller then, having just suffered through what she did and having her life upended. Something so innocent about her called to me and I never really knew why. Innocent and sweet were not my thing but I couldn't help myself. Granted she wasn't exactly some sweet pristine innocent that lived in a land of sunshine. But she was very different from me, and she had been on the verge of breaking. No part of me was ok with that so I convinced her that I was the right choice. Some days I wasn't sure I was but others it was the only thing in the world that made sense to me. She was mine and I was hers and that was how it was meant to be. The me from seven months ago would be very disgusted with this person I had become.

"Cannon," she said, suddenly very serious. "Can I ask you something?"

"Anything," I replied.

"Can I trust you?" She asked, that wasn't exactly what I expected.

"Yes, why? Is it about what really happened with that witch?" I asked because I knew something more likely had happened. If that woman wanted to know if she was a captive, she didn't need to go to such lengths to ensure privacy.

"If I tell you something will you tell your father?" She asked, watching me like it really mattered. It was obvious that she was conflicted, and I could see why.

"It's none of his business what happens between me and my wife. Unless you tell me the witches are going to kidnap you, he doesn't need to know anything. You can tell me I swear I wouldn't betray you," I assured her. It wasn't a lie but I wasn't sure it was true though. Was she more important to me than my family?

"She called me a death witch," Freddie admitted.

"Never heard that term used before but anything is possible these days. Is that a bad thing?"

"Maybe, she thinks I could control vampires."

"I think my father has always suspected that, it's part of why you are here," I told her. "He doesn't tell me everything but I'm pretty sure he thinks it a possibility. You can already kill us so why not command us too? In his mind bringing you into our lives is sort of an act of trust. Here you are under his roof with his family that you could harm. Letting you get close to us and know us means you would hesitate to use your ability against us."

"That's such a huge risk though what if I tried to kill him? Or you? I could kill you especially at anytime," she pointed out.

"You could kill me right now," I countered. "But you won't because that's not who you are. Just because you have this gift doesn't mean you have to use it."

"Do you trust me?" She questioned, still watching me closely.

"Yes," I said without hesitating. It was easy to trust her; she didn't have a deceitful bone in her body. Her heart couldn't be any purer, I could likely trust her more than anyone.

"She wants to meet with me, alone," she said.

"Absolutely not," I replied. "You I can trust but I'm not trusting some witch you don't even know. If you want to meet this witch I will go with you. No going anywhere alone, you know that."

"Just you?" She inquired and I reluctantly nodded even though it was a terrible idea. "I suppose your father was right about me being hesitant to hurt anybody here. Obviously, I don't want to hurt anybody, and I never want to do that again. But it makes sense to make me loyal this way. I'll be especially loyal once I'm having your baby. Another tie to this family it's a smart approach. Other people might go the opposite way using fear and abuse to make me compliant. Your father did it with minimal effort all he needed was you."

"It's shortsighted to go the other way, eventually a person could snap and turn on their masters. Just so we are clear our relationship is not me manipulating you and placating you. Who has the energy to keep all that up long term? You are my wife, and you matter to me, doesn't matter how you came to be mine, you are mine. And I will always protect you," I promised.

"I know," she whispered, leaning her forehead against mine.

Freddie didn't know that I would give my life for her, and I wouldn't say it. She was the only thing that mattered to me and I didn't know why. No reason to question it she had me from the moment she said yes.

Freddie

I never wanted to do anything less in my life. Therapy was a good thing; I was all for taking care of mental health but just not for me. The whole reason I evaded this before was because I didn't want to relive what happened or think about it much. How could I move on if it was always there? Apparently, it was still always there, I just hadn't noticed it until everything else was going wrong. Since this seemed rather necessary, at least to my husband, my mother and mother-in-law, I went.

Maggie Moran greeted us and welcomed us into her office where we sat on a couch. She took a seat across from us in a chair and told us a bit about herself. My urge to flee was not calmed by her friendly demeanor at all. Sensing this Cannon laced his fingers through mine the contact calming me a considerable amount. Everybody thought it was only shifters who needed a lot of affection, but vampires did too. Likely it was the aloofness of most vampires that made it seem like we don't. Cannon was always touching me, it had been that way since we were engaged. Small touches at first to ease me in after what happened but I found that it helped.

"Can you tell me what happened the night you were attacked?" Maggie asked once we were past small talk, time for the reason we were here.

"I was a teacher, I taught beginners magic at an elementary school. One night there was a meeting, and I was one of the last people to leave. The security guard walked to the door with me and waited until I got to my car before going back inside. It all happened so fast, one minute I'm opening the door the next someone grabbed me," I said.

Telling this felt like being back there that night. How ridiculous was it for the security guard to be concerned for me then the moment his back was turned someone attacked me? Cannon gave my hand a squeeze and I appreciated the gesture; he was here with me. He knew the story, I had to tell it so many times after it all happened, but I tried not to think of it now. I tried to move past it and put it behind me. Everybody in my life currently knew what happened and collectively nobody ever spoke about it.

"Um he just appeared out of nowhere, I think I screamed I don't remember. I tried to get away but he was stronger than me, at first, I only saw his face in the window's reflection. His eyes were red, and he had fangs, so I knew he was a vampire. At that time, I hadn't spent much time around vampires, and I might never have if it didn't happen. Things are kind of jumbled up in my memory about it. But I kept trying to get away, he had a knife he held it to my throat while he ripped my shirt. Panicked I threw my head back and actually managed to hit him and he let go for a moment and I tried to get away but he was faster. We were face to face then, I was bleeding from the knife cutting me and there was this look on his face… He stared at my blood, and I knew he was going to bite me. I kept pushing at him trying to stop him then all of a sudden, he froze and collapsed to the ground."

All of my life I was told that I was half vampire half witch, but I never really thought about what that meant. While I wasn't some grand and powerful witch, I always had magic. Because of that I was classified as witch and the vampire part was secondary. The problem was that no vampire was going to adopt a half vampire child. They tried to place children with people who were the same or similar in type. My parents were allowed to adopt me because my mother is a witch and they were willing to deal with my other half. Most witches and other people wouldn't want a half vampire child. I was a few months old when I was adopted, there were no records of my birth parents, I was just a foundling.

Some people go through an identity crisis when they are young and try to figure out where they fit, for me it was witch or vampire. The local vampires often keep to themselves, and I never really wanted to be a vampire. All the testing done on me at the orphanage and nobody ever realized that there was more to me than met the eye. Maybe it's because I didn't have contact with other vampires that this ability never manifested until it did that night.

"Really I didn't know what happened, I was confused and I sort of blanked out. The security guard had come back and someone passing by had stopped, there were sirens. And I just stood there bleeding with a dead vampire at my feet. Police came and my parents were there and there was an ambulance, and I went to the hospital. While I was there a representative from the vampire council came to ask me questions. I was taken from the hospital by this man who said he was an investigator of some sort. My family was taken too, people kept asking me how I killed him. But I didn't know because I didn't think I did. After a lot of testing they told me that I'm a necromancer and that's how I killed the vampire," I told her.

Finding out I had some secret magic was quite surreal, but I never had time to really process it. We were "guests" of the vampires staying in a house that was also a prison. It was shocking when Hunt Harrington himself came to meet with me. He told me that my ability to kill a vampire with a touch was dangerous for me. Vampires wouldn't like knowing someone could potentially kill them or have some kind of power over them. Most vampires aren't the undead like the old stories but some are. There were different types of vampires, I was a born vampire. As in I was born this way and I came with the special digestive system of a vampire, but I could also consume food and could go out any time of day. There were some that can only go out at night and had to die and rise again, making them technically dead or undead. No matter what type of vampires you were, we all shared some genetic traits. Apparently, though my specific make up made it possible for me to essentially suck the life out of other vampires. That vampire I killed was full blooded not a made/turned vampire, so it was especially troubling.

Hunt told me that if anyone found out I could be forced to use this ability to kill others. I wasn't safe living with my parents and teaching in the school; anybody could get to me. But he was offering protection and all I had to do was marry his son. He admitted that having me as part of his Family would make him feel easier about my situation. In his mind it was the best option because otherwise I wasn't going to be released from my prison. Did it matter that there were no charges against me and as far as the law was concerned it was self-defense? No, because I could become a problem for vampires and just the possibility made me dangerous. Never mind the fact that I didn't even know how I did it and I couldn't exactly try to repeat the process.

The advanced testing he had done told him I was a necromancer due to the presence of death magic. Half breeds were fairly common with there being a lot of intermingling between various nonhumans, but I was something rare. Some people liked to collect rare things and people, Hunt told me. Marrying his son would give me the protection and status of the Harrington Family. The fact that he was fine bringing me into his home with his family when I could potentially kill them was odd. I could kill his only son before he could stop me. At least in theory I had no idea how it worked and after what happened I didn't want to know.

My agreement only came after consulting with my parents and meeting Cannon. He was nice and we talked for a while, he promised I would be safe with him. It was what I needed to hear at the time; I wanted to feel safe. When we were released and could finally go home it was with armed guards. One thing Hunt made clear was that my time as a teacher was over, I was going to be a Harrington and that was not a job for a Harrington. There was also the matter of security which I had around the clock.

"Was it assumed that your necromancy magic only came on because your life was threatened? Or was it always there without your knowledge?"

"The tests suggested it was a latent ability that was dormant until that night," Cannon answered for me.

We had agreed that it was best not to mention anything that Ethel had said to me about being a death witch. I still wasn't sure what that was and I was too afraid to look it up. Everything I owned came from the Harringtons, so it just made sense if they were also spying on me. Did I like it? No, but I had nothing to hide, well I usually didn't. Nobody knew aside from Cannon, and I was still worried about if that had been the right call or not. There was definitely a chance I had just been feeling particularly close to him after having sex so I told him. It's not like I could tell my family who were no doubt under Harrington surveillance as well.

These days my closest friends were Ollie and Lucy, it was hard maintaining friendships with others. I hadn't spoken to my two best friends in weeks. Some of my old friends didn't understand why I would marry a random vampire or envied my change in circumstances. Plus there was the fact that I moved away to live in a heavily guarded compound where having visitors was a huge hassle. Feeling isolated was likely another contributing factor to finding myself here now.

"And it was after this whole thing that the two of you met?" She asked and we both nodded.

"Should we be talking about this?" I asked Cannon, uncertain of revealing so much to a stranger.

"It's fine, Mother assured me that you can speak freely here," he said.

"I can understand why you are hesitant, it must feel like very little good has come from surviving your attack. So you know I already am not allowed to discuss what a patient says during a session, but your mother-in-law did take precautions. There are no recording devices in this room, which was checked before you arrived. My notes on your session will be recorded without any specific detail. And I was required to sign a legally and magically binding contract just to see you today," she told me.

"Why did you agree to all that?" I asked, it seemed a bit excessive but not the least bit surprising.

"Why not? Everyone deserves the ability to get help if they have a problem and if I can help I will. You are not even my most high maintenance patient, if you can believe that. I do believe that was the appeal in hiring me, that and the fact that I also do counseling for couples," she said, giving us a suggestive look.

"Our marriage was arranged by my parents in part to keep everything a secret," Cannon informed her. "After what happened we were married 3 weeks later, there wasn't much time to adjust to anything. I'm willing to do whatever it takes to make my wife feel more secure. To answer your question, yes we met after everything happened."

"One day I was an elementary school magic teacher and then all of sudden I'm a Harrington, it has been a lot. Nobody has done anything in particular to make me feel unwelcome or anything, not really. Most people just ignore my existence, but Belinda and Lucy have been great. But I cannot stop worrying that if I do the wrong thing or say the wrong thing The Family will decide I'm not worth it anymore."

"Have you ever felt like that when you were younger? Like if you didn't get the best grades or keep your room clean that your parents might not want to keep you?"

That question left me speechless because she wasn't exactly wrong to think that. Having known at a young age that I was adopted, I never considered if it affected my actions. Did I feel like I needed to make sure they didn't regret all they did for me? Though I wasn't a difficult child it was necessary to put a lot of work into caring for me as a vampire. There were a couple of school related incidents that brought my vampire half attention. And then there was when my mother lost her coven because of me. Those were her friends, it was her community, and she left because they didn't want me. I told her it was fine that she didn't have to do it. Especially since Ollie was a full witch and she could join. Her response was simply that they weren't her kind of people anymore. Susan had been her best friend since they were in school together.

Was it possible that being an orphan was at the root of my problem? Because the Harringtons were another family for me to be part of. Of course, I wanted to be the best daughter-in-law and sister-in-law and the best wife. More than that I was now living as a vampire when I had never done so before. It's part of my designation but it was kind of just a thing I didn't think much about. Living with vampires though changed things for me, they saw the witch as the lesser half when the reverse had always been true.

"I was always the good girl, always did as I was told, always an overachiever and never got in trouble. Was it because I feared abandonment and rejection? It's possible now that you mention it, but I hadn't thought about it like that," I replied.

"Joining a family like the Harringtons naturally was a huge change for you and it presented another family you needed to fit into. Most people would feel inadequate suddenly being thrust into your situation. You were the good girl who listened to her parents and didn't break the rules, who made a career out of being a witch. Then something terrible happens to you, it's only natural that you might feel the way you have been feeling. Your life was threatened, your sense of security viciously ripped away and then you are married to a stranger moving into a big house with a famous vampire family. I imagine having a dual nature makes it harder for you to feel like you fit too. It's ok to feel this way, I would worry more about you if you weren't at least a little worried about your circumstances. And I'm assuming that should things not work out in your marriage, it's not as simple as just going back to your old life and family?"

"My father believes it's too dangerous for Freddie to ever live without protection," Cannon answered. My mind was still spinning from this revelation, suddenly everything made sense.

"How do I fix this so I can stop feeling this way?" I asked her, feeling a tinge of desperation.

"You are an intelligent woman, you know that it's not that simple," she said. "What you can do is examine everyone's actions as opposed to their words. Let your family show you that you belong with them. There is no rule that says you need to be the perfect witch for your family and the perfect vampire for your in-laws. A dual nature isn't a bad thing."

"Depends on who you ask," I said with a sigh. "What can I do to stop feeling like this? There has to be something that I can do?"

"It will take time, six months isn't really that much time in the grand scheme of things," she said.

"Is there anything you think I can do to help?" Cannon asked her. "I don't want my wife living in fear or feeling the need to escape me."

"The fact that you are here with her now I would think proves that you want to support her. But I'm guessing something else happened more recently? Can you tell me about that?"

"My family is hosting a nonhuman summit which has some mandatory family involvement. One night a vampire attacked Freddie and tried to bite her, she didn't tell me exactly what happened. Just that she wanted to leave the party so there was an issue when I was obligated to stay," Cannon explained.

"Why didn't you feel like you could tell your husband the truth? Did you think he would be angry with you or blame you?"

"I didn't want to tell him who it was because it was a member of a prominent family and the summit is important," I said then sighed. "And I guess I was afraid he would think it was my fault like I must have done something. It's the second time a vampire has attacked me this year, it feels like it's my fault. The summit is so important to the Harringtons, and I wasn't sure anybody would care."

"Freddie," Cannon said, looking at me. "None of this is your fault and I'm sorry that I failed you. He deserved far worse than what I did for hurting you."

"I know," I said, my voice coming out barely above a whisper. Just because I knew it didn't make it any easier to handle.

"Should I ask how you retaliated against this person?" Maggie asked, looking between us.

"Had his fangs removed," Cannon said like it was nothing.

"This was what I was trying to avoid, making it worse but Harringtons don't let things go," I said.

"His fangs will grow back, it's not like he's going to starve to death, what I did was a kindness he didn't deserve. There's something wrong with that family, they have never been right."

"I just want to be done with all of this but vampires think I'm weird and there's nothing to stop it from happening again."

"I'm not going to let anyone hurt you, never again, you are my family, you are important to me. If it takes the rest of our lives, I will prove that to you," Cannon promised.

"From what I'm observing it seems like you both want to make this marriage work and that's a good thing. It's going to take time like all things do," Maggie said.

"Yes we do want it to work," Cannon said, looking to me for confirmation.

Sometimes I wondered if Cannon ever mourned the loss of the future he had been expecting. He said he was fine marrying me and all that, but I did wonder. If not for me he could be married to another pure blood vampire of high class. Everything would be so different, she would be from his world not some halfling bumbling through it all. My life changed so much but so did his, we were alike in that way. I did wonder about things from time to time, but I tried not to dwell. We were married, I was the one chosen for him and there was no going back. Divorce was a human concept; it was rare that nonhumans engaged in it. Most people only got one chance, that was why parents liked arranging marriages; they were focused on longevity and stability, not on emotion. Wasn't that why I married Cannon in the first place?

Seeing him with that vampire woman the other night didn't bother me as much as it probably should. She was everything he should have wanted in a wife. A pure blood from a good family and part of his world and of course she was beautiful. Why didn't his parents choose her? Whatever the reason, here we were now together, and this had to work. Was I paranoid and insecure? Yes, I was and I could admit that at the very least to myself. Now that I recognized some of the reasons, I might feel the way I did, hopefully I could work through it.

"Yes, we do," I agreed, holding his gaze so he knew I meant it.

Everything took time, I understood it and believed it so why did I feel like maybe we were running out of it?

Belinda

I suppose this was why my children whined about boundaries and knocking. It was not the first time I found my husband in such a position, and it wouldn't be the last. Without much care for the fact that someone currently had my husband's dick in their mouth I went to sit in a chair. This whole summit was stressful, if he chose to blow off a little steam in between sessions of time wasting who was I to judge? We did of course have a contract with a local brothel. They often provided services for the hotel, though we did have to extend an offer to a second brothel for the summit. Harrington Hotels were full-service establishments; we catered to the needs of our guests.

"What's bothering you?" Hunt asked his attention on me as he fucked the throat of the man on his knees.

"You know I would never doubt you and I share in your belief that this is important. But I'm starting to lose hope that these people will put aside their differences. They don't take the threat of humans seriously enough. History does tend to repeat," I said with a sigh.

This whole massive endeavor had been in the works for years. After everything that happened pre and post Surge everyone should want to come together. In the old days we were not working together, we were all separate factions who often stuck to their own kind. So, what happened when things changed? We had to learn to put aside differences and come together for survival. Even so, nonhumans on Earth just weren't a united people. On Mars things were very different and from the start everything was about building communities. With so many still living with long memories on Earth, even rebuilding from the ashes of the past couldn't give us that sense of community. Being separate and refusing to rely on each other or ask for help made us all vulnerable. To some humans our whole existence was an issue. Never mind that we had always been here and that we shared some similar genetic make up.

"We knew going in this would be difficult," Hunt replied. "But if it makes you feel better if this continues on too long I will step aside and let you do your thing."

"You say the sweetest things," I said with a sigh.

Everybody was afraid of Hunt, though not afraid enough if you asked me. Most of these people weren't smart enough to be wearier of me. They thought of me as just the wife, someone pretty to help her husband achieve his goals. These fools had been alive too long to underestimate me and yet they do. My mother taught me to be a weapon, and my mother-in-law taught me to be unassuming. They were both far too good of teachers, nobody ever saw me coming. Hunt was the more diplomatic and politically minded of us, together we were a dangerous combination. Pity I couldn't remind these patriarchy minded fools of the truth.

Like my husband I grew up in a matriarchy, which was always so much more efficient. Too many men were in charge these days and less things got done. It was typically men with their pride and egos that couldn't set things aside for the betterment of others. That wasn't an opinion, it was a fact I witnessed it time and again. If more females were in control, then we wouldn't be wasting our time like this, at least not to this extent. Matriarchies weren't perfect, nothing was perfect everything had its flaws. The Harringtons currently weren't technically a matriarchy only because Hunt was the Harrington in our marriage. I could only truly assume the power of our Family if he was dead. And that… that wasn't something I needed to be thinking about right now. Always, I would rather have him than power, besides heading a Family wasn't really what I wanted. If I had my way I wouldn't have stepped into this role but one does not go against the plans of their mothers.

"Did someone in particular annoy you?"

"Let's just say that some of these fools are willing to sacrifice others for their own good. How can any of us succeed if we start selling each other out? I'm worried that someone might step out of line and things will turn towards violence again," I admitted.

As much as I loved some bloodshed and a battle, this wasn't the time. The fight that occurred the first night of the summit was a petty dispute by petty people taking offense over nothing. It had been beneath me to involve myself in that nonsense. And we were trying to keep everyone alive; I might have killed them all. Being diplomatic was so tedious I would never recommend it.

"Bel," my husband said looking at me while the man choked on his dick.

"You need me?" I asked though I already knew the answer, of course he did.

"Yes," he said with no hesitation so I was up moving around his desk. I sat on the edge of the desk as close to him as I could get.

"Look at you fucking that throat so good," I said watching his eyes bleed to black. Reaching out I cupped his jaw and made sure his attention was completely on me. "Be my good boy and come for me."

Nobody would ever call my husband submissive because he wasn't. Except when he was with me, he only ever trusted me this much. Watching him let go was satisfying and the hungry way he looked at me didn't hurt. He held the head of the man servicing him and groaned as he unloaded in his mouth. His eyes never left mine even once he was finished. I really hadn't come in here for this but… maybe I needed a distraction too.

"Such a good boy," I said and he groaned again.

The man whose throat he just abused sat back after swallowing every drop and looked at me. Of course, I knew that look and so did my husband who growled. Sex work was so labor intensive at times I didn't know how they did it. But I very much appreciated their services because maintaining my husband's appetite would be a full-time job if not. It had been a long time since either of us kept any long-term paramours instead we relied on the brothel for entertainment. Getting older didn't exactly lessen your sex drive, it could in fact increase it. Two hundred and fifty-something years together and our relationship had gone through all sorts of changes.

"May I service you, Mistress?" The man asked his very hungry gaze on me. What I appreciated about this particular brothel was that their workers genuinely loved sex.

"Oh you are very tempting, I mean look how well you pleased my husband," I said considering it. "Obviously you deserve a bonus for all the tireless effort you put in."

"I'll waive my fee completely if I can please you," he replied.

"No," Hunt growled, reaching over and yanking me down onto his lap. "You can have a bonus but she's mine."

It was rare when Hunt showed more possessive tendencies, we all had them, they just weren't always obvious. We didn't need to be possessive of each other when it came to sex. What was the point of that? Both of us liked our entertainment, sometimes we enjoyed it together. But there were times when he was more possessive than others, males were often just like that. Nobody could ever come between us and many had tried over the years. Sometimes my husband just wanted me to himself and this whole summit had everyone a bit out of sorts.

"Maybe next time," I said and he pouted. "Get in contact with my assistant and we can schedule something."

"Yes Mistress," he said. "Can I be of service in any way to either of you?"

"No, we are done," Hunt grumbled.

While the man whose name I didn't even know gathered his things I sat there a bit amused. At least for a moment before I recalled why I had come in here in the first place. So many insufferable people and their selfish ways. Many of them were lucky they didn't have to suffer the atrocities of humans after the war. We weren't so fortunate, and it had nearly cost us everything. Which was why it was becoming harder and harder to maintain this facade of being a peacemaker.

When I became a grandmother, I wanted to adopt a softer approach to life. I handed over some of my duties to others so that I could experience life a bit differently. A slower pace was fine; I didn't mind it most of the time. Now though? The more no nonsense and impatient part of me was trying to make a comeback. My children couldn't have me as a soft mother, it just wasn't possible, but my grandchildren could. Because things were different now, at least they were supposed to be.

Nothing good would come should we fail at this endeavor. That was why failure just simply wasn't an option.

"Are you going to tell me what's really bothering you?" Hunt asked when we were alone. I stayed perched on his lap and his semi hard dick was still out.

"I'm tired I think," I admitted. "We have been fighting for so long but it seems like it will never end."

We had been through so much, I just wanted a break. Thus my desire to be softer and more frivolous, not unlike my sisters. Admittedly adopting this new persona had its drawbacks and it could be boring. But I needed boring and quiet no more conflict no more nearly losing everything. I knew what the weight of heading a Family was like because there was a time when I had to take on that role. If I was honest with myself, I wasn't sure I could ever do that again. The weight of it was too much for one person, heading a Family wasn't just a figurative position.

"My patience runs thin too," he admitted with a sigh.

"The report... how certain are you?" I asked, watching him closely, his expression when he looked at me said a lot. That look told me more than his words ever could.

"Very, it's more than just a threat, it's not theoretical at all. We need to be prepared," he told me.

"No wonder you are so tense," I commented. The blow job likely wasn't enough with what we had to deal with.

"If only I could fuck my way out of this tension. Alas I cannot, not even with my very talented wife's assistance."

"A few more days and then we stop playing nice," I decided. He just nodded burying his face against my neck. Familiar scents brought comfort much like touch did. Running my fingers through his salt and pepper hair had him leaning into me more. His smoke and leather scent helped my mood a little.

Until we had to switch up our tactics we could take a moment to just enjoy each other. Life was always difficult; there were always things standing in the way of everything. But you really did have to make time for yourselves. Stroking his dick as his fangs pierced my neck, I welcomed the distraction, we both needed it. And soon enough we might just be fucking covered in the blood of those that got in our way. I shouldn't have been thinking of it because it just made me want to make it happen. Blood sex was the best sex and truly it was better than dealing with this mess.

Freddie

Something was wrong with my husband. I noticed it a couple days ago, but it seemed to be getting worse. If he had been drugged, I wouldn't be surprised it was something his mother might do. She was after all very invested in us having children. Likely for more reasons than because she loved her grandchildren. Everything the Harringtons did was in an effort to further chain me to this family. Whatever was going on with him, Cannon had become completely insatiable.

As per usual Cannon was busy so I hadn't expected to see him for a while. After the meeting with the witches, I hadn't been required to go out again. So, I was laying on the couch reading when he came in. The leisurely life of a Harrington wife could get boring, so I had been reading a lot. What else was I to do with my time? It didn't surprise me when Cannon came over, and his hands were all over my ass.

Next thing I knew he was pulling off my panties. He told me once he loved that I wore a lot of dresses. For me I just liked pretty girly things and for him it was about easy access. He flipped me over quickly, spreading my legs wide without a word. His hands caressed my inner thighs as he kept his gaze on me. It was the anticipation that always got me, I loved his hands on my body. I could not look away from him; I was completely enthralled.

With a cocky smile on his face, he moved down spreading my pussy before doing some wicked things with his tongue. In no time at all he had me moaning and gripping his eternally perfect hair. I could feel his fangs as he devoured me. Was it hard to make me come? No, not at all, I was so damn easy for him, it was always that way. And I knew he wasn't going to stop; he was a very giving lover. He sucked on my clit building the pleasure and then he did something I did not expect. His fangs pierced me, and he began drinking my blood while sucking my clit.

"Cannon!" I screamed in surprise; he laughed, of course he did.

I came again and wrapped my legs around him as he kept going. Vampires were so fucking weird, but it felt so good. He kept drinking and sucking. It felt so indescribably amazing. My back arched and I felt like my body was on fire as he kept going. When he pulled his fangs out as usual, he licked the marks to close them and then he started licking me again. I could barely breathe, and he just kept going and going.

"If I come again you are going to kill me," I told him and again he was amused. His response was to push my legs apart and wide and keep sucking and licking me until I did in fact come again.

"Still alive?" He asked, finally sitting up and moving up my body until he was cradled between my still spread thighs.

"No," I replied and he laughed while pushing my dress up further.

"I think you could go again," he said, pressing against me so I could feel what he wanted.

"Maybe just once," I admitted and he leaned in to kiss me just as his phone started ringing. "No," I said, wrapping my legs around him.

"Let me see what he wants," he sighed, reaching in his pocket for his phone. I refused to move my legs, which he found rather amusing.

"We have a problem, a car is waiting for you," Hunt said before hanging up.

"Guess we will have to finish this later," he said with a sigh. "If I have to kill everyone in the room to get back to you tonight I will."

"Please do," I said with a pout.

"Don't put your panties back on," he said, his hand slipping between my legs again. "I want you bare and thinking about me."

"Fine, just hurry up," I told him. He kissed me then got up adjusting his pants where there was a distinct bulge as he walked stiffly across the room.

"See you soon," he said, then headed out the door.

There went my plans though to be fair that hadn't been planned, our sex life had just started taking over. I just laid on the couch stunned by what just happened. Did I dream that? No, my still tingling pussy said it was real but damn. Maybe I need to start reading vampire romances and vampire erotica written by vampire authors. It never appealed to me before but now I was curious.

My taste in reading wasn't tame by any stretch of imagination, but I didn't read about vampires. Maybe if I did then I might have more of an imagination when it came to sex with my vampire man. With those thoughts in mind, I sat up and pulled my dress down before picking up my tablet. What would my mother-in-law think of me reading vampire smut books? Knowing Belinda, she would say that I should be finding new ways to please her son.

The fact that Cannon was like 78 years older than me meant he had plenty of time to get creative with sex. Was it weird that he was that much older than me? For humans it would be, but we weren't human, so it wasn't uncommon. Magic in our blood meant that we would live longer lives than humans. So, couples with weird age gaps happened. Witches could have long lives, but vampires lived much longer, I wasn't sure how long I might live based on my hybrid status.

In exchanging blood with Cannon regularly it was likely that I would live as long as a full-blooded vampire.

There was something in the magic of vampires that depleted our blood, thus the need for ingesting it. Somehow the blood we drank made up for the lack, I didn't know the full science of it. But not getting enough blood was why vampires were famously thought to be pale. The lack of sufficient blood had side effects which explained literally all the old myths about vampires. My new pure blood family was fine with my nonexistent bloodline because it didn't matter. I was regularly drinking Cannon's blood, so his blood literally flowed through my veins.

Vampire anatomy was very odd, and I only knew the basics because I had to in order to stay alive. Cannon and I didn't drink deeply from each other because all the food the Harringtons had was infused with blood. Blood wine, blood coffee, there was blood in everything, the chef made some very good bloody desserts. Even the fruit was grown with blood somehow, people became very creative once vampires no longer had to hide.

While scrolling through various vampire romances the door to my apartment opened to reveal Lucy. She came in holding a bottle of wine and two glasses. Technically speaking, the doors to individual apartments did lock but they all had biometric readers so unless you blocked someone from coming in, they could come in anytime. And they did, nobody in this family had any boundaries. Was it a thing with long-lived people? Or was it just the Harringtons? I wasn't sure since the only people I knew that were centuries old were the Harringtons.

"I saw my brother leave, figured it was a good time to chat," Lucy explained as she came in taking a seat.

"Are you just here to escape the kids?" I asked and she sighed, so I knew it was yes.

"Look I love my children but they are like literal demons, I mean technically they are a little demon. Markus is half demon though we don't talk about that, he was raised by his vampire mother," she said while pouring the wine. "Oh I guess that could have been useful for you to know that you aren't the only half breed in this family. They pop up from time to time we just don't really talk about it. You are a special case being a practicing witch and all. Demons are still rather cagey since people are still assholes about their whole existence."

That was interesting information though I doubt it would change much for me. Lucy's husband Markus was often away doing whatever work he did for Harrington Hotels. So, I didn't really know him well and yet somehow that fit. There was always something about him that suggested he was a little more than vampire. For the summit he spent a lot of time working with the local demon factions. Demons were theoretically just like anybody else; it was human propaganda that made them out to be evil. Anybody could be evil, humans especially so being a demon was not a bad thing. A lifetime of said propaganda though did affect the nonhumans who still looked at them with distrust. Meanwhile a fae was more likely to eat your baby than a demon. Being designated as a demon just meant that you came from another world or dimension. Until the summit I don't think that I've ever met a demon before. As I recall it was most notably not the demons who had been involved in that brawl on the first night.

"It's fine, it's his business," I said with a shrug accepting my glass of wine.

"How are things with your husband? Is he behaving better?"

"Um yeah I guess, we've been having sex a lot. I'm starting to wonder if your mother drugged him or something," I admitted and she laughed.

"Oh that sounds like something she would do, the woman has no conscience and would say it's for his own good. But I won't suggest he exhaust his lust on somebody else," she said, giving me a look.

"I wasn't trying to make a big deal about that, I was just mortified to be in the car with your mother after what we did. Even so, Cannon says he doesn't have a mistress and he will be a faithful husband."

"Somebody is pussy whipped," she commented before sipping her wine. "Wait until you've been married for years and have kids and shit you might change your mind. Then again you have a husband that would have someone's fangs removed for you."

"Yeah I don't know how to feel about that," I admitted. After it happened Cannon told me I had just been trying not to think about it.

"Nobody messes with our family, you are a Harrington now, you need to accept that. I haven't been the best sister to you, but I'm determined to change that. This is your home, and we are your family," she said sincerely.

"Thank you," I said, appreciating the effort that she was putting in. It seemed everyone wanted to keep me in this family. "Can I ask you something um private?"

"Sure," she answered with no hesitation.

"Ok so I don't know anything about how vampire relationships work. Cannon is the extent of my experience, so I never know if things are like a vampire thing or just a Cannon thing. That said, has anyone ever um drank your blood from a weird place?" I asked, feeling the heat in my cheeks as she stared at me. Well, this was what a sister was for right? To be able to ask questions and talk about things.

"What did Cannon do?" She asked and I couldn't answer until I took a drink.

"He was um giving me pleasure and uh he bit me while doing it," I admitted. "Um he kind of drank my blood and sucked my clit at the same time."

"He bit you where?" Lucy asked, her eyes wide as she stared at me.

"You heard me," I said, hiding my burning face behind a pillow. "Is that something vampires do?"

"No, apparently my little brother is into some freaky shit," she said with a laugh. "I didn't even know you could do that, did you like it? Wait dumb question of course you did this whole apartment smells like sex. And you smell more like him than usual."

"It was weird but it felt good," I admitted. I could not imagine sharing this with anyone else, not even my own sister. Not just because she was still a teenager but because she wasn't a vampire, I guess that's why I had a vampire sister now.

"I'm far too curious considering you are having sex with my brother. Does he do other weird shit?"

"No? I don't know! I told him I would kill him, and he said that was sexy," I said and she just laughed.

"That doesn't surprise me though to be fair I doubt he believed you, too much of a good girl for that," she shook her head.

"Everybody here speaks of death and killing people so casually, it's not like that in a witch household."

"It's a miracle you survived, I mean obviously your parents love you and all that but you need community. We aren't as bothered by death typically because we are old and hard to kill. My kids though aren't old and they are vulnerable. That shit is scary, just being a parent is scary, you have someone else to worry about. I couldn't imagine my kids not growing up around other vampires and with their own family. Shifters thrive in packs, and we do in our collectives."

"The fact that your family treats me like I am a vampire is different from what I experienced my whole life. To the rest of the world, I was a witch with a side of vampirism, here I'm a vampire. I see the value of community, whenever we do have kids, I will especially appreciate that."

"I'm surprised you aren't already pregnant, how often do you have sex?"

"Uh most days I don't know less since the summit started."

"Must be nice to be newlyweds, Markus and I have never been so active. Then again if he gets to be too much I send him off to his mistress."

"You're really ok with that type of thing?" I asked because how could I not? There was no set of circumstances I could imagine where that would be ok, not for me.

"Oh you sweet innocent child," she shook her head. "It's really not an issue, I occasionally indulge too but men just have too many needs. Think of it this way men who are unsatisfied cheat, this isn't cheating we have an agreement. As long as you both agree there's no issue. We have rules like we can't fuck anyone that works for us and never bring another person into our home. Definitely never anyone who is around our children, it has to be completely separate from our lives and family. Honestly it helps things and well when you are pregnant you won't want to have sex much if at all. It doesn't mean that Cannon cares any less for you if it happens. You are young so you will learn that things don't always have to be complicated. You will understand it better once you have been married for a few years."

Theoretically I knew that a lot of things in life were complicated by the human influence we were all subjected to.

They believed things should be a certain way and put labels on things that didn't necessarily require it. They also put limitations on everything because just doing what you wanted or what made you happy couldn't be tolerated. It was actually impressive the different ways and different lengths they would go to in order to control one another. In their limited imaginations a lot of things became taboo.

Even knowing these things, I still wasn't sure I would ever be ok with different types of arrangements. Cannon said he wanted us to have a monogamous relationship. Which was not something marriage guaranteed you these days, if it ever truly had. Lucy's agreement with her husband wasn't odd at all and really vampires tended to be very sexual creatures. Proven by my husband on a daily basis. Still, I just wasn't sure I could be ok with it, but maybe I would feel different once I was older.

As Lucy was the older sibling, she likely had more experience than Cannon did. Both had been alive for over a century so of course things would be different. In my 27 years I was never overly adventurous, at least not until Cannon. Who had me sitting here with no panties on under my dress because he had *plans* for when he got back home. Would I ever get tired of that? I had to wonder because right about now it didn't seem possible.

We chatted for a while and drank more wine; it was nice to do something so simple. Just hanging out with my sister, it made me miss Ollie though. My phone dinged and I picked it up to see a message from Cannon saying he was on his way.

Cannon

I promised my wife a slaughter and I was ready to make it happen. Two of the vampire Families were squabbling over something I didn't care about, and I had to mediate. Was it wrong that I started wondering if my wife could kill a room full of vampires without touching a single one? If her ability was ever that strong it would be a blessing and a curse. With her taste still on my tongue I half listened as they complained about businesses and other things. In order for the summit to be successful it was necessary for everyone to agree and form a council. The problem was that everybody had an issue with somebody and nonhumans loved nothing more than holding grudges for all of eternity.

"You are distracted," Lisha said, watching me. One of the Families in this current dispute was hers.

"I have better things to do," I replied, not caring who heard me.

"Oh I bet, I think we all know what you would rather be doing," she said. "You and I would have made a better alliance, you know, bring two great families together. Instead, your father let you marry some nothing little half vampire. It makes no sense; having met her I'm wondering what it is about her."

"Does it matter? She's my wife and you are not," I said. Did I know this was likely going somewhere? Yes, I wasn't stupid there was a reason she was bringing this up now. It was why my father wanted me here and why he increased the guards at the house before I left.

"I'm just curious, how did you even meet such a person? By your own admission she didn't grow up around vampires. No instead was raised as a witch, that is unfortunate of course. But how could you know her?" She persisted and I knew others were listening in on this conversation. Her uncle and the head of the other family were still arguing but I doubted the sincerity in it. This was a trap that my father sent me into without warning.

What did one do when they were being set up? They wanted to know more about Freddie because there was a rumor about her. So, they decided to have this pointless argument so that I would be forced to come here. Likely they would have really loved it if I had brought Freddie with me, I mean she accompanied my mother to meet the witches. If not for this summit and my father requiring us to be seen constantly nobody would have noticed Freddie. Most of the public interest in our relationship had died down since there was nothing new and interesting going on. Parading her around in front of various types of predators and backstabbers wasn't a good idea.

"We met when I assisted her with a problem, nothing too interesting. My parents have been trying to get me to get married for years so I accepted it when they presented her as a possibility. No, she's not of a vampire Family and we know next to nothing about her bloodline, but it didn't matter to me. Of course, my parents were just happy to see me finally settling down, it's pretty simple," I said with a shrug.

Officially in the report about what happened that night she was attacked and I killed the vampire. No, I wasn't there obviously but it was part of the story my father crafted. I was her hero rescuing her and showing her, not all vampires are bad, and we fell in love and blah blah blah. Nobody would tell a different story about it, unfortunately the cameras in the school parking lot malfunctioned at the time. Memories and reports could be altered, and money went a long way.

"Stop playing games, there is obviously a reason that the proud Harringtons would let someone of a dubious bloodline in their family. She's a vampire who doesn't even smell like a vampire; she is prey not a predator. Why would you take her as a wife? If there wasn't something you aren't telling other people," Lisha said. What she really wondered was why I was never interested in marrying her.

"Don't know what to tell you and really it's not your business. My wife is a Harrington now and that's all that matters," I said then stood. "This whole meeting is a waste of time so I think I'll get back home to my wife."

"Abandon your duties for this little girl? She's so young and so fragile," Lisha said. Of course that was a threat, but I wouldn't take her bait.

"You know I am distracted tonight, we are trying to have a baby so you know have to work at that," I said.

The room fell silent then and I almost laughed. No, we weren't actually trying but we weren't preventing it either so soon it would happen. Announcing here that I was planning a family with her was an indication that yes, this marriage was real. It was one thing to be married but to have a child? That made it serious and it told these people that it was real and not some game. The long-lived loved playing games because they got bored so they did all sorts of shit that made no sense. Likely they thought that I was just keeping Freddie close as a cover for something else. That wasn't the case at all she wasn't a weapon we were hiding she truly was my wife and part of my Family. I didn't agree with all of my father's decisions, but this one had been a good one.

"People are saying that your father is hiding a weapon," Phillip Gordon said. He was Lisha's uncle and clearly tired of the charade. "Are we to be forced into submission so this plan of his can work?"

"If we could do that do you honestly think we would still be having all these meetings trying to solve disputes and all of your petty bullshit? At this point I wish my father had some mysterious weapon to force all of you to stop being so self-centered but sadly he does not. What any of this has to do with my wife I don't know, and I'm tired of talking about it," I told him. We should have hired powerful telepaths to put up a psychic field and force them to sign contracts. I really wish we could have but finding a truly powerful telepath was hard.

"This wife of yours is said to be his secret weapon," Dallas North, the other family head said.

"My wife is a vampire who happens to also be a witch, look into her if you want. I don't care, there's nothing to find," I said then paused. "Oh is this all coming from the witches? Of course it is, they hate vampires, they would love to see us all kill each other. They don't like that one of their kind happens to also be a vampire, they aren't very smart."

"Actually the Smiths have been saying this, but yes others too," Phillip said. And apparently our own people were conspiring against us, big surprise.

"Ah the Smiths, I'm surprised anyone would take them seriously but have fun with that."

"You had an altercation with Ferris Smith the other night," Lisha pointed out. Was I surprised she had been watching? No, I didn't actually care but she seemed to think I should feel some type of way.

"Ferris Smith attacked my wife and tried to drink her blood, he is lucky to still be alive," I replied, holding her gaze. That earned a few gasps from the room, even Lisha was surprised. "Has no one noticed the red in his eyes? It shouldn't be a surprise, I mean with that family's origins and all. But in the interest of continuing this summit I did not kill him, but I made it clear to him he's not welcome here. If his brother has an issue with that I haven't heard of it but I'll tell him the same as I'm telling all of you. If anyone comes near my wife you have me to deal with, and I won't be so kind should something else occur."

Something needed to be done about the Smiths, I didn't know or care what they knew, it didn't actually matter. They were troublesome and determined to make nuisances of themselves. What they didn't want was to be an enemy of my family but that was where this was headed. Their tactic of trying to get everyone else on their side wasn't a bad idea. However, it would end up leading to their downfall. Nobody actually liked the Smiths and vampires were snobby enough to want them dead just on the principle of their tainted blood. Typically, I wouldn't convince others to exterminate a whole Family based on rumors or prejudice, but this was a special case. And it wasn't just to keep my wife's secret, the Smiths were up to things, and this wasn't the time for that.

"Are we done here? Or do you actually have some issue that needs to be mediated? Why waste all this time anyway? If you wanted to know you could have just asked me. I've had way too many long days and nights to be entertaining this pathetic attempt at subterfuge," I said, holding the gaze of both Dallas and Phillip.

"You should mind your elders, boy," Dallas had the nerve to say.

"I would if you didn't act like 12 year olds, all of you have done nothing but act like children this whole summit. It's gotten so bad that you are wasting my time with gossip, look at yourselves you should be ashamed. None of you have bothered to consider why we are all here and no it has nothing to do with territory disputes, business deals or mindless gossip. If you can't do anything useful you might as well be dead," I told him. Without waiting for a reply I left the meeting room, such a waste of time.

On my way out I texted my wife that I was on my way home. I fully intended to spend the rest of the night with her. It was possible that I was addicted to her blood, I craved it. Well, not just her blood, I craved her, knowing I was going back to her was the only reason I got through that meeting. Inside the car with Desmond and my driver Ty, I started getting things together to handle the Smith situation. Starting with informing my father that they were still causing trouble. Tomorrow I would deal with this, tonight I had better things to do.

Vampires aren't known to have premonitions, though it's not impossible anybody can. Some vampires could even use magic, generally the older you got the more random skills you might acquire. Teleportation was by far the most useful magical gift to have; some vampires possessed such abilities. Unfortunately, it had never shown up in the Harrington bloodline. I knew something was off after we left the hotel grounds. Trusting my instincts I tapped a secret panel in my watch and leaned forward grabbing both men. If this worked, we might just live and if it didn't my wife would be a widow.

Freddie

I knew something was wrong as soon as I heard the knock.
Rarely did any of the Harringtons knock, a lot of nonhumans
didn't believe in boundaries. The house did have a full staff
and I knew they came in and cleaned but I had never actually
seen them do it. I was still sitting on the couch with Lucy when
the knock came and then the door opened. It was Lee, his eyes
found mine quickly and I knew something was wrong. Even
though I was in the house he still stood guard over me
especially when Cannon was gone. I don't think he ever
stepped foot in our apartment though.

"Mrs. Harrington," he said, his expression troubled.

"What happened?" I asked because I knew there was
something.

"There has been an incident," he said. I just stared at him; Lucy gasped and then turned her attention to me.

"Pull yourself together," she told me. "You are a Harrington you will not give in to emotion."

"I don't know exactly what happened but I do believe the family is gathering downstairs," Lee informed us.

"Get up, we will go down and find out what's happened. It could be nothing," Lucy said. If I didn't hear the worry in her voice, I might think her devoid of emotions.

Nodding I got up and followed as Lucy went out the door pulling on her Harrington persona as she went. Lee followed us silently and I tried not to panic. Cannon should have already been home; he texted to say he was on his way. Maybe he could have been detained by more summit nonsense, it happened constantly. When we arrived in the main entrance hall there was a lot of chaos. When I hesitated, Lucy stepped back and pulled my arm through hers and moved me along.

"There you girls are," Belinda said, waving us over to her. "The car Cannon was in went off the road and there was an explosion. I know this is hard to hear but we don't know anything for certain yet."

I couldn't speak, I could barely breathe, this could not be real. Our relationship was complicated but less so recently. I was pretty sure I was in love with my husband, and I might never see him again. But no, vampires were strong and hard to kill. He would be ok, he wasn't a young vampire, he was old enough and strong enough.

"Mother, I think you could have said that a little better," Lucy said. They were both looking at me, both worried.

"Sorry, I'm so used to being straightforward about things. We don't know exactly what happened yet so no need to get upset. No matter what we are a family we will get through this," Belinda assured me.

I often felt like an outsider in this family, I was the half vampire who could kill other vampires after all. Other than Belinda and Lucy, I didn't spend much time with the other Harringtons. My position here was a bit of an odd one as Cannon's wife. He was the heir, and everybody knew it so it set him apart from others and as his wife it set me apart. Who would want to risk his wrath by not being nice to his wife? I hadn't met the whole of The Family, but I met a good bit of them. To a lot of them it was obvious that they thought me a half blood in an undeserved position of power.

Nobody was going to say anything directly to me, but you didn't always have to in order to get your point across. Their obvious distaste and resentment was something I just had to live with. As with everything, whatever I did was a reflection on Cannon and Belinda since she was my mother-in-law. So, I could not afford to let my real feelings show now. Not when top members of The Family were gathered, it was why Lucy did not let me go now.

It was selfish to consider but I had to do it anyway. If something happened to Cannon, I wasn't sure what they would do with me. He was my minder after all, what would happen if he was gone? Marry me off to a different

Harrington? Or were we back to me being a prisoner? They would absolutely never let me go that I knew for certain. Or was this the point? With Cannon out of the way maybe I would be easier to remove from the Harringtons 'care. I knew people were asking questions about me and Cannon admitted that there was a rumor about me being a weapon. If I was a weapon, I was a useless one because yes, I could technically kill a vampire, but I didn't know how. It just happened; I had been terrified and couldn't escape.

I knew one session with the therapist wasn't going to fix all my problems, but did life have to keep putting me back in my place? How was I supposed to move on if everything kept trying to drag me back? Could I really trust anybody here? At the end of the day, they were loyal to The Family, I was just an interloper. Maybe if I had a child my place here would be more secure. But it seemed so very wrong to use the life of a child as security. Even if it was likely true, they wouldn't get rid of me then.

Restlessness clawed at me while waiting for news with my mind coming up with all sorts of scenarios. The elders were still discussing things which did not involve me. It didn't involve Lucy either, but she stuck around in the hall and so did Gunnar. Frustrated by everything, I went to sit on the steps. Gunnar was pacing and when I moved Lee relocated to lean against the wall by the stairs. Apparently, he was not leaving my side even in the house. I had to wonder if he was protecting me from The Family or would he be the one to imprison me? He might feel some loyalty to me but we both knew he couldn't disobey a direct order from the patriarch.

Part of me wanted to go upstairs and get away from everyone but I didn't move. Maybe it was time to admit to myself that I was completely and foolishly in love with my husband. It definitely was not on purpose but how much time could you spend with a person before feelings just developed without your consent? We lived together we slept together, and we had sex a lot, like a whole lot especially lately. And it wasn't just sex, sometimes we were just together.

Before the summit we did go out sometimes, like a regular couple. Most nonhumans were generally supposed to be better at not confusing sex and love, but I never said that was me. I tried really hard not to attach any emotion to anything involving Cannon, it just didn't work. He knew me, knew what I liked and didn't like, knew that I loved my family more than anything and I missed teaching. Falling for him wasn't hard, trying to avoid it was impossible. If he was gone then I would never be able to tell him, not that I should anyway.

For me to tell him how I felt was... too much. It gave him too much power in a relationship where he already held all the power. I did believe he cared about me but I knew he wasn't interested in love. There were things he said that gave me that impression. It was going to take many therapy sessions before it became easier for me to not feel insecure about being in this Family. Especially now when I had to wonder if Cannon was gone. Why was life so damn tragic? When was I ever going to get a break?

Bewitch

Maybe if I hadn't been feeling sorry for myself, I might have noticed it before. Every time Cannon was near me, I could feel him. I don't know when it started, maybe when we came back from our honeymoon? That was where we initially connected on an intimate level. Obviously, I didn't know a lot about vampire marriages, but I imagine it was the blood exchanges that bonded us. The first time I thought it would be weird but it wasn. Apparently, I have instincts that only came out in the presence of my male vampire. I wasn't sure if he could feel me like that too, we never talked about it. Because of this though I was up on my feet a second before the front door opened and he walked in. He looked more tired than usual and was dirty and there was blood on his ripped shirt, but he was alive. When his eyes found me he seemed surprised to find me there but only for a moment before he moved to me faster than I could blink and had me in his arms. At that moment I was definitely cliché enough to have run into his arms like in an old movie, but he came to me. His fingers were in my hair gripping it as he kissed me.

"Sorry I'm late," he said, leaning his head against mine.

"You're alive," Hunt said to his son, pulling both our attention to him.

"Yeah, thanks for sending me into a trap," he replied to his father. His arm stayed around me keeping me at his side as he turned to face him.

"I didn't think they would attempt to kill you," Hunt said, clearly not willing to apologize.

209

"How did you get out? It was magic fire the car was burned beyond recognition," Belinda said. Just how bad had this been? I had to wonder but I knew better than to ask.

"Had a teleportation spell," he said with a shrug. "They were waiting in case we survived, would have been back sooner but decided to get rid of the bodies and bring back a souvenir." As he said that Desmond, came in and kicked a bound man onto the floor.

"Good," Hunt said, nodding to other guards who grabbed the man and took him away.

"If that's all I would like to get a shower," Cannon said.

"Go on then," Hunt said with a dismissive wave of his hand.

"I'll get the interrogation going," Gunnar volunteered a wicked gleam in his eye. For all his fun ways, nobody would tell me what Gunnar actually did for the Harringtons. Suddenly I had a feeling that I truly didn't want to know.

"Come with me?" Cannon asked me and I nodded following as he led me up the stairs.

There was some discussion going on and I definitely felt eyes on us as we went up. Was it embarrassing because of what they assumed would happen when we were alone? Yes, but I mean obviously, I was the wife, this was my job. As soon as we were inside our apartment Cannon had me against him. He held my face and just stared at me and I couldn't tell what he was thinking. I was a mess on the inside, happy to have him back, terrified of losing him and terrified of him finding out how much he meant to me.

Bewitch

"Tell me no," he finally said. "I can't be gentle, so tell me no and I won't touch you."

"I thought I lost you," I whispered looking up into his eyes,

"All I could think of was getting back to you," he admitted.

"Don't be gentle, take what you need," I told him, holding his gaze.

Without another word he picked me up and carried me into our bedroom. After sitting me on my feet he grabbed the hem of my dress pulling it up and over my head. Seeing that I hadn't put my panties back on definitely pleased him. He unhooked my bra, and I dropped it to the floor with my dress. I considered unbuttoning his shirt, but it was already torn and a bit bloody. So, I grabbed it in both hands, ripping it apart. I was not as strong as a full vampire, but I wasn't weak either. The flash of light in his eyes and him dragging my body back against his told me he liked it. His hands were on my body again and he kissed me hard and possessive. I undid his belt while we kissed and I slid my hand inside his pants as soon as I could, making him groan.

"On the bed, on your knees ass up," he growled looking at me in a way that made my whole body blush.

Naturally I complied and was rewarded with his tongue licking me from clit to asshole and back again. When he did things like that, I would probably let him do anything to me. I loved his tongue on my body and the things he did with it. Unlike any other time we had sex he didn't make me come; I

211

was just left drifting on the edge before he moved away. Before I could make my displeasure be known I felt him kneeling behind me. Something about that moment when he entered me sliding along inside me always felt so amazing. He gripped the back of my neck as he filled me up all the way until he was fully seated inside me.

"Don't worry baby, I would never leave you unsatisfied," he said as he pulled almost all of the way out before pushing in more forcefully. "I just want to feel it when you come for me."

His words while each thrust was more forceful than the last might have done the job. He gripped my hips and fucked me hard not relenting at all when he did make me come. This was the type of fucking where you might not be walking straight the next day. He gripped my hair, pulling me back until my back was against him. It wasn't a surprise when his fangs pierced my neck nor was it a surprise when I came from it. While he drank he kept up his relentless thrusting and one of his hands left my hip to play with my clit.

Obviously, this man was trying to kill me. After I came for what a third time? He pulled his fangs out and licked the marks before pulling out of me. I found myself flipped on to my back with him inside me again and his lips on mine sometimes vampires moved way too fast. His pace was slower now though no less intense. I could feel the tension in his body right before I pierced his neck with my fangs. He let go then coming inside me while I drank his blood.

Afterwards we just laid together, and he pulled me tight against him like he was afraid I would leave. I just listened to the steady beat of his heart, he was here and he was alive and that's all that mattered. Despite everything that had been happening I never thought that someone would try to kill him. This was the perfect time to tell him how I felt about him because who knew what tomorrow might bring. But I couldn't, the words just would not come out because it still felt like too much. He already had all of me giving him my heart too was just something I couldn't bring myself to do. Even without the words and even if he didn't know it he had it, it was always his. That was what scared me the most because it gave him the power to hurt me worse than anybody else ever could.

"I want us to have a baby," Cannon said, surprising me. "I know we haven't talked about it in any serious way but after what happened today it's all I can think about. If I hadn't moved quickly enough, I would have died and left you alone and I don't like the thought of that. I mean I also don't like the thought of us having a kid and me not being there too."

"If something happened to you what would your father do with me?" I asked, needing to know that before I committed to anything.

"Married you to someone else in our family, probably Gunnar since he's vampire young and unmarried. And he does know about your abilities. Were you worried about that? He's not going to cast you out whether I'm here or not."

"What I was worried about was you but yes I did consider it, how could I not? A baby means I'm completely tied to your family, to you."

"It's a smart decision to secure your place here, I won't lie. Of course, I know it's not why you would do it but you do have to think of these things. Doesn't offend me, you should think about protecting yourself especially if I am unable to," he told me. "It's not selfish to think of yourself, and we don't have to do this just because I've been confronted with my own mortality."

"We have sex all of the time, especially recently, you realize I could already be pregnant, right? Like it's not impossible I know there's a science to it all it's not just constant sex but it's possible," I pointed out. "Which is actually terrifying because I almost lost you and I can't do any of this on my own, I need you."

Did I bury my face against him like a ridiculous overly emotional woman? Yes, and I had no shame, I loved this man, and I didn't want to lose him. Especially if I could be pregnant that didn't bear thinking of really. Did I want children? Yes, maybe it was the influence of the Harringtons, but I had no blood ties to anyone. I loved my family; they weren't my adoptive family they were just my family but maybe blood mattered a little. Would I have thought of having a baby oh I don't know seven months ago? Hell no I hadn't even been dating anyone but that all changed. I was a married woman and though I knew marriage wasn't necessary for that to happen I guess I had a bit of traditionalism in me. Likely because I had married parents who were my example of a loving relationship growing up.

My relationship didn't resemble theirs but that didn't make it bad. This was just what worked for us, even though I could never tell him I loved him. Not even just because I knew he didn't love me, I knew it would change things. I barely had a handle on how things were currently; I didn't need more change. Though there might just be one change that had been in the works all this time.

"I doubt the crash would have killed me if it's any consolation, I'm hard to kill," he said while running his fingers through my messy hair. "As long as I live I'll always come back to you Freddie, I swear."

"Why would anybody do this? Killing you would not make your father more agreeable. If anything, it would make him vengeful, and nobody wants him as an enemy."

"The fucking Smiths have been going around saying things about you, trying to turn the other Families against us. And I imagine they are still pissed about what I did to Ferris."

Though my knowledge on all things vampire was fairly new I was aware that a vampire losing their fangs was a bad thing. But in this day and age it is not a detrimental thing since you could buy blood anywhere. In long past times no fangs meant you couldn't feed. That it was an act of humiliation didn't surprise me; I could see that it made you less vampire, more human. At least in appearance and it would be a weakness. Honestly, I couldn't really feel bad for him all things considered. If he tried to kill Cannon because of it though? Then I wasn't sure what to feel other than kinda like it was my fault. Even though I knew it wasn't, guilt still came for you even when it was undeserved.

"What's going to happen now?" I asked, worried that everything the Harringtons worked for was going down in flames.

"Father will confront the vampires and then he will call for a vote with the factions. He won't be in the mood to make deals after this."

"What happens if they don't agree?"

"Honestly I don't want to know, I do have a feeling he knows something the rest of us don't. Whatever it is, it's likely to come out tomorrow, he won't want to wait."

"Is this all my fault? If I hadn't told you about Ferris, then—"

"Absolutely not, none of this is your fault you were attacked so yes I retaliated. Admittedly I didn't expect all of this but the Smiths had an ulterior agenda this whole time. They have always been a problem, one that could mostly be ignored but now they are getting bold. What they need is to learn their place. He had no right to touch you, he's lucky the only thing I did was take his fangs," Cannon said. He was still very angry about that whole thing, seemingly more so than this attempt on his life.

"So what do we do now?" I asked him and he shrugged.

"Get a test and find out if you are pregnant?" He suggested and I just stared at him, that was not what I was asking.

"Um how? I doubt either of us would be allowed out of the house right now," I pointed out.

"Likely not, but Lee can go out," he said.

"Then he would know," I replied.

"He's going to know anyway he follows you around like a shadow. Did you ever notice how he seems to appear out of nowhere? He has shadow magic; he can literally move amongst the shadows. It's actually a highly coveted ability amongst vampires, if he was from a better bloodline he would be sought after. We are lucky to have someone like that; I have no idea how he ended up here. He is rather devoted to you, so he'll never be too far away from you," he said.

"Does that make you jealous?" I couldn't help but to ask.

"No, I don't exactly like it but as long as he does his job and doesn't get any ideas then he can stay. I know I can trust him to protect you, that's all that matters. And I trust you to never encourage anything too familiar between you," he said.

"Fine you can ask him to go," I said, not wanting to go down that road. "I'm going to get in the shower, join me when you are done."

"Can I borrow your phone? I lost mine somewhere," he said and I nodded.

I tossed my phone to him on my way to the bathroom. Of course, I knew that he knew the passcode for my phone, I never tried to hide that from him. Besides, what did I even have to hide?

Cannon

Truth be told I did not think I would actually die. Some
people think vampires can't die and that we would just rise
again but that's not true for all of us. Only daywalkers are
guaranteed to rise, they were a complicated breed. Daywalkers
were born vampires who only mated with humans to create a
hybrid. They were not necessarily an act of nature, more like
just how a few Families decided to live their lives. These
hybrids though would rise should they die without
consequence. Before rising though they didn't have the full
strength and abilities as a risen vampire. What they were not
was turned vampires who always occupied the bottom rung in
vampire hierarchy.

Most people didn't know the first thing about vampires beyond blood drinking. Only turned vampires feared the sun, born vampires had no such limitations. As a born vampire of over 100 years old I was strong and my bloodline was old, I was hard to kill. Unlike humans who diminished with age, vampires only got more deadly the older we got. I was not immortal and I could die; it just wouldn't be easy. Crashed car careening off a cliff?

If I didn't break my neck or puncture my heart I would have survived. Though the fact that they had an explosive with magic fire lessened the odds. Magic fire could burn through anything including people and was hard to put out. Since I was not a fool, I did not take that risk and that was why I was still alive and well. Though I was also rather pissed off, something I tried to keep from my wife. The last thing she needed was something else to worry about.

"Are we really doing this?" She asked, looking at me nervously.

"We can wait until morning if you want," I replied.

"No, I'll do it," she said, taking a deep breath and picking up the box.

Lee had gone out to purchase what I asked him to and now we were going to see if she was in fact already pregnant. In the modern age pretty much, everybody had a birth control implant. They were devices made of science and magic that were unisex and very effective. At least for most people there were horror stories out there about things that happened to some people. Enough time had passed since we had ours removed so it was possible. It was really only a guess at how long it took to leave your system. Instead of ye olde stick a woman peed on pregnancy tests had also gotten an upgrade. Just a prick of the finger and the analyzer would tell you what you wanted to know. It was a small device, another mix of science and magic, med magic had come a long way in the years since The Surge.

Freddie took the little device out of the box and stuck her finger in the indicated spot. The good thing about these tests was that they were reusable, up to 5 times the box said. So, if it was a no now we had it to check at a later time. Obviously, I was facing my own mortality and that was why this was suddenly so important to me. My father always talked about legacy, and I finally understood it. What would I leave behind when my time came? What would be my memory? Children were our legacy; parents spent their lives building things up to give their children good lives. Through them you lived on, part of you would go on as they continued the line.

I don't think either of us breathed in the 5 minutes it took to analyze. To distract myself I pulled Freddie over onto my lap. This was of course the worst time for any of this but maybe that wasn't a bad thing. If not for what happened, who knew when I would have actually gotten serious about this. And it wasn't just about legacy and narcissism; it seemed primal and biological. Wasn't it wired into our DNA that we wanted children to carry on our lines and a spouse to grow old with?

"Oh gods," Freddie said, staring wide eyed at the test.

"I guess we have our answer," I said, though I could barely breathe.

My wife was pregnant and with that knowledge I felt a tight grip on my heart. She would need more protection now; I couldn't risk anything happening to her. My mind flashed back through all the things that had been going on recently and she had been pregnant this whole time. I was going to be a father. Yes, I was the one to suggest we do this, but I didn't expect it to happen so soon. Well ok it probably was my fault that it did happen with the way our sex life was.

"Cannon, you need to breathe," Freddie said to me. I had no idea when she had turned her attention on me because I was spiraling.

"You are so fucking perfect," I told her before kissing her. This changed absolutely everything.

The next day we were getting ready for the meeting at the hotel. Our presence wasn't requested, it was commanded, my father wanted us all there when he spoke to everyone. It was a surprise when someone was knocking on our door. Which was a highly unusual thing in this household. My family were more the barge your way in types who had no respect for boundaries. So obviously it couldn't be a member of my family so who could it be? The staff generally moved about the house, mostly unseen, so I doubted any of them would knock. So, who else could it possibly be?

Our apartment was inside our family home and inside the compound that was surrounded by walls and security. Just getting to our door required you to be allowed on to the property so it was an oddity. Before I could go answer the door my wife did, and it explained everything. Her family respected boundaries so of course her mother would knock. I hadn't known they were coming but after what happened it wasn't surprising. My father would have pulled our family in close bringing everyone back to the safety of the compound. Obviously, he felt obligated to extend that to Freddie's family, which actually surprised me. Almost as soon as the door opened her mother was hugging her like she hadn't seen her in months. It had been less than 2 weeks; the Millers were always a bit dramatic about such things.

"What are you doing here?" Freddie was asking her mother and sister after hugging them both. She stepped aside letting them in and I went back into the bedroom to grab a shirt. One did not greet their mother-in-law and teenage sister-in-law shirtless.

"Well a car arrived today and we were told that we've been invited for a visit," Vivian was saying.

"Invited kidnapped, same thing," Ollie said.

"It's for your protection," my mother said, appearing in the doorway when I came back from the bedroom. "Yesterday there was an attempt on Cannon's life and we thought it best that any family outside of the compound be brought in. Today we are meeting with the full delegation to call for a vote and it's best for everyone to be safe. There may be some retaliation against us depending on how heated things get so we extended this invitation."

"Is it so serious that they would try to kill your son?" Vivian asked, staring at my mother in shock.

"Yes and no, this I do believe was rather personal," Mother said looking to me and I shrugged.

I had no regrets about what I did though admittedly I didn't expect things to go the way they did. An oversight on my part because of course someone like Ferris Smith would want revenge for me taking his fangs. It would have been easier if I had just killed him. What this whole situation meant for the summit I could only guess. Hunt Harrington was not a forgiving man and the worst thing you could do was threaten the lives of his children. Even though we survived with minimal damage the fact that it happened at all was enough to have him rain down vengeance. All I could hope for was that none of this completely derailed all of my father's hard work.

"Oh gods, is that what I think it is?" Vivian said suddenly as she stared at something on the table. She looked from Freddie to me and back again her eyes wide. Naturally my mother came over to see what she was looking at and she gasped.

"Guess there's no point in denying it," I said because there was no putting that genie back in the bottle. Stepping up beside Freddie I slipped my arm around her waist, pulling her into my side. We hadn't really discussed telling anyone about this; we were both still coming to terms with it ourselves.

"We did the test last night, it was kind of on a whim," Freddie told them.

"I'm going to be an auntie?" Ollie asked, staring at us as her sister nodded.

After that there were a lot of hugs and excitement so much that it attracted attention from my sister. Who of course was just as excited as the other females. It was exciting and terrifying knowing that we were going to have a baby. Funny, I was the one who asked for this yesterday but now that it was reality I was a bit uncertain. Maybe that was just how people felt when faced with the reality of it, all of it was a bit daunting.

Hunt

My patience reached its end when they tried to kill my son. There were a lot of things I could let go of, but that was not one of them. I tried to do this in a way that was respectful of others and their issues. We went out of our way to accommodate these useless whiners, but I was done now. Either they signed this agreement, or I would have to start killing people. Petty nonsense was one thing, but the attempted murder of my son was too much. Nobody would call me overly paternal, however my children meant everything to me.

"She's pregnant," my wife announced when she came into my office. I just stared at her blankly, all my revenge plotting came to an immediate halt.

"Fredericka?" I asked and she nodded, that was interesting. "You realize that only makes this worse don't you? Sure, we would have had a piece of him left but our son would have had a child that never knew him. And if she had been with him?" Thinking of that had me gripping my desk so hard the wood cracked.

"Yes, I think it's something that he's also realized and it's going to make him particularly vengeful. Thank the gods Fredericka was here," she said.

"Her parents have arrived?" I asked and she nodded, good then I could set things in motion. We left my office then and headed down to the ballroom.

To be honest I didn't really care that much about Fredericka's family; they weren't even vampires after all. But I was pulling my Family in, and Belinda made a case for them. They could easily be used against my son, I might not care what happened, but he would because of that fondness for his wife. So, I acquiesced to her idea to bring them here. Which also served to keep Fredericka in the house and out of the way. She already stirred things up with the witches and I was suspicious of what really happened with Ethel Rosewood. That witch was older than I am, and I knew better than to trust her. Never trust long lived witches, whatever they did to extend their lives was never good.

Between the rumors passed around by the Smiths and their behavior I was ready for that particular bloodline to come to an end. The witches I would deal with later, first were the vampires. One of the five families was responsible for the attempt on Cannon's life. Gunnar had been rather motivated to get the information out of the vampire they captured. We knew who did this and we knew that more than one family was involved. First, I needed to address the multiple factions assembled before me in our ballroom. The room had been altered in order to fit everyone comfortably; I even had the staff provide them with refreshments. Then I stood and the room fell silent and all eyes turned to me. No need to make an announcement or call for attention, they were all waiting on me.

"I invited all of you here so that we could come together. No, I did not think it would be easy, but it was necessary. During the course of this summit, I've seen some truly shocking behavior. The humans think of us as less than and monsters, some of you seem to want to prove them right. In the spirit of cooperation my Family has attempted to facilitate agreements between various groups. We have sat through listening to your gripes, grievances and centuries old feuds. We have tried to get everyone to compromise in the interest of working together. We have worked tirelessly mediating and placating. All this while you enjoy my hospitality. So, imagine my shock that someone tried to kill my son," I said.

The room went deathly silent and suddenly I had everyone's full attention. Their petty nonsense was one thing, but an assassination attempt was a whole other thing. I would not let this stand; the guilty party would pay for what they did. If anyone made the mistake of thinking I had gone soft, they were in for a rude awakening. There was a reason I was able to keep our business up and running when the world had descended into chaos and war for over 100 years. It was not by being nice, they were forgetting who I really am. And it was time to remind them.

"As everyone knows I only have two children, my wife would have liked more but that was not to be our fate. Many years ago, in the year my son was born something happened. Humans invaded, there is nothing they hate more than seeing others thriving in their own communities. In their own history they prove that by perpetrating violence against other humans. They are destructive greedy creatures who can never be satisfied with what they have.

"In the years following the wars things were supposed to settle, there wasn't supposed to be anymore death. And yet humans came here capturing, killing and poisoning us. It shames me to admit but because of those humans I could no longer give my wife more children. They sought to sterilize us to keep our numbers from growing. Another old tactic they used against other humans. We survived that encounter and it's been over a hundred years since there has been such a major attack."

Being captured, tortured and sterilized by humans was my greatest shame. It shouldn't have happened and those who did it were long dead now. A "rogue faction", the government said with no ties to anything official. I didn't really believe that, but it didn't exactly matter. My wife and daughter had been safe at the time so at least there was that. Did I hate humans on principle after that? Yes of course, before then they were just a mild annoyance. Even during the wars they weren't much of a challenge for me. Especially not with my warrior wife by my side.

Having children though did change things, how could it not? There were suddenly people depending on you for everything. Belinda and I even waited many, many years for things to settle before devoting ourselves to having children. I did everything I could to build my family up so that nothing and no one could ever touch us again. Yet here we were when I was planning for a threat from humans I was betrayed by my own damn kind. That cut deep, but of course just because we were of a kind did not make us allies. All fang folk aren't kin folk, so the saying goes. My sight was set on the future, so I never saw this coming.

"I have been made aware of who has been plotting against my Family and who doesn't want this to succeed. It is very unfortunate that the guilty parties are vampires," I paused before turning my accusing gaze at the Smiths. Those parasites caused too much trouble, and their time had come. "Do you have anything to say for yourself Mr. Smith?"

"Your son humiliated and disfigured my brother," Jim replied, not bothering to deny it. I could almost respect him for that if nothing else.

"His fangs will grow back," I pointed out. "But since you brought it up let us speak about this incident. I'll not deny what my son did, he felt he had the right to seek retribution for harm done to his wife. Your brother attacked my son's wife and attempted to drink from her against her will."

The accusation earned a few gasps from around the room; everybody knew it was a crime. Feeding on humans in a bygone era was one thing, things were different now. Blood was freely and readily available no vampire ever had to starve. Attacking someone like Ferris did proved a lack of control and that was not something anyone could permit. Uncontrolled vampires did some nasty things to others.

This was the problem with turned vampires; they needed to be taught proper control. If you didn't teach them then they would run wild and start killing people. It was never necessary to drain a person of their blood to the point of death, not even when starving. We needed blood but excess only created a craving in you that couldn't be filled so you kept repeating the same act thinking it would be different. Being bloodsick like that wasn't dissimilar to drug abuse.

"My brother did no such thing, maybe this girl wanted him and not your son," Jim said like a petulant child.

"Very well then I'll give you proof," I nodded to my assistant who set things in motion.

Viewing screens came down from the ceiling so that everybody would be able to see. Then the video recording played from the night in question. It showed Fredericka coming out of the bathroom and Ferris Smith grabbing her, pulling her into a corner. She fought him pushing him away as he became increasingly aggressive. His fangs were fully extended and his intentions were quite clear and then Gunnar came into the frame. He pulled Ferris away from Fredericka and told her to go.

What happened was pretty clear and it boiled my blood to see this again. While I wasn't sure what to do with this girl, I didn't like it that she was hurt when we were supposed to be protecting her. We failed her and yet she did what she could to protect The Family. She could have killed him; she had that ability and she was likely scared enough. But she didn't or couldn't do it, there was much we didn't know about her abilities. Still, she attempted to conceal harm done to her at her own expense for us. Maybe bringing her in wasn't a mistake after all, she at least learned the value of loyalty.

"You were saying?" I asked Jim who sat there staring at the screen looking paler than usual. There was no way to spin this, and everyone had seen it.

"I didn't know," he said finally.

"That is no excuse, just as there is no excuse for your pathetic brother. Who, if you notice had red eyes, how long have you been hiding this? Letting him go around in public making others unsafe? If my nephew hadn't come, who knows what he would have done to my daughter-in-law. My son could have lost his wife and their unborn child because of you and your failure to control your people. And you have the nerve to attempt to kill my son when your brother is the problem? How long have you known he was like this? And yet you said nothing you brought him here amongst all these people putting everyone at risk," I said. With the fury I felt I might have gone over and killed him myself. All things considered, I would have gotten away with it and nobody would have said a thing against me for it.

"I wasn't aware that things had progressed to that level," Jim said pathetically. "If I had known then of course I wouldn't have brought him here but I didn't know. What happened is unfortunate, but shall we talk more of your daughter-in-law? The pretty little weapon you handed over to your son?"

"I would be interested in knowing this too," Dallas North piped up. There was no surprise there, I knew they were colluding.

"This again? You have seen my daughter-in-law have you not? What is it exactly you think she can do? And if she could do something worthy of being called a weapon, why then didn't she do something when Ferris was attacking her?" I asked though I wasn't waiting for a reply. "My daughter-in-law is no weapon, she's just an unfortunate girl who has survived being attacked by vampires twice. It's not too complicated, my son saved her life months ago and took her as his wife. Why is that so suspicious?"

"You let some half breed witch with no bloodline into your Family that in itself is suspicious," Dallas pointed out. "And as many of us have come to notice, that girl does not smell like a vampire. So what is she really?"

"I find it very insulting that you would bring this up but since you have I will address it. No she does not smell like a vampire, it's an established fact. What is she? A girl with an unfortunate disability, that is not her fault. You would seek to shame her for it? She is a hybrid born with no predatory instincts. When we discovered this after Cannon rescued her from a bad situation, we felt compelled to help her. Her adoptive parents are a witch and a mage, they did their best, but she is a vampire. There was really only so much they could do for her, maybe if she had been raised by vampires things could have been different for her. I don't know, none of us can know as this is how she is.

"Constantly bringing up this fact and spreading malicious rumors about her is disgusting. I will not stand for this bigotry; I had thought that was only a human practice. Obviously, I was wrong, as you all sit around trading gossip and speculation you are only contributing to the problem," I told them. "Mr. North, are you satisfied or would you like to embarrass this innocent girl further?"

"It appears that we have been misled," was all Dallas would say then he cut a glare towards Jim.

None of what I said was a lie, the girl had a clear disability and yes it was an unusual one. But she was not a weapon, she could be made into one, it was possible. At present though she was no threat to anyone or anything. It was likely she never would be, and I could accept that. As long as we kept her under our control, she would be safe and wouldn't be forced to become a weapon to be wielded against vampires.

"Any more grievances against my family? Or can we move on?" I asked the crowd at large, most of whom shook their heads afraid of my attention. "Mr. Smith since you cannot seem to control your Family I have been forced to step in and do so for you."

At a nod from me a box was placed in front of him at his table. He opened it and jumped back looking from it to me and back again. Others craned their necks to see and when they did, they recoiled. In the box was his brother's head. Nobody came after my family and lived to tell the tale.

Freddie

Hunt Harrington was by far the scariest man I had ever met.
The thing about my father-in-law was that he could look so
unassuming and welcoming even. He could look like a good-
natured person who smiled often. Then there were other times
where he looked terrifying, and you saw death in those eyes.
The shift came and went so you never really knew what you
were going to get with him. While he spoke to those
assembled at the summit, he started out with that more
amiable version of himself but as time went on that part just
fell away.

Did I like being the focus of so many? No, not in the least
bit but I wasn't surprised by any of it. Hunt was the first person
to declare my lack of a predatory nature as a disability. Until
I met him nobody ever mentioned it to me but I found out later

that others knew. One of my best friends was a shifter and though her family realized this about me they didn't want to be rude and mention it. Having it all laid out for the public though was hard. Cannon held my hand through the whole thing, and I kept my expression blank. The attacks and disability stuff I could handle but announcing to all those assembled that I was pregnant was a bit much.

I knew why he did it, he was painting this picture of me as a vulnerable person. While also giving Cannon's actions more validity. Of course, he took the fangs of the man who attacked his pregnant wife. Everything Hunt said was to paint a certain picture of things. Even mentioning what was done to him which I hadn't known. This information made his determination to make this summit a success make sense.

One thing I was not prepared for was for him to present Jim Smith with his brother's head. Cannon did not appear surprised by this at all. He gave almost no reaction to anything going on other than some subtle tension when his father was speaking about me. Maybe I had been truly converted to being a Harrington because I didn't feel bad at all seeing Ferris's head in that box. Maybe knowing now that I was pregnant when he assaulted me, I couldn't possibly find it in myself to care. Why should I? He also tried to have my husband killed so nope I was fresh out of sympathy.

"A formal investigation will take place of the Smith Family and all members. Since you can't be responsible for your Family in my capacity as head of the vampire council I will. If any other vampires are found to be showing symptoms of madness they will be swiftly executed," Hunt said and Jim stared at him. The other vampires nearby seemed to subtly shift away from him at that. "The investigation has actually already begun, my men are currently at your compound."

"This is just an excuse! You've always hated us and looked down on us, so you are abusing your power to finally get rid of us. There is nothing wrong with being a turned vampire," Jim said angrily.

"If a turned vampire learns proper control and how to behave in public then no there is no issue. Your brother wasn't a turned vampire; he was just allowed to sink into madness and become a danger to others. This isn't a vendetta; I don't care enough about you or yours for such a thing. You mean nothing to me, this is about public safety," Hunt said. His tone suggested that he was being perfectly reasonable.

"Madness in vampires can be contagious," Alice Wentworth offered with a shrug. She and her sister Ada were the heads of their Family, they were long standing allies of the Harringtons. They also owned the biggest vampire vineyard in the world.

"Very true," Hunt agreed. "I think we have wasted enough time on this issue. The reason I called for this meeting with everyone present as opposed to making this a vampire matter is in part transparency. No one is above the law here. But the real reason you are all here is because it is time to decide if we can all work together. This is bigger than any one family, coven, pack or clan, this affects us all. Have you all not noticed there are less and less humans in this area every year?

Not something we would typically care about if they weren't building up human only towns not too far away. Humans are greedy creatures and as I said before they cannot stand to see others doing well for themselves. All of us living and thriving in our own communities is a threat in their minds. They have been plotting for some time now. That is the reason behind this whole summit."

"How credible is the threat?" Someone from the shifters section asked.

"Very, if they knew why we are all here now I imagine they would have an army outside this hotel. There have been incidents where they tried to gain entry or watch from the outside, but my people have deterred them. They won't go away; they are aware something is going on but not what. Today we vote and if you find that you are unwilling to be part of this then good luck. Nobody deserves the depraved things those creatures do, and they have the nerve to call us monsters. We no longer have time to indulge in pettiness and selfishness, nothing any of you are bargaining for is worth the lives of all the nonhumans in the region," Hunt said. "We will come back in 3 hours so take some time to think this over."

At that he dismissed everyone and people started talking. Some speaking in hushed tones, some outright arguing. A lot of people left but not the vampires. Which Hunt seemed to expect as the section with us in it was suddenly closed off from the rest of the room by clear sliding panels coming from the ceiling. Before a word was said men came in to escort Jim Smith and anyone with him out, they also took the head.

"Is this where you bully us?" Dallas North asked, crossing his arms in clear defiance.

"Not at all, this is where I will cede the conversation to the rest of you. All of you already know my position, it has not changed," Hunt said. To prove his point, he took a seat at the table and pulled out his phone like he had not a care in the world.

"There is only one decision to be made," Marius Lang said.

"Who's to say that any of this is true and not just a power grab? A major one at that?" Dallas said because he was determined to be difficult.

"And if it is?" Eric Gordon asked him. "Two things can be true at the same time, Harrington can want more power and there could be a serious threat."

"Humans in the town closest to us have been behaving strangely recently," Kono Lang said. "Some have engaged in petty vandalism like they aren't afraid that we would retaliate."

"We give tours at the vineyard and there have been some disturbances and humans complaining about the wine. They accused us of stealing their blood to use as if we would desire such a thing from those lowly creatures," Alice Wentworth said.

"Harrington," Phillip Gordon called and Hunt looked at him. "We will agree to your alliance if your son marries my niece."

"Our son is already married," Belinda pointed out, sounding bored.

Was I worried about this desire to replace me? Maybe Cannon wouldn't want it, but his father was the one who made the rules. If Hunt wanted to make an alliance with the Gordons through marriage, then he could. There was no law against having a second wife. And Hunt had my family now he could force me to consent to it. Cannon said nothing but was doing so with a lot of tension. He didn't like it either.

I didn't know Lisha Gordon, but I knew people like her, didn't everybody? She was the type to try to push me out or outright kill me to be the only wife. And if I was honest, I would never let Cannon touch me again if he was having sex with her too. Would his loyalties change once he had a real vampire wife? I felt sick but I couldn't say or do anything even as my life was possibly going to be completely altered. What did I expect though really? Blood mattered most to pure bloods, and my blood was certainly not pure.

"His wife is barely a vampire, Lisha is a pure blood, she will secure the bloodline," Phillip said.

"As my wife said my son is already married, his wife is already securing the line, we knew her blood status when they married. Why would it suddenly matter now? Especially now? She is with child; she is a Harrington now. I could offer my nephew Gunnar, he's unmarried," Hunt said.

"We want her married to Cannon or we will not agree to any of this," Phillip said.

"Oh please spare us, nobody else will take that girl and you just want a spy in his house. Don't be so obvious and desperate," Vera North admonished.

"Cannon," Lisha said, rising from her seat, approaching us. "You can't possibly want such a weak wife, I can give you better stronger children. I get it you can't get rid of her right now but I'm willing to wait."

"Take another step towards my wife and I will kill you right here in front of these witnesses," Cannon said. He had that look on his face that made him unable to pass for human again and she froze.

I had seen this look on the faces of other vampires; it was hard to explain but it was like pulling away a mask. It was likely that vampires used to have a different look about them that identified them as predators but then they evolved to look more human like their prey. What better way to hunt humans than to look just like one of them? That was why vampires were considered so high up on the food chain, more than any other nonhuman they could seamlessly blend making them more dangerous. I think my lack of predatory instincts meant that I could not look like that so no scaring people for me. It was impressive that Cannon apparently scared other vampires from the looks of the people in the room. I didn't know the whole history of the Harringtons and how they came into power but maybe I should.

"Go sit girl," Ada Wentworth said, shaking her head. "Your uncle cannot secure you a prince no matter how hard he tries, let it go."

"Why is the witch deemed worthy? She doesn't even have a bloodline," Eric Gordon pointed out. Apparently, they weren't ready to let it go but Lisha did at least sit back down. It seemed her uncles would sell her off for their own gain and it was sad.

"What goes on in my family is not the concern for everyone else, move on I'll not change my mind. My son is married and will not be taking a second wife," Hunt said. His tone indicated that it was the last he was going to say on the matter.

"You have our vote," Alice Wentworth said and her sister nodded in agreement.

"And ours," Marius Lang added.

That just left the Gordons and the Norths, both who proved to be difficult. Technically as 3 families of the vampire council were in agreement, they could force the issue. But it seemed Hunt was determined to wait them out. Once again, he was on his phone like nothing important was going on. I just barely managed not to sigh, who knew sitting around could be so exhausting? My job was to sit and be quiet and I would do it even if it killed me.

Whispered conversations happened within both Families like there was some other magical option. More than once, I felt Dallas North's gaze on me, apparently, he was still convinced that I was a hidden weapon. I had to wonder what he thought I could do exactly? As far as I knew my ability only worked when threatened and only on one person at a time. Though I never had a chance to speak with Ethel again so who knew. She suggested that I could control people, morality aside I didn't know how to do that.

When Ferris attacked me, I could feel it, something in me that wanted to be set free. That scared me more than anything and it's probably why I never told anybody about it. What if I did it again and liked it? The first and only time it happened I was too scared to know what anything felt like. This was not the time or place to be thinking about any of this. My head started hurting all of a sudden not that it was going to get me out of sitting here like a mannequin.

"What's wrong?" Cannon asked because he was always attuned to my moods.

"Just a headache," I said, keeping my voice low. The pain though only seemed to get worse, and I couldn't resist putting my hand to my head. It would be nice if this stupid meeting was over so maybe I could get a break before being forced to sit here even longer when everyone else returned. Why did it just keep hurting more? Suddenly Cannon stood up, tension and anger rolled off him in waves.

"Lee," he said and then Lee appeared with a knife to Dallas North's throat. The room fell silent then and suddenly my head stopped hurting.

"It seems as though some people here think I make idle threats," Cannon said. "You would dare forcibly attempt to read my wife's mind? I should let him slit your throat."

"Why can't I read her mind? Huh? What are you hiding?" Dallas asked even as Lee kept the knife at his throat. Belinda put her arm around me and I wasn't sure who was angrier, her or her son.

"You idiot," Vera North said, shaking her head. "What is your obsession with this girl? Of course, her family would seek to protect her mind, she's a Harrington they know way too much about way too much. Look at her, she's practically a child, why wouldn't they protect her? This nonsense has got to stop."

"Something is off about her, I know it," Dallas argued.

"Do it," Vera said, looking at Cannon. Who nodded to Lee who then in turn slit the throat of Dallas North and let his body fall to the floor.

"What is your decision Vera?" Hunt asked not bothering to comment on anything that was happening.

"You have the vote of the North Family," Vera North said before cutting a disgusted look at her husband who was bleeding out on the floor. "I apologize to you Cannon and to your wife, you will have no more problems from us."

"Thank you," Cannon said, taking his seat again.

Lee disappeared again and some of the hotel staff came and removed the body. It was all done rather efficiently and without much fuss. Vampires were so fucking weird.

Cannon

In a weird way I think my father's willingness to kill his own kind won over the masses. If he didn't let vampires get away with anything or give them preferential treatment it meant he would be fair to others. At least that's what seemed to be the opinion of others at the summit. After everything that happened when everybody came back, they voted in favor of his council. No, it wasn't unanimous of course but it didn't have to be the majority ruled. And if your group didn't agree to having someone sit on the council then you would be out of the loop, and nobody wanted that. Especially when being out of the loop could mean life or death. All it took was just under four weeks and a little justifiable homicide to get things done.

Two days later though I was still pissed off. After we were released, I abandoned my duties to bring my wife home.

Nobody dared say anything and she let me hold her captive this whole time. We laid in the bed mostly in silence as I tried to combat my newly developed possessive needs. What I wanted to do was take her somewhere and hide her away forever, because only then could I be certain of her safety. It felt like I failed her again, no I didn't think Dallas North would do something so stupid. People with telepathic abilities weren't often so rude as to do what he did. Of course, he thought himself above the rules of polite society. Honestly, I had to wonder if he really thought he could get away with it? It didn't really matter now he was dead and at his wife's request he would not be rising again.

If I was a better man I wouldn't be holding my poor wife hostage, her family was still here. But I just couldn't bring myself to let go, too much had happened. At least the other Families no longer believed the ridiculous idea that Freddie was a weapon. It wasn't just the vampires that whispered the witches had been saying things too so who knew what other people thought about her. Everybody saw what happened to her at that party, it was my first time seeing it. Had I known what happened that night I would have slaughtered the whole damn Smith bloodline.

While my father had his reasons for showing the recording I hated that it made us look weak. Like we couldn't protect our own, sure Gunnar came to her aid and I got retribution. But none of it should have happened, she should have been safe. Dallas, essentially attacking her in a room full of witnesses might have been unexpected and swiftly handled, still I didn't like it. We didn't even talk about it; I just locked us away from the rest of the world. It just felt like if I stayed here holding her, nothing else could touch her. Unfortunately, we couldn't stay locked away forever, there was still one more event. Just a couple more days and life could go back to some form of normal.

"Are you going to be ok?" Freddie asked, breaking the silence.

"Your rings have a spell to keep others from reading your mind and controlling you," I told her.

"How many spells are on them?" She asked looking up at me from where she laid her head on my chest.

"There might be one I'm forgetting, I wanted to make sure you were always safe. Jewelry should be functional, not just decorative," I said. Draconian diamonds and Martian gold were both magic conductors, so any spells placed on them were strong. Sure, the rings looked nice and spoke of our family's wealth but that wasn't all they were for. It took calling in a few different favors to make it happen, but it was worth it.

"Sounds like something your mother would say."

"She did, told me I was thinking too small with just location. We can always add more if it becomes necessary."

"Are we going to talk about what's bothering you?"

"All this attention on you makes me nervous and I'm afraid of losing you," I admitted. "I don't want to take you to this fucking party, even with the Smiths gone and Dallas dead I've been feeling uneasy. Maybe it's because I know you are having my baby, that's bringing out some instincts in me I didn't know existed."

"Can we stay home then? I don't care about the party; I don't want you to worry. We can just say I don't feel well," she suggested.

"As much as I would love for us to do that, we can't, it's the last night and a celebration of cooperation," I said with a sigh.

"Didn't you promise to kidnap me when this was over?" She asked and I couldn't help but to laugh.

"Yes, I want to so much but our situation has changed a bit," I pointed out. "People are interested in you and you are pregnant so aside from the fact that my mother won't let me take you anywhere I don't want to put you at risk."

"We could take a bunch of guards," she suggested.

"Let's see how we are feeling after this celebration, and what will be required of me going forward. We did all this shit and now more work is on the horizon. All I want is to just be with you," I told her.

When did I become so sentimental? Before her I was never like this, never so invested in another person. My relationships in the past were fleeting and usually just about sex and it worked for me. I was never so clingy or possessive and yet I could just sit there with her for hours on end doing nothing at all. In fact, I wanted to do just that, I wanted nothing more than to just lay here with her. Now that I was thinking about it lately all I wanted was to be with her. I was always thinking about her and looking forward to seeing her. If I didn't know any better, I would almost think… but no that was impossible. There was just no way.

"I guess at least we can look forward to our appointment with the doctor in two days," she said. That appointment was with the obstetrician which was a whole other thing to worry over.

I couldn't help but to place my hand on her still flat stomach. Yes, we obviously knew this was going to happen eventually but eventually happened to be now. Even after days of knowing it was still so very surreal. Thinking about it though made me want to resurrect Dallas North and kill him myself. I could have that day I just didn't want to leave her side not when that asshole was trying to read her mind. And not when we were in a room full of people we couldn't trust. So I delegated the task to Lee who I suppose I would have to keep around at this point.

Because of old myths people believed when you killed a vampire they automatically could just rise from the dead. In actuality it didn't work like that, there were steps that had to be taken to prepare a body for rising. There were also steps to take to make sure the body could not rise. Vera North had opted for the ladder likely because her husband would be much worse should he have risen. Rising altered you, there was no coming back the same. And I'm sure it didn't hurt that now she was the sole custodian of the North Family. A grieving widow she was not but she was a smart woman who took an opportunity to seize power. As long as they didn't bother my wife I didn't care much about the Norths.

"It's still early obviously but have you thought about if you want a girl or boy?" I asked my wife, trying to focus on what was important.

"Not really, I'm still trying to wrap my head around the fact that we are going to have a baby at all. Do you want a son? Isn't that usually what men want?"

"Typically yes but in this family it's more likely that we would have a daughter. First born sons are rare in the Harringtons and nonexistent in my mother's family. My father was the only one in like 500 years. But to answer the question I don't mind either way."

"Do you want to know what we are having? Like when the time comes that they can identify that?"

"We could let it be a surprise, if you want, I'm fine either way."

"I think I want to be surprised," she said thoughtfully.

"Then we will be, it's rather on brand for us at this point. We didn't kiss until our wedding, and we won't know the sex of our baby until they are born," I said and she laughed.

For some ridiculous reason I had the idea for us not to kiss until the day we were married. Mostly it was because I was more focused on my wife getting comfortable with me than anything else. All we had was 3 weeks to get to know each other before our wedding so it made sense at the time. Take anything potentially sexual out of the equation and focus on getting to know each other. I didn't expect that having her close and touching her would make things difficult. For one thing I could never resist touching her, sometimes it was like my hands had a mind of their own. Maybe it was the anticipation or the fact that our first kiss happened after I tasted her blood for the first time, but I almost couldn't stop. Seemed like ever since then I was hooked on her, she was the only woman I ever craved.

"Everybody is going to think we are crazy but it's like one of the few things we don't get to choose, ya know? I mean I know humans do weird genetic stuff, but this is purely nature at work," she said. Then she sat up and I had to resist the urge to pull her back to me. "It's time for us to rejoin the world I think."

"I know," I said with a sigh.

As much as I wanted to keep her safe it wasn't fair to her for me to keep her away from everybody else. Besides our family was safe, nobody would hurt her here. Still, I felt uneasy, I hoped the end of the summit would cure that. Unfortunately, I wasn't certain it would.

It wasn't much of a surprise to find Ollie at our door. Actually, it was more surprising that my mother hadn't yet burst in and demanded we leave the apartment. I appreciated that everybody gave us some space, but that time was at an end. We had to go to this party tonight, it was important. Everything was so *important* these days but that was the life within a vampire Family like ours. We had to be seen out amongst the people pretending to care about their nonsense. At least one last time, everybody would start leaving tomorrow.

"Hi Ollie," I greeted when I answered the door.

"Um hi, is my sister available?" Ollie asked somewhat awkwardly, it was likely because she was used to having access to her sister and I stood in the way of that.

"Yeah, she's getting dressed, you can come in," I said, stepping aside to let her in.

"Can I ask you something?" She asked as we both went over to sit down, her in a chair and me on the couch.

"Sure," I replied, bracing myself for another attempt from her to get her sister back home. Though now I would have hoped she would realize that was very much impossible.

"Did your dad really give someone a head in a box?" She asked and I didn't expect that one as neither Ollie nor her parents had been at the hotel.

"How do you know about that?" I asked mostly out of curiosity, it was possible that someone in the house let it slip. What happened wasn't exactly a secret, nonhumans believed in policing their own.

"Well I first saw something about it on Witching Hour and then on The Line and I mean I don't have access but I imagine it's on The Vein too," she said.

Well, that should have been expected of course with the various people there it would make social media news. What went on at the summit wasn't necessarily completely confidential after all. Pulling my phone out of my pocket I saw

252

that it was indeed on The Vein as predicted. While we didn't live segregated there did exist social media for different types of nonhumans. The Vein was for vampires, Witching Hour for witches and other magic users, High Moon for shifters, Elements for elementals and mages and there were others for other types of people. The Line was for all nonhumans to socialize together and if you wanted to socialize with both humans and nonhumans then there was Real Social. Humans could not gain access to our social media to set up a profile you needed status confirmation so that nobody was anywhere they weren't supposed to be. Plus, there were spells on the sites as extra security measures. They had Humans Only as their own platform because everybody else was going to have their own of course they would too.

"To answer your question, yes he did but he was the man who attacked your sister so don't waste pity on him," I replied.

"That's so crazy," Ollie said, shaking her head.

Interestingly enough she didn't look like she felt sorry for him at all or like it was unjustified. In some ways Ollie actually reminded me of my mother, which was a bit terrifying. Once upon a time Belinda had been a warrior, she used to train guards for our Family as she did with hers. Now she seemed the prim and proper motherly type but anyone smart knew to be more afraid of Belinda than Hunt. Ollie was a fighter too; she took lessons in various forms of fighting. Maybe I should suggest to my mother that she take an interest in Ollie, she was family after all. Training a witch would be an interesting challenge for her and it might keep her occupied. Maybe she could spend a little less time reminding us how we weren't living up to her expectations. Though knowing her she would make time for both.

"Hey Ollie," Freddie greeted when she joined us. She hugged her sister then sat beside me on the couch.

"Apparently my father's theatrics made news," I said, turning my phone to face her.

"There aren't pictures are there?" She asked, looking between me and Ollie.

"No just people talking," Ollie answered. "Some people were talking about you again Freddie, speculating that you were the cause of it."

"They think she would be having an affair with Ferris Smith of all people?" I couldn't help but to laugh at that ridiculous insinuation. "I would like to think my wife has better taste than that."

"Obviously," Freddie said, rolling her eyes. I was trying to keep things light to avoid her getting upset over the whole situation again. We all learned a valuable lesson from this ordeal, Freddie learned that her Family would defend her. And I learned never to show mercy again; I should have just killed him outright. Good thing his death served its own purpose, his life was a waste but not his death.

"In a few days nobody will even remember any of this happened, people have short attention spans," I said with a shrug.

"And yet we have to see all of these people at this party," Freddie said with a sigh.

"You do at least get to wear a pretty dress," Ollie offered. From her expression she liked the idea of getting dressed up.

"Do you want to come to the party?" I asked and her eyes lit up.

"Can I?" Ollie asked, barely containing her excitement.

"Sure why not? There won't be many people there your age but it's not a problem," I told her.

"Oh but I don't have anything to wear," Ollie sighed.

"Don't worry about that, Belinda loves this type of thing she will bring you a dress," Freddie said "I'll send her a message right now."

My wife was underestimating my mother in this because no she wasn't just going to produce a dress. Belinda would never do something as simple as providing a single dress. I had to remind myself that it was good for my wife to spend time with her sister. Except why did I still feel like what I should be doing was keeping her here? Maybe I was losing my mind and maybe I wasn't. But if I wasn't then this feeling was warning me of something to come. I couldn't protect her from everything, but I would try.

Freddie

There was clearly nothing that Belinda Harrington couldn't do. An hour after Cannon told Ollie she could come to the party there was a stylist and racks of dresses for her to choose from. Because everything this family did was grand there actually was a whole room in the house for this exact purpose. It came with a dressing room, big mirrors and a sitting area for any viewers. Lucy's oldest daughter Luna was 13 and while she couldn't go, she was having fun helping Ollie to pick a dress. Of course, my mother and Belinda were also helping. Everything was so normal after all the craziness of the summit. It was nice to just relax a little and not worry about everything going on. I was sitting on the couch with Lucy; we both opted to stay out of the way of our opinionated mothers.

"I'm surprised my brother let you out of the apartment," Lucy commented.

"Honestly me too, he's been kinda weird since everything that happened," I admitted.

"Uh yeah that asshole tried to mind rape you, it's horrible. It was bold after knowing what happened to you with Ferris Smith and what Cannon did to him as a result. Heads of families think they are untouchable, being a custodian doesn't give you a pass to do whatever you want. Especially to someone else's Family, custodians are supposed to lead and protect their bloodlines not pick on someone weaker. He thought cause you are young you would be an easy target," Lucy shook her head.

"Did he deserve to die for it?" I asked because it had been bothering me it felt like I was responsible for his death since it happened because of what he did to me.

"Death was a kindness, he's lucky Cannon didn't rip his heart out," she said. "I know you aren't use to the brutal side of things but allowing him to live after what he did would make us look weak. We cannot afford to look weak especially now and no crime against one of ours goes unpunished."

"Witches handle things very differently," I said. Even though I was outcast I did grow up in a coven, so I knew how witches operated and it didn't involve a lot of bloodshed and violence. Things weren't always peaceful, but they were never like any of this.

"Sister dear you are a vampire," she said. "Actually speaking of being a witch I did wonder something. So that night when the fight happened and Cannon did what he did, why didn't you just use magic to fix yourself up?"

"Oh um I guess I could have but it didn't really occur to me. Most witches don't use magic for mundane reasons. Magic is an element like fire, air, earth and water, the way it's typically used is to create. Those of us with the ability to access magic as an element can shape it however, we need to within our own limitations. That said, it's controversial to use magic for mundane tasks like cleaning and such. You *can* do it but you shouldn't do it often or excessively. Some people feel like overuse of magic is why it was dying out before so most of us use it only for certain things. I don't know if it makes a difference in keeping magic this time around but it's just how things are done. They stress this in school and in covens so that we grow up not taking our magic for granted," I explained.

"Interesting," Lucy commented.

"Sorry I guess that's the teacher in me coming out," I said.

"No it's fine I really am interested I don't know much about how magic actually works. I know I can purchase a spell and spells can be sent through text message, but I don't know how any of it works. Though I don't think I've ever actually seen you do any magic."

"Probably not, I think I've always taken the lesson about not wasting magic too seriously. If we were to rely on magic too heavily then if it leaves us again, we would be worse off."

I am a witch, or at least half of one so I have the ability to use magic. Even though I don't use it much I am still a practicing witch. What I don't tell Lucy but probably should tell my therapist is part of the reason I use it sparingly. Even though I was only half a witch I was more powerful than a lot of other witches. Power for witches came in different forms but it would be very easy for me to use magic for any and everything. My limitations were far less than it should be just as my M-levels were higher than they should be. Having higher levels of magic in your blood didn't necessarily always translate to magical ability. So, who knew if that was why, vampires had higher levels in general, but I was an anomaly.

Being a powerful half breed led to the wrong type of attention. Another mark against me from the coven and possibly the real reason they didn't want me. While Susan was a higher up in that coven, she wasn't the head of it, that would be Sarah who of course didn't like me. Most of it had to do with her son who had previously shown an interest in me that I did not reciprocate. Considering the pettiness of the coven I was glad to have nothing to do with them. At least once this was over, I didn't have to see any of them again.

"If I had magic I would probably use it for everything rules be damned," Lucy said. "You couldn't just like lend me some for a little while?"

"Some people can transfer magic into other people or objects but it's temporary and beyond my skill set. I never learned craft magic or spell work; those are the types you can buy. They are popular fields to go into, but it never really appealed to me. To me it kind of feels like giving away part of yourself with each thing you sell and I just can't," I said, shaking my head.

"If you don't do any of that stuff what special tricks do you have? And don't deny it, you were obviously always the best witch."

"One should not ask a witch to perform tricks like a pet," I admonished. "Really though some people get very offended by that kind of thing."

"See this is why I need you to teach me about witches."

"There is this one thing I can do," I said knowing I probably shouldn't. It was another reason the coven wanted nothing to do with me, I had an unusual ability. Looking at the glass of water on the table I twist my wrist to the right before bringing my hand palm up. The water in the glass rose to hover in a ball over my hand.

"You're an elemental?" Lucy asked, staring at me in awe.

"No, I'm not, it's just something I can do," I said, sending the water back into the glass. "I use the element of magic to access the other elements in small ways, it's not a typical ability."

"That's so cool I would seriously misuse the hell out of magic."

This tiny thing that I could do was so rare that there was no name for it. My parents supported me learning more when they found out I could do this, but the coven didn't like it. To them it was unnatural for a witch to be able to use elemental power. Sometimes I wondered how we didn't already know that they would cast me out. There were signs if I really thought about it, they never fully accepted me. But I was a hybrid, I didn't exactly expect to feel completely at home anywhere. Lucy didn't look at me like I was crazy because she didn't know what witches were really like. It was nice to have someone appreciate what I could do and try to understand.

"If you did overuse it would just drain you, magic works off of your own energy."

"How does defensive magic work?" Lucy asked and it was a good question.

"Typically it can just happen when a witch is threatened or scared," I said. "Theoretically that's what happened the first time I was attacked and the second time I was just more afraid for it to happen again than anything. And the thing with Dallas I didn't even know what was happening."

"Seems like we have overlooked something very important when you came into our family," she said. "Mother, we should have taught Freddie self-defense."

"Oh," Belinda said, stopping what she was doing and coming over. "You are right, I had thought about it but with everything else going on I figured it could wait. But yes, Lucinda, we have failed in that area but we will rectify it. A little exercise during your pregnancy won't hurt."

"You want to teach me that *now*?" I asked, staring at her, I knew Belinda was more of a warrior queen than sweet grandma, but I was not like her.

"Freddie isn't into that type of thing, we tried out all sorts of activities with her growing up," my mom said. "I suppose it's just her nature, fighting or anything involving conflict never appealed."

"Hmm," Belinda said thoughtfully then turned her attention to my sister who had just come out in a different dress. "Cannon tells me that you like fighting Oleander."

"Uh yeah I've been taking classes most of my life," Ollie answered.

"Make some time for me tomorrow, we shall spar," she decided, stunning us all into silence.

"Mother, Ollie is 17 and a witch not a vampire she cannot spar with you," Lucy said. "No offense Ollie but this sweet grandma persona is not the real Belinda Harrington."

"I've actually heard that before," Ollie admitted. "Gunnar likes to talk and he told me all sorts of stuff." For our wedding Ollie had been maid of honor and Gunnar best man so they had spent some time together. It wouldn't have surprised me if he had been the one to tell her about the head.

"Lucinda, you are out of practice, you need to get back into the gym," Belinda said to her daughter. "Oleander, would you like me to train you? Yes, you are young and a witch, but those things are just details."

"Yes Auntie, I would love that," Ollie said, surprising me. It shouldn't have, of course she would like to learn a thing or two from Belinda. Since we were all family Belinda insisted on more familial terms being used so I called her mother, and Ollie was required to call her auntie. At this point it sort of felt normal, in the beginning though it was a bit weird.

"Good," she said then turned back to me. "You will also learn, nothing too strenuous of course but you need to know how to protect yourself. I know Cannon has your guard shadowing you, literally, but a woman needs to know how to defend herself."

"Is there anything I can say to get out of it?" I asked even though her expression told me the answer.

"Of course not, dear, you are right not to rely on magic but you should be able to do basic self-defense. This nature of yours is just a detail, yes it might very well be a disability but that doesn't mean it needs to prevent you from doing things. In fact, I think it just highlights the fact that you need to do this."

"Mom," I pouted at my mom who shook her head.

"Sorry sweetie, I agree with Belinda," she said.

Both Lucy and Ollie laughed at my misery like sisters would. It wasn't a bad idea, I just didn't want to do it, and I knew I should be afraid of Belinda. Other people gave subtle fear responses around her I noticed throughout the summit, half the people in attendance were afraid of her. Hunt was more obviously scary despite his ability to seem the opposite but nice, sweet Belinda was a whole other scary. I never felt threatened by her though, she really was good at selling her current persona. She was just so motherly for lack of a better term, of course I would feel that way though she was my mother-in-law.

The door to the room opened and Bella came running in with Milo chasing her. Of course, I couldn't help but wonder what my child was going to be like. Four-year-old Bella looked between me and her mother before choosing the run to me, her dark curly pigtails bouncing as she landed beside me. Then she climbed into my lap and wrapped her little arms around me. I could almost hear her brother rolling his eyes. Eight-year-old Milo stopped beside their mother and was glaring at his sister. It wasn't much of a surprise when their nanny came in moments later.

"She's a menace," Milo declared, pointing to his sister.

"Am not," Bella said with her face still against me.

"Literal demons," Lucy said under her breath before turning to her son. "What did she do this time?"

"She's always touching my stuff," Milo complained.

"Bella," Belinda said, causing the girl to burrow into me more. "Is this proper behavior for a young lady?"

"I want Auntie Freddie, I miss her," Bella said, being her adorable self.

"I missed you too Bella," I said, kissing the top of her head. Sensing she had an ally in me she tilted her head up to look at me with those big brown eyes of hers.

"She's using her cuteness on Auntie Freddie," Milo accused, sounding rather disgusted.

"I'm sorry they interrupted, they got away from me," their nanny said.

"It's fine I have them," Lucy said dismissing the nanny who hurried out the door. "That one is newer, thinks we torture those that displease us."

"Is that something your family has done?" Mom asked, looking between Lucy and Belinda.

"Of course not, it's just a silly rumor," Belinda said dismissively. "We would never harm our employees, that's just absurd, that's not a good way to do business."

"Can you two behave? I don't feel like hiring a new nanny," Lucy said to her children. "If I have to then the two of you will have no desserts and your playroom privileges will be revoked."

"Wasn't my fault," Milo grumbled, throwing a glare at Bella.

"Sorry," Bella said working her cuteness with a sad expression. She was frighteningly good at using her cuteness to get her out of trouble, too bad it didn't work on her mother or grandmother.

"Maybe they need to be in the gym too, burn off some of that excess energy," Belinda suggested.

"Aren't you going to be busy with Freddie and Ollie?" Lucy asked her mother who just gave a dainty shrug.

"Dearest I can multi-task, besides you are their mother you could assist, this will be a fun family activity," she said with a smile.

"Translation be prepared for torture," Lucy grumbled.

"Yaya, does that mean me too?" Luna asked, coming out from the changing area in a pretty yellow dress. It was a bit too long for her but looked nice against her umber skin.

"Of course," Belinda said.

"Are you sure I can't come to the party Mama?" Luna asked, pouting at her mother.

"You are too young," Lucy said. "Sorry, my love, but this is not an event for someone your age."

"Maybe we could find a reason to dress up tomorrow after the gym?" Ollie suggested to Luna whose eyes lit up with hope. Of course she wanted to hang out with the older teenager.

"We can have a brunch set up for the two of you," Belinda offered. "Let's get this dress fitted so it will be ready for you."

"Thank you Yaya," Luna said excitedly.

"I think I'll wear this one," Ollie said looking in the mirror at her purple tea length tulle dress.

More into fighting than dressing up, it was rare to see my sister in dresses. We were opposites in that way; I was always wearing dresses. Despite the fact that we weren't technically related we didn't look different enough for anyone to assume that we weren't. Ollie had more amber skin making her lighter than our parents and dark chestnut curls, that I might have envied. It was suspected that she was mixed race, which was typical these days and not really important. Witches still used racial identifiers and sadly race did matter to a lot of them. It might have had something to do with a study that was done on different races and magical ability. The results suggested that being more melanated gave you a higher chance of having magic in your blood. Naturally that was a very controversial thing that angered people, but it wasn't exactly untrue.

While the girls got their dresses worked on by the tailor who had come with the stylist I just sat cuddled up with Bella. Lucy and my mom were talking about something, Milo pulled out a small gaming device and laid his head on his mother's lap. It wasn't often that I got to spend time with both of my families, so this was nice. This was the life my child would grow up in surrounded by love and a little chaos. With everything else that happened so far this year this tiny little thing gave me some hope for the future. The therapist did say to let my family show me how they feel about me. Well, it was all love and dresses now but who knew what it would be like when Belinda got us all in her gym.

No this wasn't the life I expected to have but it was mine and I was happy things ended up this way. Still, why did I feel a sense of dread? Everything was fine now, obviously I was just nervous about the future. That's it, that's what it had to be. One more night and then life could finally be normal.

Chapter 26:

Cannon

Somehow, I was still able to breathe once my wife left with her sister. They were looking at dresses and in the safety of our home with Lee keeping watch, so there was nothing to worry about. Less so since they were with my mother, I couldn't think of a more deadly person than Belinda Harrington. Since I had some time on my hands, I let curiosity get the best of me. I was looking at what was being said about us on The Vein. Most of what was going on at the summit was strictly up to speculation. People knew there was some kind of big meeting going on and it was easy to guess why. Though some people on The Line suggested we were building an army. If my father could get away with it, he certainly would. As is we employed something like 200 guards locally. Though they weren't often all at the same place at the same time. There was a security team at the hotel that accounted for some and then personal guards for members of The Family and about 100 of them were generally at the compound. When the door to my apartment opened, I didn't expect Gunnar, Desmond and Ty to come in.

"How could you be sure I wasn't in here with my wife?" I asked as they made themselves at home lounging all over my living room.

"Because your child bride and her child sister are playing dress up," Gunnar answered.

"Even if we hadn't seen them, Lee isn't lurking in the shadows by your door so she's not here," Ty pointed out.

Before I was married, we used to hang out here all the time but they stopped coming over as much. Technically speaking Des and Ty were employed by us but only as a way to force guards on me. My parents figured I couldn't turn down my friends having the job. Both of them had quarters within the compound, though not all of the guards lived on site. Of course, I never minded since they were my friends, but I guess marriage did change things. All three of them were still single and if Gunnar had his way he would remain that way forever. Something my mother would never allow to happen, can't go wasting precious Harrington blood.

"Even I think that guy is too serious about his job," Des said, shaking his head. Of us he was the most serious, I was definitely second and with Gunnar being very unserious that made Ty third by default. The fact that his father was captain of our guards had a lot to do with Desmond's serious nature.

"Guess you aren't firing him after all?" Gunnar asked with a smirk that I wanted to punch off his face.

"Unfortunately no, my wife wouldn't like it and he is useful," I said begrudgingly. It wasn't that I didn't like Lee, I just didn't like that he spent so much time with my wife. Which was ridiculous, though why my mother didn't assign her at least one female guard I couldn't guess.

"Realizing Auntie Bel gave your wife the pretty boy guard just to fuck with you?" Gunnar asked, looking far too amused with himself. Sadly, I could believe she would do exactly that to keep my attention on my wife. My parents never stopped with their games and meddling.

"Why are all of you here? Just to piss me off?" I asked though I did note them giving each other glances. Whatever they came for I knew I wasn't going to like it.

"Cann, this is an intervention," Ty informed me. Naturally I laughed because they could not be serious.

"What could I possibly need an intervention for?"

"Your wife," Des said and I stared at him.

"Are you going to tell me she's dangerous and secretly planning to kill us, *again*?"

"Uh no, I mean I don't believe that anymore and if I did I wouldn't say it when you already had someone killed this week," Des replied.

"This isn't really about her, it's more about you," Ty said cryptically.

"Cannon, it's time for you to realize that you are in love with your wife," Gunnar said.

Of all the nonsense things that went on between the four of us over the years I didn't expect this. When I got engaged Gunnar repeatedly told me I couldn't possibly marry a *child bride*. Freddie was obviously not a child, but she wasn't 30 so she was way too young for me. He took great pleasure in referring to her as my child bride as often as he could even now because he was irritating. Des advised against marrying her because she couldn't be trusted. Even brought it up right before our trip down the aisle. Ty was the only one not to question our relationship, he liked Freddie and spent time with her. After her incident she finished out the semester at her school, so I assigned Ty to drive her because I trusted him.

Why they decided to drop by today to bother me I couldn't guess. Freddie was my wife; I cared for her and would take care of her. Was that not what marriages were about? There was no reason for this extra shit. What I needed to focus on was the future, not think about whatever nonsense they cooked up. A lifetime of friendship and people thought they knew you better than you knew yourself.

"When you married your child bride I had my doubts about the whole thing, as you know. Thought you were crazy to agree to it, seemed like you were just dazzled by a pretty face. Which isn't like you at all," Gunnar commented. "There's something about her we have all noticed that makes you want to protect her. Honestly, I didn't think you would fall in love with her. Take care of her, treat her right and fuck her, that made sense but it's more than that."

"We all have eyes, we see the way you are with her," Ty added and they all nodded. Obviously, they had been discussing this behind my back like they had nothing better to do with their lives.

"Both of you love each other and yet neither of you will admit it," Gunnar went on shaking his head.

"What would make you think that?" I asked curious at the possibility that she... but no we both went into this with our eyes open. Love was not part of this arrangement, and it was nothing I ever had to deal with in my long life.

"Seriously? You keep her glued to your side constantly or you watch her like somebody wants to steal her from you. Oh, and all you do is fuck her, you don't even acknowledge that other women exist," Des pointed out.

"Is it wrong to be attracted to my wife?"

"That's another thing you do, it's "my wife" this and "my wife" that," Gunnar said. "The possessiveness has been there from day one. When have you ever been possessive?"

"Didn't we all fuck your last girlfriend?" Ty asked and the others nodded, I had almost forgotten that one.

That all happened years ago now and I never felt any type of way about it. We shared from time to time, wasn't that what friends were for? And yes, I was never possessive before Freddie, even I could admit that. The thought of any of them touching her filled me with a homicidal rage. These were the people I was closest to and trusted most and yet I would kill them without a second thought. Over a woman of all things, how did that happen? Gunnar was basically my brother and if

I ever found him touching her, I would rip out his heart. I didn't want to think further on why I would have such a reaction. Yes, she was mine but it's not like she hadn't had sex before we met. Was it possible that I knew the name and face of every man that ever touched her? Maybe, did I tell myself it was for safety reasons? Unfortunately, none of them were competition or anything they were rather insignificant to be honest. Nope, I wasn't examining why I needed that information or anything else.

"Is it wrong to want to keep my wife to myself?" I asked them, noting their annoyingly amused expressions.

"We all know just plotted out our murders in your head," Ty said and the others laughed.

"Can we not talk about I don't know literally anything else? My relationship is my business," I said. Did I think that would shut them up? Nope, but I had to at least try.

"Can you admit you are in love with your wife?" Gunnar countered because he was annoying like that. "We all know you haven't even looked at another woman since you met her. In your last days of freedom, we could have had fun, but your ass was too busy following behind her. Or sending Ty to watch her because you don't trust anybody else to do it. She had four guards and one of them is a shadow walker, she was perfectly safe."

"He's right," Des agreed, shaking his head. "The little witch bewitched the hell out of you."

"She did not bewitch me, she didn't want to marry me, I convinced her that it was her best option," I admitted. "My parents made it clear it's what they wanted so I chose to go along with it. Better than ending up with someone like Lisha Gordon."

"Auntie Bel would never blood shackle her precious son to her, of course I make a good sacrifice," Gunnar shook his head.

"Even if she married you she would still be trying to get in Cannon's bed," Des pointed out.

"And I wouldn't object, he can have her, she's so desperate for him."

"My wife would not like that," I said and yes I knew I did say that a lot.

"But how would your wife feel if I climbed into your bed?" Ty asked because he was the only one annoying enough to think of doing such a thing.

"She might like it but you know he has his weird ass sexual proclivities," Gunnar said. "Heterosexuality is a crime against nature."

"Who sucks dick better? Me or your wife?" Ty asked with a laugh, I regretted not removing their access to my apartment.

"Do not ever mention that to her," I said it was the last thing I wanted to explain.

My friends thought I was weird because I preferred women when sexual fluidity was the norm with vampires. I wouldn't say that I was completely heterosexual but close enough. Labels and boxes for sexuality were seen as human nonsense. It wasn't something Freddie and I ever really discussed because it didn't matter. As far as I knew she was leaning more towards heterosexuality too. We were in a good place now I didn't want her thinking that I was fucking Ty.

"Do you really think she would care?" Ty asked with an expression that might hint at it mattered.

"Freddie likes you, no reason to make things weird. Pretty sure most people don't fuck their friends. She just doesn't need to know everything I've done," I replied.

"Considering the fact that her sister is openly disgusted by males I doubt she cares much," Gunnar said.

"How much time did you spend talking to Ollie?" I asked, of course they were in our wedding together, but Ollie didn't exactly visit that often.

"Is it weird if we chat sometimes? She's an interesting kid," he shrugged.

"Your old ass is friends with a 17 year old?" Des asked, staring at him in disbelief.

"Well technically she's family, it's nothing inappropriate."

"Do you even know what's considered inappropriate or not?" I asked him though it didn't surprise me as much as it should. My cousin could make friends with anyone and Ollie's level of maturity was likely way higher than his. Was he the one who mentioned the head to her?

"She might be a good influence," Des commented. "Anyway we've gotten so far off the subject."

"Why does this even matter to any of you? Gun is refusing to get married and the two of you don't acknowledge you are basically in a relationship," I said. The fact that Ty was leaning on Des who had an arm around him proved that point.

"Can't we just be close? Why does everything have to be a relationship?" Ty asked, rolling his eyes, it wasn't the first time he said that.

"Because life is too short and unpredictable you don't want to live with regrets," Des said seriously. "You are the only one of us to get married, maybe we are all too invested in your relationship but time for you to face the truth."

"When you went missing you didn't see her," Gunnar said. "She held herself together because it was expected but it was obvious that she was worried for you. There was a look of regret that suggests she knows exactly how she feels but might not have gotten the chance to tell you. There's no accounting for taste, but that girl loves you and that likely terrifies her. I mean look at how she ended up here and the fact that she's surrounded by vampires for the first time in her life. Married to a man she knew for 3 weeks, met you after something traumatizing happened. Let's not forget how this summit has gone for her, poor thing probably can't tell you how she feels."

"We talk all the time, she knows she can tell me anything," I pointed out.

"Has she ever said she was in love with any other guy she dated before?" Des asked and I glared at him, like I wanted to think of her with other men.

Truth was that no she never said anything like that, I knew she had relationships but not much else. It was hard for her to maintain long term relationships because of vampire prejudice. I saw first-hand from people she grew up with that they thought her tainted because of what she was. They were also jealous of her; she was a better witch than most. Being a hybrid though meant that sure she could live as a witch, but her vampire half would always be there too. So yeah, she might check all the right boxes for the ideal witch wife. But she wasn't just a witch and couldn't turn that part off. Some people were very much against mixed nonhumans; they wanted purity of bloodline and type. If you reproduced with a hybrid, you couldn't know what type of child you might have and that was worrying for some.

With vampires it was different, yes, we were bloodline obsessed but blood exchanges changed things. There was no doubt that my wife would be giving birth to a vampire, but it was possible for our child to be a hybrid. In most cases you couldn't make any guarantees with hybrids, but my bloodline was strong. Since we already accepted one hybrid it didn't really matter if our child was also a hybrid. Pretty much if you came with the correct internal configuration a vampires considered you a vampire. Funny thing was that I had heard tales of vampires having nearly human children that did not have our digestive system. I wasn't sure how often that happened, but it did.

Back to the subject at hand, was it really possible that I was in love with my wife? It seemed too ridiculous but at the same time not. Thinking back to that day when Ollie asked if I loved her sister I was honest when I told her no. Love was some fanciful notion, it was something people wanted even though it could destroy them. A relationship built on mutual care and respect made more sense. We were building a life together and now we would have a child, who we could love freely without hesitation. But did we love each other?

Sure, I thought about her way too much but that was because it was my job to protect her, I would do anything for Freddie. Hadn't I already proved that much? I would literally kill for her, and I would kill to be with her. That day of the crash I had been mostly thinking of getting back home to her. She was everything to me, my first thought upon waking up my last thought as I went to sleep. We just spent two days mostly just laying in bed together we didn't even have sex. Oh... what the fuck was I supposed to do about this? Because though I would love to deny it they were right I was in love with her. As ridiculous and inconvenient as that was, I was in love with my wife.

"Fuck," I said aloud and they laughed. Obviously, they could guess the conclusion I had come to myself.

Why did people get married anyway? Safety, security, a desire to start a family, it was about companionship and stability. I didn't exactly choose my wife my parents came up with that scheme. But I had vowed from the start to protect her and take care of her and that was what I tried to do. When did I start to fall for her? Our sexual chemistry had always been great but when had things started to change? I didn't ask for this didn't mean to do it but how could I deny it? All I wanted was to have her safe in my arms constantly. I wanted to protect her from the world that seemed hellbent on destroying her.

"There's nothing wrong with loving your wife," Gunnar said.

"Love makes people foolish, they make mistakes and lose sight of things, that's not what I need," I replied.

"What about what she needs? Have you stopped to think of that? Maybe she needs to hear you say this and know how much you care," Ty pointed out.

Before I could respond, not that I knew what to say, the door opened. Of course it was her, my beautiful wife. She was surprised to find the four of us here but smiled anyway. Before coming all the way in she looked back at Lee, who did not cross the threshold. At least somebody in the house respected boundaries. He shook his head at her clearly saying that he would wait for her in the hall. Shaking her head she stepped further inside but didn't close the door.

"Hi," she said with a little wave. While the others greeted her, I was up and across the room.

"Is everything ok?" I asked did my hands go to her sides of their own accord? It seemed like it as my thumb stroked her stomach as she looked up at me.

"I'm fine, I just came to get my dress, I'm getting ready with the girls," she said. She reached out touching my face before slipping away down the hall to our bedroom.

"Pussy whipped," Gunnar said, shaking his head. They were all looking at me because yeah, I was proving their point. Ignoring them I followed her to the bedroom where she was in the walk-in closet.

"Did Ollie find a dress?" I asked, leaning in the doorway while she grabbed a garment bag.

"Yes and your mother decided that I need some time in the gym," she said, making a face.

"I'm surprised she waited this long, she's not going to make you do anything crazy," I replied. There was no way I could talk my mother out of it once she decided something.

"You know your friends can come over, they don't have to stay away because of me," she said, stopping in front of me.

"Don't tell them that, they'll never leave," I said and she shook her head.

"So are Ty and Desmond together?" She asked, keeping her voice low in an effort to not be heard by vampire ears.

"Sometimes," I answered, watching her seemingly confused expression.

"Ty is so fun and Desmond is so serious, I wouldn't have guessed but opposites attract right?"

"Des isn't always serious just most of the time."

"If you say so, I'm going to get ready, which you should probably do at some point."

"Yeah I will," I said, taking the bag from her and hanging it on the door before pulling her against me. I kissed her and of course she opened for me as always, my perfect little wife.

Now didn't seem like the right time to say anything but maybe later. The guys were unfortunately not wrong, and I couldn't deny it anymore. I was in love with my wife. Never expected it to happen and didn't want it to but it was just a fact. Did she feel the same way about me? What if she didn't?

What would things be like between us if I told her? Enough had already changed and more change was on the horizon.

"Cannon," she whispered, pulling back. "We have to get ready but after this party I think I'll kidnap you."

"Please do," I replied, resisting the urge to just take her to bed. While the guys wouldn't care she would, and ok maybe I would. Nobody else needed to hear the sound she made when I made her come.

Being responsible I walked with her back to the door and handed Lee her garment bag. She said goodbye and left me to my aggravating friends. Of course, they laughed because I proved their point. Gunnar helpfully handed me a glass of whiskey and I drank it. What the hell was I supposed to do now? Especially when I still couldn't shake the feeling that something was going to happen. One last party and this would all be over and I could figure out if it was worth it to tell her. Did it really matter if I loved her or not? Or was I just afraid to find out how she felt about me?

Hunt

History is a lie especially when written by humans. Of
course, they lie about everything and conveniently forget
other things. For the long lived though we lived through
history and knew certain truths that the humans did their best
to bury. I was born in 1895 and when the world changed, I
was 130 years old, I had seen a lot in my time. All of which I
took into account when I planned this summit. Only two
deaths and a dismantled Family was better than I had hoped
for. Those who didn't know their history were fools. The
universe worked in cycles and patterns, similar things always
happened again that was the way of things. Knowing this was
why we worked so hard to get things together, so maybe this
time things could end up differently.

Of course, I knew our united council would still have to deal with petty nonsense because some people refused to see the bigger picture. They thought I was an alarmist and paranoid, I wish I was. As far as I was concerned the only good human was a dead one and their total extermination would benefit the planet. My wife would say that was too extreme, but it was a sentiment that others shared. Once the council had its first meeting, I would show them exactly what was really going on. For tonight they could have their party but in the coming days the real work would begin. None of us could afford to be complacent, not when we had things to lose.

When the door to my office burst open hard enough to bang against the wall, I wasn't that surprised. Ethel Rosewood came strolling in like her display of power meant something to me. This saved me the trouble of tracking down the old witch. I didn't forget what she did and I knew she likely sowed seeds of discontent in that girl. My harassed-looking assistant rushed in after her and one of her grandsons stood by the door shaking his head. At least he had the sense to be ashamed of her theatrics.

"Harrington, we need to talk," Ethel announced before sitting herself in a chair across my desk uninvited.

"Sorry, she was very insistent," my assistant said, giving the witch a weary look. Of course, she didn't know what to do with a pushy elder witch.

"It's fine," I said, dismissing her with a wave. Looking far too grateful she headed for the door.

"What are you doing with that girl?" Ethel demanded once we were alone, her grandson waiting outside.

"Nothing, she's my son's wife," I replied. If I knew that so much time would be devoted to this girl I might not have allowed her to attend the summit.

"Why is that? Why did you marry your son to this girl? Don't bother spinning your tale about him rescuing her and falling for her. There's no reason he would have been in that area. She killed that vampire that much is obvious," she said.

"Does it matter who in fact did the killing? The girl belongs to us now; she's even giving my son his first child. She is being taken care of like any other Harrington," I assured her.

That girl had been a cause for concern since I discovered her existence. My life would likely be much easier if we never found her or if we didn't keep her. When I sent her to meet with the witches, I hadn't imagined that she would get Ethel's attention, of all people. I wanted to see how she behaved with the coven that denied her. If only that pitiful mid-tier coven knew what they threw away so callously. Upon reflection though I shouldn't have been surprised Ethel would involve herself; she was the type to do such a thing. The question was why and what she wanted from this girl. Never again would I be led astray by big violet eyes and the instinct to protect one so young and vulnerable.

"What matters is how you will use her for your benefit and don't deny it. I know what she is, more so than you do," Ethel said.

"Where are you from Ethel? I know you are older than I am and I can't even begin to guess why you are still alive." Shifting the subject a little was needed for our little battle of wills.

"You know very well where my people come from," she replied, giving me a suspicious look.

"Yes but I meant you specifically, not just people who look like you."

"And what of the people who look like you?" She challenged with an eyebrow raised. "We all know Harrington isn't your real name, what is the name of your tribe? No one knows, none of your family speak it, there's no written history of your existence. Could it be that your people did something so abhorrent that the other tribes erased you from history?"

"It was a different time," I said with a shrug. "I wasn't alive then but I don't fault my ancestors for their decisions as we don't fault others for wanting nothing to do with us because of it. Too much morality and humanity gets in the way of things, we are still here and others are not. We were willing to do what needed to be done to hold on to what is ours. Was it very controversial? Yes, most would never dream of it but I assure you we weren't the only ones to take such a route."

"Of that I am aware and really who am I to judge what your family did? My ancestors were taken from their homes, transported places where they could no longer connect to the land. Their magic was stolen, and the land was overrun by greedy foreigners who stripped all the natural resources. I know that humans are horrible creatures, I never disagreed with that or the threat they pose. Though if you must know I was one of those born with roots grounded in this land and that is all you get from me," she told me.

My family's choices did set them apart from others, that's true enough but desperate times and all that. Not everybody was willing to go to extremes to protect themselves, that was the problem. Not exterminating troublesome humans was why they were able to run rampant and do all that they did. Ethel truly had no room to judge whatever she did to extend her life well beyond what it should, be required sacrifice. At the end of the day everything always came down to blood and sacrifice. What were you willing to sacrifice to get what you wanted or what you needed?

"Fine, but you know the lengths my family will go to in order to protect what's ours. The girl belongs to us, I assure you we aren't trying to harm her. She's my son's wife and nothing more, but feel free to tell me why you are so interested in her," I said, bringing us back to the point.

"Because I know what she is and I know you are ruthless," she replied.

"Truly I'm not doing anything with her she's Cannon's wife, that's all," I said, holding her gaze. If she had information, then of course I wanted it but I knew it would cost me. "Why are you so interested in the girl? Her own coven shunned her, made complaints against her and tried to ruin her life. So why are you a witch of another coven interested in my daughter-in-law?"

"The Lohan Coven is full of powerless fools, they felt threatened by her. Imagine a half vampire witch being more powerful than a full witch, their pathetic egos got in the way. A real coven would have cherished her but obviously her mother didn't approach another after what happened with this one. Which in a round about way leads the girl to you and embracing her vampire side. If she had been loved by witches she never would have become a true vampire," Ethel said.

"You aren't wrong there, poor thing needed to be amongst her own kind to flourish and she has. So again, I ask why are you interested in her? I know you must have said something to her when you locked her in that bathroom with you. I don't have all day for you to dance around the subject. There is a reason you came to me, what is it?" I asked, knowing I probably wouldn't like it. Seriously, this girl was nothing but trouble.

"Because I know what she is and it's not a necromancer," Ethel said glaring at me.

"She was thoroughly tested and they said—"

"Come now boy you know better than that," she said, shaking her head. "You of all people know that those tests are flawed and limited to what is known and what access there is. There are many who aren't offering up their blood for these tests. But it's likely the closest thing such a test could match her with."

"What is she then? Obviously, you want to tell me," I pointed out.

"Death witch," she said, like it should mean something to me.

"Precisely what is a death witch?

"A necromancer's magic is in death, they can raise the dead but they cannot truly give the dead life. But a death witch? They can take life, and they can give life, they can use souls as an element. All living beings have souls, despite what humans would have you believe. I imagine that since she is also a vampire these abilities of hers work especially well on a vampire. Seems like that would be something rather useful to a man like you," Ethel said. The way she looked at me was like she was trying to read my soul, she would find no useful information there.

Humans had this idea that nonhumans were soulless monsters, that was why we didn't deserve to live. Like with most things of course they were wrong. The function of a soul wasn't tied to some biblical nonsense or morality, it was energy. Energy that essentially powered our bodies, you couldn't live without a soul. When people allegedly sold their souls to demons what they were really giving up was the energy that made their life possible. But people stupid enough to sell their souls didn't know that. A witch whose specialty was souls? Well, that was interesting, though unfortunately useless.

"This is interesting information," I said and she glared as I wasn't giving her the reaction she wanted. "Like I said she is a Harrington now, she will be treated as such. Even if I wanted to, I couldn't make that doe eyed child into a weapon of any kind. Those witches made her too soft, so feel free to mind your business."

"Will you kill her now that you know what she is?" Ethel asked and that seemed to bother her.

"She is pregnant with my son's child, why would I kill her? What good would that do me or my family? Ultimately it doesn't matter what she is other than trouble, she belongs to us."

Sure, someone like Ethel was describing would make a great weapon. Especially against the other vampire Families, who argued over so many meaningless things. While I wasn't against employing mind control, it just seemed the coward's way. It was also a good way to end up with a knife in the back once the people you were controlling realized what you did. With this news the girl went up in value but also in potential for trouble. We already had to hide what she did and keep her guarded, now we would need to get her a whole team of guards. More trouble than she was worth this girl, but it was too late to alter the course of things now. The real problem though was someone else knew or suspected what she was.

With the rumors spreading around the summit, I couldn't be sure what might happen. Yes, I strategically made sure everyone saw her as the damsel she is. But was it enough? Even after Dallas North lost his life for attacking her I couldn't be certain. Since we had no idea where she came from, we couldn't really know who knew what about her. For all I knew someone from her past could be here and we would never know.

"I suspected she could control us as well as kill us, she sucked the life right out of that vampire. He deserved it and likely deserved much worse. Because I was aware that none of this was her fault and she's practically a child I offered her protection and a place in my family as my son's wife. She agreed to it, we didn't force her and Cannon would never harm his wife. The two of them are an unlikely match but Belinda thought it could work and clearly it has," I admitted.

"I can assume you had her investigated?" Ethel asked and I nodded, of course I did. "Locating her bloodline is important, I feel it in my bones. We need to know where she came from and who made her."

"Made?" I asked, having not thought of that possibility at all.

"Yes, I think so she did not occur by accident, a death witch is far too rare for that. I think someone intentionally made her and I don't think she was the only one. This is why I've come to you especially after that display at the meeting. I've also heard whispers about her, mostly from those useless Lohan witches but still. You need to be careful now," Ethel warned.

"Could she be a product of human design?" I asked though I really didn't want to go down that road.

"It wouldn't surprise me if she was," she admitted.

"So I have potentially brought a spy into my house? Or what do they call it… a sleeper agent? And I can't kill her because she's with child, perfect plan really," I said with a heavy sigh. From everything we learned about this girl it shouldn't be possible, but anything was possible when meddling useless humans were involved. And this is why trusting an innocent face was dangerous. What surprised me out of my aggravated thoughts was Ethel laughing.

"Silly stupid boy, you see enemies everywhere and I can understand why but you think this girl is a spy? What is there to report on really? She isn't part of your business and she's not in a position of power. Think about it, she doesn't belong here, why is she here? Hmm? Because a vampire attacked her not because she wanted to be. I mean it's obvious that she's grown fond of your boy and he's most certainly more than fond of her. Use your brain, where does she belong?"

"I would say with the witches but… ah I see what you mean. The witches were foolish they threw her away but if not for the Lohan Coven being prejudice, they could have had a weapon to use against us," I said.

Now that made sense, a human experiment gone awry, they were always getting into things they shouldn't. If they created creatures like her then that meant they probably bred a necromancer with a vampire or maybe got their hands on whatever a death witch was. If she was to be used as a weapon against vampires meant that the vampires wouldn't likely have one of her kind. We came by Fredericka by accident, or maybe even by the twisted hand of fate. There was no way she could have faked what happened; it was far too dangerous. Nobody made deals with vampires suffering from madness, that was a good way to end up dead. So ok maybe I jumped to conclusions a bit but being paranoid was what kept me and my Family alive thus far.

"That's why it's important to figure out where she comes from. If we could trace her back to her origins then we have a place to start," Ethel said.

"*We*? Why we? What's your stake in this?" I asked because honestly, I couldn't see how any of this could benefit her. Unless of course she could use the girl to further extend her way too long life.

"Because that child has been failed by witches," Ethel said as if it was obvious. "Just as you took her in because she's been failed by vampires too."

"What happens when *we* find her origins? What if she is a human made weapon? What would you suggest we do with her?" I asked purely out of curiosity, I didn't actually care what she wanted.

"Then we protect her because if someone out there is in fact looking for what they created they will eventually find her. She's an innocent and I suppose her young age and lack of predatory qualities brings out the desire to protect her. Besides that, there are so many of us lost to time and senseless human slaughter, she is special, a rarity. Not a chosen one in some silly story but something rare in this world. There might not be others like her, she could very well be the last of her kind. I'm an old woman I've seen way too much, witnesses too much death, I'll not have this girl's death on my conscience. And despite what you might say neither will you, mostly because if you go against her, you will lose your son.

Also, the respect of your family, two things a man like you needs to survive," she told me. Her expression dared me to argue but unfortunately, I couldn't, she was right.

Cannon was never going to let her go, no matter how this started he spent the most time with her. His instincts would not allow him to stop protecting her. Even if she was an enemy in disguise, he would still hold on to her because he couldn't help it. The girl made you want to rescue her and keep her safe, that wasn't unheard of. It just didn't typically happen with witches and vampires; there were others like her that weren't predators when they should be. These people gave off an air of vulnerability that made you want to take care of them.

She wasn't the only creature out there with a disability like this. Someone like this wouldn't hunt for themselves so the pack or clan or whatever would provide and care for them. I never heard of it happening with vampires, but it wasn't impossible, especially if she was an experiment and this was an unintended side effect. My family would never forgive me if anything happened to her, family was all I had.

"Then I suppose we need to get to work," I said with a heavy sigh. This would not be easy, but it was important even though I had plenty of other things to do.

Desperate times indeed when I was willing to work with this particular witch. Ethel Rosewood had a reputation, and I made it my business to know everything I could about her. I didn't trust her, but I believed that in this instance she wanted to help the girl. Probably because she was taken in by the need to protect her like everybody else. It was truly ridiculous, but finding her origins was now a priority. We needed to be prepared because unfortunately this was not the end.

Freddie

Finally, we were at the end of the summit, and it seemed to be ending how it began. I was against a wall and Cannon's hand was between my legs. Why were we even here? Honestly, I couldn't remember when he did things like this. And yes, apparently my husband did have a bit of a kink for public sex. His body pressed into me from behind and I could feel what he really wanted. As if his fangs on my neck weren't already an indicator. He didn't bite me or drink my blood, but he did keep his fangs on my neck. More vampire weird shit that absolutely worked to turn me all the way on.

"Cannon, we should get back to the party," I said rather halfheartedly.

"If they want me here I'm entitled to entertain myself as I see fit," he said before thrusting his fingers in harder. "We can go up to the office and finish this."

"I am the worst sister ever, I abandoned my sister," I said in attempt not to end up naked on his desk. And I needed to remember to be responsible or whatever.

"She's fine she was with Lucy and Lee is watching her," Cannon said.

"When did you tell him to watch her?" I asked, surprised by that news.

"When I knew I couldn't stop looking at this fucking split in this dress making me want to get you out of it," he replied. "Besides nobody gets to see you come but me."

Lately Cannon had been increasingly possessive, it surprised me. He was also almost never away from me. What happened with the vampires had done something to him and he was behaving oddly. In those two days he kept me in the apartment, I just went along with it because he seemed to need it. But I had worried he might not ever let me go. Was this a result of my pregnancy? Did vampire males get like this during such times? Something to ask Lucy later, if I was ever allowed to be away from Cannon again. The time I spent with the ladies earlier seemed to have been too much for him. His fangs returned to my neck again as he made me come. I had to put my hand over my mouth to stifle the sound. Anybody with good senses would be able to tell that we had been up to something, I really had come full circle.

"I told you not to wear this dress," he said with his lips against my ear.

The royal blue v-neck satin floor length dress I was wearing was a little sexy, especially with the high split. Which was in fact the whole reason Cannon hadn't wanted me to wear the dress. I got it a while back on a shopping trip with Lucy and now seemed the perfect time for it. When in the near future would I even still be able to fit into the dress? So, wearing it made perfect sense even knowing how my husband would feel about it. I learned on our wedding day that he kinda had a thing for thigh splits in dresses because my wedding dress had 2.

It was a miracle that I kept him from ripping the dress, my swimsuit cover up on our honeymoon wasn't so lucky. This kink seemed to be very specifically about me because he didn't react that way to anyone else. As far as I could tell he didn't even seem like he noticed anyone else dressed like this. So yes, I knew better but I liked the dress and somehow, I thought he would behave in public at least. Obviously, I was wrong but kind of in the best way.

"Fuck this I'm taking you upstairs," he growled against my neck. "Too many predators in here and nobody needs to scent your blood but me."

"Cannon, you have to behave," I told him. I turned around and he just backed me against the wall.

"I'm tired of behaving, the mission has been accomplished, everybody is going to work together. My idea of a celebration involves you naked," he informed me.

It was hard to believe that this whole thing was finally going to be over. Since we came back from our honeymoon everything was about the summit. What would life be like without this hanging over us all the time? I couldn't even imagine it since this was all I knew my whole marriage. Then again, we did have something else to focus on now. While it was easy to let Cannon convince me to ditch the party I didn't want to come to anyway, we couldn't. The last thing I wanted was his father tracking us down while we were in the middle of something. Just the thought of that made me shudder, time to be responsible.

"If we can get through the rest of tonight, I'll do whatever you want when we get home," I offered.

"Temptress," he replied, leaning in to kiss me. Of course he distracted me, he was good at that. However, when he suddenly stiffened, I knew we were no longer alone.

What I expected was to have been caught by his parents. Belinda would tell me that I needed to get better control of him and Hunt would just glare in disgust. No matter what anybody said I knew that man hated me. Despite everything I didn't hate him, I wasn't sure how I really felt about him, but it wasn't hate. Confused feelings about my father-in-law aside, it actually wasn't him who came into our little hideaway. I hadn't seen Ethel Rosewood since that day in the bathroom, but I had hoped to see her again. She did kind of drop a bomb on me and casually walked away. Tonight, Ethel was dressed for the event in a silver gown that looked good with her white braids that were in an updo. As always, her grandsons were with her both in suits and silent.

"Girl," Ethel called and I had to wonder if she actually knew my name or not? Belinda had introduced me to the witches, but the woman never actually used my name. "Didn't I tell you not to trust these vampires?"

"You did but Cannon is my husband," I said like that said everything. Maybe it did because she rolled her eyes and shook her head.

"Is there a problem?" Cannon asked, he was always suspicious of everyone.

"Stand down boy, I'm not going to hurt your wife. If anything I want to help her, we are leaving, I tire of all this. But I needed to see her before I went," Ethel said. "I spoke with Harrington already, I'm sure he said nothing about it but it needed to be done."

"What did he say?" I asked both curious and confused, didn't she tell me not to trust them?

"That he isn't using you as a weapon and I'm inclined to believe him but that doesn't mean you are safe. Now you are more vulnerable, I will assist him in finding out where you come from. I have a feeling it's going to matter at some point."

"You called me a death witch but didn't explain what that is," I said sensing this might be my last chance to find out.

"This will require a longer conversation," she said with a sigh. "I will extend an invitation for you to visit my coven, you can bring your husband and the shadow walker."

"Absolutely not," Cannon answered for me. "Elder Rosewood, do you really think I'm going to let my wife enter an unfamiliar coven? Especially now?"

"So suspicious, just like your father," she said, shaking her head.

"Gran," one of her grandsons said, giving her an exacerbated look.

"Necromancers use death magic, you don't control the dead. A death witch controls life and death, the soul is your element," she told me.

All I could do was stare at her because what? How could the soul be an element? So, did that mean what I did before was take the soul of the vampire who attacked me? I knew how elemental magic worked, after finding out what I could do my parents got me private tutors. Private because I wasn't an elemental so I couldn't learn with other elementals. Magic as an element was one thing but controlling life and death? I had asked the question, but I wasn't ready for the answer, how could I be? It felt like this was too much and my brain was shutting down. Cause really what? This shouldn't be possible and yet anything was possible through magic.

"Freddie," Cannon said, pulling my attention to him. "You already know how to work elements, this is just another element thats all. One you didn't expect but it's not something to panic over."

"Ok," I nodded using his calm tone to ground myself. Seriously too much had been happening lately.

"What do you mean she can work elements?" Ethel asked, staring between us with a suspicious look.

"Just something I learned to do, I just use magic to access elements, I can't produce them just manipulate what is already there," I explained. The look of alarm on her face and her grandsons trading looks was not my imagination.

"Right now isn't the time to discuss this," Cannon said, taking charge. He also pulled me a step back away from the other witches. "I assume you have my wife's number or a way to contact her. Since you obviously used whatever, you did to her phone to track her. Call in a few days maybe we can set up a meeting somewhere neutral."

"You should never have been sent to these vampires," Ethel said, shaking her head.

Before I could ask what that meant there was a loud boom and the building shook. We all froze, it felt like everybody in the building was collectively holding their breath. Then it happened again. Cannon wrapped an arm around me keeping me steady. Things became chaotic very quickly as more booms sounded ahead of the structural damage. Across the room the ceiling fell in. Magic spread up the walls of the hallway we were in, I was vaguely aware that it was Ethel trying to keep us alive. Though that wasn't the most important thing to me at the moment. Scanning the room I didn't see Ollie anywhere. What had I done? I left my sister, and it appeared that the hotel was being bombed. All I could think of was finding Ollie, but Cannon pulled me back into the undamaged hall.

"I have to find Ollie," I told him but he wouldn't let me go.

"Lee will protect her," he said with more certainty than I had.

"She's my sister Cannon, I have to find her! I'm responsible for her, she's here because of me," I said, fighting against him. Of course, he could easily overpower me as a full blood, but I had to try.

"Fredericka, you need to stay calm, I'm not saying we leave her here. Obviously, we have to find her, but I can't have you running around putting yourself in danger, how does that help her? Wherever she is Lee is there too and though I hate to admit it he's good at his job he won't let harm come to her," Cannon assured me.

Every worse case scenario was running through my head as we watched everything falling apart. People were running and screaming, the scent of magic and blood was in the air. It felt like I could barely breathe, tears trailed down my face as I stood there completely helpless. What if I never saw my sister alive again?

Ollie

It was like something out of a fairytale. I felt like one of those princesses that finally gets to go to the ball. Of course, there weren't really many people my age around as the delegations didn't travel with a bunch of children, but it was still exciting. While I liked to think I was very adult I knew to everyone around me I was a child. Anyone under the age of 25 was essentially a child to nonhumans. Even my sister was barely an adult by those standards, and she was married to a vampire prince. Everybody knew that the Harringtons descended from vampire royalty.

I knew I should stay with Lucy until Freddie came back but Cannon didn't look like he planned to return her. Their relationship was so weird to me and it seemed to have drastically changed since I saw them before. He told me he didn't love my sister but from the way he acted you couldn't tell. Even at our house he was always keeping his eyes on her and kissing her and touching her. My mom suggested that maybe he didn't know he was in love with Freddie and having spent time in their house I agreed. Not that I knew much about love, I hadn't experienced that yet.

Wandering around the ballroom it was exciting to see all the various nonhumans in their formal attire. There was so much color and variety in how people dressed. Some people had on clothes from different time periods. These days you typically only saw that in ancient movies and TV shows from before The Surge. Nobody really paid me any attention as I wasn't anything special. I was a witch and there were a bunch of witches there, so I didn't stand out. That was fine by me I just wanted to observe things. This was kind of a once in a lifetime type of thing, when would I ever be in such mixed company again? It was rare for such a diverse group of nonhumans to be gathered together at the same place.

"Oleander?" Someone called and I turned surprised that anyone would know my name.

Nobody called me that it was just the name I came with from the orphanage. I regretted turning and leaving Lucy when I saw who had called me. Of course, this was a possibility since I knew they were here, but I had hoped to avoid them. Susan the traitorous bitch stood there staring at me in shock. I personally never liked her; there was always something about her. Like a nasty spirit maybe, but you know hidden under this facade of niceness. Her son went to my school, and he was an entitled asshole, it wasn't the least bit surprising.

"Susan," was all I said.

"What are you doing here?" She demanded as if I was a misbehaving child.

"It's a celebration," I said with a shrug.

"You shouldn't be here, why are you here?"

"Because I came with my sister," I replied, confused by her reaction. When she made to grab my arm, a hand reached out stopping her before she touch me. Both of us were surprised to see Lee, my sister's guard, appear out of nowhere.

"Is this woman bothering you Miss Miller?" He asked, his attention on me.

"Um not sure yet," I admitted and he nodded.

"Please refrain from putting your hands on her," he said to Susan, letting her wrist go. The annoying woman jumped back like someone had hit her.

"You need to get out of here," Susan said ignoring Lee and staring at me. "This is no place for you, why would that sister of yours bring you here?"

"Because we came for a visit and Cannon said I could come," I shrugged, this was so bizarre. Lee, I noted, did not leave; he stood there watching us.

"We? Is your mother here?"

"No, mom and dad stayed at the house they didn't want to come," I answered. "I think I'm going to go find my sister now."

"No, leave her, you need to get out of here right now," Susan said. "Don't go back to that vampire house, your parents shouldn't be there."

"Well it's not like it's just them that are there, other people live in the house too obviously they weren't bringing little kids here," I said with a shrug. Looking around I tried to spot Freddie but knowing Cannon, he took her somewhere to have sex.

"*Children*? There are children living in that place? Why are there children there?" Susan asked, seeming a bit frantic, I looked at Lee, and he obviously noticed it too.

"Because they live there, um like I said I'm going to go find my sister now," I said, taking a step back.

"But they said... no it doesn't matter now. You need to leave here and stay away from the vampires they are trouble," she said.

"You know you like to look down on my sister for being a vampire but did it ever occur to you that had she been accepted into the coven like she was supposed to be she wouldn't have married a vampire? She never did anything to hurt anyone, yet you made it your whole personality to vilify her for no reason. I mean she never even had contact with vampires until one attacked her," I said.

"Attacked her? What are you talking about?" Susan asked, staring at me like she really didn't know.

"That's why she had to quit working at the school, a vampire attacked her like 8 months ago now. Before she met

Cannon, if none of that happened, she would never have had anything to do with vampires. Now it's all moot because she is married to a vampire and they are having a baby. Which I'm sure you will think must be some kind of monster because everything that isn't a witch is so awful. You were my mom's best friend; you betrayed her and did everything you could to hurt my sister. What did she ever do to you? The answer is nothing, nobody did anything to you," I said because I was annoyed.

"Miss Miller," Lee said, looking at me with what had to be concern.

"Just call me Ollie," I told him and he actually smiled.

"As I told your sister I cannot do that," he informed me.

"I didn't know anything happened to her," Susan said. "She couldn't be part of the coven, we couldn't accept someone like that. And she was always showing off like she was better than us. I had heard that she might be pregnant now, but I wasn't sure it was true. You should go find her and leave and tell your parents to get out of that house."

"Why?" I asked confused by this whole interaction. Why was she so desperate to get me to leave here?

"I'm so sorry I wish... you just shouldn't have come," she shook her head. Then she turned her attention to Lee. "You need to get her out of here, it's not safe, isn't that your job? Get this child away from here."

Before Lee could respond there was a loud bang and the ground shook. Susan looked around frantically as a lot of people seemed to be doing. There was another boom and more shaking and part of the ceiling caved in. Before I could react to any of it, Lee grabbed me and wrapped me in his arms pulling me back. Where we had just stood another piece of the ceiling fell. Susan hadn't moved, she was crushed and I screamed. Everything around us was chaos, the booms kept coming and the shaking ground didn't stop, and parts of the building were caving in. People were running around and some screaming, and some were crushed like Susan. Somehow Lee and I remained standing as the world exploded around us.

"Don't move," he told me, holding me tight against him. Somehow, we were untouched by the pure chaos going on around us. I realized that he had to be doing some kind of magic to shield us.

"I have to find Freddie," I said when the shock cleared a bit from my brain.

"I cannot let anything happen to you, your sister would not like that. We will find her, she's with her husband he will protect her," he assured me.

Of course, he was right but still I wanted to see her and know that she was ok. What was happening? This was supposed to be a celebration instead it was a horrible tragedy. When the ground stopped shaking Lee loosened his grip on me, but he didn't let me go. Everything was so loud there were screams, what sounded like gunshots and the building was still falling apart. Lee looked around then without a word picked me up and the next thing I knew we were somewhere else in the room. Could he teleport? Two more strange feeling teleportations and he stopped sitting me on my feet in front of my sister.

"Ollie!" She wrapped her arms around me pulling me into a tight hug. "I thought I lost you, I'm so sorry I shouldn't have left you."

"I'm ok," I assured her. "Lee saved me." At that she pulled away from me and hugged Lee who was clearly surprised by her actions.

"Thank you," she told him before stepping back and grabbing me again, he just nodded.

"We need to move," Cannon said, more serious than I had ever seen him before. "You can come with us Elder Rosewood or you can take your chances in the chaos."

"We will join you, thank you," the Elder Witch said. She had two young men with her.

"What about your mother and sister?" Freddie asked Cannon who shook his head.

"They will know what to do," he said before nodding at his guards who moved ahead down the hall and stopped before opening a secret panel in the wall.

All of us followed, my sister stayed close to me, and Cannon stayed close to her. Inside were a set of stairs going down but oddly none going up. At the bottom we went through a locked door into an underground garage. I didn't remember there being one but obviously the hotel had all kinds of secrets.

Ty walked over to a passenger van and put his hand on some type of biometric reader. He unlocked it and opened the doors.

"To the house?" Desmond asked, looking to Cannon.

"No," I said and all eyes turned to me. "Susan said not to go there, she was yelling at me saying I shouldn't be here and our parents shouldn't be there. Before she um she..." I couldn't finish as I could see the woman being crushed again.

"Part of the ceiling came down on that woman," Lee offered. "And yes she seemed to indicate that something was going to happen before the bombing started. It's possible that a second attack is happening there right now."

"Fuck," Cannon said with a heavy sigh. "Ok, Des come with me, everybody else stay here for now it's safe here. I'm going to see if I can find my mother and we will go from there. If I'm not back Ty, you know what to do."

"Cannon," Freddie said and he stepped over to her and kissed the side of her head.

"Stay here, nobody but my family can access this place and it's protected, if I can get a message to the house I will but I need you to stay safe. Look after your sister," he told her.

"Ok," she nodded, though she didn't look like she actually agreed.

He left with Desmond leaving us in the garage. I hugged my sister and she hugged me, who could have imagined things would end this way? I just wanted to go to a ball, this was not how fairytales ended.

Cannon

They killed the architects, so the building was unstable. A smart move to be sure, we needed all 3 to hold things together having extended the hotel so much. If not for this strategic move the building wouldn't be falling down around us. Killing the architects affected the structural integrity of the magically modified building. Essentially physics and the laws of nature were catching up with us. For them to know to do this it was clearly an inside job, someone betrayed us. The alliance was 3 days old and already everything was falling apart. Only someone staying in the hotel for the summit would have known who the architects are. This summit started with a brawl and ended in betrayal and senseless death.

Bodies lay across the ballroom; people were still running around some trying to escape some trying to help people that were trapped. All of it was chaos and everything we worked for was falling apart right in front of us. Desmond and I helped where we could while scanning the room for the rest of my family. I wasn't especially worried about them because we had all been trained to stay alive. Still, I wanted to see them and make sure they were all ok.

"Cannon!" Lucy called before colliding with me, Markus was with her, and they both looked a little battered.

"Just as your father feared the humans are attacking," Markus informed me. That wasn't a surprise, of course they decided to attack now.

"Please tell me you didn't lose Freddie, I don't know what happened to Ollie," Lucy said looking rather devastated by that fact.

"Both of them are fine, they are in the garage with Lee and Ty," I said and she nodded in relief. "Both of you need to get out of here, one of the witches let something slip about an attack at our house. Doubt there's anything they can do, the house would be locked down at the first sign of trouble, but you should take the underground road."

"Let's go," Markus said, holding out a hand to his wife who took it.

"Don't die," Lucy ordered me and I nodded as they headed off to one of the hidden staircases.

The thing about my family was that we planned for everything, there was a whole series of underground tunnels under this hotel. There were safe houses and a road that went directly from the hotel to the compound. My ancestors and my father were paranoid with reason, and the tunnels were reinforced with so much magic that even this building coming down completely wouldn't damage them. We finally found my mother in the lobby; beyond the doors a true battle was going on. It wouldn't surprise me if my father was out there fighting, he wasn't the kind of king to stay on a throne when he could fight.

"Where is your wife? Have you seen your sister?" Mother demanded as soon as she saw me.

"Lucy and Markus are headed home, there might be an issue there. Freddie and Ollie are in the garage, you should go with them," I told her.

"I do not hide from trouble," she said rather indignant.

"Of that I am aware, however Freddie and Ollie need to be somewhere safe. I wouldn't trust my wife with anyone else but you. Can you do this for me? I'll stay," I said. Anybody with working brain cells knew my mother could kill all of the humans likely by herself. If I couldn't be with Freddie, she was the one I wanted with her.

"Cannon," she said looking conflicted.

"Go," my father said when he came over Lucien trailing him like always. How he even heard us over the commotion I don't even know but somehow, he did. "The people need to fight for those they lost, they need to step up and realize what we've been telling them. Take care of the girl, the chaos makes her an easier target."

"Fine, I got separated from Kami, when you see her tell her," she said and he nodded. Kami was my mother's longtime guard and cousin who had come with her when she married my father.

"Get them sent off and then do what you can, Gunnar is capturing a human or two for questioning but the rest need to die," he said.

"Understood," I replied. "Whatever happened the Lohan witches are involved. One of them warned Ollie to leave."

"Fucking witches," he shook his head at hearing that. "Lucien."

"It will be handled," he replied, disappearing into the crowd.

"Don't disappoint me," my mother said to my father and he actually smiled. Their relationship was so weird I could never possibly understand it.

"Never," he replied and with a nod she led the way to another secret passage that went to the garage.

"We are going to lose the building," my mother said regretfully as we went down the stairs.

"With the architects dead it's inevitable at this point," I agreed.

I knew my mother would never run from any fight, so this was going to bother her. My parents were the type to fight side by side, always equals, always partners. It didn't bother me that my wife wasn't a fighter, not everybody had to be. Even if she was, she was so young and so breakable, age meant less vulnerability in nonhumans. If I could get away with keeping her in the house until she was at least 35 I would. It couldn't happen but it would be nice.

Possibly one of the hardest things I ever had to do was pull my wife aside to speak to her. Was this what love did to you? It felt like my heart was caving in but I had to let her go. Sure, this structure was safe and wouldn't collapse, it just didn't make sense to keep her here. As always during this damned cursed summit I had to leave her and clean up the messes of others. I pulled her into my arms holding her tight wishing we could go back to how things were before everything went to hell.

"Freddie," I said but she shook her head.

"No," she said, anticipating what I was going to say.

"I need you to be safe, the building is going to come down. I can't have you here when that happens."

"Come with us, why do you need to be here?"

"Because it's our hotel and people need help."

"I need you," she said with tears in her eyes, breaking my heart a little more.

"I'll be there as soon as I can, for now take care of our baby and your sister," I said, unable to resist placing my hand on her stomach. This was why she needed to go; I could not have my wife and unborn child in danger. Well in more danger than we were already in.

"Cannon I can't lose you," she pleaded.

"Freddie I love you, I know it's the worst time for this but I need you to know that."

"That just makes me think that I'm never going to see you again," she said, burying her face against me.

"When I have everything to live for? As soon as I can I swear I'll be there with you but right now I have to make sure you are safe," I said, giving her a tight squeeze.

"Fredericka," my mother said, her tone gentle when she came to join us.

"I know I'm embarrassing The Family but I can't help it," Freddie said. Looking alarmed, my mother shook her head and wrapped an arm around her.

"You are not embarrassing us, I understand how you are feeling better than most would. I know this is hard, but we have to go, there is nothing in this world that would stop my son from coming back to you. It's ok to cry and to be upset and scared, I would worry more if you weren't. Come with me and we can let Cannon help those who cannot help themselves," she told her.

I never in my life heard her use such a gentle tone of voice, but I was thankful for it. Freddie nodded, I kissed her forehead then she let my mother lead her away to the waiting van. Why did it feel like I was ripping my own heart out? She was going to be safe, and I would see her as soon as I could. Having responsibilities fucking sucked. My mother nodded to me as they got into the van where Ty was already behind the wheel. Taking only two guards was against the rules but these were special circumstances. Lee shut the doors and nodded to me before getting into the passenger seat. I couldn't help but to watch the van leave, I could physically feel her getting further away from me. Never occurred to me to ask her if she could feel me the same way I felt her.

"Let's deal with this and get you back to her," Des said his gaze also followed the van.

"Feels like this whole damn thing was cursed from the start," I said as we headed back upstairs to the chaos.

"Considering witches were clearly involved in this shit that really might be the case," he replied.

At this point nothing would surprise me. While we were gone a lot of the ballroom had been cleared but there were still some people trapped. Our hotel staff was directing people outside to safety. Nothing, not even an apocalypse, could keep our employees from doing their jobs. We helped as we could along the way then headed back to the lobby; there was a different kind of chaos on this side of the building. Mostly it seemed people were being led to the back lawn. Likely that was because there was still a violent clash going on out front. It appeared the humans were prepared to shoot anyone down that came out the front doors. Bodies laid in the driveway, some of them were humans.

Guns were always their weapons of choice because they were weak. If they hadn't caught us all off guard they would have been handled more swiftly. But people were injured, trapped, scared and some were dead. I looked to Des and without a word we headed outside. Bullets could move faster than magic sometimes, but vampires moved faster. There were others out angry and vengeful, so it wasn't hard to thin the herd of humans. Everything happened in a blur of blood and death. To humans killing involved moral questioning but to nonhumans survival was more important than morals. If we let them live, they would just cause more trouble and spread more hate. Really this was a public service.

Moving purely on instinct I grabbed the wrist of a human holding a gun and broke it. Grabbing his head I made quick work of snapping his neck, just in time to catch Lisha who fell into my arms like something out of a movie. He had been aiming at her when I grabbed him. She had been fighting a different human who was now being torn apart by an angry wolf. Blood lust and adrenaline were not a good combination in a vampire. Fighting and killing and the scent of blood in the air, it did things. So, for a moment the briefest of moments when I looked at Lisha I almost did something very stupid. Something that would in fact ruin my whole life. Thank all the gods in every damn pantheon that I helped her to stand up and took a step away from her.

"Thanks," she said, though in her eyes I could see the calculation.

"No problem," I said, turning to find Des who by his expression definitely saw what happened. Of course, he never missed anything.

Things were still chaotic but as far as I could tell all the humans were down. This was going to be a hell of a mess to clean up. So many bodies littered the ground and there were creaks and groans from the building as it continued to fall apart. The real damage would happen slowly as the magic dissipated, and the added space collapsed in on itself. Hopefully anyone still alive would be out of the building before that happened.

I spotted my father dishing out orders and directing people, so I started in his direction. There was no way to hide what happened, but the laws were a bit flexible depending on the circumstances. On Mars they had retribution laws where a person could seek whatever retribution they felt was deserved when someone wronged them. On Earth it wasn't that easy but the fact that these people attacked a hotel full of people and tried to kill the survivors made the killing justified.

They were a threat to lives so they had to be neutralized. Sure, we could have taken them alive but why would we do a thing like that? Leaving them alive meant that they could come back and destroy again. Really though what sealed their fate was that they were in fact on our property. The law stated that you could defend your property from trespassers anyway you had to, especially when your life was threatened. Police and emergency services were only just now arriving; I didn't envy whoever's job it was to deal with this mess. Before I reached my father Eric Gordon came stumbling over, he was bleeding and dirty. In a shocking display of affection he embraced Lisha, who had followed us

"Lisha, thank the gods you are alright," he said, hugging her tightly. I didn't doubt that he cared about his niece, I just doubted that he cared this much.

"I'm ok Uncle Eric," Lisha said equally dramatic. "Cannon saved me from being shot by a human."

"Thank you," Eric said sincerely and I just nodded. "I don't know what we would do if we lost you. Phil isn't doing so well right now."

"What?" She asked, actually seeming genuinely distraught about that. Her uncles raised her so of course they were close. "He was injured but he's alive," Eric said. Seriously I never in my life saw him be the least bit affectionate towards his husband so the sniffle at relaying that news was a bit much.

"We are gonna go, glad you are all ok," I said, trying to be civil.

"Cannon, are you going home?" Eric asked and I knew whatever reason he had for the question I wouldn't like.

"Not at the moment," I replied.

"Can you take Lisha home with you? I know it's a lot to ask but with Phillip hurt I just need to know that she's somewhere safe."

"I'm not going home, when I leave here I'm joining my wife at a safe house," I said. It had been a long ass day, so I wasn't at my best, so I gave out way too much damn information.

"Oh is your wife alright? Was she hurt?" Eric asked, pretending to care when we both knew he would love to wish her dead.

"She's fine, she's with my mother and I need to help out here so who knows when I will get to leave."

"Please Cannon, she is our heir," Eric pleaded. "Without her our Family has no future, I know we have all had our differences but this is important."

"Fine," I said, feeling like I was chewing glass just to answer that.

No, I didn't want Lisha anywhere near my wife, but it was my job to at least pretend to care about the other Families. Did I care if Lisha tripped and the building fell on her? Nope, I knew I would regret this, nothing good would come of it. To say no though would cause conflict when we all needed to be united now more than ever. If I didn't know better, I would almost think my father organized this whole thing to prove his point.

However, I did know better, he wouldn't gamble with the lives of so many others. Especially when we were all in the hotel when it happened. People were no doubt going to speculate about it but I knew better. Hunt Harrington would never do anything that could put his wife and children in danger. What happened to him all those years ago had lasting effects on him and family was everything to him.

"Thank you," Eric said, his sincerity slipping just a bit. The Gordons did nothing but calculate how to get what they wanted. Apparently, their mission was still to get her married to me, but that shit wasn't happening. After I agreed to this nonsense, he took her to go see her other uncle who was being treated somewhere.

"That was without a doubt the dumbest shit you have ever done," Des informed me. As if I didn't already know it.

"Now isn't the time for a rift between Families," I said. "But yeah it was pretty fucking stupid. It's too much to hope for that she might want to stay behind with her uncle?"

"If he's even really hurt, they are using this to their advantage. I could almost admire it if I didn't know what it would cost you. Uh cause what the fuck?"

"A moment of weakness, we will never be discussing this again."

"I was ready to tackle you if you moved any closer to her," he offered. That was what a good friend would do, keep you from wrecking your life.

We finally got our orders from my father and went to accomplish the tasks. The hotel needed complete evacuation, doctors and healers were setting up a space to treat whoever they could. At least magic in the blood accelerated healing, so some people wouldn't be as bad as others. Police were asking questions trying to figure out exactly what to do. All the bodies, explosives and weapons painted a pretty clear picture. Humans would no doubt cry about this and blame us when they came to do harm. Their actions were justified but ours in defending ourselves not so much. I really hated humans; they were truly the worst creatures to ever walk the planet.

My wife was safely tucked away, and I would join her soon, so why did I still feel a sense of dread? It hadn't gone away in the past few days. Something crazy and dangerous already happened, it should be over, right?

Freddie

I never imagined that my life would be like this. Of all the changes that came with being part of the Harrington Family I never saw this coming. Somehow, I managed to sleep though not on purpose. Ollie was still in bed beside me, asleep, she would probably have nightmares for a long time after this. Rolling over on my back I saw that someone else was in the room. My eyesight in the dark wasn't as good as a full blood, but it was good enough that I could see Cannon sitting in a chair. Carefully I climbed out of bed and went to him. He pulled me down onto his lap, his hair was wet so he had time to shower.

"I'm here," he whispered, pulling me against him.

"I was afraid you wouldn't come," I admitted. More than the trauma of what happened my thoughts had stayed on him.

And if I would see him again. Aside from worrying over my sister, that was more terrifying than anything else that had happened to me so far.

"Told you I wouldn't leave you," he said. "Things aren't good and they aren't going to be getting better anytime soon but we are all still alive."

"What happened at the house?" I asked, I had been afraid to even think about any of it.

"Everybody is fine, your parents are fine, nobody could get in though they tried. I'm trying to decide if I want to send you home or keep you here where nobody can find you."

"Where will you be? I want to be with you, or wherever you are coming to in order to sleep."

"Yeah I knew you would say that, at this point I would send you back to your parents 'house if I wasn't certain it wouldn't be safe. That coven did this, they were informing to the humans though I don't know that they realized that the humans would turn on them. Half the coven is already dead; the rest likely soon will be. Everyone is angry and ready to go to war," he told me.

"How many people died last night?" I asked even though I didn't want to know, I needed to though.

"Not as many as it could have been, the witches were the most vulnerable in the building ironically. Not even the other covens are considering the Lohan coven a loss so 20 or so people. The rest of us can take a little damage and heal from a lot of things. Your father went out to help the survivors. More humans died than us but that won't stop them. They probably knew that whoever showed up last night wasn't going to make it out. My father wants to have his new council meet as soon as possible. Between all that and the hotel situation, I won't have time to breathe. So, we will definitely have to postpone your kidnapping."

"Sounds like I'm going to need to kidnap you."

"Possibly, everything is such a fucking mess."

"What will happen to those still alive in the coven? The ones that didn't come?" I asked, I had some conflicting emotions about the whole thing. Yes, they cast me out and made my life miserable but once these people were like my family even if it was all a lie.

"They will be detained and questioned, the guild members too," he replied and I nodded. "Hard to know if everybody in the coven was involved or just some of them."

"I thought it was weird that Sarah didn't come to the summit, she's the head of the coven. Why would she send representatives and not come herself to something so important? Maybe not the whole coven but the elders, they had to know," I told him.

The sad thing was that I could guess why they would collude with humans, it was obvious. Witches were often positioned near the bottom of the nonhuman hierarchy. Some people thought of witches as just humans who could use magic. Sarah and Susan and others in the coven thought themselves better than other people. In their petty childish minds getting revenge on those more powerful than you would make sense. Except they forgot that humans don't see us as humans, they see us as other. While they might smile in your face and make a deal to take out the heads of every local faction, they still saw witches as the enemy.

The problem from the start was that humans coveted magic, they couldn't have it so they destroyed those that did. This was what they did, this was why history was so very important. No witch should ever forget the time when they were burning people accused of being witches. Most killed back then weren't witches at all but some were. We were never supposed to forget especially when they did it again during the wars. In the chaotic post-Surge world humans would attack other people accusing them of being nonhuman and gather a mob to kill them. They liked burning supposed witches way too much.

"Do you think the guild would be involved?" Cannon asked and I thought about it a second before nodding.

"The guild master is Sarah's husband, he wasn't there either," I said.

Yes, I knew that whatever I said would make it back to Hunt and be taken into consideration. But what loyalty did I have to these people? Sure, they were like family once, but they snatched that all away from me for no real reason. They always knew I was a vampire and it wasn't my fault that I was more powerful than them. Nothing justified the things they did to me and the constant harassment. I wasn't telling Cannon these things because I wanted revenge, I didn't care anymore. No, I was telling him because those people plotted and killed innocent people. My sister could have died just for wanting to put on a dress and go to a ball. Thank the gods that Lucy didn't let Luna come too. I could have lost my life, I could have lost my husband, and I could have lost my family. It wasn't easy trying to fit into the world of the Harringtons, but they were my family now.

"It will be handled," Cannon said, giving me a tight squeeze. "How's my baby doing?" This he asked with his hand on my stomach. That was something he was doing more and more and I didn't hate it.

"Fine, but I think we might miss our appointment," I replied.

"Trust me we will not, if I can't take you to the doctor Belinda will have the doctor come to us."

"Is that even necessary? We can wait; it's not like much is going to change."

"Have fun telling that to her, just like how you might think you are getting out of self-defense now. You aren't, she will make time," he informed me and I groaned. It was nice to talk about something else for a moment before we had to return to reality. I was probably never going to be used to the way the Harringtons did things. "That's a problem for later though we are leaving soon."

"I think I'll feel better once we are home, I just feel a little off being here," I said. Though it was likely just lingering effects from another traumatic event in my life. When I got home, I was calling the therapist, way too much had been happening lately.

"Yeah I know what you mean," he said. "Ollie you can quit pretending that you are still asleep."

"I was letting you two have a moment," she said sitting up in bed.

The safe house had clothes in a variety of sizes, so we were able to change out of our dresses last night. Ollie hadn't said much last night but we might have all been in shock. And I was pitifully crying because I had to be separated from Cannon. I hoped that she wouldn't be too traumatized by what happened. Unlike me she had been inside the ballroom when the building was coming down. She also saw Susan die, even if we didn't like her, it was still a crazy thing. Before I could ask my sister how she was feeling the door to the room opened. The last person I expected to see walking in was Lisha Gordon.

"Cannon are you—" she stopped speaking, seeing us together.

"Why is she here?" I asked my husband who had failed to mention Lisha coming with him. Lisha, who was freshly showered and wearing a man's button-down shirt and nothing else.

"She's the heir to the Gordon Family, her uncles asked if we could keep her safe for a while," he explained.

"You know Cannon, he's always trying to be the hero," she said.

All I could really think of was the fight that first night of the summit and Cannon pulling me in that hallway. Belinda had said fights brought out bloodlust. Last night I was here away from him, so it seemed my husband found another option. No, I shouldn't jump to conclusions, but he brought her here where nobody was supposed to know about. What did promises mean to people who were used to getting anything they wanted? And it was obvious from the smug look she threw at me that something happened.

"Did you need something?" He asked her while I sat there silently imploding.

"It's not important, I see you are busy," she said, then turned and left the room, closing the door behind her.

"Did you have sex with her?" I asked though I wasn't sure I wanted the answer.

"Why are you asking me that?" He asked instead of answering, wasn't that an answer itself? I felt sick, I got up from his lap on shaky legs.

"You did," I said, feeling so stupid for believing for a second that things would go right for me. Nothing had gone right in the last 8 months, and it seemed it never would.

"Freddie, nothing happened despite what you think of me, I wouldn't do that to you."

"The way you say nothing happened sounds a lot like something did."

"I love you, I told you that you are all that matters to me. Even if you don't feel the same way."

"Oh so I don't say what you want so you go fuck somebody else? Seriously?"

"No of course not, I wouldn't do that. It was nothing I swear," he said. Why didn't I believe him? Oh, it might have been the guilty look he was trying to hide.

"We should get ready," Ollie said, reminding us of her presence. "We're leaving soon, right?"

"Yeah," Cannon said, getting up with a sigh. He took a step towards me, but I shook my head and he stopped. "Freddie."

"We'll be down in a few minutes," I said, looking away from him.

"Ok," he said, then crossed the room and went out the door.

"Why do you think something happened? I mean that crazy chick was definitely in here trying to stir up trouble. But why would he have done anything with her?" Ollie asked me when I sat back down on the bed.

"Don't worry about it, this isn't something you need to deal with right now," I told her. Naturally she rolled her eyes giving me the expression of a putupon teenager.

"I'm not a child and you are my sister, the world could be burning and I would still care about what's going on with you. He looked guilty and she looked smug, you didn't imagine that I witnessed it too," she told me.

"Vampires in certain situations end up in bloodlust and the last time that happened we had sex," I explained.

"Do you love him? He told you he loved you more than once," she pointed out.

"I do, I've known it for a while but I just don't feel right admitting it. If I do, then what? It feels like too much, because what can I do if he changes his mind? Or he decides maybe he does want a second wife after all? One who will give him pure blood children, then what? Yes, some of it is being paranoid and insecure, I know that. But it just doesn't feel right to admit it."

"Once you are home you need to talk to him, he needs to tell you the truth. If something did happen, what will you do?"

"What can I do? It's always the same no matter what I'm trapped, more so now than before. Vampires aren't like us, they view a lot of things differently," I said feeling hollow. Lately life has been wearing me down so much.

Was a lot of this probably wrapped up in my issues about everything else? Yes, I needed more than one therapy session to work through all my stuff. I hadn't expected Cannon to tell me he loved me at all, ever. Hearing him say it last night felt almost like a good bye. Maybe that was really the problem because what if he loved me and I lost him? Hadn't we already had some close calls? And though he swore he would never betray me with Lisha, something obviously happened so what did that mean? How was I supposed to trust that nothing happened again? Or that there wouldn't be another pure blood to come along seeking to replace me. If it was possible at all to be replaced, then did I really have him anyway?

"You deserve to be happy," Ollie told me.

"Sadly we don't always get what we deserve," I replied with a sigh. If that was the case, I would never have met my husband or his family.

Things were supposed to be getting better but it all felt even more uncertain. I felt like I was always burdening my little sister with my relationship nonsense. Of course she would say it wasn't a problem, but I still hated to burden others with anything. At this point it seemed like my marriage was cursed. Ollie hugged me and I did my best not to fall apart completely. No more crying over this man.

Belinda

Tragedy either brought you together or ripped you apart there was no in-between. Seeing all of our hard work and our hotel go up in flames was hard. We had survived a lot to get this far so we would survive this. If the agreement fell apart because of this then so be it but I had a feeling the opposite would be true. This was the proof of what Hunt had been trying to prevent humans coming for us. The betrayal wasn't too surprising in retrospect, but it was also so tragically pitiful. Some people never learned their lesson; it was such a stupid thing to do.

"Hunt told me what you said when you were at his office," I said to Ethel. We were both sitting at the table drinking tea.

"I should have cut out the middle man and come straight to you, the real power behind the throne," she replied.

"My husband is not just a figurehead, he is head of our family."

"I am old, I know where you come from, warrior women. Without you he wouldn't have his position, and you can deny it if you want to. Before you ask, I make it my business to know about all other powerful people and where their origins lie."

"Hunt was always going to be custodian with or without me. Did my presence give his grandmother more assurance that he was the right choice? Yes, we are equals, everything we do we do it together. Though admittedly he is better with the diplomacy aspect of things, I have far less patience than he does," I said with a shrug. "Coming to me would not keep him out of the proverbial loop, we share everything."

"Fine, then I ask you the same thing I asked him. What are you going to do with the girl?"

"What would you propose? Allow her to join your coven? The time for witches in her life has passed, she is a vampire and will be giving birth to a vampire," I said dismissively.

"We do not abandon our own, she is a Harrington, the witch half of her is just a detail. The girl rarely uses her magic as is, likely because that coven made her feel bad for being superior."

"Those useless Lohan witches were fools to throw her away. Her family could have brought a discrimination suit against them for their behavior. It would have served them right, but they have far bigger problems now," Ethel said, shaking her head. "It is a pity though that your girl couldn't have gone to one of my boys, she would be of value in my coven. I suppose I feel a sense of responsibility now that I've been made aware of her existence."

"What is your opinion on what the witches did? Collaborating with humans and having the nerve to sign the agreement."

"Weak witches have always been a problem. Instead of trying to better themselves they complain and indulge heavily in envy. My guess is they offered them something they couldn't say no to," she said then cocked her head to the side. "Or they sacrificed others in an attempt to gain more magic. That wouldn't surprise me in the least."

"I can't imagine doing something like this but we are longer lived and we remember what things were like before."

Throughout history there were those that collaborated with the enemy against their own kind. Save yourself by throwing someone else into the line of fire. Because nobody ever learned the important lessons it happened during the wars too. The lesson that was obvious was that either your own got you back or the enemy betrayed you. Nothing was new or original, it all happened before, which is why they should have known better. Wasn't this exactly what I spoke to Hunt about? Selfish people willing to sacrifice others, it was inevitable. Sometimes I wondered if we truly were so different from humans? Or were we just the product of the world we lived in?

"Some people feel the vampires around here have too much power. Your husband, taking command and trying to create an alliance would naturally make some people nervous. Especially people who see themselves near the bottom of the proverbial food chain. Now anyone with a brain would know that we should be united against the humans. They will always turn on us; they prove it time and again. This is why knowing true history is so important, but the youth think they know better. Elders in that coven should have known better. And here the humans are proving that point."

"What a waste because now they have the whole of the nonhuman community against them for their part in what happened last night. Humans were lurking around but for them to escalate to such violence was unexpected."

"I imagine they must have suggested that we were building an army against the humans. Instead, we are trying to bring our individual communities together. This horribly irresponsible act may now cause a war, which is what we have all been seeking to avoid. Things go bad here, there could be far reaching consequences all over the world. Resentment is everywhere and our peace could turn on a dime," Ethel said, shaking her head.

"We were so close to this ending with minimal issues," I said with a sigh.

I wasn't sure where we went from here, but I knew the Lohan coven would not survive. It wasn't vampires they needed to worry about; it was everybody. Everyone involved in the summit, especially those that were injured or had a loved one killed, would be out for blood. The worst part was that the humans had obviously double crossed them. At least if you were going to betray your own kind you should get something out of it. But since they were still in the building when it all happened the humans clearly set them up. All of it was so ridiculous, and quite frankly exhausting because now this was our problem. Because problems were in abundance Lisha came downstairs half dressed. The fact that she looked pleased with herself meant that she had been up to mischief. Such a tedious girl and she wondered why we didn't want her for our family.

Something was going on with the Gordons, that much was obvious. Though I couldn't imagine what it was. Their insistence in getting Lisha married to Cannon made no sense. She was their heir, if she married Cannon, she could not be custodian of their family. Likely what they truly were after was a merger which was rare. The question still was why, as far as I knew, their family was prosperous. They had a textile business that was thriving and didn't shut down during the wars. Their line wasn't as old as some just a couple of centuries but that wasn't a bad thing. Essentially, they were the new money to our old money so to speak.

"What are you doing you wretched girl?" I asked Lisha as she pranced around with wet hair and in just a man's shirt. What type of child had her family raised?

"She wants to sow doubt into your son's marriage," Ethel said, shaking her head.

"I'm doing him a favor, his attachment to that pathetic witch isn't good for your family. I will be a better wife," she said without a hint of shame.

"My son has already told you that he doesn't want you and my husband made it clear that we don't need you. Why are you still pushing this? Are you really this dense?" I asked her because really it was somewhat interesting in a tragic way to witness her determination.

"Men don't know what they really want, it's up to us women to show them. You've been married for centuries, obviously you knew what to do to get your husband looking at you," she said.

"Our marriage was arranged, our Families had an alliance, it wasn't about some silly nonsense you want. Anyone can be pretty or learn skills in the bedroom; there's more to marriage than that you ridiculous girl. My son isn't interested in you and trying to interfere in his marriage will only make him dislike you more. He already made it clear publicly that he doesn't want you. Have you no self respect?" I asked the girl who I would rather run through with a stake than allow into my family.

There was a reason she was still unmarried and why we didn't choose her. A half vampire orphan was the better choice and that said everything considering this girl was pureblood. Being promiscuous wasn't the reason she was unwanted; it was because she was untrustworthy. People talked and they had things to say about her that were rather unflattering. She thought rather incorrectly that sex could get her anything she wanted. What she had been after for many years was my son and we were never so desperate as to consider her. Even having her here now was a problem but I understood why

Cannon brought her. She was the heir to the Gordon Family, and they didn't want to risk her. And they likely thought she could still try to seduce her way into my family.

"Children these days have no shame," Ethel said in obvious disgust.

"Shame has been in short supply for far too long," I agreed. "You think you can push my son's wife out? She isn't going anywhere; she knows her place in this family."

While I would like to believe that to be true, I knew our poor Fredericka was not so secure in her marriage. This horrible girl had likely gotten to her. In her current condition the last thing she needed was more stress considering everything that happened the past few days. A vampire tried to forcibly read her mind; she had to deal with Cannon's assassination attempt and now this mess last night. Where she had brought her young sister, thankfully they weren't hurt. Her parents were back at our home that had also been attacked. Even though that situation was handled quickly and efficiently, it was another worry. Now here was this girl trying to steal her husband. Cannon came down the stairs looking murderous proving exactly what we suspected.

"What the fuck is wrong with you? Why did you do that?" Cannon demanded of Lisha who widened her eyes and attempted to look innocent.

"I don't know what you are talking about but if your little witch is insecure that's not my fault. You know that I would be a better wife," she said pouting at him. "Do you even know if she's actually having your child? That bodyguard of hers seems rather attached."

"This is your final warning Lisha, stay the fuck away from my wife. Stay out of our business and quit playing your childish games. I don't want you, I love my wife," Cannon told her.

"You feel bad for her, you don't love her, you rescued her so you feel responsible that's all it is. We make sense, you and her don't," Lisha said because she didn't know when to quit.

"Like I said this is your last warning, your uncles will just have to be without an heir."

"I'm a woman you wouldn't hurt me," she said and he laughed,

"That is an entirely human thing to say, you are a full blood are you not? Male or female we would be on equal footing, so don't think that would save you," he informed her.

"We have a history, you really won't consider that? I've known you way longer than that little witch."

"Sure we have a history but you are so forgettable that if you didn't keep inserting yourself in my life I would never notice if you were gone," he said. That had her staring at him all wide eyed and open mouthed in shock because apparently it was only now that she was starting to understand.

"Do stop being so desperate, it's embarrassing to watch this," Ethel said, shaking her head. "Boy, when are we leaving? I would like to get back and assess the situation with my coven."

"Soon, everybody has been relocated to a nearby property until we can get everything sorted. Also, my father wants to hold the first official meeting of the new council to discuss what to do about the Lohans and the humans. Two humans have been captured and any of the survivors of that coven are being detained. There is a lot of attention between law enforcement, government agencies and the media, this did not go unnoticed. When we left, they were still searching the wreckage to see if anyone was still trapped inside," he said.

"You informed my coven we are here?" She asked and he nodded. Since no one was paying her any attention Lisha stomped off into the next room to pout and plot no doubt.

"They were relieved they thought you had gone up to bed already when it happened. Good thing you made that detour to talk to Freddie," he replied.

"Yes, it is," she said, sounding thoughtful.

"Are the girls awake?" I asked him and he sighed before nodding.

"My wife isn't happy with me right now but she's getting ready with Ollie," he said.

My poor boy looked so tired, he had been working so hard throughout this whole thing while trying to maintain his marriage. Only for some upstart girl to try to ruin things for him. Fredericka was a sensitive girl and was deeply uncertain about her marriage. The therapist I sent them to suggested she has abandonment and identity issues stemming from her being a hybrid and an orphan. Along with the lingering trauma and possibly some depression. No doubt growing up in that coven also did some damage.

Some might suggest what was said between her and the therapist was confidential and not for me to know. Those people don't have a Family to manage where every individual was an important part of the whole. I needed to know what was going on so I could help her, we were responsible for her. This was what a mother would do and well my children always said we lacked boundaries. It wasn't that I didn't understand them, there was just a time and a place for boundaries.

When it came to Fredericka's issues it likely didn't help that Hunt had made it clear to her that her only freedom came from marrying Cannon. But I knew my husband there was only one choice he would have accepted and she made the right one. I would not have let him lock her away, that would be unnecessarily cruel. Hunt was many things, but he wouldn't do something like that. And I wouldn't let him, which he very well knew. The reason he gave her options was so that she could feel like she made the choice. If we truly didn't care about her then he would have eliminated the problem.

Hearing Cannon tell his wife he loved her had surprised me. I hadn't realized just how deeply he felt for her. Sure, they had grown close and seemed incapable of keeping their hands to themselves, but this was unexpected. My boy was in love, that he said it first was not a surprise. Though our children didn't think love existed between us I knew my husband loved me. We just didn't need to express it the way the young did. The first time he expressed his feelings I remember just staring at him. People in arranged marriages can find love, I knew that, but I hadn't expected it. Harrington men loved hard and with devotion when they chose to love.

Fredericka didn't know it, but I could relate to what happened when she had to separate from Cannon. When the humans came invading our home Hunt locked me away in the vault. We always fought together and to this day I wonder if I could have made a difference. I was pregnant at the time; I had a difficult go with our son. He wanted me to be safe and take care of our children. When he was taken, I was the sole custodian of The Family. A family that had been ripped apart and nearly destroyed.

While he was gone, I had to take charge and get things back on track. The Harringtons lasted all these years and sacrificed so much to get to where they were, I could not fail. Hunt was a different man when he came home, and I was changed too. Carrying the weight of The Family alone was not easy, it wasn't just a metaphorical thing. But I refused to let anyone take his place, I knew he would come back to me. And he did but it took years before he came back to himself, though some parts were lost in the process. I never wanted my children to know the pain of what we went through. That my son would publicly say that he loved his wife, it felt like we did at least accomplish that.

"Whatever you did, you will fix it," I told him and he just nodded. "It is ok to love her, you know?"

"Is it?" He asked looking up the stairs while absently rubbing a hand over his heart.

"If it wasn't love it wouldn't hurt so much," Ethel commented. "Groveling usually works if that helps."

"Yeah," he said as Fredericka and Oleander came down. His gaze caught his wife's but she looked away from him. This was one thing I couldn't fix for them; they had to work it out on their own.

What came next for the rest of us I did not know, we were in uncharted waters. But I trusted my husband to steer us through it all. This was the type of thing he excelled at and he had proven his point. It was still a shame we had to lose the hotel to do it.

Chapter 33

Freddie

Somehow, I knew we weren't going to make it home. I thought I was being paranoid because of my fight with Cannon. But no, I felt it in my very soul as soon as we got on the road. And I might have said something even if I sounded crazy, I just never got the chance. Not before the screech of tires and crunch of metal and the world turning upside down. I had never been in a car crash before it was horrifying as the car rolled over again and again. How do you brace for anything when everything is being thrown around? When we stopped rolling, we were upside down. Ollie was beside me and she was my first thought, it seemed I was nothing but bad luck for my sister.

"Fuck," Cannon groaned from the other side of Ollie. "Everybody alive?" He asked and groans came from the front where Desmond and Lee were.

"Freddie?" Ollie asked, reaching for my hand, I gave her a reassuring squeeze.

Cannon was the first to get moving; he dropped from his seat onto the ceiling and kicked the door out. He crawled out and stood before coming around to my side and literally yanked the door off its hinges. I knew vampires were strong, but I never actually saw just how strong my husband was. Without a word he climbed in and was beneath me, his hand coming to my cheek. Desmond was attempting to kick the windshield out. The glass in these cars was not made to be broken; it could stand up to weapon and magical attack. But it seemed somehow, he knew just how to break it, maybe it wasn't made to stand up to vampires. His side of the car had been hit so getting out the door wasn't a possibility.

"Are you ok?" He asked like it was the most important thing in the world.

"Define ok," I replied and he looked relieved.

"I'm going to help you get out, ok? Then I'll help Ollie," he said and I nodded. Maneuvering around until he was on his back he reached up to help me.

My seatbelt was locked tight and refused to let go when he pushed the release. Unfazed by this he ripped the belt apart and caught me when I fell forward. Before I could move someone dragged Cannon out of the car by his legs. It was not Desmond who was still trying to free himself or Lee who was still inside the car. There were other people outside, I could hear footsteps. Desmond worked harder at getting himself free and with a conflicted look back at me Lee disappeared completely. Silently I used magic to free Ollie and she came down in a crouch beside me.

"Stay inside," Desmond told us before he finally succeeded in getting out.

"What's going on?" Ollie asked as we both peeked our heads out to see what we could see.

"Those are vampires," I said in surprise. Why would vampires attack us?

There were a bunch of vampires in this wooded area where we found ourselves. Cannon was fighting them; he was magnificent and brutally efficient. Was it a vampire thing that this kind of turned me on? Probably, but it was so not the time or place. Desmond and Lee were both out there fighting keeping the vampires away from us. From what I could tell there had to be at least a dozen vampires. They all seemed to have the paler skin of turned vampires, but they didn't typically come out during the day.

Looking up at the overcast sky I had to wonder but it wasn't too important now. Not when the guys were fighting and we were hiding in the car. I was not a fighter by any stretch of imagination, in fact obviously Belinda had been right that I did need to learn self-defense. Ollie had her years of lessons in various forms of martial arts. Not that it would help against fully grown vampires.

"Should we call someone?" Ollie asked and I shrugged, who could we call?

"The van didn't go off the road from what I could tell so the others know we are down here. I honestly don't even know who to call about this and Harringtons prefer to handle things themselves," I replied.

In the blink of an eye everything can change, I knew that better than anyone. My life changed completely and irreversibly in a moment like that. So maybe that's why I knew it was coming right before it did. I barely had time to scream his name before it happened. Then time seemed to just stop. One of the vampires had a gun and he shot Cannon. Most nonhumans didn't handle such weapons; they saw guns as human weapons. If they were going to fight with weapons it was with swords and knives and old school type things. But this vampire had a gun which typically wasn't something to be overly concerned about because nonhumans healed fast.

Something in my heart told me it wouldn't be like that this time. Anything could die when you pierced their heart. Though Cannon was surprised by the shot he didn't stop moving, he took the vampire with the gun down snapping his neck. The next shot came from behind, Lee handled that one but one more vampire got a shot off because apparently a few of them had guns. Cannon grabbed that one by the throat crushing it and his vertebrae at the same time. Then he fell and I just reacted, I couldn't think even though Ollie tried to grab me. I crawled out from the car not caring about the broken glass and ran to him. Three shots to the heart, nobody could survive that.

"Cannon," I said, falling to my knees beside him.

"Freddie," he said, his hand reaching up to my cheek before it fell down limp and his eyes closed. He wasn't breathing, I knew this, I couldn't hear him drawing a single breath.

"No Cannon you can't leave me," I told him even though I knew it didn't matter. He couldn't hear me because he was gone. I hugged him to me not caring about the blood, some of it was his most of it was not.

There was nothing I could do, nothing anybody could do. We never discussed rising; he could come back to me unless he didn't want that. Most vampires didn't seem to want to rise again. Belinda would know what his wishes were, but I couldn't bring myself to ask her. It was so stupid I never told him I loved him. Whatever happened with Lisha didn't matter anymore, Cannon was gone. How was I supposed to accept this? My heart felt like it was carved out of my chest with a dull knife. Breathing was hard, like I couldn't get enough air in my lungs. Tears streamed down my face, I hated it, it seemed like I was always crying lately.

"We have to go," Lee said at some point, he came over to me.

"I can't leave him," I said, not really caring about anything else in that moment.

"I promise we will come back for him but right now we need to go, he would want us to protect you," he said and sure it made sense logically. Too bad I wasn't in the mood for logic right now.

"We have to get you and your sister out of here," he tried again. He even put his hand on my shoulder, it wasn't something he had ever done before, he never touched me.

"No," I said and he pulled his hand back. Then a thought occurred to me, but it was crazy, wasn't it? "Lee, are they all dead?" I asked, finally looking up from Cannon. The silence had indicated that the fight was over, and I noticed Desmond was standing with Ollie.

"No," Desmond answered, his voice was devoid of all emotion in a way that spoke volumes. Desmond had been with Cannon for years, they were friends.

"Bring me one of them," I said and Lee actually gasped but Desmond said nothing, just did as I asked.

"Freddie, what are you going to do?" Ollie asked, sounding rather terrified at this point, my poor sister was going to need so much therapy.

"Cannon can't die, I don't accept that," was all I said.

"Oh gods, what happened?" Someone asked and I guessed it was Lisha who sounded genuinely shocked by finding us all here. "Is Cannon… oh gods is he dead? What the fuck?"

"Here," Desmond said, throwing an alive but unconscious vampire at the ground beside me. Lee was immediately on alert ready in case the vampire woke up and attacked.

Elements, Elder Rosewood said it was an element, and I knew how to work with the elements. So, I could do this right? I didn't have a tutor for this, but I didn't before either, I just learned by doing. If I did nothing, then Cannon was… no I had to do this. Ignoring everything going on around me, I concentrated on finding the right way to connect with this element. There was a buzz I could feel when I held my hand over the vampire's body. Letting instinct guide me I pulled the energy I could feel inside with a turn of my wrist.

It was much more dramatic than the last time as his body was thrashing and Desmond quickly held him down. You didn't always see magic; it was typically an invisible force like the air. There was a white light of energy that I was pulling from this stranger and into myself. After I pulled everything from him, I felt powerful as his body fell limp. Desmond took a step back clearly unnerved but I wasn't focused on him. Placing both my hands on Cannon's chest I willed the new energy inside me into him.

I'm fairly certain that no elemental worked elements like this. Magic worked through intention, so I just concentrated on Cannon being alive and whole. In a rush it left me and his body jolted as I fell back and Lee caught me. Nobody spoke or even breathed as we all waited. It seemed to take forever but I could hear his heart start to beat again, and he coughed as his lungs came back online. Desmond was the one to rip Cannon's bloody shirt open and we watched as the bullets reversed course coming out of him. It was the freakiest thing I ever saw in my life.

"What the fuck did she just do?! What is she?!" Lisha yelled, breaking the silence as she pointed at me like I was some kind of monster.

"Do shut up," Belinda told her. At some point when I was distracted others had come to join us.

"I knew something was wrong with her and you knew it too! Dallas North and the Smiths were right! What have you been harboring? Now it makes sense why you people would keep a half vampire," Lisha went on since she never knew when to stop.

"For someone so desperate to marry my son you seem to fail to notice that she just saved his life," Belinda said.

The problem with magic was that everything came at a price, especially when you did bigger magic. Small things like fixing a broken vase or doing chores were small magic, you didn't have to sacrifice more than your own energy for it. What I just did, however I did it, wasn't small magic by any stretch of imagination. So, I wasn't exactly surprised when I felt the pain. It started out like I had been punched in the stomach. But the pain only got worse, and it became rather clear what I was giving up to save Cannon's life.

"No, no, no," I said, clutching my stomach through the pain. It seemed I could have Cannon, but I could not have our baby. At no point did I even stop to consider, now it was too late.

"Magic always takes its due," Josiah, one of Ethel's grandsons said solemnly.

"What does that... oh no," Belinda gasped.

"Desmond," Lee said and he got up from the ground moving fast. "If you can save your husband then you can save your baby."

"W-what?" I asked, a bit confused for a moment until Desmond brought another unconscious vampire to me.

This time it required less effort to pull from this vampire, I tried not to think about the fact that I just killed two people. Not when I was taking the energy from his life, his soul, into me silently praying that this could work. I didn't actually know how any of this worked or what it could cost me for trying. But I had to try. Magic filled me and I concentrated on my intention, shaping magic was what witches did everyday. I wasn't exactly far along in this pregnancy, but I had to try to save my baby. My body felt cold as I took it all in, essentially bleeding him dry sucking the soul out of him. When I was done, I fell back against Lee again, I had no idea if that worked or not. The pain was gone though I had no way of knowing what that meant.

"We need to get them both to the hospital," Belinda said, taking charge. Lee stood lifting me up into his arms and Desmond put Cannon over his shoulder. Belinda wrapped an arm around Ollie guiding her back the way they had come.

"Wait until everybody finds out about this! She really is some kind of weapon or monster sucking the life out of people like that. Or does it just work on vampires? Have you been influencing us this whole time somehow?"

"If someone was influencing you then don't you think they would make you shut up about your weird obsession with Cannon?" Ollie asked her, sounding tired and annoyed.

"Nobody asked you little witch, hell for all I know you have some freaky ass ability too and that's why they brought you here! Witches are responsible for what happened last night and isn't that your coven? All of you need to be investigated and there's no way in hell that anybody will follow Hunt fucking Harrington after this. Your Family is done and over," Lisha said. Truly the woman never knew when to shut her mouth.

Belinda left Ollie's side moving so fast my eyes couldn't track it and came up behind Lisha grabbed her head and snapped her neck. Everything that people said about her came rushing to my mind. It was always Belinda that you needed to fear, Lisha should have known better. Threatening her family was not something Belinda would take kindly to. Dropping Lisha's body to the ground she returned to my sister's side.

"Mustn't leave any witnesses," she said calmly like she hadn't just murdered a woman right in front of us.

That was apparently the one thing too many for me to handle after everything else. After that I promptly passed out welcoming the darkness.

Hunt

I got the call that my son had died while I stood in the rubble of what was once our first hotel. This particular hotel had been standing for centuries and was a haven during the wars. Now it was gone, it could be rebuilt, the lives sacrificed in this mess couldn't be brought back though. It was all such a waste, and I hated to waste anything. We were betrayed by witches and vampires killed my son. The humans may have destroyed the building with the bombing, but we were worse off than I thought. All this work to protect my family and other nonhumans and what was it all for?

"What happened?" I asked my wife when I found her waiting for me at the hospital. Before she could say a word Fredericka's mother came rushing down the hall. First, she hugged her younger daughter who was sitting in a chair between two of our guards. Then she turned her attention to us.

"Where is she?" Vivian asked, looking to Belinda.

"Both of you come with me," Belinda said with a sigh. We both followed her to a more private waiting area that had a door that would close.

My wife was never rattled; she could keep her nerve in the face of anything. Right now? Now she was visibly distraught but of course she was, our son died. Our son who had it as a non-negotiable in his will that he would not rise again. It was something all vampires had to think about and weigh the risks. Rising might extend your life but at what cost? Because it wasn't something I wanted for myself I couldn't force that on my son. Touch helped so I placed a hand on my wife's shoulder to comfort her. We were not publicly affectionate people but sometimes it didn't matter.

"Where is my daughter?" Vivian asked again, looking understandably rather frazzled. Both of her children had been in this mess; she could have lost everything.

"Both of them are being seen to by the doctors, your husband is with them," Belinda said and the woman nodded.

"What happened?" I asked again, I hadn't gotten many details when she called before.

"We were headed home when this car came out of nowhere ramming the car they were in. I was in the van with Ethel, her grandsons and Lisha Gordon, Ty was driving. Before we could do anything turned vampires attacked us. Once they were taken care of some of us went down to find the others. We got there too late, Cannon was already gone and Fredericka was on the ground with him. Lee tried to get her to leave but she refused of course."

She went on to explain what she saw of the girl taking the soul from another vampire and using it to bring Cannon back to life. The more she told us the more I regretted taking this girl in. So much trouble for one so young. And it appeared that in addition to losing his life my son nearly lost his child. He still might, who knew with this girl's magic. Hell, that girl didn't even understand her own magic. What if this was only temporary? By the end of her story, she had her hand on my forearm comforting me. Touch was the only thing grounding me at that moment, I was very nearly going to lose control. Nobody wanted that, nothing good would come of it and I had enough problems.

If I was honest with myself, I would have just killed her had I been there. All the times I considered killing her and I knew I would have done it. This wasn't about the summit; this was about *her* and that was why Cannon had to die. Belinda would think things through and consider that she was pregnant with our son's child. Me on the other hand, I wouldn't have given it a second thought. And it would have been the biggest mistake I ever made in my entire life. I knew none of this was in fact her fault but when it came to my children, I wasn't rational. Of course, this girl was the very one who could bring him back. Thank the gods I wasn't there; it would have been such a mess.

"Oh I guess I should mention that I snapped the neck of that irritating Lisha Gordon," Belinda said rather matter-of-factly. Vivian gasped, staring at her, I just shook my head. "I know she is irritating but she is the heir to the Gordons," I pointed out. "She will not rise, Ethel's boys made sure of that. There was a reason, I didn't do it just to shut her up. That girl was insufferable going on and on it was never ending. Unfortunately, she saw way too much and would have told everybody what happened. Anyway, while we were gone Ethel accessed Lisha's phone that she left behind. She was exchanging texts with someone about our location. That wretched girl set us up," Belinda said visibly seething.

"We can deal with that later," I said with a sigh. There would be issues because of that but now wasn't the time to worry over it. What was done was done and had that girl risen I would have killed her anyway. The havoc she would have caused would be catastrophic.

"Freddie and Cannon are both ok though?" Vivian asked, she wasn't so good at hiding her emotions.

"They were doing some tests last I heard," Belinda said. "Ahh here she comes now."

There were few doctors we would trust with caring for our son and his rather unusual wife. Doctor Georgia Remington was one of our Family doctors and was aware of Fredericka's unusual ability. Vampire healers were rare, and I was wise enough to bring this one into the fold. She had been one of those that I had called in to examine the girl when we first learned of her. Doctor Remington joined us in the waiting room, closing the door behind her. The look on her usually inscrutable face was an indication that something was off. But she held up her hands before anything could be said.

"Both of them are fine and in stable condition though I have no idea what the long term ramifications of all this is. I've never seen anything like this," Dr. Remington told us.

"Have you ever heard the term death witch?" I asked her but also looked at Vivian.

"Ethel Rosewood informed us that's what she thinks Fredericka is not a necromancer," Belinda added. Of course, she would have had time to chat with the old witch while they were at the safe house.

"Maybe," the doctor said, then we all looked to Vivian who just sat down.

"She never told me," she shook her head.

"To be fair a lot has been happening and Ethel only approached her a week or so ago now," Belinda offered.

"Ethel also told her not to share that information with anyone, especially not us vampires," I added. "Though I imagine Cannon would know since she is his wife." Did I blame the girl for keeping secrets? No, not when those secrets were far worse than what we actually knew about her and twice as dangerous.

"What exactly did she do out there?" Vivian asked and I had the feeling she knew a lot more than we had given her credit for.

"Literally sucked the life out of a living vampire and I guess gave it to Cannon to bring him back," Belinda answered. "I don't know if doing so is what caused a problem with her pregnancy or not but she was in distress and in pain. Lee suggested that she use another so Desmond grabbed one of the last vampires still alive and she took his life."

"You know something of death witches," I stated because obviously the woman did.

"Yes, my degree is actually in obscure magic and magical history. So, I've read about things that most people have never heard of. I had wondered if somehow, she might be, but the tests were negative," Vivian said.

"Which tests? There's a test for this?" Dr. Remington asked and she shook her head.

"No but they test for demigod, they have to since those of god status do tend to spread their seed carelessly."

"Demigod?" My wife asked, staring at her as she nodded again. "Why would that be a factor?"

"A death witch is the product of a witch and a death god. Well not just witches, warlocks or whatever too. You said that you were told what it is."

"It appears that Ethel saw fit to leave some things out," I said clenching my jaw. As if on cue the witch herself breezed into the room uninvited as always.

"That wasn't relevant information," Ethel said, proving that she had been listening somehow. "Go on, girl, tell them what you know."

"Yes ma'am," Vivian said of course she was respectful of an elder witch. "A death witch is a demigod, which Freddie is not. There have been too many tests and that would have shown. However, I don't have information on what the children of a death witch are. So, it is very likely that her birth mother is in fact a death witch."

"Why do you assume the mother is the witch?" I asked out of curiosity, aware I was in a room of females.

"If there were males you would have heard 'death warlock 'bandied around because men can't possibly keep anything secret. Besides that, females create life, which a death witch does," Ethel said.

"Right, a death witch can use a soul as her element... I wonder if that's why she can manipulate other elements?" Vivian said more to herself as a thought seemed to occur to her.

"That isn't in her records," the doctor said.

"Because it's not an elemental ability, she can't produce an elements; she can just use what's already in front of her. We were told it was best not to have that in her records as it's an unusual ability," Vivian answered.

"How long has she been able to do this?" Ethel asked, apparently, I had lost control of this whole situation.

"Um, since she was young, she had a few tutors help her to learn proper technique. The witches in the coven didn't like it, but we would never ask her to hide part of herself. I think I should have known what they would do, she was too powerful too and too dedicated a student," Vivian sighed. "Anyway, like a witch can use the element of magic to create things, a death witch uses souls. They can give life but also take it. And um they consume them, at least some of them do from what I recall."

"Nothing with this girl can ever be easy, can it?" I asked aloud to no one in particular, deciding to just take a seat.

Did I not already have enough to deal with? Between last night's fiasco and this girl, I might have reached my limit. Somebody wanted to claim her, a lot of planning went into this. So, it wasn't over, they would no doubt try again. My hotel needed to be rebuilt, the council needed to meet, witches needed to be interrogated and executed. Oh, and I needed to inform the Gordons that they no longer had an heir. So much to do, but if I was honest all I wanted to do was actually see my son. I needed to see for myself that he still lived. That he wasn't altered by whatever that girl did to him.

My instincts never failed me before and again they were right. This girl who looked so innocent was anything but, she was dangerous. Not just to us, potentially she was a danger to everyone. It made sense why there were no others like her, anyone who found out would seek to exterminate them. Keeping someone like that alive was way too dangerous. And yet I was required to not only keep her alive but also safe.

"Where did this girl come from? Who in their right mind would even create such a creature? If not to use as a weapon but obviously that's not what happened. Even I look at her and see her as an innocent, and I know what she did to the vampire who attacked her. The other vampires remark that she doesn't smell like a vampire because of her lack of predatory instincts. She's essentially a vampire two times over as she consumes souls. A literal energy vampire," I laughed a humorless laugh. "What are we supposed to do with her now? What vampire was so reckless as to procreate with a witch that eats souls?"

Really, I was asking myself the question more not the bleeding heart women in the room. Both mothers, the elder witch and the doctor all looked at me like I threatened to kill her. Who the hell even knew if she could die or would stay dead. I wasn't going to point out that the only souls that girl had taken so far were all vampires. A vampire woke this up in her and if he wasn't dead, I would torture him slowly for giving me this problem. Now a vampire who consumed the souls of other vampires was giving my son a child. Well, there were once vampires that only preyed on other vampires, so it wasn't surprising, just inconvenient.

"Could one of her birth parents be trying to find her?" Dr. Remington asked, breaking the silence.

"No," Belinda answered. "If it was a parent all they would need to do is make themselves known. Nobody has been hiding her and there's no reason to keep her from a parent. In fact, they would know very well that we don't know much about what she is. Offering assistance in developing her abilities would make sense as a way to get close to her. This is something else, someone must know enough to want her."

"Tracing the girl's origins is important as I have said," Ethel said. "Yes, boy, you have a lot on your plate right now but you can manage it. I will find the witch; you only have to find the vampire. If either still lives they might shed some light on all of this. Though I still feel that she was made with reason, she makes an excellent weapon."

"Do you think it was humans? It wouldn't surprise me if that was how she came to be. They have committed many great atrocities against us, and breeding programs have been found all over the world," the doctor said.

"Your hotel, does it still have the policy for foundlings?" Ethel asked because of course she did.

"Yes, so what you are suggesting is that she was meant to go to witches. We would of course have taken her in, people even now will surrender their children at the hotel," Belinda said.

An old policy but a necessary one. Our hotel was always a place where a vampire child could be left no questions asked. We found homes for the children and later in life offered employment. Many people did not want to raise a vampire child; some just weren't capable. And some just didn't want a child. More than once a non-vampire was left behind, and we made the necessary arrangements for the child. Better this option than to allow the children to come to harm. Fredericka was left at an orphanage run by witches, somewhere a vampire would not find her. If not for her attack the girl would never have had any meaningful contact with vampires.

"Someone is watching," I said and all their attention snapped to me. "How else would they know to contact the Gordon girl? They had to have been in the hotel to know that she didn't go home. The witches didn't send vampires after her and the Smiths have all been detained. Though they make a good scapegoat, with their history of turning vampires. Even if this started with humans there were not humans inside the hotel. None of the other vampire Families would have so many turned vampires. They certainly wouldn't use vampire bullets, at least I wouldn't think so. The Gordons have been acting weirdly, but they wouldn't have put their heir in a situation that could get her killed. And they wanted her married to Cannon; killing him does not solve that."

Normally I wouldn't speak so candidly in mixed company, but these were strange times. These were all people that had a vested interest in the wellbeing of my son's wife. Who for all her trouble saved his life. Couldn't kill her, had to keep her and who knew what her child would be at this point. It would be nice if sometimes all this shit was somebody else's problem.

Unfortunately, that wasn't how my mother and grandmother raised me. No, they raised me to take charge and be a leader. And that was what I would do. But first before I did anything else I had to see my son. Needed to hear his heart beating and hear him draw breath, the rest I would figure out later.

Cannon

Death was something we all had to face eventually, everything that lived had to die. It's said that our time is written into the fabric of the universe. We aren't meant to know when it will happen, but we all came with an expiration date. I had to wonder what it meant for me to still be alive? Did the universe anticipate this or was I living beyond my time? What would happen if you were meant to die but were not in fact dead?

Even now when we know so much about magic death is still a mystery. You only find out what's next when you get there. Nothing so interesting happened to me, it was like I lost consciousness and then woke up later. But I knew in that moment that I was dying and that I had met my end. Nobody could have anticipated what happened instead of me finding my way into the afterlife.

In the last moments of my life my biggest regret was how things were between me and my wife. My eyes were on hers as I laid on the ground dying, I wanted to tell her I was sorry and to run. She came to me in tears, and I hated that this was how things had to end. When a vampire died it was possible to rise again, especially in a bloodline like mine. However, I wouldn't be the same as I was, the few Harringtons who did so came back different. Not exactly turned vampire different but close enough.

Death took a piece of them as its price for rising. That wasn't what I wanted, I didn't want to come back and care less about my wife and family and everything, that was how it generally went. Sometimes the risen weren't safe to be around, not a good thing for someone who was going to be a father. Though apparently, I almost lost that too. Had it been a week or less since we found out we were having a baby? I couldn't remember anymore time had been a mess the past few months.

"I'm sorry," I told my wife when we were finally alone. Both of us were laying together in a hospital bed because she hadn't wanted to let me go. Not that I wanted to be away from her either.

"Ok," was all she said. I was pretty sure she was still in shock by everything that happened.

"We are going to be fine, our baby will be fine," I assured her. At least that was what the doctors said, one of them being her father helped.

"Maybe I shouldn't have done it," she said, the pain in her voice rather obvious. "I didn't know I could do any of that."

"I know, but I'm glad you did," I said and she finally looked at me. "Freddie, I really am sorry about everything earlier. When I said nothing happened, I meant it but there was a moment where I considered it. Not because I wanted her I was just not in my right mind at the time. Instead of getting angry and defensive I should have made that clear to you. I was ashamed of myself for even thinking it. Don't ever think that I don't love you and that I want anyone besides you. Hell, I wouldn't even be here if it weren't for you."

My wife literally brought me back from death and it was still hard to wrap my mind around. Obviously, I didn't really see what she did, I just heard about it after. She hadn't said much since we came here, most of the story I heard from Ollie. Who was the one person paying close attention to everything going on around her. That poor kid was likely traumatized having witnessed all that she had in the past 24 hours. Surviving a building collapse, a car wreck and a vampire attack, it was a lot. And there was witnessing her mother's former friend die a horrible death in the middle of a huge betrayal. Though at least from what Desmond said she had at least been tucked away and safe during the fighting.

"I wasn't really sure about this whole having a baby thing. I think I never fully processed it and so much has happened since that night. But I was losing you and I was losing this baby and I don't know I just reacted," Freddie finally said. "Cannon I do love you I've known that for a while I just didn't want to tell you. It felt like too much like I gave you everything else and I could never escape if I gave you this too. That's stupid, right? They are just words; I was too afraid to say them. And then I realized that I might never get to tell you."

"It's ok I think I get it," I said, pulling her closer. "Usually I'm better at staying alive, vampires typically think using guns is beneath them. And those fucking bullets are rare, I was just surprised."

"Even if it was a regular gun they shot you in the heart," she pointed out.

"It wouldn't have necessarily killed me, I could probably have survived," I said. Though I wasn't so sure about that anymore, getting shot in the heart was very unpleasant. The bullets I had been shot with were specially made just for vampires. They were outlawed after the wars but unsurprisingly they still existed if you looked hard enough. Those bullets also kept a vampire from rising if you didn't get them out fast enough.

"I don't know if I can do this anymore," she whispered. She buried her face against me, and I just held her while she cried.

The last 24 hours had been a lot to deal with for anybody. For us though they were especially terrible and I didn't know how to fix that. My wife had to live with having watched me die. Even though I was in fact alive, thanks to her, she still experienced it. Eight months ago, she wouldn't have ever imagined being put in this type of situation. This wasn't about us and our messy relationship; it was about everything. We were supposed to protect her and make her life easier and instead the opposite was true. She faced multiple attacks and had to fear for her own life as well as her sister's and mine, it was way too much.

If I could go back and change things I would have only to make things easier for her. If we had never interfered in her life everything would be different. If vampires left her alone, she might have met someone else, someone safe who could have given her a normal life. If only if only if only, except I was selfish enough to want to keep her. She was *mine*; I did want better for her, I wanted the best for her. Why couldn't that be me? Before the summit, things were good between us, at least I thought they were. I hadn't known then how afraid she was, feeling like she was living with us on borrowed time. So, what was I supposed to do now? How did I make my wife feel safe when it seemed damn near impossible? Especially since I knew after what she just did things weren't going to get any easier.

"I know," was all I said while I laid there holding her. I hated seeing her cry, it ripped my heart apart more with every tear.

"Can we go home? I don't want to be here," she whispered.

"Pretty sure they want us to stay," I replied and I knew it wasn't the right answer.

"Please Cannon I can't stay here I don't want to be here," she said sounding panicked. Her heartbeat became erratic, making an alarm sound.

"Freddie, I'm not going to leave you ok? But you have to calm down otherwise they really aren't going to let us leave," I said though I doubt I helped at all. Her rising anxiety was triggering in me the need to protect her though I couldn't really protect her from herself.

"What's going on?" Her father asked when he came into the room.

"I don't want to be here," Freddie said. Her breathing became erratic to join her fast-beating heart, she was also shaking.

"Sweetheart, you need to stay calm, this isn't good for you or the baby," Bernie said.

"I feel like I can't breathe in here."

"You are having a panic attack," he told her. "It happens when your body perceives a threat real or imagined and kicks your fight or flight response in. What you need to do is slow your breathing, breathe in and out like this." He demonstrated and she followed him calming considerably.

At least until the door opened again and my father stood in the doorway. His presence only served to make her breathing much worse. I could guess why, what must she think he was going to do now? Noticing that his presence didn't help anything he disappeared from the doorway and Doctor

Remington came back in. It took some time but eventually Freddie was calm and she fell asleep in my arms.

Sleep wasn't very appealing at the moment; it was hard not to wonder if I would wake up again. As far as I could tell I didn't feel any different than I did before. Everything seemed the same, but was *I* the same? There was no one who could answer that question because they didn't know either. All the medical tests suggested I was fine like nothing had happened. All of the testing done on both of us showed no abnormalities, which was weird. Magic, apparently, didn't always leave behind evidence of its use, at least that's what the doctor said.

Looking over, I saw my father in the doorway again. Reluctantly I carefully left the bed making sure not to wake my wife. I stepped into the hall and nodded to Lee who passed me and went inside. Of course he was there, he was always there. Vivian, Bernie and Ollie had gone back to the house with my mother but would no doubt be back. If it wasn't for her worry over leaving the children Lucy would have come but I told her not to. Freddie didn't really need a bunch of visitors right now; she needed peace and quiet. And yeah, I knew my sister wanted to see me too I was just focused on my wife.

"I'm glad you are alive," was the first thing my father said to me, clapping me on the shoulder.

The man was not given to emotions or public displays of affection. If he did something like hug me I would know that none of this is real. I knew he loved us; he just would never say it. Honestly, I wasn't even sure he ever told my mother he loved her, or if he did at all. They had been together a long time, since before the world changed. I have wondered on occasion if he was always such a stoic serious man.

"Yes because of my wife," I said and he nodded.

"More about her has come to light after what she did to save you," he said. "Between everything that has happened with the summit, the witches and the humans and now whatever this mess is I'm at a loss for what to do."

"My wife will not be punished for what she did," I told him. "Leave her be, she's been through enough. I don't care what you think about what she can or cannot do and I don't care what she is. I will not let anyone, even you, hurt her or try to lock her up. I would rather see you dead than let you hurt her."

I held his gaze as I said something I never imagined saying in my life. He was taken aback by this naturally; I had always been his loyal son. Things had changed probably from the moment Freddie came into the picture even if I didn't know it at the time. It wasn't just because she literally saved my life, no it was more than that. My father didn't expect me to fall in love with her because such a thing just wouldn't have occurred to him. So, he never could have fathomed that my loyalty would be to her over him. Would I kill my father and assume control of our Family for her? Yes, I would and that truth should have shocked me but somehow it didn't.

"From the moment I laid eyes on that girl I knew she was trouble," he said, shaking his head. "Cannon I am not trying to take her from you, I never really was. If I didn't want her in this family, then she wouldn't be. Once I gave her to you, I considered the matter closed despite what I may have led you to believe. The girl is a Harrington; we always protect our own. She's proven herself more times than necessary, I'm just sorry it cost her so much to do it. Really though, what kind of person would I be to punish her for bringing you back to us?"

"I'm scared," I admitted sitting down with a heavy sigh. This was not something I would typically admit to but these were strange times.

"The hospital is secure and we will take extra precautions when you bring her home. Nothing will happen to her, you have my word on that," he assured me. "Being responsible for another person isn't easy, especially when that person is vulnerable. Once your child is born you will learn what it truly means to be afraid and to have someone depending on you. Everything you do and every choice you make becomes about these people that depend on you for everything. I've done everything I have all these years to make sure this world was safe for my children and grandchildren and obviously the work is ongoing. It's not easy, but you do what you have to for your family."

This conversation was as heartfelt as I think we had ever gotten. I respected and admired my father; I wasn't sure I could ever live up to the things he accomplished. Well not just him my mother too, they were really a force to be reckoned with. I was starting to understand my parents better since acquiring a wife. When you had someone of your own to take care of it was terrifying. Especially when a series of fucked up events happened over a short period of time. Where we went from here, I didn't know, likely nobody did not even my parents who planned for everything. Nobody could have ever planned for Freddie.

"I'm trying, it just seems like the universe is hellbent on making this as difficult as possible."

"Indeed, but you have been given a second chance, something most people are never given. Do not waste it," he said and I nodded.

"I have to get back, Freddie is awake again," I said with a sigh. I had hoped she would sleep longer but the hospital seemed to really unsettle her. The why of it I didn't know, I mean her father was a doctor.

"You sense that?" My father asked in what would be a casual tone coming from anybody else.

"Yeah," I said with a shrug on my way out the door. Usually, I could just sense when she was near and that could be blamed on our multiple blood exchanges. This, though, was new but all of my senses were hyper focused on her at the moment.

Heading back into the room I found Freddie awake in the bed with Lee sitting beside her. That was far more familiar than he had ever behaved before but under the circumstances I chose to ignore it. The man refused to leave even to sleep, he was very dedicated to keeping my wife safe so how could I complain? He had also done everything he could to keep her sister safe. I didn't know that much about Lee, but I knew through his actions that he was very loyal. As soon as I came in Lee rose and left without a word, the guy definitely deserved a raise.

"Where were you?" Freddie asked me when I came back to the bed.

"Just stepped out for a moment, you should be resting, not worrying," I told her.

"I watched you die," she replied and I couldn't really argue with that now could I? Instead, I pulled her into my arms where she belonged.

"I'm not going anywhere," I assured her. "I have everything in the world to live for and I have since the day I met you. Don't worry about anything, I'm going to take care of you."

"Yes I know it's just—" she froze, turning to the door seeing my father again. Honestly, I was so focused on her that I hadn't even noticed that he followed me. Until she started to panic again but he held up his hands in a placating gesture.

"Fredericka, please, I mean you no harm, you have nothing to worry about from me," he said, his tone almost gentle. "What you did was... I don't have words to express how grateful I am. You need to understand that you are part of this family. No matter what happens we will be here for you."

"Ok," Freddie said, calming a little but I could tell she didn't actually trust him. It was in fact a miracle she trusted me at all, especially when I was constantly failing her.

"Rest now, I will make sure that you both return home safely," he assured her. After holding her gaze until she nodded, he left the room, closing the door behind him.

"He's worried," I said when we were alone. "Family is everything to him and I know he feels like he owes you a great debt. It's our job to protect you but you haven't been protected, and you saved my life, to him it's something he can never repay."

"Are you sure he isn't just keeping me alive because I'm having your baby? I mean that's all that would matter to him, right? That's my value," she said with a hint of bitterness.

"My father is a complicated man but that is not how he sees you. You are worth far more than your ability to have children. Don't take everything with my parents at face value. They are both old and from another time and had a lot of difficulties in their lives. Both of them see you as part of this family and to them that's all that matters."

"I'm afraid to close my eyes because what if I open them and you aren't here? What if this is just some dream my mind made up to help me cope with losing you? And I know you are trying to help and that they are trying but I just need to get out of here," she said the desperation in her tone was worrying.

"Ok, if that's what you need then I'll make it happen," I promised, pulling her tightly against me.

There were obviously perks to being part of this Family and I was going to need all the privileges I could to make this happen. The quickest way to get anything done was to let my parents handle it so I did. I sent them both a text saying that Freddie didn't feel comfortable here and wanted to go back home. Within the hour we were discharged and in a car headed back home. Where her doctor father would see to her care. An army of guards escorted us, but we made it back home without incident.

Belinda

I would kill anyone who threatened my family, that was just a mother's job. Did I feel the slightest bit of remorse for killing that tedious girl? No, Lisha Gordon was a liability and protecting my family was most important. Especially knowing that she had taken part in orchestrating that ambush. She was a fool who thought these people only meant to take our Fredericka away. It never even occurred to her that they would kill Cannon to do so. She was blinded by her ambition and that made her a problem. So, I solved it and the Gordons would just have to get over it.

My son died and his wife almost lost their baby; I couldn't even muster up a tiny bit of remorse for what I had done. Though my boy and his wife were both alive, physically well and back home, I still had to worry for them. Somebody had to consider the long-term ramifications of what Fredericka had done. What kind of child would they have after this? A life barely in existence and it was magically altered in a way that shouldn't have even been possible. I was no expert on magic, but that part seemed rather obvious.

For the rest of my long life, I was going to have nightmares after seeing my son's dead body lying on the ground. It was the first time I ever froze, unsure of what to do. We had arrived just after the fighting had ended. Lisha had run ahead to help, she said, but who knows with her. Bodies and blood on the forest floor amongst the leaves the scent of blood and death in the air. And my son, my baby, dead. I barely heard that girl screaming and saying whatever nonsense she was spewing, not when my son was gone. My son who made it clear that he did not want to rise should he lose his life. For him the risks did not outweigh the benefits, especially after he found himself with a wife. Who he likely never thought to discuss it with. She wasn't a full vampire and wasn't raised by vampires her parents wouldn't have thought to consider such a thing.

Looking at her crying, holding him whatever was left of my heart broke. My son was going to have a child that would never know him that he would never see and that more than anything nearly broke me. Then there was Fredericka pushing aside her grief and fear and doing something extraordinary. As long as I lived, I could never repay the debt that we owed her for bringing Cannon back. Even though it was rather obvious that doing so had put her in the state she was currently in. No doubt he would have rather died than to let her suffer in any way.

"I demand to know what happened!" Eric Gordon said being his usual tedious self with Philip nodding beside him.

"As I've already told you, we were ambushed on our way back. What I can only assume was a gang of rogue turned vampires or Smiths attacked us. It is unfortunate what happened to your niece but there's nothing we could have done," I said with a shrug.

My husband decided it was for the best that we call it collateral damage. I wasn't afraid to admit what I had done, but he thought it would do more harm than good. Right now, we had other things that needed our attention, so I agreed. This was why he handled this aspect of things I was better at killing. After weeks of the summit my patience was nonexistent so it would be a miracle if the Gordons didn't join their niece in death. Truly that whole family was just so tiresome and a waste of time. Before all this I didn't think much of them, now they better hope I didn't find the time to give them my attention.

"How is it that everybody else left there alive but not Lisha?" Philip asked and it was a valid question not that it mattered. None of this mattered, we were humoring them at best.

"Does it occur to you that she knew too much?" Hunt asked and that had them turning their attention to him. "Let's not act like the girl was some innocent, she set things up. My son and his wife and a teenage child were nearly killed. Why?

Because someone told them where to be in order to make this ambush happen and that someone was very clearly Lisha, the proof is on her phone. So, it's unfortunate that she's dead but I'll not be losing any sleep over it, had she lived I would have killed her myself. What kind of person puts a pregnant woman and a child in danger like that? We took great risk in trying to keep Lisha safe at *your* request and how did she repay us? You are lucky that she is dead."

"She wouldn't—" Eric began but Phillip shook his head.

"She would, she wanted to marry Cannon," Phillip admitted, seemingly mostly to himself. "You shouldn't have sent her with him, it was never going to end with a marriage."

"They fought together, I saw them, he saved her and nature nearly took its course," Eric said. Well, that explained why my son was in trouble with his wife, bloodlust. "Why couldn't you just let her marry him? We were willing to accept a 2nd wife position. Yet you would choose a half blood witch with no bloodline?"

"This is boring me, why don't you explain to us why it was so important to marry her to our son? She was your heir, marrying Cannon would make her part of our Family. So would you care to explain that?" I asked, losing what was left of my nonexistent patience.

"That is a very good point, why did you want her in this Family? A treacherous girl who nobody has a kind word to say about. Did you think she could become custodian on my Family? Under no circumstances was that ever going to happen," Hunt said. He too was losing patience with them.

"Also you keep bringing up my son's wife's status, we know what she is. Do you think we were tricked into taking her? We know she has no bloodline and is a half witch, if it doesn't bother us why is it of your concern?"

"We just wanted her to make a good match," Phillip said. There was some awkward shuffling and looks thrown back and forth, they were up to something.

"Go home and lay her to rest, when we find out who else was involved we will let you know. Make no mistake while Lisha was clearly involved, we are aware she was not the ringleader of this attack. Likely she was just an unwitting pawn used for her proximity," I said. It was the kindest thing I could say about that foolish girl.

Eventually they scraped up some brain cells between them and decided to leave. Kami happily showed them out; we wouldn't want them to linger around our home. With the hotel gone we were forced to allow them into our home for that conversation. They did see the proof, and they knew that girl's character or lack of character really. If only I could believe this was the end of trouble from that Family, but I wasn't so naive. Another relative would replace Lisha and life would go on. Hopefully her replacement would be less of a liability. If the next one tried to seduce a member of my family, I was just putting an end to the bloodline.

"Your theory of them seeking a merger fits," Hunt said thoughtfully when we were alone.

"At this point they might as well be on the level of the Smiths," I said in disgust. "When have we ever merged?"

"Never in our history and we will never start."

"Any idea who that girl was communicating with?"

"Nothing yet, whoever is behind this is good at hiding but we are aware now. For now, we let people think it was rogues or Smiths. This isn't the end, they will try to take her again, we need to be prepared," he said with a heavy sigh.

"Do you think Cannon would have gone through with killing you?" I asked because I was curious, I didn't know our son had it in him.

"Yes, I blame you for this, you wanted them to marry," he replied, rolling his eyes.

"How could I have anticipated this? We were not so attached to each other for years," I pointed out.

Our son threatening his father was interesting and unexpected. Young love could be unpredictable and volatile. It had been a long time since anyone in the Harrington Family killed for a position, but it was a perfectly valid way to take over. I loved my husband, but I would stand by our son, and he would expect me to. The fact that challenges like this didn't happen under the matriarchy wasn't the least bit surprising. Only males needed to prove themselves worthy violently. I did not want to lose Hunt; I did everything I could for two and a half centuries to keep us both alive. But sometimes that was life and my boy would be justified if his father did harm to his wife.

Maybe I was going soft, maybe it was that I couldn't stop seeing the look on her face. Our poor girl who unintentionally sacrificed her unborn child for her husband's life. Magical miscarriage reversal notwithstanding she would still carry with her the cost. That wasn't something any mother would forget. Sure, they could have tried again and had a perfect pregnancy, but some scars never faded. If I could have kept her from feeling that kind of loss I would have. Fredericka was a sensitive girl; she wouldn't easily get past this. There was also the matter of not knowing what was going to happen to her magically modified fetus. Nothing was ever easy with this girl but not by her own choosing. What a perfect time for our son to come into the office.

"I heard the Gordons were here," Cannon said, taking a seat in a chair across the desk. We were both sitting behind the desk, upon seeing him I opened the mini blood vault and took out a bottle of blood.

"They were expressing their opinions on what happened to their niece," Hunt said.

"Cannon, dearest, you look awful, here drink this," I said, handing him the bottle.

At first, he looked ready to refuse, and I understood why his wife wasn't feeding so he naturally didn't want to either. There were connections between vampire spouses that nobody ever warned you about; that was the nature of blood exchanges it created bonds. While my children knew this, I doubt they really fully understood it. At least not until they were irrevocably connected to another person. Right now, his instincts had him letting his health slip and letting his concern for his wife take over. What she did to bring him back likely created other bonds between them making the connection much stronger. As I stared him down, Cannon opened the bottle and drank. It didn't surprise me when he stared at me and then the bottle.

"This tastes like Freddie," he said, looking at me with suspicion. Of course, he knew the taste of his wife's blood, he was the only one to ever drink it.

"That's because it is her blood, I have some in storage, for an emergency just like everyone else. As soon as she's awake you need her to drink blood, I'm having your stored blood prepared for her. Good thing I think ahead for any potential situation. You need to keep your strength up she will want to feed from you after so long," I told my son

As the matriarch it was my job to take care of all of us which was why I had stored blood from everyone in The Family. Periodic blood draws were just a part of life here because you never knew what might happen. Only now was I beginning to wonder, who would sit beside Cannon one day when he took over? Had Hunt considered that when we agreed to this marriage?

Allowing a half blood to marry into our family was one thing but allowing her to be custodian? It was out of the question, besides the girl wasn't made for this kind of thing, most people weren't. We would need to discuss this in depth after clearing up our current list of problems. Lucinda was the obvious choice, and The Family would never accept two males, so Gunnar was not a possibility. A mother's work was never done; we needed to plan for the future especially in light of recent occurrences.

"Cannon, I know you are reluctant but the girl needs medical care. Maybe we shouldn't have taken her from the hospital," Hunt said, his tone gentler than I ever heard it. His feelings about our daughter-in-law were confused at the moment, as usual he didn't know what to do with her. Especially now when she had given him the gift of his son's life returned. It was a debt we could never repay and now this girl was lying near comatose in her bed.

"Her father says it wouldn't make any difference, she's just asleep, not in a coma, she's breathing on her own, she's just sleeping. He thinks whatever it is she did took a lot out of her and she's sleeping to recover," Cannon said.

"She is with child, she needs proper sustenance," I said gently. "You have to think of her and your child, she can't take care of herself, you are her husband you have to make the hard choices. We aren't going to let anything happen to her, everybody wants what's best for Fredericka."

"At least let her father attempt giving her blood intravenously," Hunt suggested.

"Is he with her now?" I asked hopefully, I was very much prepared for this eventuality.

However, since she wasn't ingesting it like a vampire we wouldn't waste Cannon's blood on the procedure. A vampire's digestive system was complicated, getting blood like this might not help anything at all. A vampire needed to drink the blood to replenish themselves and raise their blood count. A low blood count was dangerous; it could lead to madness and eventual death. Though that was in a normal vampire there was nothing normal about our Fredericka.

"No, her sister is with her," he said with a heavy sigh.

"In a week the new council will have its first official meeting," Hunt said, changing the subject. "All of the Lohan witches and guild warlocks have been rounded up and detained. Gunnar thoroughly interrogated the humans he captured so we have information. We held off so that we could consider exactly what we planned to do. This attack has been officially labeled by the authorities as a rogue terrorist group with no ties to government or military. Obviously, that is a lie and of course the humans aren't happy that their idiots are dead as if it's our fault, they attacked us. Another attack is imminent so it's important that we respond before they get any ideas."

"I know what you are doing," Cannon said giving his father a long suffering look that only one's child could have.

"Subtlety is a waste of time," Hunt replied.

"I appreciate that," Cannon countered. "So are you going to kill the whole coven and guild? Freddie told me it's likely only the elders that would be involved."

"Probably not but they will be disbanded and refused membership to any other coven or guild even if they move out of the area. It would be easiest just to kill them outright, but the other witches won't like that," he said dismissively.

"Why not just strip them of their power? Bind them all so that they have to live with their shame," Cannon suggested.

"This is why I need you there with me," Hunt said. "As head of the council I need to be unbiased but you and your mother can sit as members on the council. Your uncle can handle the lingering vampire matters and if we are especially cruel, we will release Gunnar on them. But I need you focused on what's important for us all. My mission as always is to make this world a safer place for our Family. Soon enough you will have a child of your own and you will see what it's like when danger seems to lurk around every corner. Though in this particular case it in fact does, your wife still has a target on her and there's no doubt your child will too. You have to be willing to do whatever it takes to protect them."

"Which of course includes sending my wife back to the hospital where she was having panic attacks. And abandon her so that I can do whatever it is that you want me to," Cannon said. His tone was flat and devoid of emotion and that worried me. He pulled out his phone and stood, ending the conversation. "Ollie text me, something is going on with Freddie, I need to go."

Without waiting on a reply or a backwards glance he left the room. Of course we followed, Oleander and Lee were standing outside the bedroom. Cannon walked in and what I saw even gave me pause. Did that coven curse this girl? Because it seemed there was no end to her problems.

Ollie

I wanted to live with my sister again and the universe answered. What I wanted was for Freddie to come back home, what I got was us moving in with the Harringtons. That wasn't something I expected to happen but after everything that occurred the night of the ball and the following day, a decision was made. My mother's old coven was in a lot of trouble, and the Harringtons were concerned that we might get caught in the crossfire. So, we were staying with them for the time being. With the knowledge that it was possible that the whole of that coven would end up dead. While there were obviously laws and you couldn't just outright kill people in the streets, vengeance had its way of getting in under the radar. For what they did, nothing good was coming to them. If I hadn't been there to see the damage firsthand, I might have thought it excessive. But I had been there, and I would never forget it as long as I lived. For fairly obvious reasons I didn't really associate with people in the coven or that were connected to it. Our family wasn't the only one that didn't like their practices so there were more people that weren't affiliated than were.

Even though I was back under the same roof as my sister, she wasn't herself. Since she came home from the hospital all she did was sleep. Everyone was worried about her and Cannon barely left her side for a moment. No matter what else happened Freddie was always trying to push forward and find the bright side. At least she used to, so much changed when she got married. I wasn't a naïve child; I knew that she experienced something very traumatizing. Likely more so than when the vampire attacked her.

I was there, I saw what happened to Cannon and what she did to bring him back. And I also saw Belinda snap a woman's neck, which I was not allowed to talk about. Nothing that happened that day was to ever be spoken about. I was starting to understand my sister so much better living life under the Harringtons 'care. What must it have been like for her to go through this all alone?

"Freddie just needs some time," my mother said and I just nodded. That's what she had been saying and the more she said it the less convinced she seemed.

"It's kind of weird to be here and not really see her," I said. Then as if called by my thoughts I got a text from Cannon.

"I'm sorry that we can't get back home or back to our lives," she said.

"Mom, it's not your fault, it's not even the Harrington's fault, it's the coven that's the problem," I pointed out.

Of course, my parents felt guilty for us being confined here but I didn't blame them. And I knew they always worried about giving my sister and I both equal attention. However, right now Freddie was the one that needed it and that didn't make me feel cast aside or anything. I was worried about her too. They hadn't seen what I did, if they were lucky, they never would. There was talk of me seeing a therapist after everything I witnessed and maybe they were right to worry. At some point I might fall apart but right now I was somewhat ok.

"I still can't believe they would be so foolish," she shook her head.

"Cannon asked if I could come sit with Freddie for a bit while he does something," I told her, showing her the message I got.

"Do you not want to go?" She asked, keeping her words and tone very careful.

"Are you afraid of what she can do?" I asked instead of answering her question. It was a valid thing to ask all things considered and maybe this type of thing might make others feel different about her. If that was the case with our parents... I wasn't sure what to do about that.

"No, we've always known she had the potential to be powerful if she stopped hiding. It's just a shock but she will always be my baby girl, just like you. I only asked if you wanted to sit with her because I know it's hard to see her like that," she told me. "Your father says she is just sleeping and with what she did I imagine it took a lot out of her. It's been days and nobody knows when she will wake up. Also, there is the fact that she's a vampire and they are prone to long sleeps."

"That's what they think? She's vampire hibernating?"

"A theory but who knows, there is very limited information on any of this."

My parents did sit me down and explain this whole death witch thing. At least what they knew about it. Some people might be jealous of their more powerful, more accomplished sibling, I wasn't one of them. Magic was a thing I could do and do well because my sister was a great teacher. But I wasn't overly interested in magic, I liked other things too. Honestly, I didn't want to be special and different like my sister, it seemed like too much work. Though I might not have minded being a vampire, that I could work with. Added speed and strength, those were things up my alley.

"I'll go sit with her, I know it's not likely that she will wake up just cause I'm there. But if she does then I consider it a success," I told Mom.

"You are a good sister Ollie," she replied. I was trying to be, it was an ongoing process raising an older sister.

When I arrived at the door to their apartment Lee stepped out of the shadows to greet me. After everything happened he explained to me what he did in the ballroom. He could move through shadows, and he pulled me into the shadows with him that day. It seemed like shadows were their own little world, but I was not thinking too much about that. Nope, I didn't need to be weary of my own shadow. Letting myself in I found Cannon standing in the doorway to his bedroom. As expected, my sister was asleep in bed, just like she had been since coming home. We did see her before it all happened, but she just went to sleep that night and didn't wake up.

"Thanks for coming Ollie, I just didn't want to chance her waking up alone," Cannon said. He didn't even turn around, I suppose his vampire senses told him I was coming.

"No problem," I replied, it was so sad watching him watch her.

"I'm not leaving the house so if you need me just call me and I'll come back. If she wakes up, see if you can get her to drink the bottle of blood on the nightstand. Obviously, she hasn't been feeding so her blood count is low," he told me.

"Has she woken up at all?" I asked, he was the one who would know the most. Finally, he turned to look at me and he looked rough; I never saw him less than perfect.

"Yes, she has but never for long, just says she's tired and goes back to sleep. The problem is nobody can get her to drink; vampires can't go very long without blood. The next step will be to give her blood and fluids through an IV, which I hope we can avoid. Not all vampires can take blood that way we need to ingest it so that means a feeding tube and more complications," he said with a sigh. "I'm not trying to worry you but it's the reality of how things are at the moment. Hopefully it doesn't come to any of that."

The way he looked at her made it obvious that he was reluctant to leave her side. Wasn't it only a few weeks ago that he told me he didn't love her? I was there when he told her loved her. Anybody that saw the way he looked at her would have no doubt about that. He looked so tired, like for all the sleep she was getting he was getting none. I remembered all too vividly seeing him be shot and fall to the ground dead. That wasn't something you forgot, just like I couldn't forget what my sister did or the look on her face when she realized she was going to lose her baby.

"Are you ok?" I asked and the question seemed to surprise him like he genuinely had to think about it in order to answer.

"Probably not but I'm more worried about her right now," he admitted. "Thanks for asking though, I'll be fine as soon as she actually can stay awake."

"Do you remember you told me you didn't love my sister?" I asked and he actually laughed.

"Yeah I do and apparently I was just in denial about what was right in front of me the whole time. Love never seemed like something attainable for me. I was fine marrying a woman I barely knew because I never expected to love anyone.

Shortsighted of me I know, but I guess you go through a lot with a person and spend a lot of time together and feelings develop whether you like it or not," he said. "Was Gunnar the one who told you about the head in the box?"

"Kinda," I admitted, surprised that he would figure that one out. "He would neither confirm nor deny, he's really annoying."

"Yeah he is, maybe you will be a good influence," he said, shaking his head. "I shouldn't be long just call me if you need me or Lee is outside."

"Ok," I said and watching him pull himself away from the doorway was heartbreaking.

Once Cannon was gone, I went in and sat down on the bed. Freddie was giving Sleeping Beauty vibes, if only her Prince could wake her up. From Gunnar I learned that the Harringtons really did mix with some vampire royalty, so the titles weren't just because they were powerful. They didn't claim them per se but everybody knew Hunt was king. So, my sister did have a real vampire prince. It was still kinda weird that she was married now and baby and all that.

I was happy for Freddie whenever she was actually happy, I wanted everything to work for her. If only it could all work back at our house, not here in the vampire castle. Sometimes though I wondered if maybe she was unhappy for much longer than all this that happened. She was the type to put everyone else before herself. But it was hard for her being a hybrid and never really feeling like she fit anywhere. There were little things I picked up on over the years that now made me wonder. But were any of us ever really fine? Especially whenever we insisted that we were?

"Freddie?" I called when she groaned in her sleep and turned over. Her eyes fluttered open and before I could get excited that she was awake, I text Cannon. Something was wrong, her eyes were glowing white and that had never happened before.

"Who are you?" She asked in a voice that did not sound like hers at all.

"It's Ollie, your sister," I said, getting up and moving towards the door instead of near her.

"I don't know you, where am I?" She asked, looking around with her freaky glowing eyes. This was above my pay grade and yes, I knew I wasn't getting paid.

"Um hold that thought," I said, then ran to the door and opened it. Lee thankfully appeared immediately. "Something happened, please come."

"Ok," he nodded and followed me back inside. We both stopped at the door and stared at her as she stared back.

"A shadow walker vampire? And a little witch, but where am I?" She asked, still looking around, then she sat up. Looking down at herself she put her hand on her stomach. "Well that is unexpected, tell me where I am. Or better yet, who."

"Call your mother," Lee told me and I nodded, doing just that. Cannon of course arrived first and did not just stand in the hallway like we did, he went right into the room.

"Freddie?" He asked then cocked his head to the side before shaking it. "Who are you and why are you in my wife's body?"

"Another vampire," she said. "Why am I here? I don't know, I felt a pull to something, then here I was. In the body of what I would assume was a child if not for the fact that she is pregnant. Strange, she's too young for this, you really should have been more careful."

"What does that mean?"

"If you are lucky it means nothing, if not, well that will be unfortunate."

My mother came rushing in followed by both Belinda and Hunt. All of them just stared but my mother charged right on in. This was the most bizarre thing I ever saw and apparently my sister was now being possessed. Seriously could she catch a break? It was just one thing after another. Of course, because Belinda and Hunt were who they were they stepped inside too.

"Old vampires, why is a little witch living with so many vampires? Oh, but she's not just a witch is she? Her blood is old," not-Freddie said.

"This body is not yours, please vacate it," Mom said firmly.

"Fine, but I do have a feeling I'll be seeing this little witch again," with a creepy smile on my sister's face she laid back down. The glowing dimmed and her eyes closed and it seemed Freddie was back to sleep.

"Whatever that was, it was old," Hunt said, breaking the silence. "Only one incredibly old would speak so cryptically."

"It was probably a death god," Mom said and everybody turned to look at her. She had busied herself, tucking Freddie back into bed.

"How can you possibly know that?" Hunt asked, staring at her like he was seeing her for the first time.

"Logic, a death witch is the offspring of a death god, Freddie has a death god for a grandparent somewhere out there. If there was a pull it would be through blood, you are vampires you know blood connects people. Whoever that was is a death god and they didn't know about her before, but they do now. That class is what we should be worried about."

After that my father came into the room to check Freddie over but there wasn't really a change. She was just possessed for a little while. I seriously did not envy my sister, I wish she didn't have this life she was trapped in. The adults were all conversing and trying to convince Cannon to take her back to the hospital, but he was refusing. She hadn't been the least bit ok when she was in the hospital, so I understood why he refused. They decided to continue their argument disguised as a discussion in the living room, so I slipped back into the room.

I wasn't a prince or a princess, but I kissed my sister's forehead anyway. In a fairytale she would wake up and all would be well. We didn't live in a fairytale, and she didn't wake up. Magic was everywhere and sometimes even that wasn't enough. I just really wanted my sister back.

Chapter 38

Freddie

I woke up with a gnawing hunger and my fangs extended.
Never in my life did I feel so *hungry*, I never craved blood
before. Yet all I wanted to do was climb on top of Cannon and
sink my fangs into his jugular. My face was against his neck
like I had been trying to bite him in my sleep. That was new,
I never did that before as far as I knew. Pressing my nose
against the base of his neck I took in his scent. He smelled like
Cannon and home. When did I really start thinking of this
place as my home? Or was he my home? How very overly
sentimental of me. What time of the day it was I had no idea
with the blackout curtains on the window.

As much as my mouth watered to take a bite of Cannon. I
didn't want to wake him. So, I would need to go get blood
from the kitchen, we always had some there. Though

Cannon's blood would taste so much better. Thankfully I could see in the dark despite my half blood status. Actually, it seemed like I could see much better than usual, that was different. Could it be all the Harrington blood I spent the last 7 months ingesting? Whatever the reason I could see better, when I went to move away from Cannon though he just pulled me in tighter against him. Why was the universe messing with me? My fangs seriously had a mind of their own because they were extended again, or were they out this whole time? Right now I didn't know, I was just so hungry. When I tried to get away a second time he woke up.

"Freddie?" Cannon asked sleepily, looking at me pressed against his chest.

"Go back to sleep, I'm fine," I told him, though I should have known better. Of course, he sat up instead and he even reached over, turning on the lamp beside the bed. His eyesight in the dark was perfect; he didn't really need it.

"What's wrong?" He asked, his voice full of concern.

"I'm hungry," I admitted holding his gaze so he knew what I meant.

"Well yeah you haven't fed in days, your blood count is very low, dangerously so. Especially considering your condition, they wanted to take you back to the hospital and put in a feeding tube," he told me. "I didn't want you waking up in the hospital like that."

"How long was I asleep?" I asked rather alarmed at the thought of that.

"Five days, they were going to overrule me if you weren't awake by morning," he said with a heavy sigh.

"Sorry," I whispered, feeling awful for what he must have been going through.

"Why are you apologizing to me? You didn't do anything wrong; we have all just been worried about you. Do you remember anything?"

"Last thing I remember was coming home from the hospital. Is something wrong?"

"No, come here, you need to feed," he said, reaching for me. When he sat up, I had moved away from him a little, something felt different, but I didn't know what.

"You should go back to sleep, I can get blood from the kitchen.

"Fredericka, why would you need to do that when I'm right here? My blood is better for you anyway."

"Are you sure? What's your blood count like?" I asked though I knew he wasn't going to give up.

"Mother has been shoving blood rich foods down my throat so that when you woke up you can feed from me," he admitted. "You will need more than you usually take, afterwards I'll go make you a smoothie with blood and protein."

"Fine," I said with a sigh.

The truth was that of course I wanted to drink from him. It just scared me how much I wanted it but he wasn't going to change his mind. So, I straddled him leaning in and sank my fangs into his neck. His hands gripped my hips as I drank.

With his blood on my tongue, it was like the last glass of water in the desert. In all the time I had been drinking his blood, it never tasted this good. Naturally though he was turned on, but he didn't do anything other than hold onto me. Which was a bit annoying because I could feel him and drinking blood affected me too.

Were all vampires this sexually reactive to blood drinking or was it just me? I pulled back feeling a little drunk, I never drank so much of his blood at once before. There was some kind of instinct in me that told me when I should stop drinking and I listened to it. I licked my fang marks closed, and a shiver went through Cannon's body. Before I could say anything he gently put me back on the bed and got up leaving the room.

What did I expect really? After what I did I'm surprised he would even continue sharing a bed with me. Then again of course he would stick around while I was having his baby. Though I did not want to think about that or the damage I likely caused. At the time I hadn't cared about the consequences, I couldn't lose him, but I did anyway. How long had I been married now? Seven months? Eight?

I didn't even know what time it was or what day of the week, forget knowing the month. Less than a year for him to regret ever agreeing to this. But there was no way out, at least there wasn't before his parents might just reevaluate it now all things considered. After this baby came my life was no longer needed, they wouldn't hurt me now but after? Well, who knew, I had been tired for months, I wasn't sure I had any fight left in me. Cannon came back into our bedroom carrying a glass with a blood smoothie in it.

"You need to drink this," he said, holding the glass out to me. Without a word I took it and I drank because obviously he wasn't going to poison me.

"Is this your blood?" I asked because it tasted like it, that was so odd tasting him but not getting it from the source.

"Yeah, my mother had these drinks made for you to help get your count up."

I felt disconnected from him, like maybe he didn't want to be close to me. Maybe he didn't after what I had done. We were sitting on opposite sides of the bed, so much space between us. Was he disgusted with me now? Knowing I could do something and witnessing it in action were 2 different things. Who wanted a wife that could very literally suck the life out of you? That would make anybody nervous, it was such an unnatural thing. He *had* to take care of me, it was his job as my husband, and it was in the marriage contract. Plus, I was having his baby so of course he would care for me. That didn't mean he would desire being close to me.

"So what do we do now?" I asked because I couldn't take the silence.

"Is there a reason you didn't want to drink from me?" He asked instead of answering, wasn't it always like this?

"Do you not want to touch me anymore?" I asked and he just stared at me.

"Why do you think I don't want to touch you? Where the hell did that come from?"

"Just seems like you want to get away from me. But I get it you feel obligated to stick around. After what I did to those vampires, of course you don't want to be near me."

"Freddie," he said, shaking his head. The next thing I knew he was sitting leaning against the headboard and I was on his lap. He took my face in both hands and just stared into my eyes. "You saved my life and our baby, how could I fault you for that?"

"I killed those vampires," I whispered.

"If you hadn't Des and Lee would have," he said with a shrug.

"I've killed 3 people in less than a year," I said. Until that night all those months ago I had never even been in a fist fight. Now I was racking up a body count, and I wasn't sure how to feel about that.

"Freddie, you did nothing wrong, you did what you had to at the time. Hell killing in the name of The Family only makes you more of a Harrington now. You saved my life; I owe you everything for that. It doesn't bother me what you did because obviously you did it to save lives. I wouldn't care if you were out casually murdering anyone who looked at you sideways.

"Why should it matter? I would help you hide the bodies if you needed me to. You are *mine* and you always will be nothing could ever change that. It's a lot to take in knowing that you took another person's life, there's no way around that. Just know that they obviously were not good people as they ambushed us and were fully intending to kidnap you. They could have killed us all in the car crash. What they wanted to do was kill me and take you, that's why they came prepared," he told me.

Theoretically I knew all of this but accepting everything that happened was hard. This wasn't supposed to be what my life was like. I was supposed to be safe instead it seemed I was in constant danger. How had all this even happened? Ever since my first encounter with that vampire whose name I didn't even know my life had been so up and down. Becoming a Harrington was supposed to make things change for the better but it seemed to only make things worse. The urge to flee was so strong but I had nowhere to go as far as I knew my family was here and nobody was ever going to let me leave the house again. Plus, I wasn't that stupid, I knew it was dangerous, still I didn't want to be here.

"Do you want me to call the therapist?" Cannon asked and I just stared at him. "I can feel you pulling away from me with all your thoughts racing. What she said about you feeling like everything in your life is uncertain because you were adopted makes so much sense. You keep trying to run from me and think the worst of every situation because it scares you. It's obvious your parents were perfectly fine with you as their daughter. Just because you are a little different doesn't mean they need you to prove yourself worthy. Freddie, I love you, I'm not going anywhere I'm sorry it took so long for me to figure it out. When you were upset in the hospital, I told my father that I would kill him if he tried to do anything to you."

"Why would you do that?" I asked, staring at him in shock, he wasn't wrong I panicked a lot.

Obviously, I was going to need to see the therapist many more times if I ever hoped to break this habit. To be fair though, until vampires became part of my life, I didn't find it necessary to panic constantly. Vampires seemed to be at the root of all of my problems likely because of unresolved issues I had about being a vampire. I did not grow up as a vampire; I was raised no different than a witch. My vampire life began when I married Cannon, I never really had to think about it much before it just was a thing I had to live with. Had I been treating vampirism like a disease that I had contracted? So much to think about and work on in therapy, if I was ever allowed to leave the house again.

"Because I'm not going to let anybody hurt you, though obviously I've failed at that time and again. You deserve better, if you want me out of your life, I understand I haven't kept my promise," he said, sounding defeated.

"Cannon I don't blame you, how could you have prevented any of this? You are right, I'm scared of pretty much everything. I almost killed our baby, and I don't really know that what I did was a good thing, I was just desperate," I admitted.

"Why does it have to be good or bad? It just is, it's just something that happened. Obviously, I know very little about magic, but I can't see any of it as bad when I'm here because of you. Our baby is still here because of you and yeah things went a little wrong. But we can't dwell on that, we are alive that's all that matters," he told me.

"I guess," I sighed, still feeling rather off. And even though I was on his lap I still felt a little disconnected from him. Did I break something between us when I brought him back?

"Is there a reason you don't want to drink from me?" He asked and I just stared at him, but he looked serious.

"You are the only person I've ever drank from, why would I not want to now?"

"Just seemed like you were really against it. Maybe my blood isn't best for you anymore, I mean we don't know what could have changed in me."

"Cannon, I wasn't rejecting you," I said this time taking his face into my hands. "I've never craved blood before I wanted to bite you as soon as I woke up. Hell, I still want to bite you right now and I already fed from you."

"Why didn't you just bite me?"

"Uh cause you were asleep and I didn't ask you."

"Why would you need to ask to drink my blood? When have you ever had to ask me?" He questioned, maybe he had a point. At the time I did feel out of control. "Drink from me whenever you need to or want to."

"Ok," I agreed, feeling a little silly about it. "Cannon, I love you."

"I love you too," he replied without hesitation

I realized I never actually said it to him and I didn't want to waste any more time. Anything could happen so why not say what you meant? I snuggled against his chest, and he put his arms around me. There were probably a lot of things I should be doing but I wasn't going to. In that moment all I wanted to do was be with him. He was here, he was alive and that was all that mattered.

Cannon

Every day that I woke up now felt like a gift that could be snatched away at any time. No matter what I did I couldn't stop worrying that the next time I closed my eyes would be the last. Should I still even be alive? Dying was not something I would recommend, it wasn't something you just got over. Maybe it would be easier if I didn't know what happened, but I did. My life was continuing on because of some crazy magic none of us really understood. Aside from the worry over if this was temporary or not, I didn't feel any different. Physically nothing had changed, I was in perfect health.

My life irrevocably changed, and it was like nothing ever happened. If I didn't know for certain that it did, I wouldn't know, there was no proof. Nobody who wasn't there and a select few family members even knew it happened. Of course, the doctors would never say a word about it, and it wasn't on record. Because if Freddie could bring me back from death, then she could potentially do it for anybody. And that was dangerous. Everything was always dangerous with my wife.

"I should have come with you," Gunnar said when he came up beside me. I was on the balcony getting some air, the apartment was full of people.

"You had your own mission," I replied without turning to look at him. Did it surprise me that my cousin felt guilty for not being there? No, of course, he did for all his unserious ways Gunnar was the most loyal person I knew. "Besides I had Des with me, it wouldn't have mattered."

"I could have done something," he argued because he couldn't help it.

"No, you couldn't, it was a set up you would have just ended up dead. I'm still here," I said, finally turning to look at him.

When you needed something, Gunnar always came through no matter what. Nobody ever took him seriously except for when it was needed. He was very good at getting information out of people by whatever means necessary. Seeing him work was a bit terrifying; I almost pitied those humans he captured. If he had been there that day, he was the type to take a bullet for me. I mean Des would too, but it hadn't been necessary. And if we were all honest, I don't know if my wife would have done what she did to save anyone else. Not that she wouldn't want to, she just was especially motivated by my death. Besides, I didn't want anybody else to die for me.

"Des should have done his damn job," Gunnar muttered.

"What did he say when you told him that?" I asked though I already knew just like I knew he would confront him about it. These were my people, and they were really predictable.

"Said he would have taken your place," he admitted. Yup just as I expected, that's how Des was. "I think he's also terrified of your wife."

"That doesn't surprise me," I replied. "Are you? Ty is more practical about most things so I doubt he would be."

"Of course Ty isn't, he likes weird shit, but I don't know what to think about her. She saved your life and was willing to kill to bring you back. It's not so much what she did, it's that she's still so innocent and non-predatory."

"Everything changed and nothing changed, using magic isn't going to make her a predator no matter what she does with it. She's probably more freaked out by all this than anybody else."

"I get that, but are you both ok?"

"Yeah, I guess, things are just a little weird right now," I admitted.

All those days I sat by her side ignoring the rest of the world, I had too much time to think. Think about what would have happened had I stayed dead. My wife was already fragile; I wasn't sure she could have coped with the loss. Despite what she thought, our family would take care of her. They wouldn't just take our baby and kick her out. She probably didn't remember but there was a clause for my death in the marriage contract. If I was gone, she still was to be taken care of as a member of this family. Just telling her these things though weren't going to erase the fears.

I thought a lot about what I would do with my second chance at life. Mostly I wanted to focus more on what was truly important. My father and his machinations came after my wife in priorities. Sure, one day I would head The Family, but right now other things were important. Sometimes I wondered if that was what I wanted or just what was expected of me?

Two male custodians in a row already made the elders nervous. For that reason, I had to always be the perfect son and heir and prove to them I deserved my future position. Male custodians had on occasion led this Family astray, so they were extra careful about that. Part of me wondered what they would have done had I stayed dead? Who would step up and take charge when my parents retired?

"If you were dead I would not fuck your wife," Gunnar told me and I laughed. "Not just because she could suck my soul out, but she's yours. They would make us get married, I just would never touch her."

"Why cause I might come back as a ghost and kick your ass?"

"We've fucked the same people before but I don't know this is different. It would be a betrayal, and you know I wouldn't do that."

"I can't believe I'm going to say this but if that ever happened, if she's happy then it's fine," I said with a shrug.

Yes, thinking of them together still filled me with rage but life goes on. If I couldn't be here, then she deserved to move on with someone else. And because I know my family it would be Gunnar, things like this have happened before. Generally, only if you are young, if you lost your spouse when you are older you wouldn't be pushed into another marriage. One of my cousins inherited her sister's husband a decade or so ago. They made it work because what else could they do? Freddie was very young so they would not let her remain a widow, especially with a baby. My kid calling Gunnar daddy, another thing to be filled with rage over. But if I could feel things then I was alive and that was good because none of that was going to happen.

When a vampire rises their emotions are all out of whack. Some of them get dialed all the way up or disappear completely. One day they might love their spouse the next day they might kill them. And far too many times they kill their own children. Why? Everybody says your soul splinters and death takes part of it for payment. But was that true? What did any of us really know about souls? Something we really needed to consider now.

You think your soul is a vital part of who you are but is it? When I died my soul presumably left my body and another was put in. Were the parts of us that made us ourselves actually just part of our bodies? Maybe your brain stored your personality and shit. Damaging a brain could change you and make you act differently. Was a soul just a battery that animated us? Yeah, I had way too much time to think. But even after all of this I still wouldn't want to rise because the cost was never really worth the extension of life.

"You think she would want to just move on? That girl loves you for some reason. In fact, she loves you enough to bring you back from death. Don't think she would move on," he pointed out.

"We aren't talking about this anymore because I don't want to be forced to kill you," I said and of course he laughed.

"I really am glad you aren't dead, woulda said it sooner but you were busy."

"All I want to do now is keep her inside for the rest of our lives. When she wouldn't wake up... I don't know what I would do without her," I told him.

Last year at this time I was not thinking about marriage or any of that. My life was pretty much work, hanging out with the guys and whatever Family stuff I had to do. Now it felt like my whole life my whole being was devoted to this one person that I hadn't even known a full year. And if the gods were merciful, we would be having a baby. A baby that might inherit their mother's strange abilities. That was something I didn't even want to think about. My parents were right to want to track down her birth parents because we did need to know more.

"She's here, she's safe and Auntie Bel won't let her leave without at least 50 guards," Gunnar said then shook his head.

"Can't believe you let yourself fall victim to love, couldn't be me."

"Tell that to my mother," I replied. There were no circumstances in the universe that would get Gunnar out of marriage.

"Who would even want to marry him?" Ollie asked when she stepped outside. Like the 106-year-old adult he was Gunnar stuck out his tongue at her.

"Plenty of people would love to get their hands on me," Gunnar said. "However I don't want that shit, look at Cannon he follows your sister around like a very aggressive puppy. Never happening to me, I'm happy being single."

"Why do you need to get married anyway?" She asked because she was young and a witch, she had freedoms we did not.

"Because in order for The Family to prosper it needs to grow. And being part of the Harrington bloodline means we have to keep the line going. Others might get away with it but not the bloodline family. And you know for the usual reasons nonhumans want to replenish our numbers," I explained. "Also marriage is a good way to make alliances."

"That's how we got Markus," Gunnar added and I shook my head. While that was true there were other reasons my sister was given that particular husband. Everything worked out, they had been married 15 years now.

"Vampires have too many rules," Ollie decided. "Anyway I came out here because my sister is looking for you. Well maybe not looking per se but I think she needs to see you and won't say anything about it."

"Ah, ok I got it," I said then stepped back inside ignoring the bickering that started up between Ollie and Gunnar.

As soon as I stepped inside my wife's head turned to me. She was struggling a bit with my un-death. What she feared was that she would lose me again or I would run out of soul to power me. Both of our mothers were also there and Lucy. I was struggling too if I was honest, I was also worried I was on borrowed time. Watching her lay beside me unable to wake up was also weighing on me. What if she went to sleep again and never woke up? What if she was possessed again? I needed to call the jeweler and see if anti-possession could be added to her rings. Her mother told her about the whole possession thing, and it appropriately freaked her out.

"Hey," I said when I sat down beside her. My sister helpfully vacated the seat without a word.

"Hi," she said looking up at me with relief. Right now, being away from each other was difficult.

"Almost time," I said and she sighed as I wrapped an arm around her.

Soon the obstetrician would arrive for our first appointment. Of course, my mother had arranged it all so that we didn't have to leave. Sometimes privilege was very useful. Were we both a little nervous about this? Yes, life does go on.

Chapter 40:

Freddie

The realest truest form of magic was hearing your baby's heartbeat for the first time. Thanks to the wonders of tech magic and med magic with the placement of little monitoring pads I could listen to my baby whenever I wanted. Of course, a Harrington offspring would be afforded nothing less. A monitor a little bigger than a watch was permanently attached to my wrist and various pads were applied to my skin to monitor things. It was compact and very efficient, that was the beauty of tech magic. I would basically be monitored every second of the day, but I didn't care. How could I? I could hear my baby.

Lately it felt like all I did was cry but I couldn't help the tears. Especially since I almost lost this, something I was never going to forget. Earlier I mostly managed to keep it together while everyone was visiting. After I woke up, I just laid in bed with Cannon for a while until my dad came by to check on me. Now here we were two days later listening to the tiny heart beating inside our baby.

There was a science to getting pregnant, it obviously happened completely by accident often enough. But obviously I knew there were certain times and certain conditions to it. The problem though was that vampire females didn't technically menstruate like other females of a species might. As I learned when I was younger, vampires in general did not bleed unnecessarily. Everything in my physiology was made to keep blood inside my body. Unless wounded vampires didn't bleed and even when wounded we didn't bleed as much as others would. It was all very complicated, at least to me with my lack of a medical background. Apparently, it wasn't uncommon for a vampire female to be unaware that she had conceived for the first few months.

Determining when ovulation was going to occur could be tricky and it wasn't a monthly thing. For a healthy vampire female, it could occur every other month or every few months, monitoring was required to know. But there were also times when like others of the nonhuman variety that a female might go into what was called heat. Which basically was a strong desire for sexual satisfaction. Such things could affect a male who may have a biological reaction to said female and biology did its thing making them want to mate. Lots of sex happened and 9 times out of 10 there would be conception.

Based on these facts it could be estimated that I was about 16 weeks along. Which lined up with a very interesting weekend away Cannon and I had before the summit. So, I was 4 months pregnant, much further than I expected. The last few months were not easy at all; it was in fact the most difficult time in my life. On the bright side I learned that unlike some others morning sickness was not a vampire issue because vampires were just built different. It was something about our ingestion of blood that made that make sense. And the fact that a vampire body did not willingly give up blood. If one was throwing up blood, then there was a serious problem.

We were getting a crash course in vampire pregnancies from the comfort of our own bedroom. While my dad was not an obstetrician he was there because he actually had some midwifery experience. His medical career was an interesting one, he spent some years working with midwives. Also, his mother was a midwife, a lot of water mages went into the medical field. My new obstetrician was Doctor Emily Chen; she was a vampire. There weren't many vampire doctors mostly because people got weird about that sort of thing. Most vampire doctors only treated vampires because vampires felt safer with vampires. Like to like and all that, a lot of people felt that way. Just as nonhumans didn't trust human doctors and vice versa, everybody preferred care from the people that understood them best.

"Would there have ever been a sign that I was pregnant had we not taken the test?" I asked curious about that because it was rather weird to be four months pregnant and just find out.

"Sometimes there are, sometimes there aren't, I've had someone find out at six months," the doctor said. "You are very young so it's not a surprise that you saw no indications. After 20 or so weeks I do believe, your husband would start hearing the heartbeat. Can't be certain what your senses might pick up but it's possible for you to be able to hear too."

"So everything is normal?" Cannon asked the question we all needed an answer to.

"While this is my first witch and hybrid pregnancy there is nothing that appears to be different than it should be. I understand your concerns; Doctor Remington filled me in on what happened. This is why we will keep you monitored so that we will know about any slight change. I can't promise everything will turn out perfectly but as far as we can tell the pregnancy is proceeding as any other would," she told us.

"I will personally be keeping track of your monitors," my dad added.

"Any other questions or concerns?"

"Before I knew I was pregnant I did drink wine," I admitted.

"As long as you weren't drinking excessively it doesn't affect anything. Our metabolism is fast enough that no harm would be done. Besides I assume blood was in it, some people believe blood wine to be good for a pregnant woman. You will find that elder vampires have all sorts of ideas about what you should be doing. Most are fairly harmless but just be careful with any advice you receive from someone without medical training," she said.

For the most part I didn't really interact with the elders of the Harringtons. They just seemed to ignore my existence and that was fine, I didn't want their attention. So, it was very unlikely that they would be dishing out advice to me. Belinda and Lucy would though, they loved to advise me. I don't think I would mind too much because I had no idea what to do with a baby. None of my friends had children, not that I saw any of them recently. The only baby I ever spent a significant amount of time around was Ollie but that was 17 years ago. Even Lucy's kids were older so nope no babies. And yet in a few months I was going to have one of my own.

"Before I forget your mother-in-law did ask if you would still be able to do some light exercising. The answer to that is yes just nothing too strenuous," she said and I groaned. Of course, Cannon laughed so I glared at him.

"Nothing is going to get you out of it, once Belinda decided something it's gonna happen," he said.

"It's good to stay active," my dad added.

"You too? Why is everybody against me?" I asked, pouting a little, Cannon put his arm around me and I leaned on him.

"You should be more worried about what she's going to teach your sister," he said unhelpfully.

The last few days had felt so depressing really. I was scared all of the time I hated when I couldn't see Cannon and neither of us was getting much sleep. We survived so why didn't it feel, I don't know, better? Everybody was around since I woke up and I found out I was possessed while I slept. Of all the ridiculous things that happened to me that might be at the top. Cause really what the actual hell? My mom told me what she knew of death witches and that didn't make anything better. When Elder Rosewood told me what it was, she didn't really explain. To be fair a building was collapsing around us so there wasn't much time.

Yesterday we had a virtual appointment with the therapist because I wasn't doing ok. Neither was Cannon though he would never admit it. It would just be nice if things could just go back to normal. But the truth was that things were never quite normal, not for us. Of course, I worried that this thing that I was would change things between us and with everybody else. Our family was great, and they were trying to be helpful and supportive, it was just hard. How do you help someone who doesn't even know what help they need?

My life wasn't any safer than it had been, it was much worse. Somebody was willing to kill my husband and everyone else around me to get to me. That was something I just couldn't wrap my mind around. Along with the fact that Belinda and Hunt were actively searching for my birth parents. I had enough problems; I couldn't even spare more than a stray thought on that situation. Because what if they found nothing? Or what if they did find something? Both options were equally potentially upsetting.

"Why don't we go ahead and get a look to confirm that everything is progressing?" The doctor said accepting a machine my dad handed to her. He was playing the part of a nurse for the day. Since he was already going to be here and the Harringtons were weird about letting people onto the property. My parents hadn't exactly said when they planned to go back home but Belinda assigned them permanent quarters so there was that.

I thought hearing my baby's heartbeat was pure magic, but seeing them? More tears, it was so annoying to be so weepy but like I was really going to be having a baby. Like I knew that, but all of this made it so much more real. Seeing images on the ultrasound machine was amazing. Like most things it came in portable because medical tech magic was all about convenience. Dr. Chen and my dad said things, trading medical terms, and I just stared at the screen. Cannon did too and he leaned down kissing my forehead. We made a person together; it was so crazy I could barely believe it.

"We might be able to tell what the sex is if you want to know," the doctor said.

"No, we decided we want to be surprised," Cannon answered.

"Do your mothers know that?" Dad asked and we both shook our heads. "That will be an interesting conversation."

Everybody always wanted to know this type of thing, but it was the ultimate surprise. We were having a vampire that was all that mattered. But I had to wonder if there was such a thing as a third-generation death witch?

Belinda

There were moments in your life that just never left you.
When you lived long you acquired many scars, and it felt like
you lived many lives. I didn't understand why some elders
don't like to speak of the past until I became a mother. There
were things we didn't talk about, even my children didn't
really know. I had been giving it a lot of thought, and it was
time for me to speak with my daughter-in-law. She wasn't
having an easy time after what she had been through. It was
understandable and to be expected really.

"Fredericka, dear, can we talk?" I asked when I found her
actually out of her apartment for once. The open courtyard was
a good place to sit and enjoy some peace and quiet. She didn't
spend as much time in the shared spaces of the house as the

others did. It was likely because she still didn't feel like this was her home.

Another thing I needed to work on, I wasn't doing as good a job with her as I had thought. I was distracted by the summit preparations and then the summit itself. What she needed was more attention and I failed her in that. No wonder she didn't feel like we wanted her here; nobody had ever truly gone out of their way to show it. The therapist said that we needed to show her that she belonged.

"Of course," she responded as expected. Poor thing probably felt like she couldn't ever tell me no.

"I've been doing some thinking and I think I should share with you an experience I had early in my marriage," I said. That perked her up a bit, the children were always interested in knowing about the past. Us elders generally were trying to move on from it, never forget but also never dwell.

"You know we aren't really much alike right? I mean you were like a warrior princess and I'm very conflict adverse," she pointed out.

"Well yes, we are different, we grew up very differently but at the end of the day we are both still women. And there are certain experiences that only another woman can understand," I said and she stared at me. "As you are aware I was married only 5 or so years before The Surge. What you don't know and neither Lucinda nor Cannon know is that at the time I was pregnant."

"I thought you were waiting until it was safe to have children?" She asked, staring at me because that was what we told everyone. If you say something enough then it almost becomes truth.

"After we lost the pregnancy, yes we decided to wait, it was a dangerous time," I said with a sigh. "The Harrington Hotel has always functioned as a safe haven, a sanctuary and even a way station for those not human. There were times when they also helped certain humans. From what I've heard things were quite different before colonization.

"All this I'm saying so you understand what was at stake when The Surge happened and the history of our Family. For a long time, there was an obscuring spell on the land around the hotel that helped in keeping things safe. When The Surge happened, things devolved rather quickly as people began to change. The humans seemed far too ready to take action against us and we were unprepared. We all felt it in the air that something was coming, and we were warned but then it just all happened. And here we were, The Family called upon again to provide safe haven."

Those days had been dark and only got worse. One would think planes falling from the sky due to electrical failure all over the world would be the worst. That was just the beginning, many vehicles stalled out stranding people in all sorts of places. Everything that could go wrong did. And I was a newly married girl far from home with a family I barely knew for 5 years. All I wanted was to go home but I was pregnant, I had a chain keeping me here. Hunt wasn't going to stop me from leaving, physically he couldn't as he could never beat me in a fight.

"I was young and thought myself invincible, I wasn't thinking I just saw people in need. They were on their way being chased by humans. My instincts had me acting without thinking and as a result I lost my first child, it was a girl. Part of the reason I was chosen for Hunt was because my family has a history of mostly female births. And yes, I know it's not exactly up to the female what the sex of a baby will be, but it increased the odds. While they trusted Hunt to lead The Family everybody was happy with the idea of us having a daughter to be next in line.

"What I'm trying to say is that sometimes things happen that are beyond our control. It doesn't make you any less and it doesn't mean you won't be an amazing mother. Obviously, our situations are very different, and you were able to turn things around. I just need you to know that it's ok and you did nothing wrong," I told her.

"I know better though we don't do big magic, not without a cost. Most of the time I don't do much magic at all even though I'm a practicing witch. Always so careful not to rely on magic or overuse it and look what I did," she said. There were tears in her violet eyes, it was going to take time to adjust to this.

As her family we needed to be there for her, no doubt her emotions that were already fragile could barely hold together after this. Finding her alone had been surprising since my son was usually hovering over her and her family still in residence. Well, she wasn't completely alone though she should have been safe in our home. Lee was off keeping to the shadows at least allowing her the illusion of alone time.

"Sometimes life is just not that easy, it would be nice if it was. You did what you needed to, you saved your husband's life. Would you rather not have done that?" I asked, there weren't always easy or right choices.

"No! I couldn't let Cannon die, especially when it's my fault."

"How could any of this be your fault?"

"They wanted to take me; they killed him so that he wasn't in the way."

"Yes, that is very well likely the truth of things, we are still investigating. However, their intent and actions are not your responsibility. And no matter what the situation is I know my son he would give his life to protect you."

The relationship between the two of them surprised me and very little surprised me anymore. I knew over time things would progress as they got closer, but I didn't expect it to happen so fast. Maybe they were always meant to find each other. Things like that happened, soulmates were a real verifiable thing. If that was the case, they would always find each other in every life they lived. Something to consider though finding out the truth of that wouldn't necessarily be easy. Was it needed though? They were already in love, maybe this was one time I shouldn't meddle.

"I never wanted him to give his life for me," she said, her voice barely above a whisper.

"That, dearest, isn't your choice to make," I said and she stared at me. "Someone who loves you will always seek to keep you from harm, whether you want them to or not. This is something you will have to make peace with; you don't have to like it but it's a fact."

"I'm not like you, I'm not strong and can't hold everything together, I've literally been doing nothing but falling apart."

"While it would be nice to think that I am impervious to everything, that's not true. Before Hunt I had been considering marrying someone else," I admitted that got her attention. "The trouble with some males is they like to dominate and a woman who refuses to be dominated is a fun challenge. That type seeks to break you, publicly admire you only to privately beat you down. I was so young, and I thought we would be equals, that wasn't what he wanted. Obviously, it didn't work out, he's been dead a long time."

"You skipped this when you told me about your engagement," she pointed out. On her wedding day she asked me about my arranged marriage, so I told her the usual story.

"The past is the past he was never important anyway. I'm just using this as an example to prove to you I don't always do the right thing. And I was much older than you at that time so I had no excuse," I replied.

When Hunt came along years later, admiring my skills, I was weary of him. He was there to pick a wife out of my sisters and cousins, I wasn't interested. Of course, he picked me, but I refused to make the same mistake twice. We didn't know that our mothers had already decided how things would go for us. My children think I meddle, but my mothers were the true meddlers. They set us up and pretended to let us choose each other. He did convince me that he didn't want to control or dominate me, so eventually I gave in. No, it was more that he wanted *me* to dominate *him*, but that I was not going to share. They didn't need to know everything and probably wouldn't want to anyway. Hunt promised we would be equals and that is what we have been.

"Was it hard to leave your family to come here?"

"Yes, much like you I never wanted to leave, and I never wanted this position. My meddling mothers didn't accept that and well here I am. What was hardest was when things went bad, I didn't know if I would ever see my family again. It took a long time before I saw any of them."

"I can't imagine living through that time, you had a lot going on," she commented.

"Yes, it seemed like everything bad that could happen did in those early years. When I lost my child, I could not cope, I blamed myself for what happened. Hunt wasn't always the way he is now but back then he was amazing. I felt broken and like a failure, told him to take another wife. It was all so dramatic, but he refused to leave me and refused to let me wallow in despair. Eventually I moved past it, I never forgot and never stopped mourning. But life goes on even when we fall apart.

"You did something extraordinary, something no one else could have done. I don't know a lot about magic, but I do know that at least. These things you are feeling won't just go away, unfortunately things don't work like that. Just remember that you are lucky you were able to save your husband and your baby. Just try to remember more about what you gained than what was nearly lost," I told her.

There was a reason I was happy to give my son a softer wife. He needed someone to protect, that was who he was. I never really had to worry about if they would suit or not. They just needed time though apparently not as much as I expected. Young love was a good thing; it would only grow stronger as time went on. Nobody could fathom why we allowed this marriage to happen, but it was simply because it made the most sense. Things obviously hadn't gone the way any of us planned but in life you had to learn to pivot and carry on. Fredericka knew the love of her family but grew up in a world where she was forced to hide things about herself to fit in. That was no longer the case she didn't have to hide here with us, but she was conditioned to and that would take time to overcome.

I would never stop seeing my son lying there on the ground dead. No part of me blamed this girl for any of it. How could she control things that she didn't know of or understand? Whoever sought to take her from us was to blame. Whoever they were would learn not to mess with my family. They weren't going to give up but neither were we, she belonged to us now there would be no prior claim.

My son was alive because of this unlikely girl. He had a future and would have his own child. All of it was down to this one girl who was quite frankly too young to be dealing with any of this. Waiting to bring her into The Family hadn't been an option, but maybe we should have done things a little differently. Too much was happening too fast; there were too many things we did not consider that we should have.

"I worry that what I did won't last and I will lose them both anyway," she admitted. That did not surprise me; we didn't know nearly enough about her abilities.

"We can't know what will or will not happen, thus far the doctors believe it to be permanent. There are no indications of complications, and you are both being constantly monitored," I pointed out. "I understand why you are scared and you have every right to be. But you can't let fear rule you otherwise you will miss out on life."

"Thank you," she said and I nodded. "Do I still have to learn self-defense?"

"Of course you do, we will start off with something light. A woman should always know how to defend herself. And you will want to protect your little one. Being a mother isn't for everybody; it can be terrifying. I still worry about my children, though Cannon more so than Lucinda. He very nearly did not come into this world, everything during that time was difficult.

Even people without your unique abilities have to worry about various things."

"Just seems like anything bad that could happen somehow happens to me," she said with a sigh. "Does being a mother ever get easier?"

"No, no matter how old they are you still worry over your children. And you do what you can to help them along but at some point, you have to let go. You are one of my children now, I worry for you too," I told her. Somehow that surprised her, but I couldn't see how. Had I not made it abundantly clear since she came to us that she was my daughter?

Bringing a hybrid witch into the fold hadn't been seen as a good thing to a good portion of The Family. They didn't know about her abilities and couldn't understand what her value was. Why would we allow our future custodian to marry such a person? They didn't need to know what she could do or why I decided to make that decision, they needed to just fall in line. She was ours end of story; her background and lack of a bloodline didn't matter. Though if the death god who possessed her were to be believed she had an old bloodline. It didn't really matter, once we decided that she was a Harrington that was it. As one of the custodians my word was literally law, so they had to accept it.

"Did the therapist speak to you?" She asked, looking at me with a little suspicion.

"I will not apologize for needing to know what's going on with my children," I simply said.

"Is that why you are being nice to me right now?"

"When am I ever not nice to you? We are speaking because some things need to be said. What I wish is that we knew you were struggling so that we could help you. For me it was always likely that I would leave home when I married. You were not prepared for that, and you weren't prepared to join a family like this let alone a Family. There is nothing wrong with having some troubles, you just didn't have to suffer alone."

"I don't really want my mom to know; I don't want her to feel like she did something wrong. It's just me," she said with a sigh.

"Tell her how you feel, it's better than trying to spare feelings. She is your mother she loves you, she will feel worse if you don't tell her and she finds out later," I pointed out.

"Is being an adult always so hard?"

"Yes, dear, it never gets easier."

"You know they are up there listening right?" She asked, referring to Hunt and Cannon who were on the second level having their own conversation. Maybe it was time for my children to know some things from the past.

"Yes, little is secret in a vampire household," I said. "Are you going to be ok?"

"Maybe, I appreciate you telling me all this though. It helps," she said.

"I would hug you, but I think it would alarm my son too much," I said and she laughed like intended. We weren't those kinds of people; her family was though so she wasn't lacking in such things. "Come let us go collect our men, they like to think we women are the overly sentimental ones, but I beg to differ on that."

"When did you know you loved him?" She asked as we headed for the stairs. Oddly enough I heard my son ask his father if he loved me, she just assumed it.

"He said it first; Harrington men are like that when they love. It took me a while though, one day I just realized I couldn't see my life without him. It didn't hurt that we fought side by side protecting our home during the wars. Things like that bond you, our mothers were unfortunately right about us."

"Did they ever let you forget it?"

"No, and my mother is still reigning over things, much to my sister's dismay. She still calls from time to time to give me critiques."

When we joined the men as always Cannon was pulling her right to him. Lucinda wasn't so affectionate with her husband in public so maybe that was why it was such a shock. Looking at them together I knew we made the right decision, no matter what came with that choice. An idea occurred to me as I stood beside my husband who looked a little less disgusted with them than usual. Nearly losing our son had done a number on him, so I silently slipped my hand into his. Touch was a good thing it helped ground you. He said nothing, just brought our joined hands up and kissed the back of mine. Of course, he knew what it cost me to share my story. And he knew all the things I could never share.

Cannon

I was another year older, but the jury was out on if I was any wiser. Birthdays for a lot of the long lived weren't much of a thing. After a certain point most just celebrated the milestones. At 106 years old I didn't need a celebration but that didn't mean I didn't have things to celebrate. This time last year I never could have imagined that I would be married with a baby on the way yet here I was. Less than a year and so much had changed. The fact that I also died was enough to have me rather contemplative. It was crazy how much life could change in 9 months. And how much more change was on the horizon.

Waking up and finding that my wife had left the apartment made me feel odd. We were basically attached at the hip since everything happened. Sleep was a precious commodity these days, we both had nightmares. Some of mine involved being lost in a void, trapped in the dark unable to escape. Others were of the last minutes of my life and ones where my wife never woke up. Our newly formed co-dependence let me feel like I had some control over things.

When I found my wife, she was in the courtyard talking to my mother. I was upstairs and they were downstairs, so I didn't want to interrupt. My parents kept secrets, we knew that, but I didn't expect this. Though I suppose I understand why my mother would tell my wife about this and not me and Lucy. In a weird way I appreciated her willingness to be open with Freddie, she truly did see her as family. Maybe this could help her to see that she had a place in this family.

"Why didn't you ever tell us this?" I asked my father when he joined me. Turning to look at him I saw some uncharacteristic emotions in his expression. Sometimes I did wonder who he might have been had the world not changed.

"It's not something we talk about," he admitted. "Think of how your mother is, any feelings of weakness are hard for her. Before you say it, no I never thought her weak. But she was just very hard on herself. I wasn't there with her when it happened. The first thing my mother said to me was that if I couldn't be what Bel needed that I couldn't see her. Never did I blame her, but she did blame herself. All of it was a long time ago, she thought it best to leave the past where it was."

"Do you love her?" I asked and he stared at me in surprise, it wasn't something I would typically ask.

"Of course, I don't feel the need to cause a scene about it," he replied, giving me a look. "Maybe I was more of an affectionate person when I was young but so much changed. Especially when the humans came destroying our peace. I wasn't the best person to be around when I came home, I was broken. Part of me didn't want to come back here after what they did to me. If I had fought harder or did things differently maybe everything could be different. The Family was in good hands; your mother could have continued on as custodian. That was of course why they chose her for me, because she was strong on her own. What did she need with a broken man?"

"Why did you decide to return?" I asked, curious just how open he was willing to be.

"It was the coward's way to run, I could never be that I wasn't raised for that. So even broken I returned to find her getting things back on track after what happened. You were 3 months old the first time I laid eyes on you. She didn't want to tell me she almost lost you, I don't think she would have come back from that. When I told her what happened she was horrified, we had plans for more children but there could be none. I told her to take another husband, one that could give her what I could not," he told me.

"Did she tell you that you were being stupid and to never suggest it again?" I asked and he laughed nodding.

"Of course, I also told her she could stay leading, but you see how that went. Your mother has always been the strongest person I know, I wouldn't be here without her," he said. The look he had when he gazed into her direction was definitely loving. "She told me after I was back that you would lead The

Family, not Lucinda. Another male heir? Seemed impossible but she was certain it would be you and here we are. Somehow, she got my mother to agree to it, everything was in motion before I knew anything of it."

"You didn't have an opinion on it?"

"I trust my wife, if she tells me this is what's going to happen then I make sure to make it happen. Remember I was raised by two very opinionated women, I know when to fight and when to shut up. Have you thought about your future?"

"Are you asking because Freddie can't be matriarch?" I asked, it was something I had to think about.

"Aside from the fact that she's a half blood and practicing witch, she's too soft. Nothing wrong with that, you needed a softer wife. But it does present a problem," he said, measuring his words carefully.

"Lucy is the obvious choice," I said, watching him for a sign of his opinion.

If I was honest, I always knew Freddie wasn't meant to be custodian matriarch. There was too much responsibility that came with that position. Too much worrying over what everyone was doing and how their actions might affect The Family. My sister was our mother's daughter, she could handle it, but the question was did she want to? It wasn't an enviable position, and most didn't want it. The requirement for custodians was that at least one person had to be a Harrington by blood. So technically anybody could join me in reigning over my family.

Because of our roots in matriarchy, it was expected to be a female that did this with me. Like my mother my father's mother chose him to take over for her. Even though she had a daughter, but my aunt didn't want the job. In fact, her personal legacy was starting the first Harrington Hotel on Mars. Which due to the wars had her completely cut off from The Family for almost 200 years. Good thing vampires lived long, one of my cousins was heading the business there now.

"Yes, she is," he agreed looking thoughtful. "It's not an immediate problem, we can think on this for a while."

"Did you actually want to be custodian? Or was it just because your mother decided?" I asked since my father was being uncharacteristically open at the moment.

"Yes, I admired and respected the women of this family but I had something to prove. For myself I needed to prove that a male could in fact do the job and not wreck everything. That last one really did a number on things, and they weren't eager to trust another male," he explained. "Things haven't been perfect but I think I managed to prove myself. Though I'm sure my mother would say there's always room for improvement. It was all I knew and what I was raised for. There was never really a choice in it for me."

"This isn't me insinuating that I don't want the job, just curious," I said and he nodded.

"The young are often too curious for their own good. You know what you need to, other things are best left to time," he said his gaze on my mother.

The women were done talking and had come up to join us. I spied Lee moving in and out of the shadows, keeping watch like always. Sometimes the elders and their insistence on keeping the past in the past could be irritating. They would tell you things and make sure you knew history so as not to repeat the mistakes of others. But they got cagey about other things, living so long I guess wasn't easy.

Nonhumans lived longer than humans in general and even longer since The Surge. Magic in the blood slowed the aging process. I wish I could have known my parents before, life changed them. It had been 250 years since The Surge, it was 2275 now, so many things happened in that time. When I was an elder, I didn't plan to be so weird about the past. Though who knew what changes I might go through in the coming years.

"Have fun listening in on a private conversation?" My mother asked, giving us both a look of displeasure. If she was really mad, we would know it, so she didn't care as much as she said she did.

"I was just looking for my wife," I said. As soon as she stopped next to me, I wrapped an arm around her, pulling her to me.

"I did leave a note," Freddie pointed out.

"True, but next time just wake me up," I told her and she just nodded. Likely she understood the reasons why without me explaining it.

"The two of you have been through so much," my mother said thoughtfully. "Cannon, why don't you take Fredericka downstairs."

If there was one thing I did not want to do it was take my wife *downstairs*. When she said that she wasn't just talking about another level of the house. There were all sorts of underground chambers and tunnels here. It came from my family residing on this land for so long. They had plenty of time to just be doing shit. Without her saying so I understood what my mother wanted and why. Freddie of course looked between us confused.

"What are we doing?" She asked, looking so damn innocent. Oh, she was going to hate this but there was no getting out of it. It had been years since I went down there.

"After all that you have both endured in the past few weeks you need a reset. We have a chamber where you can be revitalized and rejuvenated," she told her without explaining a damn thing. It was kind of something you needed to see to believe.

"Is it like a spa or something?" Freddie asked, so innocent, she was about to learn some hard truths about this Family.

"Something like that," my mother said. If I wasn't mistaken my silent father had the nerve to look amused, unbelievable.

"Go on do as your mother says," he had the nerve to say. They knew why I was reluctant and they were rip the bandage off kind of people.

"Fine," I sighed, choosing not to argue.

My wife was about to get a crash course in the power of a vampire Family. All families kept some kind of well of their bloodline's power. Ours was massive, there was a reason we had always been able to keep this land no matter what. If she thought vampires were weird before...

Chapter 43:

Freddie

I knew vampires were weird, but I never imagined they were this weird. How could I do anything more than stare at my husband who brought me to this secret subterranean room? There were many rooms in the house I had never been inside; this one was just different. The walls and floor were made of some kind of smooth black stone with red striations. In the center of the room was a large pool, there wasn't much to the room, otherwise just a couple benches and a shower tucked into a corner. What was throwing me off was that this room was full of magic. It was in the walls and the floor and just everywhere in this room. Vampires for the most part did not practice magic but that didn't mean they couldn't make magical things happen. And of course, the largest concentration of magic was coming from the pool.

"How does this room have so much magic in it?" I asked, turning to face my husband.

"Honestly I don't know the whole mechanics of it but it's a type of stone that conducts magic. Very rare and not of this world," he replied.

"And the blood? Where did that come from?" I asked because I couldn't even begin to calculate how someone might have a pool of blood. A pool that wasn't small and vaguely reminded me of something like an underground hot spring, but full of blood.

"There is no good answer to that question, it's been collected over centuries. Essentially this is our anchor to the land, years of sacrifice and blood magic made it so that we can never lose our land. Everybody thinks the hotel was where The Family lived in the distant past but that's not true. Our center has always been right here," he explained. "In the very old days strong magical binds were the only thing that could protect your land. Was it a controversial practice? Yes, so many couldn't or wouldn't do it even in the face of invasion. I assure you we are not the only ones who have spilled a lot of blood to hold on to what is ours."

In theory I knew about land ties, but I never really gave it much thought. The Harringtons had been here a very long time so it made sense that they would use that kind of magic. Especially given the history of what happened with colonization. Magic tied your whole bloodline to a location, but the cost was staggering. This pool of blood had to have been added to regularly over the years. How many people lost their lives so that they could hold on to their legacy?

"Cannon, I am not getting in that pool," I told him. How could I?

"In my lifetime there haven't been any sacrifices made here, so it's fine."

"*Fine*? How can you be ok with this? People died, a lot of people and some of them were witches."

"Never said witches didn't hate us with good reason," he said with a shrug as I stared at him. "Freddie, this whole thing was a necessary evil, maybe it was wrong, maybe not. We weren't there, we can read about what happened here, but we can never know the full truth because humans lie. And anyone who is still alive from that time likely won't tell you much. It's not just sacrifices, some of my ancestors contributed their blood and lives to this. They believed in it so much that they volunteered for it so that this family would be protected. So that we never lost our home, the home our child will grow up in."

Morality when it came to nonhumans was vastly different from what humans practiced. Knowing that, I understood why this wasn't an issue for anyone in The Family. They were being pragmatic about it; there was a problem and they solved it. Life and death to nonhumans meant different things than with humans. The problem was that humans had infected the world with their skewed views. Knowing this it shouldn't bother me so much, but it still did, I couldn't help it. But I did understand it, I just didn't have to like it. There were many practices that nonhumans performed that might seem questionable. Who was I to judge?

"Why do I have to do this?" I questioned though I knew the answer. Basically, it was because Belinda said so and we all did what Mother wanted.

"For healing and rejuvenation," he said, sounding like his mother. "After everything that has happened Belinda thinks it can help you feel better."

No, I wasn't exactly back to myself, a lot had changed. Some things that I hadn't told Cannon or anyone else about. Physically I was fine, I had monitors permanently attached to me that would sound an alarm to any issue. I wasn't sure how bathing in magical blood was going to help anything. Most of my problems were in my head but I suppose Belinda did know best. But just because I drank blood did not mean I was perfectly ok with being covered in it.

"Can we just lie and say I did it? She doesn't have to know," I said and he laughed. Of course, we both knew better, the vampire matriarch knew all.

"Typically in this family it's customary for a bride to bathe in the blood before her wedding," he said far too casually. "I convinced her that given the circumstances and the fact that you didn't grow up around vampires that you wouldn't want to do it. This my love has always been your fate."

With a groan I let him help me out of my robe and lead me over to the pool. Sure, I could fight it and say no, I probably should, but this was my family too now. And ok maybe I was a little curious, still freaked out and mildly appalled but curious. Blood called to vampires it was just a fact and there was enough magic in that pool to call to the witch in me. As nonhumans our blood had magic in it that was what made us different. This pool radiated magic in a way I never felt before.

Cannon climbed in first because if I had to do this, he was doing it with me. My first step into the blood I could feel tingles of magic on my skin. It was strange though not unpleasant as I continued in and let the blood cover me. Drinking blood was one thing but being in a pool of it? That was something else entirely, it felt so strange. And that was without the tingles of magic buzzing on my skin. Cannon wrapped his arms around me, pulling me deeper into the pool until it completely covered me up to my shoulders. No reason to think about just how deep it was or what it meant for the amount of blood it took to fill this thing.

"Is it supposed to feel like this?" I asked him because the magic felt pretty intense.

"What does it feel like?" He asked with his body pressed against mine.

"Like magic? I don't think I can explain what I'm feeling."

"We probably don't feel the exact same since I'm not a witch. To me it does indeed feel like magic but also power and a connection to my ancestors who gave their lives so that their descendants would always have a home."

"I don't even know what it's like to be blood related to anybody, so I doubt I feel your ancestors."

"I think this suggests that you are very much part of our line now," he said, his hands slipping around to my stomach.

"Right now is a convergence of sorts where the past and future are meeting. Obviously, I don't know what it's like not to have blood ties but now you will."

Without another word he turned me and lifted me up so I could wrap my legs around his waist. My arms were wrapped around his shoulders as he took us in deeper. Seriously, how many people died to make this happen? Even understanding why, they felt it was necessary I couldn't completely divorce myself from the reality of it. When he stopped, we were covered up to our necks. Did I imagine an extra magical zing against my jugular? Considering we were in the magical and body temperature warm blood of the literal ancestors, anything was possible.

"Do you think blood is an element?" I asked and wasn't surprised by his shrug.

Taking one of my arms away, I held my hand above the surface. Doing a slight gesture moving my hand back, forth and in a circle a small sphere of blood rose up and rested against my hand. If blood was an element, then were there blood mages? Something I should investigate, though maybe not; I had enough problems. Because what could someone that could control blood actually do? Maybe something to ask my father about, he was my go-to for this kind of knowledge. Thinking about this though was helping to keep my mind off the weird consistency of the blood. It definitely wasn't like moving in a pool of water, it was thick and the warmth of it... nope just nope.

"Guess you have your answer or it's the magic in the blood that responds to you," Cannon commented. "Have I told you lately that you are magnificent?"

"You treat me like I'm your own personal goddess come to life," I pointed out.

Since I woke up Cannon would not leave me be. Sometimes he had a near worshipful gaze as he looked at me. He took being an attentive husband to a new level catering to every need I could possibly have. And it wasn't just his actions he constantly praised me for this and that. If I didn't know better, I would almost think him under a love spell. But no, it was a combination of dying, coming back and nearly losing everything.

"Because you are," he said with no hesitation. "How weird do you think it would be if I told you I wanted to lick this blood from your skin?"

"Um very, because should this blood be consumed?"

"Why not? It's blood, I wouldn't be the first or last to ingest it. Vampires do not waste blood, everyone in our family has had a little."

"No words for that one but uh does a pool of blood make you horny?"

"Yes, does it not affect you? Seeing you covered in blood was not something I knew I needed until now."

Before I could come up with a reply he kissed me. We were naked so I knew he was hard, pretty much the whole time we were in there. Honestly, I didn't blame him because the magical tingles felt so... enticing? Euphoric? Arousing?

Whatever it was, the magic tingled everywhere so he wasn't alone, but I was just trying to ignore it. It wasn't the only thing I was trying to ignore, because this blood had more of an effect on me than I wanted to admit. He walked us back to the side of the pool but didn't get out. Instead, I found my back pressed against the smooth stone.

"Cannon, should we do this in here?" I asked and sighed when he slipped inside of me.

"Why not?" He asked as if I was being totally unreasonable for asking.

"Um because it's your ancestor's blood and basically the well of power for your whole family?"

"Don't know if this will help or not but I'm fairly certain I was conceived in this pool."

All I could do was stare at him because there were no words. How many Harringtons had sex in this very pool? Nope... I didn't want an answer to that though I wasn't that surprised. Sex could be its own kind of magic; it likely strengthened the magic. But did I want to have sex in a pool of blood that my in-laws had sex in? Ok it was over a 100 years ago, but it was still so... what was a better word for weird? Strange? Odd? Bizarre? With him thrusting inside of me I stopped thinking of synonyms.

"Vampires are so weird," I said before kissing him.

No more thinking, just feeling him inside of me and those damn magical tingles. He licked blood from my neck, and I realized maybe I was weird too. Because I liked him licking the blood from my skin especially when his tongue licked a trail down between my breasts. When he sucked my nipple into his mouth, I moaned my fingers gripping his hair as he used his tongue to tease me. Maybe I did like him licking the blood from my skin, apparently a new vampire kink had been unlocked in me. Testing this out, I licked his skin and he groaned, thrusting harder inside me creating more ripples on the surface of the pool.

"Fuck, I'm going to need you covered in blood more often," he said. His lips found their way back to mine, I sucked his tongue, tasting more of the blood. The magic in the blood had tingles spreading through me, I almost felt drunk from it.

"Cannon," I whispered and he looked into my eyes with a look of understanding.

"You feel it too?" He asked and I nodded, unable to begin to describe what I was feeling. "I love you, you are my everything, tell me you are mine."

"Are you sure?" I asked, answering his unspoken question, this was not something I ever expected.

"Of course," he said with no hesitation. "Mine, you are mine, say it."

"I am yours," I said and gasped when he thrust harder. "You are mine."

"I am yours and you are mine," he said, holding my gaze.

Without much thought to it I went for his neck, and he went for mine. We drank from each other at the same time, our bodies moving frantically against each other. Not since our wedding ceremony had we drank from each other simultaneously. Then it had been a simple taking from the wrist just a sip really. Our first taste of each other as man and wife, it had been beyond my imagining. This? Well, this was something else entirely, this was its own magic.

Mating happened differently for different types of people magic; blood and intent were always what made it happen. You couldn't mate by force or coercion; it wouldn't take if you did you had to both want it. A mating was more than a marriage; it tied two souls together; it was binding your life to another's. It wasn't a common practice in these modern times because nobody wanted to deal with the consequences of it. Sometimes you shared power with each other and not everybody was a fan of that. You could make each other stronger or weaken the other, it was complicated like that.

This wasn't something they could really teach you in school when it happened, *if* it happened, your instincts would guide you. Being mated was not what I ever expected to happen for me, certainly not before Cannon and for obvious reasons not with him either. But here we were in a pool of blood that likely amplified everything tying ourselves to each other in a way that even death couldn't break. In this life and the next we would be tied together drawn together and maybe we already had been in a past life. That was the type of thing we weren't meant to know.

The orgasm was the best I ever had, and my body felt like it was completely engulfed in magic. We both pulled back but didn't close the punctures. First, he kissed me, our blood mingling on our tongues, our bodies still in motion. Then he used his fangs to slice his thumb and I followed. Both of us rubbed our blood in the punctures we made on each other, mixing our blood together. Again, our lips were on each other's my fingers were in his hair getting it rather bloody. His hand was at the back of my neck knowing even in that moment not to get blood in my hair. After we both came a second time he pulled back and just stared at me. This wasn't supposed to happen; this wasn't what our relationship was and yet… it felt so right. Was this truly meant to be?

"Mine," Cannon said, his eyes on mine his had gone vampire black. As I looked at him the human-like mask slipped, and I saw the scarier face he sometimes wore. I probably should have been scared but I wasn't, I just leaned in to kiss him.

"Mine," I said no part of me was ever afraid of him. How could I ever be?

We kissed again, it felt like I couldn't get enough of him. Without breaking our kiss, he picked me up again and carried me up the steps. He didn't take us far, lowering us to the heated stone floor. There was magic here too; it tingled against my skin. We were both covered in blood and all I wanted to do was lick it all from his skin. I pulled back from our kiss just to lick his neck.

"Fuck, you are going to be the death of me, aren't you?" His hands moved over my body, and it just felt so good. "Give me this pussy I need to taste you."

"If you want that then I want it too," I said and he raised an eyebrow.

"I would never deny my wife anything, so come sit on my face, baby."

"Are you going to do that thing?"

"Like that do you? Of course, I wouldn't ever want to displease my wife."

We moved around and he pulled me down on his face before I could do anything. His tongue... I was moaning while he buried his face between my legs. I licked his dick from root to tip and was rewarded with him sucking my clit. A few more licks just to tease him and I took him into my mouth. Seriously, licking blood from him was so hot and I didn't know why. Sucking the tip, I swirled my tongue around it and he locked his arms around me making sure I couldn't move. Then he did exactly what I wanted him to, his fangs pierced me, and he drank my blood and sucked my clit at the same time. My body jerked as I came moaning around his dick. Hmm I wonder... but no I couldn't. Could I?

My fangs pierced him just below the head and his whole body shook. He moaned so hard I felt it on my clit. Drinking blood in general was rather orgasmic; you really couldn't help but to come from it. Especially when you were engaged in sexual activities. I sucked and he gripped my hips hard enough to bruise. Pulling out my fangs I was ready to swallow when he came in my mouth. Not to be outdone he sucked my clit so hard that I swear he was sucking my soul out. Which was a ridiculous and ironic thought to have.

Licking my fang marks closed I noticed that he was somehow still hard. Seriously? Was this because of the blood?

Before I could think too much about it I found myself on my back and he was on top of me inside me. With his eyes on mine the whole time he fucked me slow and deep. Even once we both came, he didn't stop he just thrust harder and rubbed my clit until I came again. He kissed me as he came too.

We were covered in blood and sticky, but we laid on the floor together. My head was on his chest, but I was pretty sure in all this I got blood in my hair. For a little while we stayed there in silence. I still couldn't believe we did this. Mating was so serious, we really should have thought it through. What even happened when vampires mated? With magic users you could share power, with shifters it was about connection. I had no idea what it meant to be mated vampires, and I didn't know who to ask about that. Would Lucy know? Was she mated? With shifters there were marks, I hadn't seen a vampire with mating marks.

"Stop thinking so much," Cannon told me because he knew me well.

"Can't help it," I said, sitting up and looking down at him.

"Let's get cleaned up and then we can finish this upstairs," he said. He sat up then stood holding out a hand for me.

"Finish? You want *more*?"

"I can never get enough of you." He pulled me to him and kissed me again, his hands all over my ass. Distracted by my sexy naked husband I almost didn't see it.

I had been doing my best to ignore it, but it was always there it wouldn't go away. Since I had no idea what it meant I hadn't said anything to anybody about it. If I said it then it would be real and I didn't want it to be. Didn't I have enough problems? When I saw the cord, I stumbled in surprise, but Cannon was there with his excellent reflexes. That thing was not there before. But now I knew for certain what I was seeing, and it terrified me. How could I turn it off?

"Are you ok?" He asked his gaze, taking me in no doubt ready to whisk me away to a doctor at any little thing. Too bad the doctors couldn't fix what was wrong with me.

"Yeah I'm fine it's nothing," I said and I had to force my gaze away from the cord that he could not see. Lying to my husband felt wrong, if I was going to tell anybody shouldn't I tell him?

"Let's get cleaned up then," he said, his tone even. Of course, he knew I lied, I was keeping something from him. Vampires were good at knowing that kind of thing with their supernatural senses that I lacked.

"Something happened and I didn't want to tell you," I said and that had him stopping in his tracks. "Talking made it real and if it's real I don't know what to do."

"We will shower and then we will talk," he said and I just nodded.

Pretty much I was on autopilot letting him lead me as we washed the blood from our skin. I was still a little stunned by what we did and washing off the blood didn't take all the tingles away. Part of me wanted to climb my husband and sink my fangs into him while I ride him. We just had sex, possibly a few times I wasn't even sure anymore. So why was I still so horny? Right, it was because we mated, I forgot about that fun fact. Just what I needed right now when I was also freaking out because I just couldn't ignore it anymore. I had to tell somebody so why not tell Cannon? Even if it made him regret mating with me, I would tell him the truth.

Cannon

I might have just made the biggest mistake of my life. There was no going back from this, and it was hard to think straight when all I wanted to do was fuck my wife. Of course I did, we just mated and biology was going to do its thing even though we had already accomplished the job of procreation. That was what happened when you mated you were driven to fuck until conception occurred. Who the fuck knew what happened when you did it in the wrong order. All I knew was that every second I spent with my dick not in her was maddening. Even after we both came multiple times my dick was still hard. It was hard to focus on that when I knew something was wrong with my wife.

Starting with the fact that she lied to me, right to my fucking face. That pissed me off but the conflicted look in her eyes calmed my anger a bit. No, we didn't talk about this, we didn't plan for it and it happened. So, what now? Live with the fact that my wife clearly regretted truly tying her life to mine? Marriage even with our contract wasn't exactly forever. When you mated though that was it, this was the ultimate soul tie, and it was rather literal. Mates often died together because one dying would kill the other. So yeah, it wasn't the best idea, and it was part of why it wasn't a common practice. People still did it, but it was a huge risk. I never thought I would do something like this and yet here we were. And she regretted it.

"Should we not have mated?" I asked her once we were out of the shower sitting on a bench in our robes.

"No, probably not," she said, her voice barely above a whisper.

What could I do? There was no going back and mating like marriage didn't guarantee you a life of happiness. What it was happened to be the deepest connection a nonhuman could make, and it wasn't reversible. Obviously, I didn't force her; it wouldn't have worked unless she also wanted it. But did she feel like she had to? I thought we were past all that but maybe not maybe that was just my wishful thinking.

The only woman I would ever love, and she didn't feel the same. Never was I so reckless and impulsive, not until I lost my damn mind and fell in love. Which was probably the dumbest thing I ever did. I didn't regret it though; I loved her and that could never be a bad thing. What this meant for our future I didn't know, but we would have to just get through it. Maybe it was just the wrong time, so much had happened.

"Ok," I said because honestly I had no idea what else to say. This was a disaster.

"Cannon," she said, suddenly turning and staring at me. "It's not what you think, I don't regret being with you. This felt right, even though I never thought something like this would happen for me."

"I'm confused, then what is the issue? Did you feel like you had to do this because—"

"No! It's not you it's *me,* I don't know if you should have done this with me," she said making no sense. "Something happened when I woke up, well not immediately after. I thought it would go away but it hasn't."

"What is it that's happening?" I asked, trying to keep my tone calm and patient.

"I think I can see your soul or something, not just you, it's everybody. There's like this light in everybody, I can see it in me too, I know it sounds so weird. Unless I'm hallucinating that's what I've been seeing and it won't stop," she confessed.

"Ok I didn't expect that," I said, shaking my head. "Why do you assume it's a soul?"

"Because when we came down here you had a light and I had one separately, now there is a link like a cord between us."

"Is this a bad thing? I get that it's freaking you out because it's unexpected but is it affecting you in any way?"

"Not really just very disconcerting, I don't know what to do."

"Do you want to tell anyone else about this?"

"Not really, at least not right now."

"Then it will stay between us," I said, pulling her closer against me. "When you are ready we can figure it out, we really don't know what type of abilities you might manifest as you get older. We don't know nearly enough about what a death witch is and what that means for you."

"Why can't things ever just be easy?" She asked with a heavy sigh, there was rarely any easy to spare around us.

"Easy is boring," I said, kissing the side of her head. "Though boring would be nice right about now."

"Boring would be amazing," she sighed.

"Are you sure you are ok with what we did? I know witches don't often mate," I said. Was I still worried that she was having regrets? Yes, the last thing I wanted was for her to be unhappy again.

"It was never something I thought would happen for me being a hybrid and all. And I didn't expect you to want this type of thing, it's such a big commitment. But how could I regret being tied to you? I'm already tied to you in every other way, why not this too? However, I'm worried that you will regret it because of this new weird thing," she admitted.

"Why would I regret it? It's magic, I don't understand magic. My wife is a practicing witch, I kind of expect things to be different. I was just worried that you didn't want this too or you felt like you had to do it," I told her.

Being married to a witch meant there would be some quirks that wouldn't be present otherwise. My wife was a powerful witch even though she pretended not to be. What she did with the blood was not something I ever heard of someone doing before. I knew about her little tricks with elements and that her parents got her lessons because of it. When we went away on our honeymoon, she demonstrated the ability and the reaction from another witch told me just how rare it was. She was so used to hiding and shrinking herself for others that she truly believed a new ability would change my mind about her. We definitely needed to see the therapist more often. Freddie deserved to be free to live without the judgment of others who were just jealous of her.

"It wouldn't have worked if I didn't want to and I promise it worked probably too well. The magic and blood worked to make the bond stronger. We probably shouldn't have done that here and ugh we made such a mess."

"Don't worry about the mess, there's a team that comes in to cleanse the blood and chamber," I assured her. "As for mating in the blood I think it was the right decision. I want us to be connected, I want to do more than just feel when you are near. Doing it here felt right, I wasn't even planning to do it. But all I could think was that I needed to make you mine in all ways."

"This is what I want, I love you," she said leaning in to kiss me. If we kept kissing, we were never going to leave this room.

"Let's get back to our place so we can finish what we started," I suggested and she nodded.

It occurred to me that if my wife could use her magic to influence elements and it worked on blood then she was more dangerous than we thought. All living creatures had blood pumping in their veins... Could she manipulate the blood inside someone? Probably best not to ask, wonder or ever speak of such things. Already we had to deal with her ability to use souls. But now I had to wonder were there actual elementals whose element was blood? Nope, I didn't need to know I just needed to take my wife upstairs.

"How do you feel when you see these lights appear in everyone?" I asked her in the elevator on the way back up to the main house.

"Hungry," she whispered. And that was likely what scared her most of all. It sure as hell was fucking with me.

Ethel

I had seen a lot in my long life but nothing like this. When the Harrington girl brought her husband back from death, I wasn't there to see it. However, my Josiah was so I used his memory to see. As soon as I saw that girl, I knew she was powerful and that she could be useful. The problem of course was that she was half vampire. That was unexpected, hybrids were interesting beings. People whispered things about the girl during the summit. Those traitorous witches had nasty things to say about her.

Looking into it it was very obvious what their issue was. They were weak, she was not and because of them she hid how powerful she really was. I had seen a death witch before, long ago I would never forget it. There was a subtle hum their magic gave off that most people would not notice, I wasn't most people. And then there she was proving exactly what she is. It was as if the hand of fate set her in my path. Why else would I have found her at that party just before the bombing? If we hadn't been there, we wouldn't know what she did. The Harringtons would kill to keep that secret, proven by Belinda.

We were exactly where we needed to be and now, I was tasked with helping them. Poor girl should be reunited with her mother, who could properly train her. Harrington surprised me by not seeking to use her, he wasn't one to waste an asset. Though I suppose I understood why, she was so young and you couldn't help but want to protect her. That's why she was dangerous, she made the perfect predator. Except that she wasn't predatory at all, it was so strange the make up of this girl. When she was older, she might change, anything was possible.

After that whole ordeal I was happy to be back at home. There was a brief council meeting before everyone disbursed. The traitors were already in custody and being questioned. If it was up to me I would burn that whole coven and their companion guild. But others cared too much about potential innocents. We would meet again soon though it would be through video conference.

Humans were already whining so there will be much to discuss. Sooner or later, they would attack again, and we would be ready for it. I almost swear Harrington set that bombing up to prove his point. But it wasn't necessary and it was a waste of life. And the man was famously all about his family, so no he didn't do it. Fate was working overtime these days and up to something.

"Gran, why are you getting involved in vampire business?" Josiah asked, watching me with suspicion.

"It's not vampire business, the girl is half witch," I pointed out.

"A powerful half witch who is also a vampire, married to a vampire and part of a vampire Family. She is their problem not ours," he pointed out.

"I need to know where she came from, something isn't right about her. This isn't her fault of course but there's something there I can feel it, but I don't know what it is. Besides we help other witches in need, she was cast from her coven."

"Probably the best thing in the world to happen to her so her family isn't targeted," he said. That whole debacle was rather unfortunate, witches conspiring against nonhumans with humans.

"True, still I feel like witches have failed her too often in her life. She was raised a witch but to get protection she had to surround herself with vampires."

"Can we be honest Gran? I think I know why you want to help this girl," Josiah said. He even had the nerve to look me right in the eyes like he had some authority. "You want her because she can give life but she's not going to be able to do what you want."

"You saw with your own eyes what she did," I pointed out. Why bother to deny what we both knew to be true?

"Yeah she brought her husband back that just died, he was dead for like 10 minutes. She is young, untrained and pregnant, she cannot do this," he said. His tone was gentle yet firm, my boy was growing up trying to parent me.

"I know, she's very young and vulnerable, she can't help. But somewhere out there she has a mother who is a demigod," I said. His expression changed then as he considered what I was saying.

"A demigod who might be grateful to you for reuniting her with her daughter," he nodded. "Good idea but if she doesn't want to meet her daughter? Somebody gave that girl up, it could have been her mother."

"It wasn't her mother, how do I know this? Because someone that powerful would not leave their child behind. If they didn't want the child, they would kill it. Besides you forget humans were involved, they left the child with witches instead of vampires. Everyone knows you could leave a child at that hotel, humans wouldn't. Humans are also stupid enough not to realize a baby vampire needs blood. She was a few months old when they got her, somebody was feeding her blood before that. It's simple logic my dear boy," I told him.

Yes, I gave it a lot of thought and looked at it from every angle. The records showed that she was well taken care of when she was left at the orphanage. They guessed how old she was they couldn't know for certain. A healthy baby, a baby that the orphanage quickly realized was a vampire. I looked at all the factors and all the information Harrington had on her. Investigators were hired to look into her origins but there were no birth records and no bloodline match in the system. No missing children reported from what they could find.

"So how do we track down a demigod witch?" Josiah asked because my boys were good and knew to just fall in line. "Witches go missing all the time and nobody cares to look for them, that's where we start. We investigate witches that have gone missing between 27-30 years ago. The identifying marker being violet eyes, if the girl has violet eyes, she got them from somewhere. It's not likely the vampire father had them, though I do wonder about him. How can there be no match? Vampires are obsessed with their bloodlines, that's so unusual. Maybe if we find the witch she can lead us to the vampire if we are really lucky, they will be together," I said. Though I didn't think so, I didn't understand how a demigod death witch could procreate with a vampire at all. It was such a waste to do so unless of course they didn't do it by choice.

I did want to help Fredericka, she needed it and witches did her wrong. There would be no prying her from those vampires, especially the one she was married to. Though I was very interested in seeing what their child would be. But I did have my reasons for getting involved, entirely selfish ones. Death was an inevitable inconvenience for most people; we couldn't all live forever. Immortals were rare, immortality was not something to envy.

Sometimes we lived too long of a life. And sometimes those we loved didn't live long enough. Why did death have to be the end? Why was there a limit to magic? Maybe just maybe there was some way to get around death and the key to that was this girl.

Hunt

Humans were either food or enemies, there was no in between. Some would say it's "not all humans" but I beg to differ on that point. The slightest thing could have them turning feral, I knew that for certain. Something as simple as one child doing better than another in school could breed resentment in those horrible creatures. They would assume that a nonhuman might have used trickery or magic to get ahead, never considering that they were just intelligent or hardworking. Wasn't the way they treated their own throughout history proof enough that humans were the monsters? Some of us might look scary but we were not the ones doing the things they did or killing each other over minor differences.

I knew what they wanted, it was obvious really. Fighting for territory was a tale as old as time. And it was something humans were constantly doing because they could never be satisfied with what they had; they always wanted more. If someone had something they wanted of course, they would steal it because humans are a plague upon this planet. They wanted to push us out of the region and take over; they wanted us gone. I would never allow that to happen. We would not give up a single millimeter of our territory; I would see them all dead first.

Proving to the other nonhumans of the region that there was a threat was easy. They saw it for themselves and experienced it and even lost people to it. Some of them would likely wonder if I had planned it somehow. No, I didn't plan it and tried to prevent it, but I couldn't lie that it worked in my favor. Now it wasn't a theoretical threat, it was an active one that they saw and felt. The loss of nonhuman life was unfortunate, but this was a war, there would be casualties.

Anti-magic sentiments had been going on since reconstruction, some people hated that magic made things better. They whined and clung to science even though it was more like magic than anything else. Things that could not be understood were categorized given a name and researched to death in an effort to replicate it. Like humans studied science and they studied us, *I* studied them. My family had been here long enough to witness a great many atrocities committed by humans. We always watched and never forgot, unfortunately no amount of science or magic could explain these strange creatures.

Was it possible that just to be safe I had planted a spy in their midst? Yes, if I didn't keep an eye on them who else would? No matter how they tried to study us there were just things they could never know. So of course it was possible to fool their magic detection systems. The instructions I gave were to blend in and watch not to participate or rile things up. It appeared though that those damned witches were the ones stirring things up.

That coven was weak; they were greedy like humans for more. And what did they have to show for it? Most of their delegation was dead and any who hadn't been here had been rounded up for questioning and execution. Any who were found to be innocent would have their magic bound so they couldn't get themselves in trouble. Was it fair? I honestly didn't care; it was either this or we killed them all. While we had to appear to follow the silly human laws in reality, we handled things ourselves.

"Buildings can be rebuilt," my wife said when she came to stand beside me. "It's not the first time the structure has been damaged."

"True but never this much, I suppose at least all the spilled blood will help with our rebuild. Sacrifices made to our future," I replied.

"Ethel called, she's very invested in finding out where our dear Fredericka comes from."

"Oh I bet she is, that old witch is always up to something. It would be foolish to waste a resource, if it comes to it, we can kill her later."

"Did you not once accuse me of being the bloodthirsty one?"

"Yes, you are much worse than me when you want to be, I am just without patience for anymore nonsense."

"Fair, but we do need to ask ourselves what the connection between this disaster, the Smiths and what happened on that road is. Because we both know it wasn't the Smiths that arranged that, not after you gutted their family and locked up their patriarch," she pointed out.

"They wanted us distracted so that they could take her, the question is why? Nobody should know what she can do, unless of course Ethel was right and this was an experiment. Someone was riling up the humans and obviously someone whispered to the Smiths but where do these other vampires come in?"

Nothing really made any sense but maybe that was by design. Distract, confuse, and then take what they want. Obviously, they were just lackeys sent out to fetch her; they had no useful information. Only two of them survived and the one who had seen what Fredericka did was terrified. They hadn't known but *somebody* knew. One act of kindness and here I stood with my hotel in ruins, and my son was almost lost to us. It would all be so much more interesting if she was actually the one behind all of this nonsense and was sent to destroy my family. Of course, the thought had crossed my mind a time or two. Nothing could ever be so easy, could it? Though how she turned my son into a lovesick fool who would threaten to kill me for her was impressive.

"We have the reports back on those vampires," Belinda informed me.

"Did they find markers for their bloodlines?" I asked and was surprised when she turned to me with a troubled look.

"They found something strange with the bodies recovered," she said. "Finding out where she came from is a priority, something was wrong with those vampires. I mean we knew that because what self-respecting vampire would use vampire bullets on another vampire? But there is more to it."

She handed me a tablet I hadn't noticed she was holding. On the screen was what was discovered during the autopsy of the enemy vampires. I almost dropped the damn thing reading over what they found. They didn't just autopsy the vampires that died during the fight, they did the ones the girl killed too. Maybe our daughter-in-law wasn't as innocent as she appeared to be. Maybe I shouldn't have let her into my home and family because now she was completely untouchable. And it was all my fault.

I hate cliffhangers, so I'm sorry...

Book 2: Bedevil

Coming 2026

Sign up for my newsletter to keep up to date with what's going on

britandrews.substack.com

Brit Andrews

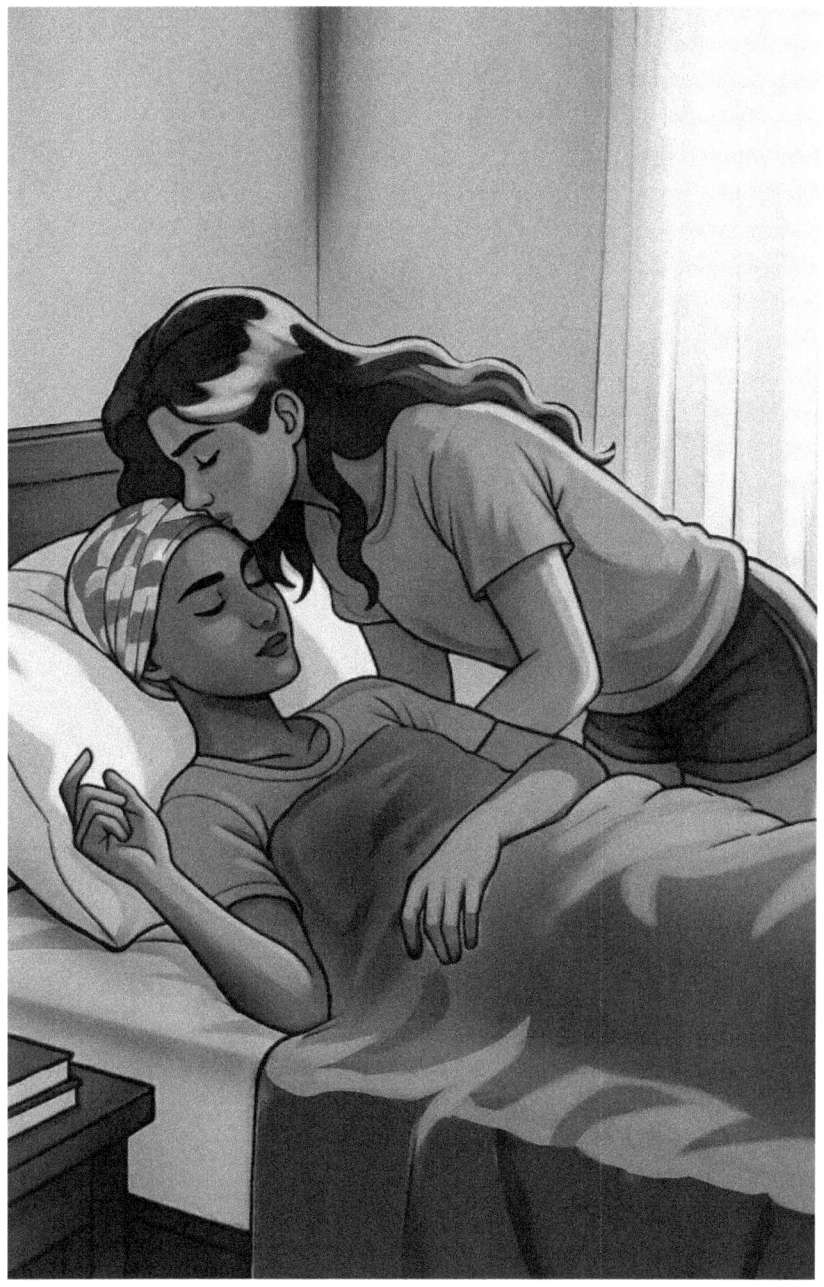

Brit Andrews

Acknowledgments

First, I have to say thanks to you for picking up this book and giving it a chance! I would appreciate it very much if you would leave a review.

I would like to say that Freddie and Cannon's story was expertly planned out but that's not what happened. My writing process is pure chaos. This all came from a dream I had, and I just started writing. This was back in March of 2024, by the end of April of that year I had most of it written. Instead of finishing I started the second book and finished neither. So, the good news is that I have half a second book already. And I promise not to procrastinate for a year before getting it out. Feel free to nudge me a little.

The date of my release is actually on what would have been my Grandpa's 99th birthday he was born 12/26/1926 so I had this idea that next year on 12/26/2026 it would be his 100th birthday and my one year book anniversary. So Happy Birthday Grandpa. To my Grandma and Grandpa, I still miss you every day and always will.

I have to thank my Mom, who has always believed I would be a famous author. Not quite famous but I finally have this author thing going. To Andrew, who has always encouraged me, thanks for begrudgingly reading several different copies of the same story that I promise one day I will actually finish. Also thanks for putting up with all my chaos and sticking with me for all these years. To the rest of my family: sons: Jayden and Rhys, siblings and nieces I love you all even though none of you read. But I'm still holding out hope that the girls might like reading.

To my Sestra Renee, thank you for always being my first reader no matter what nonsense I came up with. And for being my best friend since our days at CAPA. To Kaila, my unexpected bestie, I could not have done any of this without you. Tell Korra I said Hey Bestie!

Can't forget my beta readers, ARC readers and street team, thank you all so much for joining me on this journey. I very much appreciate you. Special thanks to Simone who stuck around with me to the end of the book.

Hope to see you all in the next one!

About the Author

Brit Andrews lost a book when she was 8 years old and has been writing stories ever since. She is a lifelong reader who has always loved all things paranormal, supernatural and fantasy often with some romance in there. It took her 30 years to decide to get serious about publishing a book, but she got there eventually. Somehow, she survived 38 years in a family of non-readers. Brit lives in Pennsylvania in a house full of shenanigans and boys. If she's not reading or writing, she can be found sewing and making book character pops.

Find me in the usual places always @binkabrit

www.instagram.com/binkabrit/

www.goodreads.com/binkabrit

www.threads.com/@binkabrit

www.tiktok.com/@binkabrit